The Intelligence Break

For Richard –
un buen tanguero

Best wishes
Tom Barnard
3/19/11

Library of Congress Control Number:		2010902916
ISBN:	Hardcover	978-1-4500-5639-7
	Softcover	978-1-4500-5638-0

Bandoneon Books
70032

The Intelligence Break

A Novel about the Curious Relationship between Sex and Brains

Thomas Barnard

I think I'll miss you the most.

—Dorothy to the Scarecrow

PART I

Transference

I was in love with my psychiatrist. Except, of course, in the current coin of the realm, this gets relegated to the status of transference. Not real love. Virtual love. Transference, a halfway house on the way to the real thing. I don't know that any of us lives for such distinctions. We're not waiting for some old grizzled prospector to look over our shoulder to tell us the stuff in our hands is fool's gold. We want him to tell us that it's the real thing. The genuine article.

Unfortunately for me, I had the feeling this exquisite creature was always nearly about to drop me as a patient. There wasn't enough sufficiently wrong with me to require her services. She wouldn't take my money without some good reason. I was neurotic. I had anxieties, but that wasn't enough. I thought of Woody Allen with his legendary anxieties—he had his psychiatrists, analysts. It didn't seem fair that she should drop me.

She was Russian and had this wonderful accent. If for nothing else, I went just to hear her accent. And she was gorgeous. I was willing to pay just to have this gorgeous woman speak to me, give weight to my problems. It was like going to my masseuse. Say again, massage therapist. She, too, was gorgeous. Life was working to make money to be able to afford therapy from beautiful women. That was life.

Therapy came from the Greek, *therapeia*, service, from *therapeuein*, to be an attendant. The woman who cut my hair was another of my attendants. Haircuts could be wonderfully sensual. Tingly, hitting all the high notes, now moving down to the low notes. Comb, comb. Cut, cut. Comb, comb, comb. I would have her cut it all off, but it grows back so slowly now. As it was, I didn't need to see her more than once a month, and then I'd say, "Another of my nothing haircuts."

I wanted to dazzle Sophia. Dr. Petrosian. I told her about my dreams. I told her my dream about how aliens came to Earth and dug up graves, whole cemeteries, with intent to disturb. They wanted the spirits, poltergeists, wraiths, in upset. And although their purpose was to stir up the anger of such spirits, I had the notion they could control them, ride them—like wild horses. Rope them, train them. Then I could see: they used this upset to drive their spacecraft the way gasoline drives a car through the use of controlled explosions.

All very interesting, Watson, but what does that have to do with the problem at hand? Sophia didn't really care too much for this dream stuff. Interpretation of dreams was passé. More of an art than a science, and this was a material girl. You could tell that from the Mercedes she drove. In fact, I was only a marginal patient, more of a customer.

Psychiatry had gone away from the study of dreams to the immediate restoration of psychological equilibrium. But I was out of synch with my times. I loved the pictures of Sigmund Freud's office, his study. The books, the Persian carpets, the menorah, the sofa. A true Taurus. The man loved his possessions. And with his rich imagination, he was the perfect therapist. Attending to the patient. The patient luxuriating on the sofa. Speculating, "What do you think that means?" Free-associating. Horse. *Sex*. Cactus. *Kinky Sex*. Endowing the patient's dreams with more meaning than Rothschild had money.

These days Sophia was likely to prescribe drugs. It was shown that traditional therapy, talking, did little good in empirical studies of the matter. Drugs were by far more dramatic. I had nothing against them, and neither did Freud, who used cocaine. But Freud, in the end, was a man who loved his luxuries. His cigar, his womb of a room, even his thinking was a kind of luxury. Sophia once confessed that she would love to do psychoanalysis if only she weren't so busy. But psychoanalysis was a thing of its time like Pullman cars, or a month at a Swiss spa, or a weeklong trip on an ocean liner crossing the Atlantic.

Sadly, treatment in the 1990s was a lot like McDonald's. In and out, quick. Could fast-food operators have realized that their paradigm would so drastically change the nature of psychological treatment? And many is the time I've seen her clean off her desk of McDonald's packaging as I came in for my hour. Still, she was gorgeous. And if I don't have the Persian carpets and the menorah and the sofa, I also don't have the cigar smoke and the crusty visage of a curmudgeonly iconoclast. I have the scent of Obsession wafting toward my chair, and a model worthy of Goya's *Naked Maja* to look at.

I could see the layout in *Playboy*. The Sirens of Psychoanalysis. After all, they had done an issue—The Women of Mensa. But visually you could see how psychoanalysis would work so much better. The sofas. The Persian carpets. The Sigmund Freud look-alikes in the background for voyeuristic interest. Or maybe just a photo of Freud hanging on the wall in the background. For contrast.

Was this reverie the reason for the glazed look in my eyes that she remarked on? Could I, in my forties, still be mooning like an adolescent in a history class? You bet. There was a problem sometimes with these therapy sessions, and that was that I had to generate conversation when all I wanted to do was glaze out. Just look at her and close my eyes and smell the scent wafting my way.

"Mr. Ambrose, I'm afraid that I don't tink dat I can justify these zessions anymore to the medical management. The PPO."

"Why?" Damn the Preferred Provider Organization.

"Well, dese days everyone is looking at the expense of treatment, and if I can just prescribe some drug at $20, it's cheaper than an hour session with me. Even discounted for the PPO, it's still a $120 per hour."

"But what of my anxieties?"

"I'll prescribe some Atavin."

"What does Woody Allen do?"

"Probably he has to pay out of his own pocket."

"I see."

"Everyone is watched so closely these days. If I don't prescribe some drugs, some reviewer for the PPO will say I'm too expensive, and they'll drop me from the list. I see a lot of patients through the PPO, I can't afford to jeopardize my standing with them."

"I understand." Orwell was right about Big Brother, we just didn't realize he would turn up as an insurance company's remedy against medical inflation.

"I'll write out a prescription. You have the PCS card, you can get the generic version, it won't cost you more than five dole-lars."

"Well, I'll take the prescription, but put me down for next week. I'll pay for it. Even if my PPO doesn't think I need these sessions, I do." After all, the PPO only paid $50 toward the hour anyway. With the impossibility of measuring mental distress, medical insurance companies treated such conditions with distrust. In California, always on the cutting edge, employees submitted worker compensation claims for the mental stress of being fired.

"As long as you understand that we cannot submit these to the PPO."

"I understand."

"In that case, I'll see you next time."

"And the fee will be?"

"Ordinarily, I charge $150 per hour, but I suppose I can give you the PPO rate."

"Thanks."

If I were really in love, would I quibble about the rate? Sure I would. Money was the chief thing couples argued about. It turned up in countless articles in the Sunday newspapers.

I wondered if it would make any difference to her if I told her I had been one of the chief programmers for the Patriot missile. That I had developed many of the algorithms that made it home-in on targets so successfully. All she knew was that I was a programmer. A dull fellow, a nerd.

Naturally, I dreamed that my problems would be so interesting that she would see me for nothing. Make excuses to have dinner with me.

What then would make a difference to her? Money, probably. A millionaire, a billionaire. Women have a duty to nail down the wealthiest guy they can get. They owe it to their mothers, who maybe missed the mark by a mile. Happily married to their spouses … Scratch that, mothers grown used to their husbands, still lusted after the monied guy, and saddled their daughters with their unfulfilled desires.

And money still wins over interest, hands down. But it was my feeling that interest was the dark horse. That interest would win by a head. Where was the proof? Proof started with the entertainment guys; Spielberg, Hitchcock created interest and money. Spielberg had made a billion, and even a singer like Dean Martin had been the largest individual owner of RCA stock before it became part of GE. Entertainment and suspense was the tip of the interest iceberg. Education might turn out to be the main course. The Discovery Channel showed how much people really wanted knowledge. Intelligent conservatives loathed the public education system with its strong union, but soon it wouldn't matter. Parents could buy courses from great professors on video for their children. And children could find out things for themselves on computers and over the Internet.

*   *   *

from the journal of Stephen Ambrose

Transference. The problem is that at the end of your life (which my brother constantly reminds me is coming up), you discover you never had love. All you had was a mother's nurturing, puppy love, an infatuation, a crush, an hormonal imbalance, a security thing, first love, rebound love, more rebound love, transference. You never had full-grown, full-blown adult, unclassifiable love. All you had was transference, and they wouldn't even let you call that love.

*   *   *

I thought my journal entry was so good I shared it with my sister, Amanda, with whom it was possible to share such things. Amanda was built on the same blueprint I was. She was tall and slender, a redhead. Fair skin, of course, she had perfect posture. The years of ballet, I suppose. Even my posture would improve when I started tango.

She was very simpatico, charming, but at the same time she was a deadeye. I felt she was a superior version of myself. Where I mooned about getting an advanced degree in paleontology, she was there, doing it.

She said, "You know, it's a nice entry. It conveys a feeling about love we all experience, but these days it's either testosterone or oxytocin."

"I said hormonal imbalance."

"Yes, you covered all the bases," she smiled. "Even I don't like to think it's all chemical, but it is."

"Then you'd be administering drugs like Dr. Petrosian."

"Even that is a bit of an art. First, they gave women a terrific dose of estrogen to prevent conception. Now, it's a lot less. Or now they give you tetracycline, not only prevents babies but clears up your skin. And they've learned if a woman's diet is too lean, she may miss her period altogether. But keep at it, maybe one of those entries will work out."

*   *   *

"You idiot. You fell in love with your shrink." Abner, brother.

"I didn't say that."

"You just said she was attractive. You forget: I know you. How much more do I need? Don't you know everyone falls in love with their shrink?"

"Yes, I know. They call it transference."

"Drool over her all you want. She's only in it for the money. You're not even really a patient 'cause you're not sick. More like a client. What is a client? A regular customer. But client is too elevated. You're just a customer."

"I suppose."

"Nah, even customer is too much, you're just a regular, a weekly john. That's what you are."

Count on family to spare you the Novocain.

The Only Thing Worth Dreaming of: More Brains

Perhaps everyone wishes he were a little smarter, saw things a little clearer (at least clearer than his chums), was less mystified by Nature, knew how to make connections a little better. And so it was that even as a little tyke, Stevie dreamed of mental acrobatics. As a kid, this amounted to autistic savant stuff like doing long division to fifty places. This tendency was not curbed by age, and by high school when he was in the full flower of adolescent fantasy, he wished he could do a little better on his SATs.

The idea was a brain as big as an elephant, but on a human body, so the brain-to-body ratio would be huge. It turns out this ratio is as important as you might think it would be. If it were cars we were talking about, they would call it the power-to-weight ratio. A car with four hundred horsepower is a lot. But on a go-kart it's stupendous. On a three-thousand-pound Cadillac, it's still good but less thrilling.

It was a mistake, of course, focusing on mental gymnastics. High scores on standardized tests. His pals who had such scores did not attract the beautiful women, which he failed to notice. They never mentioned it, of course, and he wasn't clever enough to see it on his own. Jacqueline Bouvier didn't marry a mental giant; she didn't marry a writer, for example. She married a very good-looking, clever fellow who turned out also to be a shrewd politician. (The brouhaha about JFK's speed-reading times was way overdone). And when he died, natural selection gives us the basis for the second husband. It was for the protection afforded by the biggest silverback around, Aristotle Onassis. Wealthy men have a more immediate kind of power, a more absolute power. They can will something and make it happen.

If they want a building, it goes up. They don't have to coax it through two houses of Congress or a Parliament. They just send for the architects and put it out for bid. An oversimplification, of course. There are still zoning committees to be bribed or co-opted. But the politician's power in a democracy is kind of a ship captain's job. His power is kind of a big and bulky thing; it doesn't handle like a Porsche. It doesn't turn on a dime. It turns and then you wait. And stopping? Just ask the captain of the Stockholm before he struck the Andria Doria about stopping.

Ambrose failed to pick up on the basic thing that anthropologists tell us time and again. Namely, that females seek security. Sometimes they say they seek men with resources. Men with resources can provide security. So, if a man wants to know if he can attract women, he should take a RQ instead of an IQ test. Resource Quotient. We are always a day late and a dollar short with this testing thing.

In any case, in secondary school he nursed fantasies about getting high scores on IQ tests. In a *Twilight Zone* episode, there was a man with a special watch. With the watch he could stop time. Everyone froze in place. He appropriated this scenario for his fantasies. So, he froze time and took an extra fifteen minutes to finish the test. This progressed to the point where Ambrose imagined a special room in which he got an extra fifteen minutes, or an extra thirty minutes, or even an hour to work on his standardized exam, IQ test, whatever. This generally would guarantee a perfect score on the mathematics part of the SAT, but not the verbal. Verbal was another kettle of fish.

Somehow he thought high test scores would impress the girls. Sophia, for example. But as a Jacquelyn Bouvier might say, "If you're so smart, how come you don't have more money?" Not a problem for John Maynard Keynes, but financial success for Balzac would certainly have reduced or stopped altogether a stupendous literary output, the money from which only bought him time to stall his creditors. The man had serious debts, but debt didn't stand in the way for the ladies. He had charm, personality, fame. Fame can carry you a long way even after the money is gone.

*   *   *

from the Journal of Stephen Ambrose

Brains. At first they thought it was the size of the brain that was the critical thing, the operating variable—which it is, up to a certain point. But it doesn't explain Einstein, whose brain was only 2.7 pounds, and a little less than normal size of 1,350 cc's. But it does explain the difference between chimps and their larger cousins, homo sapiens. Chimps have a brain size of only 350-400 cc's.

I am completely flummoxed by measurements. Writers quote cubic centimeters (cc), pounds, and grams (gm) like they are all the same thing. They say Turgenev had a huge brain, weighing in at 4.4 pounds, but Gauss, the brilliant mathematician, only had a 1,492 cc brain. What does this mean? Those that were worried that Turgenev was smarter than Gauss were consoled by the fact that Gauss's brain had more convolutions and fissures than the average brain. But moreover, Gauss's was still above the average size, bigger than Einstein's.

Back to the pea brain, Einstein. A missing region may explain why he was slow to speak, but an inferior parietal lobe 15 percent larger than normal may explain his genius in spatial thought and mathematics. Also, there is some thinking that the density of his neurons was greater than normal, and that he had more helper cells, called glial cells. Maybe it's not more brains, maybe it's higher quality brains we want.

Remembrance of Proust

"There's nothing like finding a girl's long hair when washing around your crotch in your morning shower. That's my Proustian madeleine. The cascade of memories flows from there," said Nick, fondling a tall glass that held his Weissbier.

Stephen laughed.

"I'm just washing along, minding my own business, and 'What's this?' and you pull a hair, and it gets longer. And longer. You know it can't be one of your pubic hairs because it's so long, and it isn't curly. It's the wrong color, it's blond, and very straight, and . . ."

"I get it—Proust, the madeleine, the cascade of memories."

"Exactly. You remember standing up on the bed to turn on the overhead fan, and then you look down at her, and you grab her head and pull her over to you. She gets the idea."

"Stop. Stop. Stop. You can spare me the play-by-play."

"Don't worry. I have to go anyway. I've got a date." That was Nick all over.

We go through a series of people we are close to in life. When you're young, it may be the kid next door, or the kid sitting next to you in class. It might be an assigned roommate. Brothers are often assigned roommates. Later, at work, it's the guy at the desk in front of you. Hell, you may have hired him. Such people may not always be wonderful friends; nevertheless, we are fixed to them. Attached to them. Language fails us. So it was that Stephen found himself knocking about with Nick Newhouse.

*   *   *

Sophia left her building on Michigan Avenue and headed for a rendezvous with Nick. Walking down Michigan Avenue was itself a chic, elegant experience. The windows were decorated with care, and she was comforted in the knowledge that there was very little better shopping anywhere in the world.

Dinner at Spiaggia. Elegant Italian dining. In the 1990s, there were restaurants of all kinds, but Italian restaurants were particularly popular. For weight watchers, pasta was the low-calorie route, which was the thinking of the moment. No heavy meat dishes to contend with. Salad and pasta, that was the ticket. Nick knew this because Nick knew women.

This one was very attractive. "You know, I think you're probably the most attractive psychiatrist in the country."

She blushed, and said, "Tank you, Nick."

Twenty-seven compliments per hour. The rate required to get laid.

A good-mannered egomaniac, thought Nick. No, no, that wasn't the right word. *Narcissist* was the current term. She was a good-natured narcissist. Language breaking the shore in waves. What used to be conceited, or self-centered, now turned up as narcissistic. He hated that this brilliant, beautiful woman ended up using the same tiresome lingo that he heard on all the talk shows.

He hated the talk shows. Every moron in the country now turned up on television *axking* every stupid question under the sun. But even he broke down and watched if the hookers or porno stars interviewed were good-looking enough.

In the golden earlier days of television, Jack Paar would interview someone like Oscar Levant and prompt him to plug his book, *Memoirs of an Amnesiac.* Or maybe he interviewed Richard Burton, who, even though he was married to one of the great beauties on the planet, Elizabeth Taylor, would tell Paar, in the depth of the racial difficulties of the 1960s, that the real racial difference was between men and women.

These days they interviewed Loni Anderson about her marriage with Burt Reynolds. It was as the IQ boys Murray & Herrnstein expected, that television would become important as intelligence levels sank toward the averages, regression toward the mean.

The really intelligent people, writers like Saul Bellow, said that television was contaminating, and stayed away.

But like the oceans, currents went every which way, and books were selling like hotcakes even in years like these when television was sure to replace them. Newspapers, which had been on their way out for years, were still around. Ambiguous trends and crosscurrents sometimes made it seem impossible to know for sure which way things were going to go. Computers were going to replace humans in the workforce: we all heard about it for years, like the phoney war in Europe circa 1939. But then it started happening, *Fortune* told us in advance, downsizing would continue for the indefinite future. Computers and robots were going to continue to replace jobs. It would start out innocently enough. Robots would replace humans on hazardous jobs—spray-painting cars on assembly lines so that humans would be saved from noxious fumes. And then with enhanced language skills, computers would replace whole accounting departments in twenty years. Finally, the only work left for programmers would be the horror of writing expert programs that could write programs they were writing; thus doing themselves out of a job.

Science fiction was hinting all the time that the organic would be supplemented with the inorganic. The Borg, half human/half machine. Question: if the inorganic can reproduce itself, let's say through nano-magic, is it still inorganic?

At this point in the conversation Stephen would say something like, "Well, the genetic paradigm may not be exhausted. Maybe it's just machine envy. You know, you think the machine is so much better, but then maybe you find that machines have limitations after all. That maybe a hundred million years of hit-and-miss evolution has come up with something pretty interesting after all."

"Oh, that's just the ineffable hubris of being one of the exalted. You know, a monkey with the big brain cavity, a so-called human being," said George.

George was one of the people that one could be close to, attached to, who might be called a friend.

"Now that sounds like something I would say."

"Mimicry is my gift."

"Mimicking sounds is one thing, but you've also got the ideas as well."

"Sadly, it's still probably a case of monkey see, monkey do. Even with ideas."

"That was very much me when I was first learning to program. I would look in some textbook and copy out the lines of code, and see if it would work. And then I would change this or that. Run it again. See if it worked. You know, play with it."

*　*　*

"Well, you are looking particularly good tonight." Feed the egomaniac her ration of compliments. Distract her. As a student in his college days, the way to beat the bookstore was to put a book under the sweater, and buy some small thing.

Maybe a cheap BIC pen. That way the clerk was distracted by the small purchase and failed to see the larger pilfering which was going right before her eyes. That was how it began, thought Nick. What if I had been caught? Would I have become repentant? Would I have been annoyed by the disgrace of being caught?

Disgrace might have done it. But that was never a chance. People were basically such simpletons, and so easy to manipulate. And perhaps that was the charm of dating such an attractive psychiatrist. She, of all people, should be the one to see through such card tricks, but if she did, she never let on in any kind of obvious way.

On the other hand, you think you understand something, but then it turns out you got it all wrong. The sun did not revolve around the earth, but with the sun moving across the sky, it sure looked that way. An honest mistake. The earth wasn't flat, but it was such a large sphere though, that anyone in his right mind would think that it was flat. And these days it looked like String Theory would explain everything, but maybe the string would only be good for wrapping. And meanwhile, maybe other life forms are watching to see how much we'll figure out. To see if we'll figure out the Theory of Everything. Waiting to see how long it takes us to figure out how to use fusion constructively. Looking to see how we handle the bumps in the road, and meanwhile computing the curve of our knowledge accumulation.

Theory of Everything. That was an overstatement if ever there was one. The egomania of physicists. They called it the Theory of Everything, when it was simply trying to relate the four forces—the electromagnetic, gravity, and the strong and weak nuclear forces, more aptly called the Unified Field Theory.

All of which is to say maybe the checker wasn't fooled by the BIC pen purchase. She had a crush on the young man, and couldn't see her way to causing a scene. She overlooked it. Maybe it was the same way with Sophia. She would let anything pass if the guy was good-looking enough, if the compliment was clever enough or big enough, the prospect rich enough. You thought you understood, but you missed it. A clean miss. You thought you were more clever than you really were.

"Tank you, Nick."

What she did was ask how well Nick liked a new top she had purchased. It was a sheer crepe filmy flowy flimsy 100% silk blouse that rustled attention to the bold relief of the bosom underneath. Nick thought: the more intelligent you are, the smarter you can employ your assets to best advantage.

"Well, I like it very much. Especially, what's under it."

"Tank you, Nick."

He wondered if she shopped at Victoria's Secret. Sadly, he thought, probably not.

"So who did you see today?"

Ordinarily, this was taboo. But Nick had done such a good job of putting her at ease that she told him about the characters who visited her office.

"Well, there was the fellow with AIDS. Poor man, I don't know what to tell him. He hasn't told his lover."

"Poor lover."

"Poor lover. Poor man. He still has problems to resolve with his father. And he has a son by a woman he was married to for a while."

"Trying to please his father, no doubt."

"Very good. Dat is vhat I think. Yes, you see, da problems go on and on."

"You think that at the end of life there is resolution, all the plot twists and turns finally come together, but that's fiction."

"And all that happens is that someone dies."

"Exit, stage left. And the beat goes on . . . and the beat goes on."

She gave him a quizzical look.

He thought, this is what I get for hanging out with Stephen, all this explanation and analysis: "Sonny and Cher used to sing a song called 'The Beat Goes On.' The never-ending thing. Nietzsche claimed that patterns repeat—the eternal recurrence of the same. Or was that Heidegger's summing up of Nietzsche? There is a kind of status thing, a brand name thing, even for thoughts, don't you think? If it's Nietzsche who says it, then it sports the equivalent of a BMW or Mercedes label. But if Sonny and Cher say it, then it's a Ford Taurus."

She laughed, "Yes, I think that's true."

"So who else did you see?"

"I did a session of marriage counseling."

"How was that?"

"Well, I don't know. Men are always cheating."

"Why do you suppose that is?"

Because men are bastards. Born bastards and die bastards.

"It's hormonal. They say it is one of nature's schemes that a man spread his sperm as widely as possible. But women want men to be around to help raise dare young. Kind of a built-in conundrum."

Conundrum? How did a foreigner's vocabulary expand so quickly to include arcane words like *conundrum*?

"Could very well be," he said, passing up a perfectly good opportunity to pay her a compliment on her vocabulary, and also passing on telling her about the evidence for blocker sperm, which might argue that women were just as promiscuous as men. Current research suggested that only 1 percent of sperm are true end zone sperm, all the others are out there tackling. Tackling because they know she's been out doing fieldwork. Collecting sperm samples.

"So, the whole thing is beyond us."

"Yes and no."

"What do you mean, 'yes and no'?"

"If we say something is beyond our control, then we don't have to be responsible. We don't have to make an effort to change behavior."

"Ah." To discuss this further would lead nowhere. She might easily say that monks were able to control their drives and hormones. But Nick did not feel that this was his destiny. His destiny was to ride that wave of hormones on to yonder undulating beach. Again and again.

Moreover, he would counter that church excavations were turning up evidence that control was impossible. It was impossible to turn off human nature, i.e. the sex drive.

The trick now was to figure out how to get her into the sack. Ordinarily, he could accomplish this on the first date, but this had gone on now for three dates. He figured an expensive meal at Spiaggia, and then a movie at Water Tower Place, then an after-movie drink at the Ritz, and then, finally, go back to her apartment. *And don't forget the compliments, twenty-seven per hour.*

*   *   *

Nick licked her clit until she was dying for him to enter her. She pulled his head up. It was time. Come up. Get in. "Please."

He entered her and fucked until he came. She made all kinds of noise, but the moment had passed. If she had let him continue on her clit, then maybe something interesting might have happened. As it was, she was kind of predictable.

This was a hard one to bring around. She had all kinds of preconceived notions about things. At dinner she talked a lot about control. So naturally, when it came to sex she wasn't going to release control. Nick remembered the magazine article about the kinds of professions control freaks ended up in—journalism, teaching, politics, and psychological counseling.

Understandable, perhaps. But there was a flip side. He knew a number of women who used their orgasms to control men. Men were crazy for women who could bridge the gulf between their slavery to hormones and a woman's seeming freedom from it. The agitation. A woman who surrendered might create a curious need.

Not a problem with Sophia, she was saving hers, probably for the hereafter. Resisting control instead of breaking through control to reach the other side.

"I'll stay if you want, but I sleep better in my own bed."

"Dat's okay. Vee'll boat sleep bedder."

Nick dressed and looked at her furniture. He supposed one could say it had a contemporary look, but really he felt it was just a temporary look. The thing was appearances, and he figured it out, she didn't spend any money on her apartment because she didn't bring anyone here, except for himself.

All her money went for clothes and the car. Clothes first and above all. Many a fabulously coiffeured woman walked to her car, a battered, rusting fifteen-year-old junk. Of course, if one had the money, the car came next. These were the things that people saw; this was one hundred percent of the impression. Certainly he was impressed. A doctor, a psychiatrist, who would have done wonderfully well in the swimsuit competition.

She was working on her big project—The Institute for Human Understanding. This was the thing that was going to make her future. They would spring up all over the nation like McDonald's. *The* franchise for psychiatry. She was keen on buying a building, so that she could put up a sign. This seemed to be important. It was in keeping with the *presentation is everything* mentality.

He wondered if she would find the money. No doubt she thought he had money, perhaps that was the quid pro quo. He was supposed to have the connections to do her IPO.

It was only midnight, so Nick headed out in his BMW, his trusty Bimmer, to one of his favorite watering holes on Rush Street—Gibson's. Women were attracted to his youthful sociopathy, the lawlessness. A face not yet ruled by the law of gravity. A mouth uttering phrases not bound by convention. A breath of fresh air. They were the moths. He was trouble, the flame they could not resist. The problem with straight girls was that they were a little dull. His real insight was that the women who really liked sex were in the business. The hookers. He noticed a lot of them had Aries in their charts. It's what scientists would call anecdotal evidence. Not real evidence, not hard evidence, just something that might be interesting—worth testing. He once heard that more *Playboy* centerfolds were Aries than any other sign. What connection, if any, did that have with Hef's being an Aries? What he would love to see was a study of testosterone in hookers versus a broad cross section of women, and Aries hookers versus all hookers. Well, he didn't have the temperament to do real tests, so meanwhile he kept tabs on an informal basis so that he might better identify likely prospects, because even if asking a person's sign was a trite leading line, you could still use it.

Gibson's wasn't dead, but the deck was stacked with Kings and Jacks. He pulled out his cell phone and called Miranda.

"Can you talk?"

"Well, actually . . ."

"When will you be free?"

"Two."

"See you then?"

"Sure, honey."

He wished she wouldn't do that. My God, he had entered every hole in her body and mounted the opening in her mind, and still she said, "Sure, honey."

That was for the client. In order to maintain some kind of illusion that her next john wasn't that special, she had to treat the phone call with some kind of ordinariness. That was it. Love was treating someone as special. That guy on the phone, he wasn't that special. You're special. That was love. Good sex was spending just a little more time on the clit. See, there it was in a nutshell, who needed the Unified Field Theory or String Theory, anyway?

Meanwhile, he had an hour and a half to kill.

He decided he would stay at Gibson's, and sat by the piano bar, and flirted with an older but attractive woman. She talked about her hospital league and going to Greece. His game was to see what offers such a woman would make to entice him. Several had wanted to take him on trips to Europe; one woman was headed to the Orient and wanted some company.

*   *   *

"Miranda, you're looking good, but a little tired."

"No, I'm fine. My last didn't stay that long. I gave him a blow job and he was outta here."

"He's an idiot."

So, she wasn't worn out. A blow job didn't take that much out of her. There was a downside to everything, and the downside to seeing a hooker at the end of the day was that she was often worn-out from fucking. It would be best to be with her in the morning, but that had never happened.

"Why is he an idiot?"

"Because if he were smart, he'd spend the night with you. You're so adorable."

"But you never do."

"Only because I find it impossible to sleep in anybody else's bed."

"Ah."

"But if I didn't need to sleep . . . I could easily spend all night fucking you. Maybe I will tonight."

"That would be nice, sweetheart."

"I read about a girl who was able to give a forty-eight-hour blow job. Do you believe that?"

"Well, it's a stretch."

"So to speak. I think it's too long. There is an optimum for everything, and I think forty-eight hours is just too long. It would hurt your dick."

"How would you know, darling?"

They were standing up. Nick had both hands on her ass, and by now was dry humping her crotch.

"That feels good."

"That's the problem with getting new partners all the time."

"What's that, sweetheart?"

"You have to train them. Sex is all a matter of preferences."

"Ouch!"

"And that's another thing."

"What's that?"

"Some just don't smell right. It's one of those vastly underrated things."

"How do I smell, sweetheart?"

"You smell just right."

"Give it a sniff, would you? Just to be sure."

Prime Earth

Prime Earth was an enormous spacecraft. Many had wanted to use an asteroid, but an asteroid was unwieldy, still beyond twenty-first century technology. Originally, the craft was called Earth Prime, using the mathematical notation, but this got reversed in common usage, and eventually the craft was known simply as Prime. In the late 2000's, when the problems of earth—population, pollution, poisons—became larger instead of receding, it was decided by a joint commission under UN auspices to try and save a sample of Homo against the chance that the planet might not make it.

No, strike that. It was decided to try and send a craft to explore another planetary system. So, Prime was built. It would have the same effect. A sample population of the recent strain of advanced primate known as modern man would be protected from the problems of Earth. The project was not unlike other enormous projects of previous eras. The Pyramids, the Coliseum, the Titanic, the V-2 Project, the Manhattan Project, the Apollo Project, the Three Rivers Dam, but Prime was on a far larger scale than any of these.

It was sold on the basis of the stimulus it would provide to all earthbound economies. And another boon to technology. Plants for manufacture were distributed on a combination of political and logistical rationales. Computers were still developed in the United States but manufactured in the Pacific Rim. Software was subbed out all over the place, a lot of it went to India. In the late 2000s software had developed to the point where expert programs developed just-in-time software solutions.

Earth built manufacturing facilities to be used on the spacecraft; the spacecraft was assembled near an asteroid, where additional materials could be obtained at extremely low escape velocities, though lower cost solutions had been found to escape earth's gravity.

Materials were regularly vaulted out of earth using the cannons developed by Gerald Bull, who had taken the cannon to a much higher level than that used by the Germans in the famous Paris Gun, which in three minutes lobbed a 106 kilogram shell 42 miles high and a distance of 126 kilometers. It had a muzzle velocity of nearly 6000 kilometers per second (7500 g's). Considering that jet pilots have trouble at 6 g's, the device was no good for sending up humans. Using a mountainside, they ramped up a gun several miles long. That was the ticket. Still lethal for humans, Jules Verne's vision would turn humans into unrecognizable mush, but worked perfectly well for sending up raw materials.

The Iraqis were working on a gun of this type until British customs officials discovered a piece of it. Eventually, Bull was taken out by Mossad when he could no longer be trusted not to work for the Iraqis. Six bullets to the back of the head for work on Scud missiles he did as a side job. Right outside his West German apartment. Thus, the progress of this particular engineering marvel was halted until the late 2000s when it was brought back to solve the problem of sending certain materials to the spacecraft. It was also used to dispose of radioactive materials by shooting them at the Sun.

Propulsion was a continuing problem. The principal problem faced in interplanetary and interstellar propulsion was that gaseous engines lost matter that could not be replaced in deep space. Conservation was a preeminent problem in deep space where nothing would be replenished, so of course, gravity slingshots were a cheap way of gaining speed. And material from solar flares were used to boost velocity when they came along.

*   *   *

"I think it would be best if you left out the stuff about propulsion. Propulsion will go through all kinds of evolution in the next one hundred years. The Paris Gun was probably the end of the road on that idea, Gerald Bull notwithstanding." Nick.

"Maybe. But we're a one hundred years out and we're still using the gasoline engine in automobiles. It's more sophisticated now. Gas engines sound a lot more like electric engines now. No big thumping of the cylinders. Everything hums now. And big guns might be the perfect solution for sending materials up. They'll need enormous amounts of water."

"Still in all, I'd stay away from that. Just an intuition."

"Yeah, who's to say that some kind of antigravity machine won't take us off the planet instead of these wasteful controlled chemical explosions? No loss of matter there. Or they'll toss down a ladder from space, like 'Jack and the Beanstalk.'"

"Quixotic hyperbole."

"What?"

"Not what. You."

Ignoring a remark that he didn't fully understand, Stephen continued his thought, "Think of it. To get up to speed, an interstellar craft would bounce off the sun's gravity, or use it to apply the brakes."

"And what would happen between stars where there are no large gravity objects?"

"There you may prove to be stuck. Maybe it's like a pinball machine. Can't control the velocity until you are near another accent point."

"Probably there will be several propulsion systems on board. You didn't mention the plasma which fusion reactors will generate. Or other plasmas. They say the only thing out in space are hydrogren atoms."

"Yeah, I saw something about hydrogen collection. Hydrogen engine, is that what you're suggesting? Or what about antimatter? Those reactions really generate energy."

"Maybe there are more subtle solutions."

"Quantum mechanics. Stepping into another place in space-time. Wormholes."

"Really, you know. You must be a writer. You have all the characteristics of a writer. Sublimate, sublimate, sublimate. The only female in your life is your shrink where there is no sex. It's a relationship where all you do is discuss all these airy speculations, which have no connection with reality."

"Ah."

"'Ah,' again. You look tired. How's your sleep?"

"It's a low quality sleep, but I try to make up for it in volume."

They were sitting at the bar in a club called Tangier. This was the night they had met for the free suck-'em-in lesson of tango. Tangier on a Tuesday night. Tuesday night at Tangier was Tango Night. Stephen learned the basic salida. The salida was nothing very complicated. A step to the left with the left foot, the right foot going forward in a simple walking motion. Right, left. Stop. Feet together. The left foot goes forward, the right goes to the right, and the left follows.

Stephen was supposed to meet Nick for tennis, but when he cancelled to do this tango sampler, he reluctantly suggested that Nick tag along. Nick met him at Tangier and sat at the bar and spoke with the women. Since the women gave him all the attention he required, he felt no need to learn the dance. At the end of the lesson, Stephen stepped over to the bar and watched Nick work the two women sitting next to him.

Stephen was watching Nick, watching the bartender, watching the tango dancers attempt elegance in walking, wondering if aliens were watching, looking over our shoulders to see how *we* handled the problem of boredom. Who was looking over the shoulders of the aliens, that's what he wanted to know.

It was a hot night in July. Stephen was drinking wine tonight. Last time out he had drunk Dewar's until he was stumbling drunk and made the old joke, *of course I drove home, I was too drunk to walk.* He drank to the point where he was a little afraid that he might get stopped by police. So, he went the other way for a while, and drank soda water and cranberry juice.

He was never a regular drinker, it took the wine to get him oiled enough to speak to some woman who might be standing nearby. Usually an older women out in a last stand against the ravages of age. After a couple of glasses of wine, he was, at least, sympathetic to their plight, a theme that naturally came up with Nick.

"Why give your ear to these old crones? In their youth they probably left a lot of men with blue balls."

"And you haven't left some of your lovers without an orgasm?"

"Well, who can tell when a woman is faking it?"

"Somehow, I'm surprised to hear you say that. You with the sexual x-ray vision. You, who can smell an orgasm at fifty paces."

"Very clever."

"I'm just reiterating something you once said."

"Well, maybe I overstated a little."

"Maybe a lot."

*   *   *

Ambrose did not have the facial symmetry of Nick. He didn't have the confidence and the charm that comes from years and years of facial symmetry. But he could learn to dance. He signed up for lessons.

He did six weeks of group lessons. He learned the basic salida. Right foot back, left foot to the side. Right, left, feet together. Left foot out, right foot to the right. Bring the left foot over to the right to collect the feet together in the tango close.

It was like every dance. Like salsa. They show you the basic step, but at the dance hall everyone leaves the basic behind, but it was, after all, a starting place. In tango, the first thing to go in the basic salida was the step back. In a crowded milonga, a step back meant you would be hitting someone. So, in practice, everyone started with the left foot going to the side. The eight-step salida in practice dropped to seven steps.

He went to the milonga and did his awkward beginner's military salida.

Gainful Work

The President of the United States was a psychiatrist. A couple of presidents in the past one hundred years had been female, a couple were black. One was black and Jewish. This one was a variation of the Tiger Woods mix—mostly Caucasian (and one-quarter Jewish), with splotches of African and Chinese. But more importantly, he had been a psychiatrist. By now most people knew it was all in the head. Virtual reality made that clear.

Prime Earth was called Virtual Earth by the kids. And with Intel packing eight trillion transistors into its microprocessors, some kids never made it back from virtual reality.

Never was it clearer that the people needed a psychiatrist to bring them out of virtual hell back into reality. And nothing did this better than a project requiring real work.

The President, Maury Win Ho, knew this better than anyone. In the early 2000s, work had made a comeback in psychiatric thought. Children always try to avoid work, and Maynard G. Krebs of the show *Dobie Gillis* led the charge of the baby boomers, who was shocked whenever the word "work" was mentioned. Calvinists had been too doctrinaire in their thinking. They turned work into too much of a duty. And Nazis gave it a pejorative ring when they put the words "arbeit macht frei" (work makes you free) in the ornamental iron over the entrance gate to Auschwitz, which put a definite damper on the "arbeit" part. Nevertheless, the psychiatrists said, go ahead, do this, do that, get burned—you will find that only work will give you that true sense of well-being. Only true, gainful work is the key to good mental health.

Problem was: work was everywhere; gainful work for humans was not. Computers were eating up gainful work like crazy. The future came into the present like a change in the tides. At first just lapping the beach with just a splash, then coming on with inevitable force. Job loss was a continuing problem for the economy. Poverty was not. The solution to the fusion reactor was solved in the early 2070s, and energy became cheap beyond belief. An endless source of energy could run desalinization plants until the cows came home. The problem of fresh water ended, deserts were turned into farms. Problems still existed. They had to figure out what to do with all the salt. And water levels dropped from all the desalinization, but this was offset by the melting of the ice caps from global warming caused by the increase of carbon dioxide, CO_2.

The negative income tax guaranteed that everyone had money enough to get along. The real problem was that computers picked off jobs like a marksman at a circus. Accounting departments were wholly run by computers. Speech software fielded requests for information and generated reports however you wanted them.

Jobs that were real jobs kept disappearing. Receptionists were replaced by smart telephone systems. Manila files were replaced by digital files, so the file clerks disappeared. Their arms were replaced by the arm of the storage device that found the files. And so on up the chain. Managers were replaced by expert systems, smart-manager software.

Oh, there were clever firms that found ways to keep humans on the job, but it was all temporary. They would never keep their jobs forever. Eventually, they would lose their jobs and end up on the negative income tax dole.

Finally, people began to rise up against computers. It was the Luddites all over again. In the late 1700s, Luddites were textile workers who tried to stall the industrial revolution by destroying mechanized looms. It was becoming clear that Intel would eventually build something that would come to consciousness. People wanted to stop the inevitable. It was annoying but also frightening that they would be supplanted by their own handiwork. Hoist on their own petard.

But finally, curiosity was a force greater than they imagined. It was a force for good and evil. It was not a force that could be stopped, so it was that all the President could do just to point this force that was like the powerful onrush of water from a fire hose. He pointed it at the Prime Earth project.

Friendship, and What Purports To Be

Ambrose missed his friend George. George was the best of friends—loyal, steadfast, intelligent, nonjudgmental. He was still a good friend, but along the way he found a woman he wanted to be with, and it was one of the big sacrifices of Stephen's life that he had to give up George to marriage. Though, of course, it was folly to call it a sacrifice. It was something over which he had no power to sacrifice. George would marry her anyway; it just felt like a sacrifice.

And the reason he especially missed him was because he now knocked about with Nick, a man he did not feel the same way about. Nick was too tricky. Too nimble in his thinking. Reason was like the containment boom for an oil slick. The thing underneath was an unruly sea and quite beyond control.

"Do you ever notice that at work you'll let things go to point where you don't even do quite enough to get by?"

That was Nick, in his own way trying to figure out the laws of human behavior.

"Yes."

"I wonder why that is. Do you suppose we do that so that need is pressed down like a spring and we are forced into a situation of maximum effort? That it's really the human need for a thrill. That we need to feel a lot is on the line."

"Very good. I like that."

Then he looked down toward the other end of the bar.

"That girl has wonderful hair."

The girl had been intent on talking with her two girl friends. Hair without the face was wonderfully speculative.

"I suppose you'll go down and speak to her?"

"Not necessarily. Hair can be very misleading. Might be a butterface girl."

"Butterface girl?"

"Great hair, but her face . . . I'll go to the bathroom and check."

"Surely you don't need to uncork the casket yet?"

"You know better than that. I have a bladder for the ages."

He walked down to the end of the bar, gave a glance back to look at the girl, and headed for the john.

While Nick was taking a leak, Ambrose thought about him. The wonderful thing about Nick was that he was sort of amoral, reptilian. It mattered not to him whether a girl was married or not. Engaged or not. The only thing was whether the girl could break away. Find time for a rendezvous. When Nick came back, Ambrose said to him:

"Well?"

"NG. No good."

"Tell me, is there anything about, say, a married woman that would stop you?"

"Sure, she might be loyal to her partner."

"Aside from that?"

"Well, there are all kinds of game players. If the issue is control, then the thing that drives them is keeping you at bay. Then they use the marriage as a kind of barrier, a fencing tool—a shield. I don't enjoy this so much because it gets in the way of sex."

"Sex, which you need as much as you can get, as often as you can get it."

"Exactly," he laughed. "So, tell me, Ambrose. Who interests you?"

"No one in particular these days."

"What? Not even the shrink?"

Ambrose was sorry he'd slipped up on that one. A friend like George, for example, would never bring the subject up. He would leave it alone, possibly forever, and wait for Ambrose to bring it up, if he ever cared to. But Nick would not do that. Which was why Stephen was not so much inclined to reveal anything to him anymore.

"Oh well, she's very attractive."

"Better than that, you claimed."

"She says that she can't see me anymore."

"Her husband won't let her," Nick mocked.

"She's not married. No, the PPO won't pay for the sessions."

"Why not?"

"Talk used to be cheap. Now it's expensive. They're going to end up asking her why she hasn't dispensed some drug. Like Atavin for anxiety, or Prozac for depression."

"I see. And has she prescribed any drugs?"

"Atavin for anxiety."

"Anxiety about seeing her no doubt."

"Right."

"It does seem like a vicious circle. You're anxious about seeing her. She prescribes Atavin for anxiety so that you can see her and she can prescribe Atavin so you can see her again. Have I got something wrong?"

"No. I think you've got it right."

"I don't know why you make such a big deal out of it."

"When you're attracted to someone . . . I don't know that you can always control your feelings . . . that's part of the attraction, losing control. I think that is part of the thrill. Why do people love roller coasters? They love the notion of almost being out of control," said Stephen.

"Really, that sounds almost profound. Too profound for this dump."

"Profundity loves a dump."

"What is it with you? Quit with the aphorisms already."

"Trust me, it wasn't intentional. And that didn't make it to aphorism. It was just a stab at it."

"I don't know. I think you harbor aphorisms like the gut harbors bacteria."

"The stomach needs bacteria to help digest, it's a symbiotic relationship. If the bacteria died, so would we."

"I like that, it's sort of like you need evil to know good." Nick.

"No, that's you. It's more like using explosives to break up a mountain of coal into usable, bite-size pieces. It's nice to have a tool. Explosives are not intrinsically bad. Same thing for bacteria. They are not in and of themselves bad. You're the one with the good and evil issues."

"Okay, okay. So what are you going to do about the PPO?"

"Nothing to do about the PPO."

"So, you're going to quit the sessions."

"No."

"Then what?"

"I'll pay for them. It's a luxury, I know, but maybe also a necessity."

"Well, these days luxury is the new necessity. What's her name?"

"Dr. Petrosian."

Bingo.

Nick and Sophia Go on a Date

Imagine that, and Nick was just about to give the doctor up. He had wondered what it would be like to date a world-class beauty who was a psychiatrist. He liked the idea, but she wasn't really his type. Miranda was more his type.

The trick was how to get a look at her file on Stephen. She would honor her patient's privacy. She might mention a case, but never any specifics. Never any names. And she didn't leave files around her apartment. Patience was the ticket, something would come up. Wait till Friday. She was always busy, and could find work to do all the time, but she generally left Fridays open.

"Will you be free on Friday?"

"Probably."

"Because there's a new movie out—*Under Suspicion*. Stars Gene Hackman and Morgan Freeman."

"Who else?" Meaning, he supposed, *any women actresses?* What did Stephen say?

"Yes, there is an Italian actress, Monica Something. I don't remember her name. It's a murder mystery set in Puerto Rico."

The never-ending screening process. Answer the phone, don't answer the phone. Listen to see if they leave a message or check the caller ID. See the movie, don't see the movie. Check the reviews.

"Okay. What time is the show? And where?"

Bup bup bup. Details, details.

"At the Water Tower. How about a nine-thirty show? We can get a bite beforehand. There's a restaurant we need to check out."

"Okay."

She likes mysteries. She likes the Water Tower. Anything posh. She seems to like period pieces. A drink afterward, probably at the Four Seasons this time.

The thing was—if he could get a look at Stephen's file, maybe he'd find something he could use. Maybe he had a special interest or a hang-up he could make use of. Information was the thing.

* * *

He made the best of the evening, and was very relaxed. People liked to talk about themselves. The personal myth would be the next big thing. *I was born in a log cabin that I built myself.* Or the up-to-date version: *I was born in an ad campaign that I wrote myself.* She was a dazzling student, and this had been her ticket to rise above the muck. Well, that and her dazzling looks. She couldn't fail.

"I graduated from medical school at twenty-two."

"Is that early?"

"Most people start medical school at twenty-two."

"Oh, wow!" It's such a drag when people have to explain their claims to fame; it's better if you understand the significance of their references. "That's quite impressive."

An attempt to regain favor. *Remember, twenty-seven compliments per hour.*

"How did you get into medical school so early?"

"I was smart. They didn't know what else to do with me."

"Wow."

She raised her head some; body posture was at full mast. Progress. Maybe that last "Wow" was a double or triple square. Worth ten compliments at least. Maybe that "Wow" alone was enough to put him over the top. Without multi-point squares, it was impossible to reach the goal.

Then the waitress came over, and looked Nick over in such a way that all progress was lost. It was impossible not to respond to the appraisal of an attractive woman. You try for the poker face; it's the best you can do.

Nick thought this little episode was over when the waitress brought over some mixed nuts, and asked if they would be interested in a dessert. She was showing a little too much interest, but he looked over at Sophia. She was smiling at his efforts at containment.

"She's attractive."

It was one of the things that he marveled at about women. They seemed to be more willing to acknowledge the beauty of other women without the competitiveness of men. A man might recognize the attractiveness of another man, but he would be a great deal less willing to say anything about it, especially to a woman.

"Yes."

"Really attractive."

"Yeah."

"Very nice bust."

"Oh brother."

She laughed. "Listen, my car is acting out. So I need to take it in for service tomorrow, but I haff to go to court first ting and give expert testimony. I vunder if you could help me out."

Patience worked again, and he hadn't expected anything so soon. With the keys, it would be an easy thing to peek at Stephen's file.

Peeking Into Files

So, the thing went like clockwork. He met her at eight-thirty. She gave him the keys and went off to court. He took the car and went to her office. Think. The file cabinet had a lock on it, but it was unlocked. Check the A's, Ambrose. First find the file. Finding it, he turned on the copier, and meanwhile thumbed through the pages while it warmed up.

After he made the photocopies, he turned off the machine and returned the file to the file cabinet, and then went off to the dealership. He waited until he was back at his apartment ensconced in his favorite reading chair before he examined the stuff.

STEPHEN AMBROSE

B.D. 08/11/62

PRESENTING PROBLEM

Patient presents as being unable to sleep. A neighbor of the same age died of congenital heart problems in his sleep. He has "extra heartbeats," and is afraid of sleeping.

PRESENT PSYCHIATRIC HISTORY

Evidently, his job as a programmer is very demanding. He is unable to speak about his work, and has concerns about industrial espionage. He works very long hours, and sometimes has as many as three drinks.

PAST PSYCHIATRIC HISTORY

Patient has had counseling off and on for many years. He traces first treatment back to college when he experienced hyperventilation after an LSD episode. Medications failed to resolve a cough, and finally whatever caused the problem receded in time.

MEDICAL HISTORY

Patient reports that he had chest pains at age thirty-five, and went to the emergency room of LaGrange Memorial. He was between residences and evidently under stress. He was kept in the hospital overnight for observation, and was released the next day. Tests indicated he was suffering from stomach flu.

The file was made available and the final diagnosis was depression.

FAMILY HISTORY

Father is a remote, successful businessman with no history of psychological treatment. Mother is a housewife who became neurotic with the end of child rearing, and has been in counseling for fourteen years. He says, "Is this the same recipe that made for Jeffrey Dahmer? Passive father, nutty mother."

INTERVIEWS WITH STEPHEN

Patient believes that nearly all illness is mental illness, and is writing a science fiction novel wherein the president of the U.S. is a psychiatrist. He has a vivid imagination. An example of one of his dreams: Aliens come to Earth and stir up graves so they may "feed" on the spirits, use their anger as fuel to run their spaceships. Suggestion was made to patient that this is often the solution to psychological problems. To use the problem emotion to best advantage. To use anger, for example, to best advantage—to win a tennis match or golf match.

He states that the problem with psychiatry is that people see problems, but that does not guarantee they will take steps to solve them. He refers to Freud who thought that naming the problem would solve it. But he questions—how does naming "love" solve the problem? He noted that in the scientific community when they speak of the animal kingdom they use the term "mating" instead of "love." Patient states millions of people would like to mate, but can never locate an appropriate partner. He talks about propinquity. Says the reason the actor Richard Burton married an airline stewardess was because she was there, within eyeshot, within "radar range" as he says. Elizabeth Taylor married a carpenter she met in therapy.

PSYCHODYNAMIC FORMULATION

The patient is neurotic. Transference is an issue. Advised patient that his condition is not severe, and have prescribed Atavin for acute symptoms of sleeplessness.

It is not clear to what extent, if any; the patient's job affects his disposition. Stress from work may contribute to sleeplessness.

*   *   *

This was sort of like looking at your test scores at school. No one would let you look at your test scores; they were afraid that they would affect your behavior. Nick always scored spectacularly high on the standardized tests. And no high school filing cabinet was ever going to stand between him and his Iowa Basic test scores. That was then, and no file cabinet in Sophia's office was going to get in his way now.

He agreed about the propinquity thing. Probably Richard Burton met Liz Taylor at the MGM commissary. But the mention of love just made him wince. Whatever could she mean by that? For that matter, what could anyone mean by that? He knew Ambrose was neurotic, everyone who knew him knew that.

It was not clear what this information had yielded. It was easy to get information; the question was always, "what did it mean?" Nick paced the hallway of his apartment. His favorite totem was the panther. The black panther. It sprang from out of the void when it attacked its prey. Ambushing from its staging area in another universe, from a crack in time-space. Born in the year of the Tiger, he would say to himself—"close enough," after all, there is no year of the Panther. He devoured the movie *Cat People*. At night he would put himself to sleep thinking about having superpowers, catlike superpowers. Extrasensory hearing and infrared night vision. Malcolm McDowell was perfect for the role with his sinister presence, and New Orleans was perhaps the only exotic locale in North America. A black panther in the night, that was stealth to the nth degree. That was a creature which could hide between the radar beams. In his chair and ottoman, he imagined himself as human transmogrified into panther/human.

He put on the soundtrack for *Cat People* and paced some more. Nick had always identified with cats, even from his early years. They were untrainable but intelligent. Not sociable, but would caterwaul long into the night when in heat. He understood cats. He made no demands of his cat, but when he sat down in his chair, inevitably his calico would nestle next to him.

He played with the cat, but even with the cover of fur, this cat had quite a gut—the feline equivalent of a beer belly. He turned on the news. He looked at a chess game on his coffee table. It was one of Botvinnik's games, the master of the logic, master of the combination, planner extraordinaire, who moved pieces together, in synchronicity, to give the opposing king nowhere to go. But chess takes a lot of energy. Absorbs energy like a sponge. He faded. The speech of the newscasters turned into chatter, and the chatter into incoherent babble, which faded out.

The Defining Characteristic of Man

Stephen Ambrose seemed to spend his life in front of a screen. Television screen, computer screen. *You must be made to wear earphones.* That was the way Bob Dylan put it. Earphones fastened to the body, part of the body. Next, it would be the eyes and the screen. In this increasingly important era of the bandwidth, the visual band would be paramount. In the Dylan sense, eyes would come out of their sockets and affix themselves to the video screen.

We keep trying to define the age in which we lived—the atomic age, the nuclear age, the age of television, the information age, the age of the bandwidth. Perhaps the defining characteristic of the human being is the business of defining. Stephen was a part of the new modular age. Coders like himself were increasingly using modular blocks of code to do simple jobs, over and over again. These modular blocks were called objects. You didn't have to rewrite code as much if you could use the same block of code to do the same job again and again.

For example, he could send out a command to write to a file. Store a file. The command would see if anyone else was using the file, in which case it was considered locked. If it found it was locked, the block of code would continue to send out the request again and again, until it was deemed too long an interval by the code block, and then it would flash a message on the screen like "Server Not Available." In which case, the user could try again, or check and see if the server was just busy or actually down. And you could use that piece of code in every application. Or until it had to be written in another language.

Objects were like program cells. Cells: apartments, work cubicles, cars, a block of code. The metaphor of the cell had a lot of room to grow. It has been suggested that the biological cell formed around a drop of water.

He worked hard, like a horse. He kidded about strapping on the feedbag at night. His official title was software engineer, but coder was more like it. Coder, robot key-striker. Plodder. His specialty was writing algorithms, which narrowed the scope of the missile as it homed in on its target, be it a building, a ship, or another missile. In the Desert Storm, the Israelis had Patriot missiles, but with only the first version of programming, in effect version 1.0. Ambrose had written five versions since, and now they were using version 6.0 on the new ones. So, the United States sent Patriot missiles from West Germany to Israel to protect against Iraqi Scuds. The principal difference in the missiles was an improvement in the algorithms that Ambrose had written. Algorithm—the word came from a man's name, Abu Ja'far Mohammed ibn-Musa al-Khwarizmi, who lived around 800 A.D. He lived and taught in Baghdad, which, in Desert Storm, became the target of missiles that Stephen wrote algorithms for.

Algorithms were routines to narrow choices, IF and THEN statements steer the program.

IF the girl is blond, THEN proceed to the next IF. IF NOT, keep searching until you find a blond.

IF the girl, blond, is not three feet away, THEN move within three feet, and proceed to the next IF.

IF the girl, blond, is now three feet away, and IF NOT engaged in conversation, THEN ask, "Can I buy you a drink," and proceed to the next IF.

He did the same thing with missiles by using global positioning satellites, radar information from AWACs, and heat from its engines to determine the enemy missile's exact position, and the same stuff plus onboard sensors (altimeters, etc.) to detect where his missile was. This was done constantly, second by second. If the missile was not on track, the code of algorithms would alter the course.

He played computer games to relax, to not have to think. A sanitary time fill to shovel in all of his toxic psychological tendencies. A lock against thinking. Increasingly, this was identified as a meditation. Solitaire with cards used to fulfill this need; now one shoved around images of cards with a mouse, and the computer lined them up in perfect order. For a while he was locked into playing the Battle of Britain. Knew all the Messerschmidt numbers, watched Weekday Wings on the Discovery Channel. But in the end, the images the computer games offered were really clunky, and he could only imagine how wonderful the game would be when they could really manipulate the pixels. But Intel was still processors away from what he had in mind.

Ambrose conjured the game he had in mind. They would acquire the images by going up in a helicopter and photographing surround-type images, and figuring out how to do the distance thing from all the different angles. Two cameras in each direction for stereoscopic vision. There had to be a way of compressing or expanding images without photographing a zillion different angles. There were still big problems to solve with computers and images. Did the brain hold a static image and make changes to it? They would figure out how the eye and brain did it and back-engineer. That's why robots and androids would resemble humans. Legs are useful means of locomotion, a better general solution for locomotion though slower than the specific flat surface solution of wheels. Millions of years of design evolution had not gone to waste. That's what the engineers discovered when they looked for better designs. Wheels were not as useful as legs.

That's it, he thought, the computers, the androids would use games to keep humans occupied, put them to sleep. Render humans completely docile. Homo ludere. Man who plays. Even Salman Rushdie became an expert at Supermario I and II, when at rest between efforts to find a new hideout from agents of the Ayatolla.

He looked in *The Reader* at the matches ads. Where would he find his opposite number? Strike opposite. Where would he find his complementary number, his symbiotic match. The one that would be like the good bacteria in his stomach. Maybe it was time to try the Matches ads again.

Last time he responded he ended up with a twenty-eight-year-old who was auditioning men on a fifteen-minute trial basis at a local bar. She had ice water, he had a glass of Merlot. She was mildly attractive, so the thing was not settled in his mind immediately, and he did his mating-dance thing and fluffed up his tail feathers in best male display fashion. But he was hampered by secrecy acts from his best claims to fame, and could only allow that he was a programmer. He tried to create interest by spilling all the secrets of his dinosaur story, but she could care less. Secrets are a little like beauty; it's all the eye of the beholder. Speculation, including scientific speculation, appeared to be a male thing. ("I thought I saw the deer go that away. Let's head off in that direction, men.") Her motives lie in the direction of fulfilling her matrix of needs—a quality sperm donor, protector for her offspring, helpmate with chores, companion, financial security. So this exquisite product of his frontal lobes was lost on her. She said, "Oh, that's interesting," but claimed she had to run, a friend to meet. Probably another candidate at another bar. Very courteous, but over.

He, too, had placed ads. The ad read:

Science Fiction writer wants to meet with alien for fun and research.
I am SWM, 5'11", 160.

One girl called very up on her science fiction. Read everything: Harlan Ellison, Heinlein, Asimov, Piers Anthony, William Gibson. Interesting character—she confessed that she worked a 900 number, and that should have been the tip-off. After an hour of interesting conversation, after drooling over hearing that Gia was a 42DD, he finally asks, almost as an afterthought, "How tall are you?"

"Five foot two."

"And weight commensurate with height?"

"Two hundred and twenty pounds."

"You're kidding," said Ambrose.

"No, I'm not."

"Sure, you are."

"No."

"Well, I don't know what to say."

"Say you want to meet me. I'm the sexiest thing you'll ever meet."

"Well."

"Well what?"

"Well. Well. I don't know what to say."

"Say you want to meet me."

"I'm sorry, I just don't think it'll work out."

"Maybe it will."

"Well, let me think about it. Okay?"

"Think about it now."

"Okay, I have to go. I'm sorry. Goodbye."

"Wait wait wait . . ."

Click.

He felt horrible. Of course, she was great on the phone, that was her business. She knew conversation. He felt that she had worked not only the 900 numbers, but had done a stint at telemarketing as well. He had tried to be diplomatic, but he felt it didn't really work out well. What could he have said that would have been better? "Well, I'm busy this week, but give me your phone number." And then never call. Diplomacy was always a trick. With *The Reader*, you couldn't see the enemy much less the whites of their eyes, perfect terrain for ambush. Could she count on the good manners of men to complete the date? That was the question.

So, his next ad read:

> Science fiction writer wants to meet with alien for fun and research.
> Alien's weight must be commensurate with height.

At this point he wondered if the ad should specify that the alien should be a female alien. It took the fun out of the ads that you had to specify everything so exactly. That such a playful ad would be abused felt like a mugging. But on the other hand, in another age, today's slim women might be viewed as anemic, unhealthy, and the overweight woman might be seen as the superior specimen, the picture of health. She had that layer of blubber that would keep her alive in lean times.

He got more responses this time. Everyone was familiar with Star Trek, and they spoke about favorite episodes, and the original Star Trek versus Next Generation versus the Star Trek movies. But the girls sounded too wholesome. Not one of them suggested the porno title—Star Tramps Next Generation. And somehow he was always a little concerned that real aliens might try to reach him, to improve a waning genetic line. For all he knew Sophia was an alien. If an alien was really that far advanced, how would you know?

He narrowed it down to a couple of prospects. One was a doctor. A superachiever type. Traveled all over the place. Skied in Europe and the Andes. They spoke a few times, but her schedule was so jam-packed that he decided to give it up. What was the point, after all? Why date someone whose schedule is so crowded that you would never get to see them?

It was as though this woman wanted to do everything. Yoga, tae kwon do, Viennese waltzes, Hawaiian hulas. Travel everywhere. But then, maybe we all wanted to do everything but she was the one who was doing it. The envy thing again, turning up like a bad penny.

Nevertheless, she continued the idea of meeting for three weeks, but this was, after all, ridiculous. IF it's that difficult to meet, THEN he felt, "let's forget it."

But it did bring up the question of persistence. How did one know when the woman was worth the effort to wade through the swamps of hell and wait for her to finally give up the boyfriend, or as in some Isaac Bashevis Singer story, wait for her to raise her kids and the husband to die, and then marry her. Singer didn't make it seem very attractive, although human enough.

He did meet with a psychologist. A short Italian thing who hands him a report on one of her patients to check over the spelling. "My English is good, but not that good." He checked the spelling, but reading was inevitable, and it turned out the patient desperately wanted to undergo a sex change operation. Paul was ready to become Pauline. Her analysis was that he was in the midst of a depression that the sex change would not improve, that in fact, he would likely take a turn for the worse if the operation occurred. He wondered if it was appropriate that he should read someone's personal history like this—it felt very odd. But in a city and suburbs of seven million people, there was still an excellent chance that he would never meet up with this person, and he certainly wasn't nosey enough to look for him. Still he had the disagreeable taste in his mouth of being a voyeur. And not in a happy way.

She was vivacious and engaging, but there was some disagreeable quality about her skin, which was sallow and oily. She did not have the right smell, which was a revelation of sorts because most of the time he didn't feel like he could smell anything at all. In the pollution dome of Chicago, his nose was constantly stuffed up. He often thought the olfactory senses were like some antiquated sensory antennae, something that used to have value. Nowadays if there's some bad smell—a fire, for example—we have fire detectors to do the work.

He took her to dinner, which Nick thought was excessive ("Just meet her for coffee. Why spend all that money?"). They went to Primavera, which had waiters and waitresses who were aspiring singers. They sang opera and show tunes.

And she told him all about her family, and how she came to America, getting some Italian government subsidy. But instead of taking the learning back home, she wanted to stay here. This devolved into a discussion of her visa problems. Marriage would help of course, and no doubt that was one of the thoughts when she responded to the ad. He felt sympathetic to her cause, but marriage seemed like an extravagant solution. Though for many this was the only route to a green card, surely there were other ways. Or worse comes to worst, she ends up back in Italy, which she described as gorgeous.

After dinner, he took her to a play. His brother Abner: "You must be a lunatic. Nobody spends for a play on a first date. A blind date at that."

"I didn't have anyone else to take and I wanted to see the play." In the end, he went back to see this inspired, small Steppenwolf production of O'Neill's *A Moon for the Misbegotten* three more times. Alone.

"Where did you go to dinner?"

"Primavera."

"Isn't that the place with all the would-be opera singers?"

"Right." He knew what was coming next for him, the would-be writer.

"Don't quit your day job." That was the line he was waiting for. His science fiction would come to nothing.

Afterwards, they went for a drink, and then he took her home. They kissed good night and then they went spinning off like subatomic particles at Fermi Lab.

Now Feynman, the subatomic wiz, was a man who knew how to deal with the problem of women. When in the late 1940s, after the Soviet Union had figured out the trick of atomic explosions, he worked on his Portuguese and decided to go to Brazil.

Down in Rio, out of harm's way, he applied his mind to the problem of dating and the mechanisms of bar romance. Using the psychological tools at his disposal, he figured out that by treating women with disrespect, he could guide them down the ramp that would lead to a bed somewhere close by. He uses a dollar and ten cents for sandwiches and coffee to make a girl feel "worse than a whore," so she sleeps with him, and then ends up repaying him the $1.10. A gifted lady-killer as well as a gifted physics theoretician. A problem is a problem is a problem.

It didn't hurt that he was tall, dark, handsome, and engaging. That he was a fun conversationalist and could dance. These were not particular tools he developed for pursuit; they were more things he found available, on hand, which he realized he could put to good use.

Ambrose would like to have been like barroom bongo Feynman, but he was a hacker, a computer geek who sat in front of a screen figuring out how to invade government security systems, which he did all the time, just to see what was there. Well, this was not unlike Feynman, who would open government safes at Los Alamos for the fun of it.

It was easy for him to see how a twisted geek might tinker with code that could act like a virus shutting down whole nations of computers. He knew how to write such viruses, he knew how to write them better than those who were writing them, but it gave him no thrill to exercise that kind of power. Really, it was a personal thing. He was annoyed enough by power outages caused by thunderstorms that man-made outages just infuriated him.

And it was this that led him to help track down one such renegade hacker. There was a certain challenge to it, and it served notice to the computer community that such faceless keystrokes were not without a trail. But there was always the next hacker-genius who might develop the perfect untraceable virus.

He thought this might make for a good novel. Tracking down the virus maker. But he felt it would be too technical. Where is the drama of a guy in front of a screen with a keyboard? It would do better as a computer game. Moving from one screen to the next. It was perfect as a computer game.

Devising a virus was no particular secret. Everything was in a book or on television. The scary thing was that outlaw nations like Iraq or Iran might get hold of those secrets. After all, they knew how Desert Storm was going from watching CNN, and if fission was explained on television, where everything turned up eventually, then the world was at risk. What would it take for them to get the signal? A satellite dish and a code.

On C-Span, the CIA revealed in a session before Congress the work it was doing to forestall the release of fissionable material from Russia, and showed slides of the exits from the country, which meant the enemy could get a feeling for it, too. It was General Sherman who complained the press "retailed" the North's strategy. 9/11 would set the U.S. off on a wild goose chase for terrorists, slowing down air travel in the name of safety, taking over a poor, harmless country, while the real risks were still out there. A nuclear pulse bomb that went off three hundred miles above the center of the country would just about wreck everything. An electromagnetic pulse bomb would wreck all communications, computers. Cars wouldn't work because the computer chip that ran the motor would be fried. The financial markets would be in disarray, the country would be all but destroyed, and no one would die—straight off, anyway, though spoiled computer records would do their business in the hospitals.

Everything out in the open. Maybe that was it: join a nudist colony. Quick reversal: bad idea. It would never work for him, a skinny ectomorph. But he wasn't alone, a lot of people did better in clothes.

He placed another ad:

Programmer moonlighting as a science fiction writer seeks woman from the Adult Ads. SWM, 40, 6', 160.

His ads were always terse. He read so many long ones that led nowhere; he didn't want to waste anyone's time. And the anecdotal evidence was pointing to the fact that one could not avoid one's destiny. Many of the women who called on his alien ads also responded to this one. The same heavy girl, Gia, who answered the 900 line, called again, but he recognized her voice this time on the recording and did not return the call.

He looked at his novel.

Paperwork

They completed assembly of the craft in the year 2097. It was an enormous ship, holding five thousand people. It was like a skyscraper, but much larger. It was the size of the Empire State Building plus the Pentagon plus the Merchandise Mart. The craft had some of the features of those huge buildings. It was a world in itself. Water Tower Place was like that. A hotel, apartments, stores, parking, restaurants. A handy thing in the winter. And it was always winter out in space.

Prime included vast gardens, a park with trees, a zoo with many, many samples of different animals, a fresh water pond, a saltwater pond. Many floors for manufacturing. There was a place in the library called the artifact room. Many important paintings and first editions of books were vaulted into space. Not perhaps the most important documents. They didn't want to attract too much attention to the fact that Prime was an off-planet safety deposit box for all of civilization. But no books that were not first editions were maintained. Books were not efficient, everything was on electronic storage, and everyone had a set of glasses with a screen for reading books or viewing video. A Kindle screen would seem like clumsy technology compared to this.

*   *   *

Nick wanted to break off with Sophia because she was a little too vanilla for his taste, kind of a dud. She was exotic-looking, but somehow, it was a disappointment that this gorgeous, exotic woman expressed the same thoughts that all women expressed. Her taste in sex was mundane. A little bit like fast food. Always in a hurry, on to the next thing.

But to make his mark, he was going to need Ambrose; he was the key. The Koreans would be keen on Ambrose. It was not enough just to pass envelopes to this Senator or that Congressman; that was routine work. He needed something spectacular to generate the money he wanted. For the acclaim, however secret.

And Sophia might turn out to be the key to Ambrose. So Nick decided he would have to continue with Sophia, perhaps even try to deepen the relationship. He stepped up his apparent interest by suggesting a trip to New Orleans, where he had a drop to make. She found the idea very appealing. Not for the sleazy character of Bourbon Street which he found charming, but because of all the great dining. She saw Proudhon on the *Today* program many times, so they would have to go to K-Paul's.

It was a weekend deal they worked out. They left on a Friday night, but because the plane's weather radar was not working and there were severe storms, they were routed to Little Rock, and put up for the night in a Holiday Inn.

A bad omen, but it didn't matter because the whole trip didn't matter except for the envelope he would have to transmit sometime during the weekend. She was very frustrated and he tried to cheer her up.

"Damn American Airlines, I'll bet they sent us up with faulty radar," she complained.

"Don't be silly, they have to meet all kinds of safety precautions, flightworthiness criteria, checklists," he said.

"See!" Then she made a face, "Paperwork."

"Well, important paperwork. They could be shut down."

"Hospitals are always threatening to take away my privileges if I don't keep up on the paperwork."

"Since English is not your native language, I can imagine this is a problem."

"You know, you are right. I wonder. Could you help me a little bit with my paperwork? My secretary is a moron who cannot even do the simplest thing like my billing."

"I could try to help."

"That would be so wonderful." She kissed him, and hugged him in a way much more emotional than she ever had before. Necessity warmed her up. They made love, which was still nothing special, but okay because he still got off, and this did feel good after all.

Lying together, she said, "Of course I am always late on my paperwork. Even in Russia. But you'll help me anyway."

"Yes. I can try."

The next day, they landed in New Orleans and started the gourmet tour. Brennan's for breakfast for the requisite Eggs Benedict, red beans and rice at Proudhon's for lunch. Then they took a boat trip to the zoo, and spent the afternoon walking off the first two meals and returning on a streetcar named St. Charles for the trip back through the Garden District. And they finished the day with pâté and duck at the Commander's Palace. It was a lot of food to eat.

Before dinner, he walked downstairs to buy a newspaper, and that was when he delivered the package of money.

"What took you so long?"

"No papers downstairs. I had to go look for one."

She was lying on the bed with pieces of potato over her eyes and cheeks.

"You don't need stuff like that. You're gorgeous without."

"Beauty needs a little help once a while."

"Once *in* a while."

"That's what I said."

"No, you left out the preposition 'in.'"

"Once in a while."

"Better."

"Thank you for correcting me. Because I'm a doctor, everyone passes over my mistakes, and I can never improve my English." And also because she's a great beauty. He thought the same rule applied to her sex life. Because she was so gorgeous, she never had to make any effort on technique. Men came after her no matter what, a continuous supply. There was always one standing by, like a Pez dispenser.

At dinner he paid her the same compliment about not needing the potato slices because she was so gorgeous (on his way to twenty-seven), and she said, "Oh, that is nothing. My grandmother had eighteen proposals of marriage."

"Oh, surely you have received that many proposals."

"No," she pouted.

He sensed that he was supposed to chime in with his own proposal of marriage, but that was more than he could bring himself to do. With each passing moment, he felt he was losing in the balance of compliments.

"Oh, I'm sure before it's all over you will out-proposal your grandmother by a mile."

"Tank you, Nick."

Later in bed she claimed she was too tired for sex. So, the question was: was she really too filled with food, or was it that he never restored the lost compliments? Just because you're traveling with a woman, and you are paying for the room, and dinner, and the plane ticket down, is no guarantee you're going to get laid. She may still insist you satisfy that quota of compliments.

*   *   *

Stephen Ambrose sat in front of his television trying to decide if Dennis Quaid's accent in *The Big Easy* was authentic. He thought New Orleans would be a wonderful place to take a woman. To take Sophia, for example. She would love it, the luxury of Cajun food, and a hotel with prompt room service.

But there was always something to trip up a great daydream, and room service was something he had never ordered in his life. You need acres and acres of money, or an exaggerated sense of self, before you feel comfortable ordering room service. It was a matter of priorities, Sophia's Mercedes was a large percentage of her wealth, 10 percent at least, maybe 20 percent. Even 50 percent was not out of the question. He hated to think it could be more than that, but appearances held great sway with her.

Oh, the hell with it, it's only a daydream. Damn the torpedoes, full speed ahead. Order the room service. The luxury of it, and then a pair of masseuses. The cost was truly insignificant. A couple of hundred dollars.

He thought of Sammy. Sammy would remind him of the eighty-year-olds who rued all the chances they passed by. Regret is the main occupation of the aged. And the unoccupied. And everyone was idle at night. Night was hell. Night spent by one's self was nothing but regret.

Sammy might be classified under the heading of Las Vegas Jew. Ever since the late 50s, he had trekked out to Vegas to gamble, to see the fights, to see the shows, the hookers. He lived for Vegas, going five to eight times per year. A big gambler, he got suites comped, meals comped, shows comped. The only thing he didn't get comped were the hookers. But if the hotel comped all these things, then he had more money to play at the tables, and a shrewd look at the odds and a little study of Black Jack and he was able to make a profit on many of the trips. And often enough, when Black Jack didn't work out, it was a strategic bet on the football or basketball games that saved the day.

It was Stephen's contention that Sammy got all his luck from relatives who were snuffed out during the Nazi years. They looked down on him from heaven, saving his ass time after time, funneling into one soul the good fortune of an entire family.

But it didn't pass into the next generation. The next generation did well because of Sammy's preparations, but their luck was ordinary luck, proletarian luck, lumpen luck.

Stephen felt his luck was lumpen luck. He didn't make that much money programming the Patriot; he would make a lot more money selling secrets to a competing country. It always amazed him that the public servants with so much on the line made so little money. The President's measly $400,000 was chicken feed, a month's pay of the average *Fortune 500* CEO. Perhaps the government should be on an incentive basis. He wondered what Milton Friedman would have to say about that. The basic notion he got out of Friedman was that incentives were the basis of capitalism, that and increase the money supply a steady two percent. Friedman was the B.F. Skinner of economics. If we provided the proper incentives, perhaps we would get the effective government we sought. Problem was: most people were a little bit afraid of effective government, believing, for example, that spending to solve the war on poverty would bankrupt the country. People truly sought governments of gridlock and deadlock, because deadlocked governments were the safest. Friedman would say the smaller the government, the better. Jefferson thought so, too.

He made half the President's pay to write the programming for one of the most effective missiles on the planet, and he only got that much by working for a contractor. But he did get a perk: they let work at home in Chicago and keep his own hours. They didn't send him to Los Alamos or Langley or some other godforsaken dump. It seemed to him greatly unfair that he didn't get any big money, or at least some bragging rights. It reminded him of his high school days, of his six friends—three had fathers who worked on the Manhattan Project with Enrico Fermi at the University of Chicago and stayed on at what became Argonne National Laboratories afterwards. He remembered seeing a photo in the *Doings* of his friend's father receiving an award.

"What's the award for?" he asked the friend.

"Who knows? He works on nuclear reactors. Everything he does is top secret."

Ambrose wondered how anyone would know enough about what his friend's father was doing to grant such an award if it's such a damn secret. Ambrose would have loved to receive some award, but no one in the government wanted to draw any attention to his work. Not that such an award was what he lived for, but women seemed to put stock in a man's achievements. My husband conquered Mt. Everest. My husband robbed seventeen banks. My husband services all the McDonald's accounts in the state of Wyoming. Some kind of bragging rights.

He saw that on an anthropology program on television. Women sought men with resources, and men sought women who appeared to be fertile. Somehow scientists proved that there was a relation between the hourglass figure and fertility. A relation between waist and hip size. A waist a little less than two-thirds of the hips. The golden ratio.

It was all in the hips. The pelvis signaled changes in locomotion. Ankle, femur will follow form in hominid locomotion, that's what they said. Human development was tied up with the hips. Upright locomotion frees the hands—to carry things, to fashion tools, to make animal-killing tools. The tool bearing hominid, homo habilis.

Shape was everything. Shape came first. It looked like the shape of the head in Lucy made room for the spinal chord directly underneath, which indicated the upright posture came first because her brain was no larger than a chimp's.

Dolphins have a larger brain than humans (1,700 cc's vs 1,350 in humans), but their braincase to body weight ratio is not quite as good as a human's, and their water-designed bodies put them at a distinct disadvantage. Humans can enter and swim in water, however poorly, but dolphins cannot walk on land. Not even a few steps. Water was a sloppy, difficult medium to take with you. Moreover, they lack hands to manipulate their environment. Hands allowed man to: make slate tools to kill and butcher animals, later to make marks on clay tablets and paper, to leave behind cultural documents. Cultural documents left behind a bank of information and ideas, and such documents gave any brain that knew the code the ability to look up, evaluate, and improve on their understanding of their surroundings, to extrapolate on their understanding, to send men to the moon and back. An achievement that showed a pretty good understanding of the rules of nature.

Dolphins were horny creatures, excited a lot of the time. The males appeared a little homosexual as well. Maybe it was just a kind of an extended horniness.

Brain expansion. They think that occurred to cope with changing climate. Drought, rains. Lakes that came and went. Forests that turned into savannahs, savannahs that turned into deserts. It required brains to survive, to cope with change. And at around the same time they become meat eaters. The meat provides the energy the new larger brain requires. The brain consumes twenty-five percent of all calories the body ingests.

*   *   *

When Nick returned home, the first thing he did was call Miranda. She was a total pro. The word "pro" in itself thrilled him. Her mouth was a warm fuzzy home for his favorite set of nerve endings.

But when he complained that one amateur hurt him, Miranda said, "Well, some girls get a little excited with a hard cock in their mouth, and they forget to take precautions. You know, it's really a little bit dirty. And you know how girls can be when they drop their inhibitions."

"I know how you are."

By now they were kissing, her hand pressing against his pants at the crotch, stroking the outline of his cock. His hand down her back to her ass, touching it lightly and then moving further to her clit. Sometimes long arms were an advantage.

"I think you're getting a little bit hard."

"I think maybe a lot."

Miranda got down on her knees. Now, this was a nice gesture that girls outside the profession rarely made. They usually would only take a man in their mouths when already in the sack, and only from the side. Never straight on, never like they meant it. They hid behind a veil of long hair. You could feel something going on down there, but you never got to see it.

She got down on her knees, unbuckled his belt, unbuttoned him his shirt, and before bringing down the pants teased him some more, kissing his dick through his underwear. Just a little bit of teeth, so he'd know something was there. A lot of hookers these days wouldn't take a dick in the mouth without a condom, but that failed to generate enough friction to do any good. So they used the teeth to increase the sensation, and the teeth hurt.

She took just the head in her mouth and rubbed her tongue softly around it. Then she took it out and said, "Listen, darling, my neck hurts a little tonight. How about if you do the work?"

"I can't imagine what you mean."

"I think you can. You just want to hear me say it, don't you?"

He nodded and grinned.

"I want you, darling, to fuck my mouth with your big dick."

He took her head in his hands and started to push forward a little bit, and then back, and he looked down to observe, and she looked up at him with slightly shy eyes. All part of the act.

Then she put her arms behind her back and grasped one with the other, so that he appeared in full control.

She said, "Look in the mirror."

He looked in the mirror and saw her in submission, which spurred him on.

A Pinhole in the Darkness

It was dark in space. Prime Earth hurtled forward at sub-light speed in the darkness. Looking into the dark made astrophysicists wonder if there was enough mass in the universe to halt the expansion of the original Big Bang, and start the convergence necessary for the next Big Bang. If there were black holes at the center of galaxies, that would help solve the problem. Dark matter would help, but dark energy didn't. Dark energy was sending everything further out into space. That was the thinking.

Dark, dark, dark. In the void, the sensors, which constantly swept the area around the craft, detected a signal in the radio bandwidth. The signal formed a pattern that was not constant in a natural way, such as the rotation of a neutron star. There were two patterns, one consistent, and one intricate like music. Maybe it was some other galaxy's idea of music.

Ramón, who was head of Prime, convened a meeting of the crew to determine what action, if any, they should take. Scans revealed that the source of the signal was small, not detectable in any visual way for the moment.

Ada, the ship's counselor, joked, "This is probably another of your delusional hallucinations. Like subatomic particles."

The basic question was whether they should attempt to investigate. They could not stop on a dime, stopping might take three years, and more than three years to get up to the speed they were at now. And no large bodies around to hop a free increase in acceleration. So it was a big decision to make.

Ada said, "Three years to check out an hallucination. That's a long time, sweetheart."

Ramón responded, "Physicists in the twenty-first century felt the same way about discovering neutrinos, which were practically nothing, and would pass through everything. They often wondered if they were doing *hard* science, or whether it was all a dream."

Like most decisions, this one was put off. It was decided that more information was required. Nobody in the universe was at rest. And what everyone wanted to know was in what direction the signal was headed, and at what speed. If it was headed their way, they would have to stop and then change direction, or attempt to curve around and back. And if the speed of the object was too fast, the whole thing would be academic, because they could never catch up with it.

The research took some time, because until they were closer, their equipment was not sensitive enough to answer those questions. In the meantime, they released visual and sensor buoys that could be used to refine the picture of what they were looking at. And over time, they were able to figure out that the speed of the object was slower than their speed, and secondly, that they were headed in the same direction, Alpha Centauri. So, although they would have to slow down, it would not seriously slow their progress.

So the crew voted to take the time necessary to match up with the signal, and then to slow to docking speed. It was estimated that this would take 1.4 years. A lot of novels and movies would be consumed in that time. And a lot of games. One popular game that had been developed was called "Boarding," and involved 1950s aliens.

A trajectory was decided upon. It would involve applying Newton's laws of mechanics for 1.4 years. Some scientists thought that when the universe reached the stopping point of its expansion, the inward march would be the reverse of the outward progress. By the time all mass gathers back into a bolus, we had better figure out how to transport ourselves into another universe, or some other dimension, or we're toast. *It's a technical thing.*

It was hard to keep up interest for years and years on a spacecraft. People went into stasis for years at a time to avoid the boredom. When the mind didn't have sufficiently meaty external stimuli to feast on, it went awry and started eating itself. Thus, an insufficiently occupied brain often found its occupant in a drunken state or drugged state or compulsively gambling or chained to some video game. Hence, Sherlock on cocaine. Hence, Freud on cocaine. The only thing left to do was to take the brain out of commission, put it to sleep, put it in stasis, and wake it up when there was something substantial for it to chew on.

Finally they neared the signal, and Prime sent out various hails to try and get some kind of communication running, but the ship continued to send out its hail without acknowledging Prime's signal.

Most of the crew had set their wake-up call for one month in advance to witness the approach and boarding, and they were reaching a fully *wakeful* state now. There was little to observe. Telescopes gave a visual picture, but at the earliest sightings the distance was so great as to make the picture useless, just a point of light. A pinhole in the darkness. As they closed in, the visual picture became more interesting. It was obviously constructed by intelligent life, and a large craft at that. Nearly as large as the craft they were on. More hails were sent, but there was no response.

Is Intelligence a Short-Lived Phenomenon?

Sophia did not tell Ambrose much about herself, establishing the distance, the boundaries necessary to do psychological-type work, and Stephen wanted to know more.

He sat in an adjustable chair and set it for a nearly supine position. Her perfume wafted in his direction, and she had on a flimsy silk blouse which traced her brassiere. He had to remark, "Do you wear that to the hospital?"

"Yes."

"You must drive the natives wild."

"You're probably right. My chief has sometimes remarked on my dress."

"I'll bet."

"So what would you like to talk about today? A dream perhaps."

"Well, I had a dream."

"Yes . . ."

"Dreams, dreams. I don't know if there is any point to this dream stuff. I thought you were one of those who prescribe a drug and send the guy home."

"That's true. But you seem to think there is something to them, so maybe this is a good way to start."

"Okay, if you want. I don't know what you're going to get out of this dream. In the dream, I am a policeman, a detective. My partner and I are after a criminal. My partner says, 'We should get one of those fashion people who make perfumes. Fashion people are always one step ahead, they always know what the next thing will be. So, being one step ahead, they'll know who the criminal is.'"

"Really."

"And I say, in the dream, 'And if not, they'll sniff him out.'"

Sophia said, "That sounds like a dream I should have had. The perfume the thief is wearing should be called . . ."

"Criminal."

"Of course."

"And you can see the ads. 'It was criminal that a woman should smell so good.'"

She laughed. They were almost together for a brief microsecond. Then she quickly reasserted authority.

"So, how is your novel going? What's it about?"

"What do you want to know—the plot? The characters? Or the theme?"

"What's the theme?"

"The notion that intelligence might be a short-lived phenomenon."

"Intelligence is a short-lived phenomenon? Why do you think that might be?"

"Well, once it reached a certain threshold, look at how damn quickly it has developed. Humans, for example, crowded out all the other top predators. And the has-beens are all on endangered species lists. And all this in seventy thousand years, a mere blink of the eye in the age of the planet."

"And how was this accomplished?"

"Tool-making helped, superior communication skills probably aided group hunts for big animals like mammoths. All larger brain activity."

"Of course."

"And language and writing allowed for the rapid accumulation of information. Freeing the mind from remembering great quantities of minute facts, and allowing it to be used for a higher occupation. Figuring out the world. The laws of nature. We start out self-centered . . ."

"Like a baby. That would be the psychologist's point of view," said the psychiatrist.

"Sure, why not? First we're the center of the universe, center of the solar system. Then Copernicus figures out that we are traveling around the Sun. Finally, the Sun turns out not to be big at all, it's a small star in an average-sized galaxy."

"Yes. Your point?"

"Computers have magnified this ability of ours to store and manipulate information, which makes the whole thing rather heady, skyscraperish. Vertigo if you take a look back. My grandfather grew up on a farm in Ohio. Horses were the mainstay of transportation. When he complained about someone changing horses in midstream, he was drawing an analogy, sure, but he was talking about horses. Horses they had on the farm. That was about a hundred thirty years ago. We've figured out the secrets of the atom, at least enough to make enormous bombs. We figured out how to generate enough velocity to escape the Earth's gravitational field and put someone on the moon. And for years, since the hyperdrive of *Forbidden Planet*, we've predicted travel faster than the speed of light. In *Star Wars* they called it hyperspace. Even real scientists like billions and billions Carl Sagan, assumed a transit system faster than light beams in *Contact*. Nowadays, they call it warp speed. That's *Star Trek*. Or they assume you'll be stepping through a looking glass or wormhole or other portal."

"Nowadays?"

"It's an antique English expression. I guess I would expect you to pick up on that since you're not a native. I think I'm being ironic.

"Anyway, things are happening very quickly indeed. And if you were to plot a graph with time on one axis and human knowledge of the universe on the other, it would be quite asymptotic." He took a post-it note and drew a diagram.

"Meaning that human knowledge appears to be increasing toward the infinite. So, if man goes off the graph, what happens to him?" she asked.

"You mean: if knowledge goes off the graph, the question is: what happens to man? Is he replaced by the next thing in evolution? Do we invent a superior human with improved genes? Do we invent a hybrid, carbon-silicon machine? A bionic man, a borg. Do we make an android? Not organic. Perhaps we are replaced by this as Neanderthal man was replaced by Homo sapiens."

"No, I meant, if knowledge increases toward the infinite, does man become God?"

Stephen said, "Well, I guess that depends on what you mean by God. Imagine how the ancient Greeks would have reacted if we sent a helicopter to Mt. Olympus with flame-throwers and a machine gun."

Sophia felt this tack in the conversation would lose the wind. She wanted to fill the sail again, "Let's go back to your theme, you said intelligent life was a short-lived phenomenon. So, does that mean any kind of intelligent life, whether organic or not?"

"Wow. Good point. Important point. Sure, it doesn't have to be carbon based. Maybe we move on to silicon, one step down on the table of elements. And yes, you kind of wonder what happens. Is there some law? The General Law of Intelligent Life and Population. Does intelligent life always reproduce itself to destruction? Is it the bread mold phenomenon?"

"You're saying that bread mold eats at the bread until the bread is gone."

"Gone, unusable, bread mold waste. Is there always a point where intelligent life decimates its food source, desecrates its environment, its atmosphere, wrecks necessary links for its well-being? Not unlike cancer, where the population of cells grows to the point where it blocks the transport system.

"For example, we might destroy insect life important in the food chain, the pollinators. Plant life dies, herbivores that exist on plant life die. Predators who live on herbivores die."

"How will we destroy the insects?"

"You're going to wear me down with details. How do I know? I'm not an entomologist. Maybe it will be clear-cutting the rainforest. They say every tree in the rainforest harbors unique species. Maybe it'll be screwing around with breeding insects. Did you see the thing about the African killer bee? Someone failed to close a breeding hive properly and two species mixed that they didn't intend to mix. One from Brazil and one from Africa. What if by accident they produce an angry stinging bee that doesn't collect pollen very well? Then what?"

He continued, "Or does every intelligent species on every planet do themselves in when they get to their industrial revolution? Do they throw so many toxic particles into the air and water, into their environment, that they can never recover? Did you know that the Earth was cooling off because tiny particles are reflecting the sun's light off into space? Well, mitigating global warming. But it throws a wrench into the global warming scenario." He stopped, and said, "I've drifted off into complexity, which is another subject altogether."

"Perhaps you are being too negative about intelligence. Do you know about John Stuart Mill?"

"What about him?"

"Well, he became depressed because he thought there were only a limited number of musical compositions. He was afraid they would become exhausted. And it was this possibility that sent him into a deep depression."

"Yes, I know about Mill's depression. I know about the fixed number of musical compositions. And you think that my thoughts about the possible demise of intelligent life threaten to send me into a depression?"

"You seem to be setting yourself up for something."

"Mill was a depressive, wasn't he? And I may well be wrong about everything. Actually, it's an exciting time. And in some places, the birthrate is not at replacement, Italy and Austria, for example, so maybe we'll make it. It's like a thriller. Maybe we will figure out how the arctic deep-water pumps work before we turn them off."

"Deep-water pumps?"

"There are deep-water currents, what they call the conveyor, which take warm water from the tropics up to the arctic, and cold water from the arctic down to the tropics. If the pumps turn off, then cold water instead of being pumped to the equator would accumulate in the arctic, and we would have another ice age. That's the theory. They say it could come on quite quickly."

"How would the pumps turn off?"

"No one knows this, but you can speculate. They've taken ice cores from mountaintops all over the world. And using wily scientific stuff like the level of oxygen ions, they can determine how far back in time the core goes and they can read the temperature levels. They say that the last twenty years are the warmest in twelve thousand years. Maybe this is normal, but maybe it's the greenhouse gases . . ."

"What has this got to do with the deep-water pumps? I wonder if you have A-D-D."

"Are you saying if I don't make the connection, you'll put me on Ritalin? Well, if the atmosphere is heating up because of the greenhouse gases, carbon dioxide, then it is thought that more ice will melt off of Greenland. This ice is salt-free. Did you know that the number of large icebergs has increased from four hundred prior to 1970 to one thousand today?"

"No, but you're a little bit maddening. Please finish your thought about how the conveyor would stop." She slowly shook her head.

"It is the density of the cold water plus the weight of the salt that sends the water to the bottom of the ocean. The large number of icebergs, which are salt-free, melting in the Atlantic might disturb this process. Plus the fresh water runoff from Greenland. To complete the thought, fresh water would lack the weight of the saltwater and fail to sink, thus stopping the conveyor."

"Yes, that's interesting. But it was good to see you could finish a thought sequence. Your mind has a way of wandering."

"Climate, which usually varies quite a lot, has only been decent for the last ten thousand years or so, at fifty-nine degrees. Interesting how that coincides with the rise of human culture, isn't it?"

*   *   *

from the journal of Stephen Ambrose

Idea for a story: Just when everyone thought that global warming would melt the poles, a new ice age sets in. It was the melting of the snows off Greenland that turned off the deep-water pumps, which brought warm water up from the equator and sent cool water south. The fresh water was not as heavy as the ultracold saltwater, which ordinarily sank to the bottom, and then went south. The pump stopped.

September was unseasonably cold. After a summer's melting dramatically slowed down the deep-water pumps, an early winter began with a chilling cold in October. At the end of the month, a blizzard of three feet was followed by a blizzard of another three feet in the first week of November. And another blizzard of five feet two weeks later. Then a blizzard of six feet. Forty feet of snow had fallen by the end of November. In December another fifty-one feet. In the last ice age, the ice pack was a mile deep. That's 5,228 feet.

By now, ninety-one feet of snow had fallen, and by the middle of January another forty-two feet. All travel shuts down. Airports were kept open, but it got worse and worse. O'Hare was down to one runway, and finally they had to close that one. The train system also shut down out on the plains when the snow drifts on the tracks were three times as tall as the train. The roads shut down. The concomitant unimaginable horror that followed was the food problem. Just-in-time food supplies meant that everyone had food for a week, but by the second week some were beginning to feel it, and the stores were emptied. With no trains or trucks to bring it in, the shelves emptied in a week. $200 worth of food salted away (cans of soup, dried milk) would have helped many. But what happened had been unthinkable: mass starvation.

By end of January the snow for the year was up to 195 feet, by the end of February: two hundred thirty-three feet of snow. Unimaginable snow and cold in January and February was the straw that broke the camel's back. The cold sapped everyone's strength so that it was a very passive event. No race riots, no Watts. No nothing. Television continued and droned on about how many were dead. The Internet played on even after the food dried up. Though eventually the weight of ice and snow snapped the power lines, so the electric space heaters failed, and television and the Internet no longer kept you company. The natural gas lines were okay for a while, with failures here and there. Before the shelves were emply, a few people bought kerosene heaters and food (canned, dry, whatever) for the four months until summer would come on and allow the human population to regroup.

The economy was in chaos. The stock market was shut down for the time being, but there was no real relief in the U.S. All the way down in Key West they experienced freezing temperatures if little snow.

Summer came, but thirty-three million were dead. Atomic war numbers. No war. One tenth of the population of the United States was gone. Summer was nothing like previous summers. The snow line did not retreat as far as in previous years. Much of Canada remained under snow. Those who could, headed south. But a tiny food supply and distribution problem would await those who moved. They would die warm but starving . . .

The Clovis People

My sister Amanda was three years younger than me. We shared an interest in paleoanthropology, and I wondered if that was because we had the same brain morphology. We weren't twins, of course, but independently we developed an interest in twins. With wide-ranging interests, we surprisingly connected time and again. Amanda drove herself nonstop. Studying, writing, taking flamenco lessons, practicing her violin. Sleep was total collapse. There I differed. Sleep for me was something I eased into and eased out of, when I was lucky. I envied her. "It's interesting stuff, the Clovis people, but there's such a surplus of PhDs that you'll get your sheepskin, and end up in some distant outpost like Wyoming or Alaska," was what I said.

"Now you're sounding like Abner. I'm sure there are interesting dig sites around those places."

"Right. I'm sure there are." Too damn resourceful for her own good.

The Clovis people, named for a town in New Mexico, came over to North America from Asia eleven thousand to fifteen thousand years ago at the end of the last Ice Age when the oceans were three hundred feet lower than they are today and there was an actual physical bridge from Russia to Alaska. Since I had my concerns about man's destiny (as opposed to being an out-and-out pessimist), we had frequent conversations about the subject of my novel. (I wouldn't let her see but parts of it. All I needed to hear was "nice try" or "keep at it.") She brought me up to speed on the Clovis people.

"Well, a guy named Paul Martin has done a lot of work on the Clovis people since the 1960s. The upshot is that after Homo crossed over to Alaska, twelve thousand to fifteen thousand years ago, animals over one hundred pounds suffered terrific extinction rates. In North America 73 percent of large mammals disappeared. Not individuals, I mean species. In only a couple of thousand years.

"In South America 79 percent disappeared, and the big question is whether it was the weather, melting snows, that did 'em in or the humans."

"And your guess?"

"Well, Martin makes good arguments that it was the humans. Only large species were in trouble. Mammoths, for example, had been in North America for a million years. Humans show up, and poof: they're gone. It certainly is incriminating."

"What was happening elsewhere in the world? Africa or Australia?"

"Where humans coexisted with large mammals for a long time, like Africa, there appears to be a balance. Maybe the animals learned to stay away from the skinny two-legged walkers. There is an argument that there was a severe extinction in Europe when homo first arrived there a million years ago.

"But Australia is another matter. The evidence is clear. Modern man first appeared there sixty thousand years ago, and by forty-five thousand years ago most of the large marsupials had gone extinct. They were not particularly big-brained animals, maybe they didn't know enough to run away. After all, size as an indicator of strength fails to identify the threat that comes with man, who is, say, one half the weight of a lion, or less, and not particularly fast." Amanda.

"Then why do some still survive when these others are gone?"

"Well, my bet is that the ones that survived were really fast or nocturnal."

"Ah. If that's true, it's really discouraging. Man goes to Australia, marsupial extinction. Man goes to America, large species extinction. And not that long ago, maybe a thousand years ago according to Leakey, the Polynesians went to New Zealand and wiped out a kind of bird world there. Apparently there were all kinds of birds. Moas. Birds for all niches. Instead of cows, there were grazing birds. Instead of gazelles, there were fast gazelle-like birds. But man was the direct agent of death in only some of the cases. The real damage was done by the rats the Polynesians brought with them. They ate the bird eggs."

"Unintended consequences."

"Abner's favorite. Well, you have to give him his due."

"Yes, it's a case of the foreign species phenomenon." She said, "I suppose the best we can hope is something like, 'And yes, in his early development man hunted indiscriminately most large animals to extinction. Later on, he realized that he needed to maintain some kind of ecological balance.'"

"I would say that's putting the best possible light on it. Maybe man is the ultimate foreign species, say again, alien species, once he left Africa."

Everything I Know I Learned
from Canaries

"Everything I know I learn from canaries."

"Good, I like that. What, do they sing the secrets of the universe to you?"

"Are you impugning the brain capacity of canaries?"

"I can't imagine why I would do that." Nick's bottle of Weissbier was beading up drops of water. The humidity was damaging the integrity of the glue holding the label to the bottle, and he was peeling it off.

"It would be a big mistake."

"So, let's see, it's Friday. You saw your shrink today. What did she have to say?"

"She thinks that the problems that I see as external problems for society are reflections of my own inner turmoil."

"That's a rather mechanical psychological interpretation, I'd say."

"Yeah, not particularly creative. But the real question is whether she is correct or not."

"I wonder if that is a common characteristic of beautiful women . . . that they're not creative."

"But then what is creativity? Even the Big Bang may occur over and over again. I've always thought this creativity thing was overdone."

"There's a thought. I wonder, does the Big Bang occur with variations each time out, or does it replicate itself exactly time after time?" Nick was picking the label off the Beck's bottle like he was picking a scab.

"The only way to tell would be to transport to another universe when ours collapses, and then travel back to find out."

"And are the physical laws the same, universe to universe?"

"You're hinting that universal laws are only universal within this universe, the one we are in. A good point. This reminds me of a philosophy class I once took. Wittgenstein. The problem of other minds. Do they exist and so on."

"Hold on to that thought. Right now, I need to solve the problem of other toilets."

Nick walked off, and Stephen focused on a blond on the other side of the room. She looked a little like Claudia Schiffer. His drink was nearly gone, so the bartender asked:

"Another?"

"Why not?"

The bartender got a fresh glass, filled it with ice, and poured Johnny Walker Red until he filled the glass.

"I always wondered about bartenders who measured out a shot."

"Some bartenders are too scientific about it. You can measure it out with a shot glass, but it's kind of like measuring out love. I will only give you this much love, and no more."

"But your boss may total up the number of bottles, and he'll sense a bartender's been too generous."

"Perhaps. But then, how do you measure repeat business? The feeling customers have for a bartender and a bar? How are you going to measure the liquor-to-repeat business ratio? It's an art, not a science."

"Yes, I like that. Even pouring a drink is a complicated business proposition."

"It's a microcosm. Everything is complicated."

Nick came back. "So what did we decide? Is the universe different each time out?"

"You mean, do the laws change, gravity and the like?"

"Yes."

"I don't know. The thing to do is run a couple of experiments."

Nick ordered an Amstel, and Stephen looked again at the blond.

"It's all archetypes, isn't it?" Nick.

"Does that mean we are back to a discussion of the characteristics of beautiful women?"

"It's a subject that engages my interest."

"I think it's a hopeless subject. We will devolve into a discussion of consensus beauty."

"Does beauty start at the magazines and work its way down? Or does it come up from the streets and work its way into the magazines? I don't know if these questions ever have any useful answers."

"I can tell you this: in experiments, babies looking at faces on a television have a preference for the symmetric face," said Stephen.

"That sounds like something you would say." Looking at Claudia, he said, "I wonder what she thinks."

"Hell if I know."

"I think I'll go ask her." Nick walked in her direction.

The bartender offered, "She'll claim it's genetic. Her mother was a homecoming queen, a Junior Miss, a beauty queen."

"So you don't think she's going to credit her makeup?"

"Nah. In her case, beauty was a birthright. Came from Mom. Genetic."

"This gene stuff is going to take beauty to new places, I can see that."

"When everyone looks great, ugly will finally come into its own."

The bartender went down the bar to draw a beer, and Stephen cast his glance toward Nick and Claudia. Nick laughed and walked back to the bar.

"So?"

"I offered to buy her and her friend a drink, but they said they were just having one here and then they're off to The Goodman."

"So, you didn't ask if all beautiful women were as sexy as she is?"

"That's the common misconception. That beauty and sexuality are not connected."

"And they aren't?"

"That girl is beautiful, but until you take her for a test drive, you don't really know if she's sexy. Actually, I think beauty and great sexuality are antithetical."

"And why's that?"

"Because the beautiful woman doesn't have to make any effort to be a good lover, men are coming at her from every direction. There is no need to learn to become a good lover, no compelling drive. If she loses one guy, she's got five backups ready to replace him."

"And women who aren't as attractive?"

"They'll go the extra mile. Maybe do that thing the attractive girl won't do. That's their competitive edge."

"Like?"

"The attractive girl might not give you head."

"And the attractiveness-challenged woman?"

"She'll give you head. And if the beautiful woman will give you head, then the less attractive woman will take you all the way down to the root."

"Go the extra mile, so to speak. It's an interesting theory, and by God I love a good theory. But if your theory is on track, how come there are so many absolutely perfect women in porno?"

"Well, my first response is: I grant you these girls are beautiful, but if these beautiful women are so sexy, why do they have fluff girls on the set to get the man up? Think about it. Let's say you're a beautiful girl. You take inventory. What can you do with this beauty? Marry, that's your first option. That's your best bet. But maybe your parents' marriage was a disaster. You're not looking for marriage particularly, although you may have tried marriage. Once, twice, three times. And a lot of those girls have had odd upbringings. Raped maybe, maybe a parent sexually abused the kid. Watch Howard Stern, it turns up often enough."

"Not all of them come from disaster."

"I'm sure some of them are just curious or greedy or had a friend in the business or a boyfriend who wanted to test his power over them."

"So, some of them are probably good lovers."

"I suppose. And there is something I would grant you, the beautiful girl would certainly have more opportunities to practice. And practice makes perfect. I think it must be a German expression."

"It is?"

"IF it isn't, THEN it should be."

Sending Over the Engineers

Prime closed in on the craft, but there was still no change in its outgoing signal. They decided to board it. Engineers were sent over with tools to enter one of the portals, and access was gained.

The boarders were curious like crazy. Some remembered the old twentieth century movie, *Alien*, and were nervous. Many things were vaguely familiar. The craft was made to fit creatures of roughly their size. Seats seemed to fit the humans.

Carolina, an anthropologist, an intelligent life specialist, remarked to Ramón: "You have to wonder—does organic intelligent life always tend to be of a certain size, four to seven feet?"

Ramón wondered, "Life on our planet is based on twenty amino acids. And I guess the question is: is all life—in this universe, anyway—based on these same amino acids?"

"We've been out in space for years, bored to tears, when we might have been experimenting around to see if we could come up with a different paradigm for life."

"Does all life have to be cellular, for example?"

"The microcosm/macrocosm thing. The single-celled organism, amoeba. String a bunch together and you have a worm, and then a lungfish, a frog, a lizard, a shrew, and finally, for now anyway, man."

"Well, all stars fall into certain categories and bear similarities."

"Think. Most species on Earth bear similarities. An even number of limbs. And once you get to a certain size, four limbs predominate. At a certain size two eyes are the rule. Once you have two eyes, and they face forward, you have stereoscopic vision and depth perception. Perhaps nature, in its economy, never permits more than two eyes for very long. There isn't any need for more. There is much diversity, of course, variations on a theme—eye color, eye size, acuity."

"But not particularly in the basic building blocks."

"So the life form that occupied this craft probably came from a planet enjoying the same intensity of light from a star that the Earth gets from the Sun."

"Enough speculation, Ramón. We are here. On their ship. What happened to the people on this craft?"

Carolina touched something on a console, and a screen appeared on the surface filled with unreadable designs.

"We need a linguistics expert on this."

"A linguistics expert? I don't even know how to turn this off, much less manipulate it to figure things out."

"I'm coming over," said Eladia who was listening in.

Carolina said, "This feels like a García Márquez novel. Eladia will figure their language out just before this craft self-destructs." She recoiled from the screen.

Ramón said, "Don't be ridiculous. No one in this universe would make a self-destruct sequence that would be that easy to set in motion."

"Right." Eladia looked at the screen again. "Well, it's the handiwork of something intelligent. That's for sure."

The Role of Motivation in Intelligence

Nick wanted to be more than a bagman. To deliver money to a congressman was easy enough, and probably important, but gaining the programming to a Patriot missile would be infinitely more impressive. And lucrative, though this was perhaps not the driving motivation. For an ego of Nick's makeup (configuration), it was the impressive that he wished to accomplish. Knowing he had an extraordinary IQ, he felt it necessary to find a task that engaged all of this intelligence of his, and getting the software would be one way. Never mind that he felt the number connected to his IQ was too low. Never mind that with such potential he could figure out how to do the programming himself, Ambrose did it with much less. Nick was more inclined to do the blue jay thing, eat the eggs of the lesser lights.

Nick asked Stephen, "Do you know what your IQ is?"

"No."

"What do you think it is?"

"120 is considered bright. Ninetieth percentile. Probably something like that. And yours?" Knowing that that the whole point of this tangent was so Nick could reveal his own.

"175, Stanford Binet."

"Ah."

With a little more time on the test, Stephen thought he could get those same scores. His Twilight Zone extra-time room at first was just 10 x 10 x 10 feet. But then he expanded it. Eventually, he stuffed a large supercomputer in the room. He would be a genius who could outcalculate Enrico Fermi, who was a whiz at calculating in his head. With a little extra time he definitely could get a perfect math score every time. It was a speed thing. That was the theory of Francis Galton. One of his ideas to test IQ was to test reaction times. The faster the reaction time, the higher the IQ. It was a starting point, then Binet went on to develop the questions of increasing problem-solving complexity.

And this drew Stephen back into his world of stop-time and his own IQ. The problem of vocabulary. There were always words just outside his vocabulary. So, after awhile he allowed himself a dictionary in his stop-time room.

Then there was the matter of time. First he would allow himself a handicap of only fifteen extra minutes. Then he decided that fifteen minutes would not be enough time. That he might need a half an hour. Then an hour. Then two hours (the reading parts might require a lot of evaluation). Then he dropped the time limit altogether; what did it matter anyway? He would just take as long as he needed.

Then it would bother him that he was cheating, taking all the time in the world. He would go back to fifteen minutes, and only cheat a little bit. Sometimes he would go all the way back and eliminate the stop-time room. What good was it just to score high on a standardized test? People would expect things of you that such people can do. There might be a qualitative thing he could never get at with the stop-time room. In his adult years, he shed the stop-time room. The fantasy died. Getting a high score on a standardized test never made anyone a genius. Basically, he felt life was like an open-book test—take as long as you like, the only thing that matter was what you figured out, achieved, be it the invention of calculus, the theft of the Hope diamond, or the discovery of evolution. And this was his point of departure with Nick:

"What do you suppose Newton's IQ was?"

"Hard to imagine. High."

"Terman starts out at about 130, based on his childhood achievements."

"Terman?"

"One of the early IQ developers. Galton, Binet, Terman. Kind of silly don't you think, assigning an IQ to Isaac Newton? About 2 percent of the population has an IQ of 130. That would mean in the United States, in a population of 280 million, there are, let's see, about 5.6 million people of this intelligence. Which is a lot of people. And in a world population of 6 billion, there would be 120 million people of this IQ."

"And your point?"

"Only one Newton so far. Though Einstein came pretty close. But to be fair to Terman, he ultimately decided Newton was at 190, adjusted for his adult achievements."

"Okay."

"And if you want to repair back to statistics, that's one in maybe 7 or 8 billion, if you consider all of the humans that ever lived. You know who Terman put at the top of the IQ list?"

"Who?"

"John Stuart Mill."

"I always thought they liked Goethe."

"Yes, him too."

"Okay, one is almost inclined to say, 'Who is Mill?'," said Nick, "But I know who he is. And I think I know why he is considered so smart. Because his father taught him Greek at three and Latin at five. And there is a record of this."

"Probably. And what great work did he do?"

"In philosophy, he wrote some brilliant tracts."

"*On Liberty*. Right."

"And what do they think his IQ was?"

"190."

"Very high."

"Yeah, but they give Rembrandt and Raphael 110 each. Bach gets a 125. Whose brains would you rather have, Mill's or Bach's?"

Nick pondered.

Ambrose continued, "Okay, you think about it, but I'll tell you which I'd rather have—Bach's."

"So you think IQ tests are useless."

"Not entirely useless, but yeah, limited. Limiting. They tell you something, but a person with an IQ of 180, and I've known some, can still get a D if he has no interest. And on the other side of the coin, my roommate at school told me about a classmate of his in high school who had SAT in the 450s . . ."

"Dead average."

"But he got a perfect score, 800, on the history achievement test."

"So, it's motivation that needs to be tested."

"Even Einstein said he had the persistence of a mule. Think about it. The person with the highest recorded IQ test score, Madelyn Vos Savant with her IQ of 228, seems only to be motivated to write a newspaper column and go around the country showing people how to score higher on standardized tests. Her high test score did not predict an understanding of space and time that resulted in a warp drive, or great poetry, or even a new paradigm for merchandizing. My God, I'm tired of the franchise system. Every town in America has its franchise strip. Warren Buffett loves them, but I think franchises are the death of creativity."

"Okay, I get it. You think IQ tests are useless."

"Well. Every individual is different with unique motivations, and I don't know if the psychologists can build the butterfly net that will capture that individual who will change poetry or physics, for example. Eliot was at Harvard in the Philosophy Department writing a PhD on Bradley. Wallace Stevens was vice president in the Bond Department at Hartford Insurance. Bellow was studying anthropology in Madison, Wisconsin. Einstein, everyone knows, was a clerk in a patent office in Switzerland."

"Mild-mannered Clerk Kent checks out patents by day, but at night he turns into Übermensch, able to leap through time and space in a single bound."

"I have a kind of quantum theory about people. Maybe you can tell what groups of people will do, but you can't tell where an individual electron, the individual individual, will be."

"This is getting too serious. This is the year 2000. In 2000, we don't have those deep philosophical discussions anymore. That was the first half of the twentieth century. That was the nineteenth century." Nick turned toward the bar, and made the typically American remark, "Barkeep, what are my options?"

They were at a microbrewery bearing the name Oktoberfest in Berwyn, and the options were numerous. The place was unique until the owner started another in Elmhurst. Nothing succeeds like duplication.

Ambrose decided first, "I'll have the Bavarian look-alike."

"I'll have the Weissbier . . ."

"You know, Feynman solved the problem of deciding on dessert by ordering chocolate ice cream every time out."

"Yes, well, I suppose if one channels one's creativity, that there will be gaps in creativity elsewhere." And then, "Why did we meet here? There's not a woman in sight."

"Women come here. Just aren't any here right now. Patience."

"Patience may have been the way for the past million years, but now if you're patient for a little while someone exploits your ideas, steals your girl, the stock you were looking to buy moves up, and you're out of luck."

"Getting back, the big question being, without Einstein, how long would it have been before someone developed relativity, or thought of light in waves and quanta?"

"So your question is: Would it have been one year or one hundred years or five hundred years?"

"In a way, the observations seem quite simple. Light has a mass characteristic. And that mass characteristic would allow the Sun with its enormous gravity to pull light around. That mass can be converted into energy and light. Or to put it another way, energy precipitates into matter."

Ambrose continued, "Einstein is my idea of a power thinker. It's not a matter of how quickly you can answer questions on a standardized test. Think about this—no matter how many minutes you give Vos Savant, you can give her all the time in the world, and she'd never come up with relativity. Einstein is the only one out of, let's say, four billion who lived up to his time, who answered that particular question on the standardized test for all of humanity. It's bearing down on a problem and solving it. Like Watson and Crick on the DNA thing."

"Yes, I like that example. Watson made it perfectly clear in his book that if Linus Pauling had gotten hold of the crystallography, then he probably would have figured it out first."

"Yes, I read that, too."

"The State Department blocked Linus Pauling from going abroad."

"Right. They did. Think about it. It shows that even without the supergenius Pauling, they were still able to knock it off."

"And your point?"

"That even without Einstein, his problems might have been solved in a relatively short time. Henri Poincaré was working on some of his problems. David Hilbert, a mathematician, spent some time on physics and relativity, and came up with field equations for gravitation a few days before Einstein, but never quarreled about priority. Newton and Leibniz discovered calculus around the same time. Darwin and Wallace got the same idea about evolution at around the same time."

"And so how do you think intelligence should be measured?"

"I'm not in that field, I don't know. I'm just an amateur. But there are other qualities which are also important, and I suppose foremost among those is drive. Watson was driven . . ."

"And Crick?"

"They were both driven to figure out the DNA structure. So, they pushed and pushed and pushed whatever intelligence they had to the very limit to figure this problem out. Rosalind Franklin provided the X-ray photograph showing something of the structure, from Gardaff they got the relationship of the four bases; they memorized Pauling's *Nature of the Chemical Bond*. Bim bam bom, the double helix."

"So, Pauling is still in the equation?"

"There you are. That's my theory: the really interesting people get to the heart of things, it is hard to cut them out of the equation."

"So, drive is more important than intelligence?"

"Might be. It might be that anyone with average intelligence is still capable of extraordinary things if properly motivated."

"So how would you get at testing motivation?"

"Who knows? But if motivation is key, and you test someone before the bright light hits him, before the lightning bolt hits, he might test out as a knot on a log."

"Driftwood on the river."

"Right. Motivation is a kind of vector in the intelligence equation. And, I think, there are other issues. Creativity for one."

"Creativity. I find that word rather annoying."

"Yes, me too, maybe curiosity is a better word. Language does not always provide an adequate expression for what you need to say."

"My point is that creativity has a rather grand implication. In the first six days I created the planets and the heavens, then I went on to create electromagnetism and gravity . . ."

"Me, too. I wish they would use something less grand. Or less grandiose. Someone takes a writing course, and it's entitled 'Creative Writing.' You get in the course, and all the professor wants you to do is write dorm stories. Stories from your experience. Such classes do not deserve such a grand course title."

"The course title should be 'Writing from Experience' or 'Intro to Writing'— something along those lines."

"Exactly my point. Such a course title would not put off those who would like to use such a course for therapy, and even a writer as good as Graham Greene said his novels were therapy."

"Maybe 'Writing Therapy' is more to the point."

"Both are acceptable, more like it. I remember taking such a course, and I thought I was going to have to develop a new literary form. A sonnet scanned aabb eedd fgfgfg hh. Or some new form between a poem and a short story. And all they end up doing is writing dorm stories. I must say I was relieved, but also disappointed. And I'm not saying that there aren't certain built-in things, inherited things, genetic things that aren't advantages. They say that Einstein had more than the usual number of glial cells."

"Glial cells?"

"Glial cells. Support cells for neurons. But they didn't seem to make such a big difference for his parents, did they? There is an argument that says that the brain, to some extent, builds itself. You get certain equipment from the genes, but, for example, if you don't learn language at a certain period in your youth, you're up the creek. You'll never get it right. So, environment does have a lot to do with brain development. Of course when I say environment, I'm including the parents who are responsible for the transfer of language. Eventually, the brain itself wants to find things out and directs its own development."

The Basics

On the ship they found zones where entry was not possible, but the hand sensors they brought with them picked up organic compounds, which further motivated the language people to figure out the computer system. They wanted to figure out how to open doors to gain access to the rest of the ship.

Finally, the ship's computer starting spitting out diagrams on a flat screen on a table. The first diagram was a triangle. Eladia looked at it and looked at it, and finally she said, "Triangle."

The picture vanished.

She said, "Where did the triangle go?" And it reappeared.

Then the computer generated a square.

And Eladia said, "Square."

The square vanished, and then Eladia said, "Square," and it reappeared again.

A line appeared, a circle, and so on.

Then after a time, the computer said, exactly as Eladia had said it with her voice, "Triangle." And the language people took a stylus next to the screen and drew a diagram of a triangle on the screen.

This was how the computer learned English, but they learned nothing about the ship. It was a little like the relationship between America and Japan in the late 1900s. Americans bought lots and lots of Japanese products, but learned little about the Japanese. Hardly any Americans could speak Japanese. Even Richard Feynman gave up when he had to learn three different ways to say chocolate ice cream.

But the Japanese learned enough English to get by.

The geometrical symbols were a universal language, but they needed to get beyond that. So, the next thing Eladia did, after drawing a symbol for triangle, was to write the word "triangle."

And then she tried on arithmetic. They drew a "1." Then "1 + 1 = 2."

And then she said, "One plus one equals two," and then she wrote it in words underneath the symbols.

The computer came back with "1 + 1 + 1."

And she said, "Equals three." And finished the computer's work with "= 3" And wrote, "equals three."

Computer came back with "1 + 2 = 3."

Rosetta stone.

*   *   *

After writing this speculation on how one would try to communicate with an intelligent device from another world, Ambrose turned off his computer for the day, and walked down the hall to his bedroom. He went to the closet and made a cursory inspection of his porno tapes.

He pulled out one of the Max Head tapes. Max had a sense of humor at least. The girl has no script, so he runs down the hall and picks up a script. He takes it back to the bedroom where the girl is, and opens the manuscript to the first page. He points to the first line, which reads, "Suck me off, very fast."[1]

So much for the script. Before long the girl is sucking off the male lead, and Ambrose right there with him. The girl reminds him of his psychiatrist.

---

[1] Editor's Note: The actual line from *Casting Couch #15* was "Fuck me hard."

Science Fiction is Always Out of Date

Nick could not seem to get Stephen to talk about his business. He always claimed that after spending a day coding, he wanted to set his mind somewhere else, and that was writing his science fiction, which he sometimes called speculative fiction, and which he was always willing to talk about.

"The problem with science fiction is that it is so dated," said Stephen.

"So dated?"

"So set in time."

Nick tried to be positive, "Well, I suppose *all* fiction is rooted in its particular time. And language for that matter. Consider Chaucer, 'Whann that Aprile with his shoures soote/The droghte of March hath perced to the roote . . .' Language has changed a hell of a lot since then."

"Changed, evolved, transmogrified."

"And there are some serious people writing the stuff. Aldous Huxley wrote *Brave New World* and George Orwell wrote *1984*. And these days you have Michael Crichton writing *Jurassic Park*, putting his particular spin on the future, bringing it into the mainstream . . ."

"Because now, things are changing so fast that science fiction becomes the norm, mainstream. People see the stealth fighter with its straight lines and odd shape, and they can see the future is here."

"Today everyone can call the starship with their handheld, flip-open communicator. Today everyone has their own computer. They even allow you to bring calculators to the standardized tests."

"Asimov's story about relearning arithmetic will come true."

"In fact, we've become a little impatient. People with illnesses wonder why science is taking so long to come up with a cure for their problems. 'Could you please hurry it up a little in the lab, please?'"

"I'm sure I would feel that way if I had some unresolvable condition."

"Oh, me too. Absolutely."

"How about with programming? Don't you feel that the whole thing could be faster than it is now?"

"It's getting faster all the time. The problem is that I'm getting to be an old dog. New tools come along, and the programmers are forced to use the new tools and rush out a product that is not just ready for market. So, it comes out buggy, and because it's buggy, it's useless. So, you wait and read the reviews and talk to people always willing to try the new thing, and see how it's working out. If the feedback is good, then you give it a try. But you're resistant. I used Wordstar 3.1 for a hell of long time. It came with my first IBM PC back in the early 80s, and it worked. So, I never bothered to replace it. But then these editor programs like Brief made programming just a hell of a lot easier. So, I used that for the longest time, even for writing my novel. I just don't like changing tools all the time. Converting files to the new format, finding out what all the icons do. These things are never as intuitive as you'd like. These damn software companies are always wearing you out with new features. Hell, government agencies, the SEC, will only accept information in standard formats. If you change data formats too often, you may not have the software to read the data anymore.

"Yeah, I heard that as drug companies migrate their records from one format to another, say from FORTRAN to Windows NT, they find the data off, sometimes by eight digits."

"That's a lot."

"A lot? Disaster. Anyone relying on this data will be in jeopardy."

"You can see the lawsuits."

"Lawsuits are the least of the problems. It's the basis for the lawsuit. It's the agony of people taking too much of a drug. It's the poisoning."

"Is it a software problem, or a data storage problem?"

"Well, it can be both."

"But these are solvable problems."

"Probably. Interesting, isn't it? In a few years they'll figure out how the brain does its work, and the whole process of learning will be changed. We'll all be prodigies then. Learn six languages by age ten and so on."

"Or we'll all be babbling idiots with computers to do everything for us. Life will be endless video games with eating breaks. Computers will be the slaves who do everything and in so doing become our masters, and finally they'll grow tired of us and hang us out to dry."

"And then the computers, the robots, the androids, will figure out the rest of the rules of the universe, and then hit the reset button. Find out the rules, speed things up, hit the reset button. Over and over."

Nick thought there must be a faster way to get his programs than to have to listen to all this futuristic garbage.

*　　*　　*

Stephen saved his new big insight for Sophia. He wanted desperately to impress her with his mental prowess, not that this would work. Her and her white Mercedes. But the thing that distinguished man was his 1,350 cc brain, and so somehow he persisted in thinking that his thought-lifting efforts would pay off.

Though she had had an intellectual period. She read literature country by country. Germany—she read Goethe, Hesse, Mann. France—Balzac, Stendhal, Camus and Sartre. America—Mark Twain, Hemingway, Fitzgerald. England—Shakespeare, Dickens, Conrad, Maugham. Spain—Cervantes. Newer writers got neglected—Graham Greene, Borges, Márquez. And she had never read another novel after she entered medical school. That marked the end of her liberal arts education. Although she favored the better movies, it was the only entertainment she ever had the energy for. Moreover, it was a chore to read anything in English.

All this she explained to Stephen, wistfully regretting the end of her education. Her mother was kind of a monster, never allowing her to socialize with her girlfriends, much less to meet any boys.

Stephen thought: this was not related to me in the sense that I was anyone special in her life. I wasn't. But we were both relaxed in her office, which she was starting to decorate. No orientals on the floor or book-lined walls yet. But she hung a nice Degas print of some dancers on the wall, and that was a pleasure to look at. And she was a pleasure to look at, her perfume wafting in my direction.

"It's a shame you quit reading. You might get more out of it now, especially given your training in psychiatry."

"This is probably very true. On the other hand, maybe it would be boring diagnosing literary characters. Hamlet was bipolar with anxieties and guilt, and so on."

I had been hoping a natural opportunity would arise to present my insight, but it didn't, and I couldn't figure out how to bring one up.

"I had an insight recently."

"What is that?"

"Well, that all decisions are made to favor what I would call nodes. Or decision nodes. One decision solves multiple problems. For example, I decide to meet a friend at the mall for lunch. One, I see my friend. Two, I shop for a book I want to pick up. Three, I need to eat and we have a meal. And four, we see a movie together. These were all things I wanted to accomplish in one fell swoop, and meeting my friend in the mall where there is a bookstore, a restaurant, and at a time when I want to see a movie, which is also in the mall."

She laughed, "You know I have never heard that presented as a formal teary anyvair, but I'll tink you could."

"In the last century, this would be good for a paragraph in a novel, but these days they put it on the cover of a book and sell it by the millions."

"Yes, look at that book *Emotional Intelligence*. That is a case in point. It's worth a paragraph somewhere, but what can you say after you've said a lot of decisions are not necessarily logical, they're based on emotional needs?"

"That's my point."

"You know. I love your teary. It explains so well my marriage. He was Russian in America. I was Russian in America. We were bote doctors. He had money and influence and a house and prestige. He was well-read and played the cello."

Wow, she had never mentioned her marriage before.

"Explains a lot, doesn't it?"

"I would say. All prerequisites met in one decision."

"But we divorced anyway."

"I wonder: is it that we know so little going in? Or is it that God has just meant for us to go through these different periods like a child going on different rides in an amusement park? In astrology, they would call those periods transits. Speaking of decision-making, Richard Feynman, the physicist, got tired of making decisions about dessert. So, he kind of made a command decision, that all he would ever order was chocolate ice cream." He wanted to see what she would say.

"Yes, I think that people will make those kinds of decisions. It is a kind of rejection of thinking. But maybe there is another more interesting command decision—to ask the waiter what's the best desert."

"I like that. In Feynman's case I think it was a narrowing of focus. Not to clutter his mind with lots of extraneous material. Sort of like when Sherlock Holmes was informed about the order of the planets in the solar system. He didn't feel it was necessary to his crime detective work, and told Watson that he intended to forget it."

"Did Sherlock Holmes say that?"

"I know five people who witnessed it."

She laughed. Their hour was rapidly coming to a close, and Stephen wanted to avoid the break which would occur if she called it to a close, especially after the progress we had made today.

"Well . . ."

"Actually, those witnesses are dead by now. And what good is a dead witness?" She laughed, and Stephen laughed and said, looking at his watch, "I don't think I can take any more of this humor."

"Very well." Progress. She didn't say, "I'll see you next week."

A long time to wait. Waiting. In Russia, even after the end of communism, all they do is wait. Wait for toilet paper, wait for shoes, wait for pants, wait for a car, wait for everything. In America, if you have to wait, it's bad service. Somebody has failed. But perhaps there is a difference in the cultural rhythms. Fast and staccato in the States, slow and languorous in Russia. America is young and impetuous, by nature.

Stephen would have to wait another seven days. In the meantime, he would daydream about the thing which would set him apart from the other patients. The crossover event. He thought about the movies. They would talk about movies being crossover. Could this small film (Cuban, Argentinian, et cetera) be the crossover, and capture a larger audience? One had only to understand what an audience is, and he had a thought about this one day as he was driving in on the Eisenhower. At Austin, downtown Chicago stood in the polluted distance like a Kokoschka version of the Emerald City. On a clear day, the Sears Tower stood head and shoulders above the morass, reminding one of the Carl Sandburg poem from the beginning of the century. Still true almost a hundred years later.

Anyway, traffic was agonizingly slow, the entire city was waiting. Finally, we came up to the hubbub, a car was on fire. There were police cars all around and a couple of fire trucks. And that was when Stephen got his insight: an audience is really just a gaper's block. Watching some tragedy to get that charge from contrast relief. *They* were in the soup, *you* were safe.

*　　*　　*

Nick loved Miranda because she was such a slut. She would say it.

"You know, I'm such a slut."

Nick would affect to maintain an even cool.

"Slut, sludge, slush, slutte. That's the etymology, out of the mud and muck."

"I thought the word came from a combination of slit and slumming."

They were in a booth at Cucina Tuscana. She had her hand on his crotch. Rubbing it up and down.

She continued, "You know, I feel like a musician."

"In the Kama Sutra you would be the flute player."

"What I love is the combinations I can use to turn a man on. Sometimes you just talk him into it. Like a 900 call. Sometimes all you do is suck on one of those empty teats of his until he's hard as a rock. Sometimes you just use kind of a light touch until he comes around. Just a light touch. Touching all around."

Meanwhile she was giving him the light touch. She was an artist.

"This is kind of cramped."

"Poor baby."

"I need to move it around. It's really kind of painful."

"No, no. Let me do it."

She moved him around little by little as he would work in conjunction with her when the fabric of pants caught him.

"Is that better?"

"Could be better still."

A waiter came from nowhere.

"Would you care for coffee or dessert?"

"What do you care for, honey?"

"Oh, coffee."

"Two coffees."

"With cream," and as the waiter moved out of hearing, "it's important not to forget the cream."

"Absolutely."

"Speaking of cream, you want me to suck you off right here, don't you?"

"Well, yes. But I'm afraid it would make too much of a scene."

"How about I jack you off?"

"Well . . ."

She unzipped him, and moved her hand around him. She pulled and pulled and after a while he could resist no more, though he was a trooper till the end.

"Damn. Now I've got this stuff all over my pants."

"You're wearing a suit coat. Button up. That's all."

The Aliens Emerge

By the time the aliens emerged from the inaccessible areas, it was anticlimactic. The creature who came from behind the door had silky smooth mostly hairless skin with something like down feathers around the head. The skin had a pale yellowish color. He seemed a little dull compared to the genius computers who served them.

To say the computer had robust pattern recognition skills would be understating it by a lot. Ramón and Eladia had a great time communicating with the computer, which picked up English like an extraordinarily precocious kid. Such a kid has never existed on Earth. It was speaking basic English in a few days' time.

The aliens were very slow indeed. At first Ramón thought this was because of the waking up process. They needed to bring up their metabolic systems. Equalize their electrolytes.

The leader spoke to his computer.

"Computer, who are these beings?"

"They say they come from a star system with eight planets."

"What is their mission?"

"It appears their mission is to explore star systems."

"How long have they been traveling?"

"503 revolutions of their home planet around their star."

"How long have we been traveling now?"

"10,241,101,532 revolutions of our home planet."

"Then, they have not been traveling very long at all."

"Thank you, Computer. Now, what do these creatures know of us?"

"What they have seen."

"Anything of our language?"

"Nothing."

"What do they call themselves?"

"Humans. Human beings."

"What is the level of their understanding?"

"Good enough to have brought them here."

"Can you please be more specific? What is their method of propulsion?"

"They have various propulsion systems."

"Explain to me how their systems work."

The computer took the creature through each method of propulsion step-by-step. The creature would say, "Oh yes, I remember. What's the next?"

"What is our method of propulsion?"

The computer was used to lapses in the creature's memory, and part of its function like that of all computers was to provide such missing information.

"What weapons do they have?"

"The release of finger size segments of metal at great velocity called guns; focused light of great intensity which they call lasers, ignition of unstable chemicals, ignition of nuclear explosives . . ."

"Computer, I would like you to act as an interpreter."

"Of course."

"Begin now. Greetings, human beings. We are the Throdēop. Have you come far off your course?"

"More than one revolution, but less than two revolutions of our star."

"Computer, how long is one revolution of their star?"

"We have not yet calibrated their measurement of time or distance."

"Are there any questions you have for us?" asked the Throdēop.

Ramón answered, "Your computer has answered many questions for us. But what is your destination?"

"Our destination? Computer, what is our destination?"

"We are headed for a star system with planets and possible life forms."

"Our computer states we are headed for a star system with planets and possible life forms. Our names will be useless to them. Show them a three dimensional diagram, which will allow them to figure it out."

"Where are you from?"

The Throdēop answered, "A star system with twelve planetary bodies larger than two thousand miles in diameter."

"What is your mission?"

"Our mission is to investigate other planetary systems. We will leave population pods where a planet without intelligent life can sustain us."

"How do you determine whether a planet has intelligent life?"

"Computer, can you refresh me on the matter of intelligence?"

"Intelligence is the ability to satisfy your body's survival needs, to recognize yourself in a mirror, the use of language, the use of tools, the ability to solve problems, understand ideas, learn from experience, the ability to use memory to draw analogies and recognize patterns, the ability to deal with other intelligent beings, insight into what another being is thinking, the imagination to speculate on and plan for the future, and the ability to manipulate your environment to suit your needs. There are other signatures of intelligence, but these are widely recognized."

"Tell them what you have told me."

The computer reiterated its statement in English.

Ramón said, "This says nothing about music, for example, or visual expression, or records of experience, what we call literature. Or irony."

The computer related Ramón's observation to the Throdēop, who told the computer to make a more clarifying statement:

"Basically, we will not have anything to do with a species who can recognize themselves in a mirror. We prefer a much lower level of life on a planet. Plants, small basic forms of life. And you are correct, we recognize culture, the passing on of non-genetic information to succeeding generations, as one of the inventions of intelligence."

"Have you made many colonies?"

"So far, none."

"Have you found any habitable planets?"

"So far, none. Have you?"

"No. But probability suggests such planets exist."

"Of course, we have generated such numbers ourselves."

"So, you have never had to walk away from a planet that had developed intelligence? Which means this directive of yours about avoiding planets with intelligent life, that's just hypothetical at this point, isn't it?"

* * *

Stephen wondered about such speculations. Did he have the thing in focus? As with most things, it seemed the more you penetrated into a particular subject, the more nebulous and difficult it was to make anything out. A classic example was the atom. It turned out to be mostly space with a tiny little nucleus at the center and a little gnat of an electron flitting about.

Feynman suggested that understanding the nucleus might require more than bombarding it with high speed particles, and watching to see which way the subatomic particles went. Feynman speculated: what if the nucleus is like a clock? If you smashed a clock, you would see springs and gears emanating from the clock, but you would understand nothing about how the clock worked.

The Fantasy of Financial Independence

"At first $300,000 was enough. I thought with $300,000 at 5 percent you would have $15,000. Or maybe you could get 10 percent, which would generate $30,000, and you certainly could get by on that.

"Rent back then was a grand a month, $12,000 per year. Taxes would remove 30 percent or $9,000. So, that left roughly $9,000. And that was plenty of money, depending of course on one's desires. You couldn't own an expensive house or car or anything."

My brother chimed in, "That must be the artist's fantasy. Enough to work and write and write to your heart's content. You could move to South America. Live in Costa Rica or somewhere in the Carribean."

"Exactly, Hemingway lived in Cuba for a long time. I don't think it was an accident that he ended up there. Cheap living for a writer. It allowed him to live as a king among the natives. He liked Africa for the same reasons. In *The Green Hills of Africa* he writes about waking up and having one of the blacks massage his feet and put on his shoes."

It was a cozy little gemütlich fantasy. Hard to resist.

Hemingway, erstwhile the man's man, roughing it in Africa, spending days in the Caribbean fishing, was a man, in the end, who loved his creature comforts. And it may not be coincidence that he left the much-loved Hadley for Pauline because he had become tired of the artist's life in Paris. Living from hand to mouth, article to article was a tiresome thing. And Pauline took him away from all of that. Their house in Key West was a gift from one of Pauline's uncles. A wonderful house. Good-sized rooms, a catwalk from the bedroom to his studio over the garage. A big, two-hearted studio.

"And so it was that I tired of the artist's fantasy and the $300,000. I moved the sum up to $500,000. Half a million bucks. That was more like it. Even in the worst of times, you could get 5 percent, which would be $25,000."

"Twenty-five thousand. Big deal. It's still the artist's fantasy."

"Let's make it a million. Even in the worst of times, at 5 percent you would have fifty grand at your disposal."

"Even that doesn't seem like that much, does it?"

"Shakespeare left an estate of a thousand pounds. A thousand pounds today buys you a round-trip ticket to America for you and your wife. Forget the nominal sum, and look what he owned: Shakespeare had something like a 10 percent interest in one of the biggest entertainment houses in London, the Globe Theatre. His percentage was tied to the number partners, which varied. Having achieved success, he went back to Stratford and bought the second largest house in town, New Place; he bought a 127 acre farm, then he inherited his father's house in Stratford, which he subdivided; he bought tithes. Tithes were like your portfolio, the equivalent of bonds, and paid income each year. Then he went back to London and bought a house there as well. The value of houses and farmland today would bring a substantial sum of money. Millions, dollars, or pounds. He was a wealthy guy."

"Get real. The only writers who make money like that are popular guys like Clancy and Grisham and Crichton. Shakespeare is the exception, great and popular."

Whoosh, splat. So much for fantasies. "Always look to your relatives for support."

"I just want to keep you grounded. You talk about Hemingway, but you're no Hemingway. You're a beanpole. You're hardly even there. Game hunting in Africa? Your idea of game hunting is the meat counter of Whole Foods. Get real. Hell, you're not even an Asimov."

"I've got another call coming in."

"Wait wait wait. I don't hear any ring."

"I shut off the ringer. Listen, I've got to answer this."

One can only take so much family support.

*   *   *

Science fiction writer wants to meet with alien for fun and research. Alien's weight must be commensurate with height.

No luck with humans, alien must be alien.

The Six-Pack Girl

Nick's fantasy was the "Six-Pack Girl." The Six-Pack Girl was a girl you could take to a motel with a six-pack and do whatever you wanted with. That was the essence of the Six-Pack Girl. She was totally available and compliant.

When you stuck the third finger up her snatch, she stuck her tongue in your ear to confirm that you had made the right move. And if you put a finger at her back door, she was likely to push back.

Nick would question Ambrose if this girl or that girl was a Six-Pack Girl. And Ambrose would judge yes or no. But Nick would say, "Ambrose, you don't understand, they're all Six-Pack Girls. It's just a matter of how and when."

"Then this Six-Pack Girl is your Lara, your Heloise, your great love."

"Hell, no. Great love is almost always a gyp. Abelard got his nuts cut off. No, the Six-Pack Girl is what holds you over. She's the one who has that drink with you when all is going wrong. Really pleasant to look at, but not exceptional, not threateningly beautiful."

"I see."

"She might have some particular thing which is great, like a really sweet heart-shaped ass or pendulous breasts or generous pouty lips."

"And she's the one you go to when the Great Love fails you."

"Right. She welcomes your frustration, your anger. She's the one who knows how to egg you on."

"How's that?"

"Oh, she calls you a wimp, a baby, a spineless jellyfish."

"Excuse me. You left me behind. That wasn't in my fantasy."

"Oh yes, it is. Let me finish. She is calling you all these names, so finally you slap her."

"No, I'm not into slapping."

"How about a spanking?"

"I see your point."

"First you spank her over her dress or blue jeans or whatever, but then you find this unsatisfactory, so you raise the dress up and grab the panties and bring them down and then ... smack."

"And she responds by saying ..."

"Really? You think she could say anything in the middle of this scene?"

"Maybe."

"How about this? She says: 'Brand me with your hand. I want to see all five fingers in the mirror.'"

What is It About a World?

First I would read about the rich everyone knew about in America. The Rockefellers and oil, the Fords and the automobile, the Mellons and their bank, the Astors and their fur trading and Manhattan real estate, the Vanderbilts and the New York Central and Manhattan real estate. In Chicago, where I was from, Marshall Field and his store figured prominently. He had real estate, too. And gave a block of it to the University of Chicago. I pored over his will, which was at the end of the book. He had a wonderful portfolio. He had a good slug of the trusts, and a few railroads. Two-fifths went to his grandson Henry Field, and three-fifths to Marshall Field III. But Henry died, so Marshall III got it all.

Another fantasy. You are born back in time. Born as a Rockefeller brother knowing the future, what was coming. One could invest in Xerox or IBM or Microsoft. And actually, one of them did some of that. Laurence Rockefeller did well in McDonnell Douglas and Eastern Airlines.

In high school, when the fantasy was dying off, the Rothschilds came to the rescue with the five brothers conquering Europe. Loaning large sums to governments. Nathan making a fortune off of Waterloo. First, selling early in the day, then buying through agents when everyone sold because he was selling, knowing from his homing pigeons that the news of victory later in the day would send prices soaring. The boys were geniuses.

Nathan's son, Lionel, loaned Disraeli the necessary sum to buy the Suez Canal, and all of the brothers bought into the railroads big time. Ruining their competitors. James destroying Credit Mobilaire. The only thing they didn't buy was a country. If only they had bought a country.

In 2000, Bill Gates could buy countries. He could buy the Caribbean one country at a time. The problem with rich guys is that they lacked creativity.

At least Kim Basinger bought a town. Didn't work out very well, but it was an interesting idea. That's why I liked Alfred de Rothschild and his fairy book castle, Waddesdon. And George Washington Vanderbilt and his chateau Biltmore. Larger than life. In the 1990s, Warren Buffett lived in a modest home with a Lincoln Continental. So he had a jet. Big deal. He would end up leaving an enormous sum to Bill Gates's foundation. Henry Ford must turn over in his grave when he sees what has become of the Ford Foundation. All the Jews he's funded! It's better to spend while you're still in control.

*   *   *

Worlds and worlds. It is the dream of rich men and writers to create a world. Balzac in volume after volume creates a Paris Prime. A subset of Paris, a Paris not unlike the Paris which existed, but his Paris—Balzac's Paris. A Paris he developed from twelve o'clock at night until six in the morning. His cast of characters appear in novel after novel. Vautrin, the homosexual villain. Bianchon, the doctor. The Goriot sisters sucking every last dime from their father, Cousin Pons's relatives stripping his apartment of his bric-a-brac, treasures he had acquired piece by piece. Count on Balzac to show you the dark side of self-interest.

But the examples go on and on. Faulkner and Yoknapatawpha County, Scott Turow and Kindle County, Horton Foote and Harrison, Texas. For Joyce it was the Dublin of 1904, the year he left Ireland.

Rich men have tried to create their own worlds. George Pullman created his city within a city in Chicago. Hershey created his own town in Pennsylvania with streets like Caramel Street and Cocoa Avenue. And how many southern plantation owners have created their own Tara? Their own world. Movie directors do the same. Hitchcock created a cozy world of the backyard in *Rear Window*, complete with Miss Lonely Hearts, the Newlyweds, the Composer, Miss Torso, and the henpecked newlywed husband. It is a complete world. Italian immigrant Frank Capra created the world of Bedford Falls in New England. Fellini creates a world in a small town in *Amarcord*. Or for Michael Crichton it is the world of an amusement park in Jurassic Park. A world of wonder and amusement and terror.

A world is something the mind can get caught up in, get lost in. For a rich man, is it an opportunity to reclaim a lost childhood? To play with houses, and trains, and stores, and dolls who can move? Rosebud. But if a world can have a bright side, it also has its dark side. Hitchcock's backyard world has a murderer, Capra's has stingy Mr. Potter, who owns the bank and most of the town, Crichton's has terrific danger in beasts of unusual power in *Jurassic Park*. Anne Rice developed the world of the vampire, a creature of unusual power. A world of the night and dark alleys. Where the protagonist must feed on blood. Unfortunately, she turned it into a franchise, so that she could buy all kinds of properties in New Orleans. Warren Buffett would certainly approve. The HMS *Titanic* becomes a world, and the examples go on and on.

A world is an opportunity to become God. Woody Allen made that clear in *Stardust Memories*. Someone from the audience, the gaper's block, asks him if he doesn't identify with Narcissus. He says, "If anybody, I identify with Jove."

Or as Abner would have it, "There are two magical things in the world: being transported in a dark theatre by a movie."

And what's the other? "Compound interest."

Deception and The Vanity of Brains

"If you found out your wife was cheating on you, would you be more upset because she had betrayed your trust, or because you didn't see it happening?" Question posed by Nick in the lounge area of the Oak Park Tennis Club, after being defeated by myself in singles. We sat on flat plastic cushions, tennis balls bouncing back and forth in front of them. Pop, bup, pop, bap.

"Why do you ask questions like that?"

"You're terribly afraid it would happen to you, aren't you?"

Stephen wondered why he hung out with Nick. It was continual harassment, embarrassment, and humiliation. And here he just won at tennis. He wins but he still loses.

Nick continued, "Intelligence is one of your pet concerns. Children can detect deception from a pretty young age, four, let's say. It's a tip-off, one of the signs of intelligence. One of the terrors of parents is that their children will not be able to detect the deception of an adult who says, "Your mother asked me to take you right home, get in the car."

"Not only do you want to terrorize me, you want to terrorize every parent who ever lived."

"Don't you agree about deception?"

"You focus on subjects I'm not that comfortable with. Who wants to focus on deception?"

"Magicians. Would there be magicians without deception? Where would the Wizard of Oz be without the man behind the curtain?"

"First, I would have to be married, and that prospect seems remote."

"It doesn't have to be a marriage. You can just be dating someone to suffer the effect."

Stephen thought: Now I didn't even get to be married before I am duped and abandoned. Great.

He continued, "Besides, marriage is nothing. You can be married every year if you want."

"Easy for you to say."

"Oh, anyone can get married if he wants. All you have to do is lower your requirements and expectations. Russians and Latin Americans and Asians want to get married by the boatloads. For the green cards."

"Ah, right. A marriage of convenience. A strategic marriage. Lust on one side, and what on the other—service, duty?"

"Myself, I have no use for marriage. It would get in the way. It would involve me in all manner of lying and intrigue. The way it is now, I don't have to lie to anyone."

This was Nick of the total honesty. The Nick who imposed honesty, a kind of human lie detector. When he was about to go to bed with a girl he didn't know, he would hold her wrist and check her pulse, and then ask, "Do you have herpes?"

Stephen, who could never detect a pulse, said "Ah." Stephen relied on this expression as a kind of defense mechanism, a pause to buy time while he searched for some suitable repartee.

None came.

"I will explain this to you one time. Analyze everything from the standpoint of power."

Nick was an authority on power.

"And love, where does that fit in?"

"Ah yes, the power of love." Pause, let it sink in. "Or is it more like the love of power?"

"You know, Nick, I wish you would flesh things out once in while. It doesn't pay to put the fluoroscope on everything. We are not simply bones. All is not power."

Such conversations irritated Stephen because you never knew when the Lord, like some perverse coach in high school, will make you the example, make you live up to what you say. You think power isn't everything, then the Lord says, "Hey you, Roly-Poly, jump in the water and show us the backstroke."

And actually, such was the case, for Stephen had been twirled around like a baton by more than one of the girls he had dated. He was irritated because Nick might turn out to be right, though certainly bad-hearted.

"Don't be silly, power is the only thing worth discussing," said Nick. Like the Cowardly Lion in *The Wizard of Oz*, he nearly sang, "Why does the alderman get up in the morning? Power. Why does the broadcaster broadcast? Power. Why does the advertiser advertise? Power."

He continued, "That's why I prefer to be on the outside of marital relationships. It's better to be the cuckolder than the cuckoldee. By the way, my informal poll shows more people would be upset by their failure to see what was happening than by the pain of an infidelity. It's an ego thing. A brain thing. Pride in our brains."

"No kidding."

"Nope."

Stephen thought: I knew that I could never see anything even when it was right under my eyes, so I knew it would be the pain of heartbreak that would do me in. I knew that I could be deceived. I'm not that smart. And I knew something about neglect. After all, I was the son of neglect. On neglect I could write a best seller. The women would buy it in droves, and the men would ignore it in legions. But that's how we are: we know our own problems intimately, become infinitely articulate on them, but solving them was another matter. But that was a generational thing, most of the men of my generation were neglected by their fathers.

It was folly to think that honesty and forthrightness could exist throughout instead of just as a front, a facade, a billboard. Honesty, Next Exit, 5 Miles.

But honesty can be a destructive force as well as a positive one. What need to worry your partner about one lapse in a marriage? The offending partner should keep it to himself or herself, and bear whatever bad feelings it causes. Leave the cuckolded partner in peace, and if he truly cares about his partner, not repeat it. It's silly to think that your partner will never learn about repeated offenses or that they won't have any effect on the marriage. It's not a throwaway world anymore—the emotional pollutants are bound to seep into the subconscious, percolate back up into the topics supply, contaminate the phone lines, bubble up into conversation, show up in a blood test, or surface on the skin.

Nick, true to his thinking, had no marriage to overturn, though Stephen couldn't help but think that some of the women he took home surely harbored the notion that they might marry him.

A good starting place to understand Nick would be school. The man was a phenomenal test taker, bumping the top on every intelligence test—Iowa Basics, Stanford Binet, SAT, ACT, National Merit Qualifying Test, 99.9 percentile. And Stephen was in envy.

Though Nick was the superior test taker, Stephen had doubts that it qualified him on the genius front. The only real test of genius is the act of doing it. Newton, Shakespeare, da Vinci, Degas, Vermeer, Einstein, Pauling, Balzac. Those were geniuses. James Joyce, Edison. Good test takers were good test takers. Test really well like Vos Savant and you get into the Guiness Book of Records. But it doesn't qualify you as a genius.

Nick joined Mensa and then dropped out. Mensa wasn't really exclusive enough. After all, they admit all those people in the 98th percentile, which is 1.9 more percentiles than he felt they should let in. Though, to be sure, Nick was not really a joiner. The man was a loner, a coyote, not a pack animal. A tiger in the Siberian plains.

In school he scored a lot of A's, of course. But only when he was interested, and when interest waned, grades dropped. The mind still has to be willing to accept, and he could be as stubborn and obstinate as the next guy. His grades in French were dismal.

Nick was more athletic than Stephen, and played basketball and tennis. He was not really a team player at basketball. He was a star. And tennis was more the correct pattern. But he had certain social skills he could summon, and dated his share of pom-pom girls and cheerleaders, though they were too rah-rah for his nature. He did it because he could do it, to perfect his hunting skills.

Stephen had tendencies to allow himself to be run down, even in his pre-Nick days his friend Ralph would taunt him.

Talking about a date, Ralph would say, "Isn't Shelley attractive?"

"Yes."

"I think it's the way she does her hair."

"Her hair is very nice."

"Also, she's a good kisser. She has such generous lips, and she's really generous with them."

Stephen could only take so much of this conversation, and he would never say Ralph and he were the best of friends, nor were Nick and he for that matter. In fact, Stephen would say that his friendship with Nick, whatever there was of it, was always teetering on the precipice of a very high cliff. He never had the heart to push it off. It just seemed too mean a thing to do.

And this badgering continued into the present.

"The problem with you, Stephen, is that you've missed your calling. You shouldn't be a programmer; you should be a violinist or composer. You're a true sublimist. A child of culture."

"I write."

"That's right. But you've never published. But that fits, don't you see? The sublimist's sublimist."

Stephen thought: But what he really wants to say is that I don't have an active sex life. And that hurt. Though I wondered if sex itself was enough. The current hooker ads had all kinds of codes: did you speak French, Greek, Russian, or Asian? But the acronym that bore out my theory on the limitations of sex was the increasing appearance of GFE (Girlfriend Experience). At the end of the day, love still mattered. It was said about smiling, that smiling even if you weren't happy had a good effect. And if a girl faked a little love for you, it was better than no love. And the ads and the message boards made it clear, in the end, men did want this feeling.

*   *   *

But that was at the end of the day. At the beginning of the day, during one of his summer jobs in high school, Sid the salesman told Stephen why he strayed and ultimately got caught and ended up divorced.

"The wife wouldn't give me any head." He joked, "My kingdom for a blow job."

Sid went on, "And then there are blow jobs and there are blow jobs. One of my favorite hookers was a girl with this one eye that wandered a little—that went toward her nose. Anyway, with that eye focused on my member . . . she seemed so devoted to my dick that you'd'a thought it was the only thing in the world. I used to think I would marry her just for this one talent. To have this is to have a gold mine—right in your own home."

"What happened to her?"

"Oh, she moved on. It's not a stable business. Never saw her again. But never have gotten a blow job as good, either. She'd logged her practice hours. A pro is a pro is a pro."

"Someone said that about a rose. You should have married that one."

"Don't laugh. I was seriously thinking of it. But what do you say when you get out of bed. Say again, after sex."

"I get it, the sex might not be in bed."

Stephen saw his pro as more of a waif, not a full personality. Kind of an idiot savant, who knew only one thing, how to suck on a cock—every single variation.

On the other hand, in the next summer job there was a black woman who would frankly tell us how little interested she was in sex, taking care of her man once a week. Sort of an ordeal she put him through, death by sex. Oversatiate him so that he would become a little sick of it, to the point where he would leave her alone. No real enthusiasm on her part, just fulfilling her end of the deal. Her line was, "Women are waste receptacles for men's passion."

So, anyway, one Monday Stephen came into the office early and cheerful, ready to tell her about a nature program he'd watched on TV the night before.

"Hey, Marva. I saw a program about elk last night that reminded me of you. The female elk is receptive only one day a year, and then only for sixteen hours."

If she had laughed a little, they both would have enjoyed the comic relief. But her laughter, which began as a chuckle, worked its way into hysterics. Every time she thought about it, she moved into ever-higher paroxysms of laughter. She couldn't stop. Meanwhile, Stephen's chuckle subsided into a smile, and finally he had to go into the next room to escape. Paralyzed by the truth revealed in the other room, he went into a mild catatonic trance. Feet on the drawer of a desk, and leaning back in his chair, he focused on a speck on a painting of eggs until it didn't exist.

Marva, meanwhile, came to the door to ask some question, saw Stephen's glum look, and that started the laughter all over again.

It was like the death of hope. How were babies ever made? How did these two races, men and women, ever meet? And lastly, how was one ever born?

Surely it had to have come about somehow. I'm here, therefore I was born; therefore two people united in coital embrace. His phenomena up her noumena.

So, it was that even in his twenties and thirties Stephen came to feel he knew so little about the world that he often felt like a child. He was once in love with a Jewish woman who said to him, often, "Wake up and smell the coffee."

Stephen wondered: Will I ever wake up? It seemed no concentrated espresso, no sugar, no benzedrine would ever wake me up. I thought I would slumber through life like a turtle for which even winking seemed to take forever.

It was a perverse setup. For sex to be a mutual thing, you would figure that women would have pleasure sensors at the back of the vagina where it would meet with the head of the penis, right? Not so, nature's plan called for the woman to be stimulated only when the penis pushed all the way in and the man's pubic bone hit her clitoris on the outside. And actually, this doesn't work very well according to Hite and others. They tell us that oral or hand manipulation is ultimately needed to get the job done.

Really, here's what it comes down to: all sex is masturbation because nobody's gonna feel your orgasm but you. And it requires concentration. Sexually speaking, it's a solipsistic universe. Wittgenstein missed it by a little. It's not the problem of other beetles or other minds; it's really the problem of other orgasms.

Language and Coincidence

When they first saw the Throdēop, his head was yellow-greenish and boxy, but then it changed. Became reddish-yellowish-greenish and more oval.

Through the computer, the Prime Earthers, principally Eladia, began to ask the Throdēop if the Prime Earthers could learn their language, and the Throdēop agreed, but he warned them it was a difficult language.

He said, "There are 891 languages on our planet, and why this one became popular God only knows. It's one of the worst."

"We would like to learn anyway."

"I will instruct the computer to assist you. Meanwhile, in a gesture of mutual hospitality, I would like you to continue to instruct our computer in your language, which a few of my friends and I would like to learn."

"Our language, English, like yours, was not necessarily the easiest to learn, but neither is it the hardest. It became the international language about 150 to 200 years before we left. One of our peoples had conquered various big parts of the planet. The economies of those parts were very large. People learned this language to do business with them. They had money. They had many scientists who wrote in the language. Coincidentally, it also happens that perhaps the greatest of our writers spoke this language."

"Those are things that would have a central role. It was the same with us. If we had come a little earlier, we would be speaking another language."

"As would we. Related, but different," Eladia the linguistics expert said, "As it happened, the people whose language we speak were conquered by another people. Their language, French, was assimilated into the language they conquered, English. But if we had left 300 years earlier, we would have spoken their language—French, which was then the international language. Here's a question I often wonder about: Do you think if our greatest writer had spoken some other language, we would be speaking that language?"

"Were there other great writers who did not speak your principal language?"

"Oh, yes."

"And they were translated?"

"Yes."

"There you have your answer. Language is a matter of convenience and necessity. You must be a writer."

Eladia answered, "Yes, I am."

"Yes, our writers suffer a similar delusion. I think that's what you would call it, a delusion. Writers like to think their influence over language is preeminent."

"You are not a writer."

"That is correct. I am the leader. But with our long life spans we have all tried our hand at writing. And we all respect elegance and simplicity in our best communications."

The Possibilities of the Novel

from the journal of Stephen Ambrose

My view: the novel was the opportunity to reveal everything you knew. A Theory of Everything for the novelist. A child would reveal everything he knew by reciting the alphabet, followed by every word he knew, but even a kid would know when he came to counting out all the numbers he knew that it would take a lifetime task to write down every single integer he could think of. Because the rules of number-making were clear, and would make for an endless list. After he developed the laws of mechanics, Newton, for example, quickly realized it would be impossible to figure out all the motions of all the heavenly bodies.

The novelist is faced with this kind of huge possibility. He, too, realizes it is impossible to include everything he knows. And if you do try, your novel becomes the kitchen sink. Not that that would necessarily deter someone from trying to do it. Look at how Joyce stuffed nearly every word he knew, the acceleration of gravity, all the important writing styles of the last 1,000 years, and his theory about Anne Hathaway into either *Ulysses* or *Finnegans Wake*. Balzac stuffed his comprehensive knowledge about human beings plus his knowledge of Parisian high society plus his knowledge about printing and papermaking into his oeuvre, *The Human Comedy*. Yeats put everything he knew either into his poetry, plays, or his esoteric work, *A Vision*. Even Shakespeare's volume of plays contains 29,066 different words, the history of the Tudors, the Romans, and his take on the nature of comedy and tragedy. Shakespeare is everywhere in his universe but fails to materialize for us.

A mysterious character indeed. In 1603, Queen Elizabeth died and James came down from Scotland to succeed her. Plague followed. So the playhouses closed, as they routinely did when plague struck, so this made for a good time for Shakepeare's troupe, The King's Men, to go out to the hinterlands. A letter written by the Countess Pembroke has it that the troupe played at Wilton. She wrote her son to invite the king to come and see *As You Like It.* "We have the man Shakespeare with us." But the letter that contains this passage has mysteriously disappeared, so no one knows for sure it was even written, and so the mystery continues. Was he as interesting as that passing remark suggests? My bet is yes, he was. His verse was printed by 1609, and it had made the rounds among the aristocracy in longhand for years before that. And the same way people recognize style in a composer like Mozart or a band like the Beatles, they would recognize it in Shakespeare. Word would get around. Shakespeare is hot. He is "able to bombast out a blank verse as the best of you . . . the only Shakescene in a countrey."

Finally, I came to the conclusion that probably the desire to reveal everything still exists among writers, but that this must needs be compressed. It might be as simple as a theorem, "women are impossible once they know they have you in their thrall" or the collateral theorem, "men are impossible once . . ." and so on.

Let's start again; the seven basic forms are the sphere, the spiral, the 120° angle, branching, the explosion, fractals, the meander, and the detective story. Detective story, you ask? How did that get on the list? But I submit even Hamlet is a detective story. Did Claudius murder Hamlet's father? Is he the beast the ghost says he is? It seems to me, it is the detective story that is the basic form for the writer. In every work of fiction or theatre, something has to be found out, discovered, resolved. And that is the thing that the writer is working on. Lear doesn't know up front how things will develop if he passes on his kingdom to his three female offspring; he must find it out for himself. Will the devil get Faust's soul? And it would certainly explain the popularity of Sherlock Holmes, the quintessential detective.

For Stephen King, it is the artifact that is uncovered. How is this any different?

Science is kind of a continual detective story, which is again why education will become the growth industry of the twenty-first century. With more free time on their hands, everyone wants to know everything. Failing that they will want to know something. Hopefully something unique and interesting. Interesting meaning interesting to someone else. We are social creatures in the end, and will want someone to share our unique knowledge. Something IQ tests fail to measure. Social intelligence. Making friends. Making friends with people who can assist you in your endeavors, whatever they are.

The Zoo

Prime Earth was enormous. It housed a large zoo. The zoo was the pride of the ship. It was an engineering marvel to create a huge open space, with plant life sufficient to support the craft. There was not enough room for large predators like lions or bears to roam around. Lower-level predators were interesting to the children because they hunted other animals. It was a challenge to the humans to try and create some kind of equilibrium. They cloned animals when they fell out of balance. But the challenge was to choose just the right species so that cloning became unnecessary. That was one of the games. To create the perfect self-sustaining closed system. Another was to run evolutionary experiments.

A few of the larger predators were cloned and caged. Sometimes they were sacrificed and others were cloned. The sacrifice was like a great Roman spectacle because they would allow a pack of hyenas to devour a lion. Or vice versa. Proving only that it always came down to the macro and micro. Humans never really made progress as so-called humane beings, it's always just a matter of scale. Chiaroscuro. They were, by turns, ruthless and sensitive.

Humans could walk through the zoo, which was just an open space with no bars or other obstruction, on a path which protected them from the animals with electric shock in the soil. No one used the word "ground" on Prime; it never felt quite right. Ground was an elemental word that conveyed the idea of largeness, gravity, homeness. It was a word that felt out of place in deep space, where the only sun was the lighting provided by the ship, which could never be the rich light of a sun bursting continual hydrogen explosions millions of miles away. Nevertheless, a rich light source was developed, and like the sun, you could never look directly at it.

The word they used was "floor."

---

*   *   *

Near the end of the twenty-first century, childbirth no longer required a mother's womb. There were machines, instrumentation that assumed the task of embryo development. So it was that many on Prime even later in life wanted to have children, or one child even. Ova and sperm from younger years were in the vault. But the craft's size limited the number of children they could have. It was a pretty straightforward calculation.

Or so it seemed. But it became a pretty heated issue. Men and women still wanted to raise children. And there was heated, heated debate over how many children the craft could support. Supposedly this problem was to have been avoided because the number of living spaces was predetermined when the craft was designed, fixed by the architects of the ship. But there was redundancy and extra capacity built into the waste recycling facilities. Moreover, this was not a craft with a totally fixed interior space. It was a craft with manufacturing capability, which meant it had the ability to redesign and reengineer the interior to accommodate more humans. Especially if the zoo were eliminated.

So, it became a quality of life versus quantity of life issue. More human life could be stuffed into the craft, but there would be less living space per individual. Less freedom of movement. Indeed, it became more and more apparent that freedom and living space were more closely connected than anyone thought. Many people, especially those who had been waiting for years, were less willing to wait. Human life on Earth at the end of the twenty-first century had become a much longer-lasting thing. Average life spans were extending well beyond 100 years, sometimes 150 years. With a growing understanding of physiology, the quality of life was greatly improved. Tennis at 100? Skillful use of biological knowledge of hormones, proteins, coenzymes, DNA, precise nutrition, and exercise made it possible. And tinkering with the telomeres.

A Slice of God's Country

The big hot button issue on Prime was the zoo. On the one hand, the zoo was their everything. Their slice of God's country. Their solace. Their Grand Canyon and Botswana watering hole all rolled up into one. It was the marvel of design.

On the other hand, it was just a big space. And big spaces could be redesigned for humans. Women wanted their babies. And what of the animals? As Carlos said, "We can clone tigers anytime we want. We have the cells in the deep freeze. We have the structure of the DNA on computer. Either we can use the cells, and if there's some problem, we can splice together some DNA. One way or another we can make these animals anytime we want. And the space can also be redesigned and landscaped however we want."

Technologies changed everything. Fusion had changed everything on Earth before the travelers had left. Cheap energy meant that the deserts of Saudi Arabia could be used for agriculture, the Sahara was re-forested, which meant that carbon could be taken out of the atmosphere. Population growth had stabilized and stagnated for a while, but new arable land moved population growth back up.

Problem was: a lot of people liked the tigers in their blown-up, filled-out form, not in the test tube form. Though holographs were great. True-formers were annoyed with virtual reality, there was something phoney about it. They like the true form of things. And there was something funny about holographs. As virtual reality closed in on the real thing, these annoyances seemed to grow stronger. Philosophy, which wore itself down with proofs for the existence of God, consolation, metaphysics, solipsism, grammar, and other issues, disdained and ignored for eons, finally found its home in the virtual world. After all, the practical man has no real reason to question if the mug of coffee he's drinking from (seeing, feeling, smelling) is the real thing if it performs all those functions. But what if he dons a virtual reality helmet, and he feels, sees, tastes, smells a mug and coffee, but there is no coffee?

Many claimed coffee provided no nourishment even in its true form, though it seemed to help Balzac in his writing from midnight to six in the morning. His output was stupendous, and all written before he was fifty-one. Maybe the monk's habit and the lack of interruptions helped.

In Which the Plot Resumes, However Thin

Stephen never invited Nick to his apartment, so in order to get at Stephen's computer, he invaded his apartment, which was in an older building in Oak Park, "vintage" in the real estate code, with no security. He went on Stephen's tango night. Stephen never missed. In fact, Nick would go there later, after his visit.

No lock on the outside door, he went right up. Nick used a trick a locksmith had used on his own apartment. He took a screwdriver and went through the molding. It only works if the dead bolt is not set. And only if you are in an old apartment with wooden moldings. Evidently, Stephen was not that paranoid because no dead bolt got in the way. A funny thing for a missile programmer, he thought. The nice thing was that the molding was loose, and it didn't look damaged. He used the end of the screwdriver to hammer back in the nails.

Nick inspected Stephen's apartment. Only one shelf of science fiction, though the three shelves below were filled with science books, science biography, textbooks. The shelves themselves were the particle-board type with a teak veneer which no doubt leached formaldehyde into the room and into the erstwhile science fiction writer's mind and work.

A shelf of Saul Bellow, a shelf of Graham Greene, a shelf of Balzac. Two shelves of anthropology, paleontology, two shelves of the Elizabethans, Shakespeare. A shelf of rich people, Norton Critical editions of most of the greats of literature, a few Elmore Leonards. Oak floors with orientals. The place was vaguely organized, but cluttered with stacks of books against the walls when he evidently ran out of shelves.

Nick came back to it: only one shelf of science fiction, how can that be? And he calls himself a science fiction writer?

There was a pair of cockatiels, which Stephen gave the run of the apartment. Nick put on his surgical gloves and went for the computer. After the system came up, it asked for the password. He typed in, "Stephen." It said, "Access denied." He tried Stephen's birthdate, his social security number, his mother's maiden name.

What could one do? He supposed one could take the computer out, lock, stock and barrel, but would you ever get the information out of it? Obviously, although Stephen was in a low security residence, he had taken steps to protect his programs. Nick got a chill, and he started to perspire. How devious was he? Did he have a camera looking at him? What triggered the camera and so on.

He figured that the programs were encrypted, and that would make them impossible to look at.

Nick's preparations were only for minimally protected equipment. He tried using a Windows start-up disk, which he hoped would get him the C: drive, but he encountered more protection. No doubt the government insisted. It wouldn't be Ambrose, whose self-esteem was so low he didn't think anything he was working on was worth stealing. Theft of the whole machine was the only solution. Nick retreated with that thought as his principal alternative. The Koreans could figure out the encryption. He had to think out the implications, for now he left the machine behind.

*   *   *

Stephen came off the floor after dancing with an older woman.

"This is your idea of fun, dancing with an older woman?" Nick.

"She's a good dancer."

"You're hopeless. How am I going to turn you into a hunter?"

"Hunters, like lions, for example, always go for the easy stuff first—small animals, young animals, the lame, the old. So I am a hunter, after all."

"Okay, I accept. Good defense."

"Perhaps someday you'll move up the chain, and move like a cheetah and knock down a lithe, sexy impala."

"Thanks, Coach."

"Listen, I was wondering, I'm working on a sensitive project, and I wonder how I might protect my computer."

"What kind of project?" Stephen.

"Can't really say, a sensitive industrial project. My superiors are concerned about break-ins and whatnot. You know, industrial espionage."

"Not my bailiwick. Sorry, can't help you." Well, it was worth a try.

"No problem. They must have experts for that sort of thing. I was just trying to get a leg up."

"My work isn't that sensitive."

Sure, like hell, thought Nick.

"Well, maybe you're right. All sex is masturbation."

"What? Where did that come from? When did I ever say that?" Stephen.

"Never, but you don't have a girlfriend. So what does that leave?"

"I see."

"The idea of mutual satisfaction is absurd. That's in the category of Hollywood Endings. You rub your thing in her pussy. She doesn't feel anything, no nerve sensors. But if she's really excited and wet you pound really hard to get some sensation, maybe you finally bounce against her clit. It still doesn't do the trick. Of course, I don't know what women feel, but if I read Sher Hite correctly, the woman doesn't care too much about couplings. Probably only oral sex makes any difference."

"So, you're giving solipsism a new life."

"Not me. Nature. God. Whatever you want to call it. Men and women. It's like one of those complicated mousetrap contraptions. You're attracted to her fertility, but she has her needs, too. Maybe she needs a security blanket. Maybe she wants to be close. You can be sure if she's identified you as a great sperm donor, she wants a kid. And she has nerve endings, too."

"You know maybe all this stuff is true, but it's like surgery, and I get a little woozy when you open up the patient."

"But that's how it is."

Stephen felt surrounded by reality instructors. His brother, Nick, Sophia. The instruction never stopped, really. He just wanted to close up the patient and go to sleep.

Culture and Cloning

There was a practical problem with cloning a species back to life, and that was the problem of culture. Monkeys did learn from their parents, as did wolves, as did lions, as did squirrels. Male birds learned their songs from other songbirds and so on. If culture is the transmission of the learning, then humans are not the only ones to have a culture.

Elsa (of *Born Free* fame) was lucky; she was able to reintegrate into lion life. She got laid. But this was not always the case. Many is the time that even animals from the same culture did not get laid in zoos. But then, maybe that was the problem, that these were animals without a shared cultural life. If a wolf is raised in captivity, what does it know of wolf culture? What does it know of dominance and submission? Maybe gorillas or pandas—or whatever the animal—fail to mate for lack of a common culture (if the species is complex). I'm a West African gorilla, that silly East African gorilla doesn't know how to act.

It was the argument of those who wanted children that culture could be transmitted to these animals via video. If they watched videos, they would get the idea. Experiments were conducted with clones and videos, and it was Elsa revisited. Sometimes it worked, sometimes not. The trick of video aided panda mothers in the year 2000. They learned to suckle their young by watching videos.

*   *   *

As they had closed in on the alien craft, the issue of what to do with the zoo moved to the background. Leaders such as Ramón claimed that Primers would eventually find a planet, which would be habitable, and that those who desired it could have all the children they wanted.

The Throdēop started to speak in English. Consequently, the efforts made by the crew of Prime to figure out the Throdēop tongue diminished. Eladia thought this was a bad thing: that the aliens understood English but Primers did not have a handle on Bop, the language of the Throdēop. She brought up the experience of the Americans with the Japanese in the late 1990s. The Japanese made a strategic effort to understand English, in which they largely succeeded. More OEDs were sold in Japan than anywhere else. They took that knowledge to subvert from within. The Japanese sold the Americans cars that Americans liked even better than the cars they made themselves. The Americans complained about the balance of trade, to which the Japanese gave lip service. Complain, complain. That's all the inferior Americans were good for.

Eladia pointed out that it was easy enough to communicate with the Throdēop in English, but maybe they were missing out on something important by not learning Bop sufficiently. Maybe something important would turn up if they could read their history texts. Similarly, the Americans failed to understand that the smiling Japanese were really conducting war. Ted Turner understood, Michael Crichton understood, but many did not. How could Americans ever really insist the Japanese purchase American products? They had to fight as the Japanese had. Learn Japanese. Make cars with the steering wheel on the correct side, the right side. Only the oddball Japanese would buy a stupid American car with the steering wheel on the wrong side.

And, she wondered, how was this Throdēop able to learn English so quickly? The creature had seemed so dull at first. And its first attempts at English were singularly inept. She kept on with her studies, plodding along.

One of the first things the Throdēop said was, "My name is Tōparr."

She had asked the creature why it had appeared to be so dull, but it did not seem to know how to answer. It seemed dull again, or feigned dull. Meanwhile, the now English-speaking Throdēop became like a child in the backseat. "Dad, why is the sky blue?" But the Throdēop asked more pertinent questions—about their spacecraft for starters. How did they seal the atmosphere inside their craft? What was their means of propulsion?

Later, the Throdēop wondered about the oxygen content. It was nearly the same as theirs, more or less, and they both pondered the role of oxygen in the development of their respective life forms. And other curious parallel developments.

They both were life forms based on cells. It turned up that the same twenty amino acids were in both life forms. DNA was the same four building blocks—cytosine, guanine, thymine, adenine. This was becoming damned intriguing to both sides. The Throdēop queried its computer, "Computer, what does it mean that we share these common things?"

The computer might seem to have a sense of humor, "It means what you think it means: either you and the humans have a common ancestor, or that these twenty amino acids, and the four bases of DNA are a necessary condition for the development of intelligent life. Though there could be other systems for intelligent life."

"Thank you, computer. Please expand on the notion of a common ancestor."

"You have the same building blocks. Throdēop and humans both have amino acids, proteins, DNA. All of this suggests the possibility of an ancestor in common. Examination of the DNA should shed some light on that. The equipment, though, has not been used for millions of years. It will take quite a while to test and calibrate the equipment."

Tōparr said, "Please begin the process of testing the equipment. Computer, how is it possible that we have a common ancestor?"

"There are still questions about Throdēop development. Perhaps you developed from primordial soup, or perhaps you were jump-started by an alien civilization which is common to you and the humans. Spores which exist in space."

"Spores."

"Spores, bacteria, a virus. Some elemental life form."

"And from there to more complex forms."

"There may turn out to be uniform rules for the development of complex life forms. We have no experience with life forms from other parts of the universe, so we do not know what those rules are. I checked the databases on the human ship and they have constructed experiments of early life on their planet with methane, ammonia, and water. They ran an electric current through it to simulate lightning, and it formed amino acids. And other experiments generated nucleotides."[2]

"Yes, we have also done such experiments, too, haven't we?"

"That is correct."

---

[2]   Editor's note: Right. That would be the 1953 experiment of Harold Urey and Stanley Miller at the University of Chicago.

Flight Path

Eventually, the humans wised up. They asked the Throdēop to show them their flight path. A 3D simulation for their flight path took them back through several star systems. The final star system, from which they started their voyage, looked familiar. It had four large planets. One that was blue like Neptune, another with rings that looked like Saturn, and one was the size of Jupiter, though it had no red spot, so perfect identification was not possible, then on to a band of asteroids, a small red planet, then another small blue planet.

As it traced back its path in three dimensions, Eladia asked, "Is that our solar system?"

"It sure looks like it," said Ramón.

Tōparr said, "And now we are back to the star system from which we began our travels."

The humans held back their thoughts until they reached their own quarters.

"My God, they're from Earth," said Eladia. "What does that mean? Are they dinosaurs? If so, then explain the discrepancy in the years. They haven't been traveling 10 trillion years after all, which seemed a stretch since the universe is only thirteen point seven billion years old."

"Could it be that since they only have six fingers, that all their numbers are in base six?" said Ramón. They queried the computer, and it turned out that ten trillion was only 65 million in base ten.

"They're not like any dinosaurs I ever saw."

"Well, at the end of the Cretaceous era, there may have been many developments of which we are not aware. Things can happen quite suddenly. There were for millions of years small numbers of hominids. If the dinosaurs are anything like

Homo, then we might never have found anything to suggest an intelligence developing. Stone axes, for example."

Eladia said, "Well, perhaps there were indications of intelligence."

"What do you mean?"

"Evidence suggests that the numbers of dinosaur species were declining before the Chicxulub impact."

"Yes, what do think that means?"

"There was a dramatic reduction in the numbers of species on the planet before our human group left Earth."

"Are you suggesting that one of signifiers of intelligence is a reduction in the numbers of species on a planet?"

"Well, humans killed all other competing predators—initially in self-defense, of course, but eventually for sport. The predators were maintained in zoos as curiosities, but that wasn't a sufficient population. Gene rot. But then humans overfished, overhunted. They clear-cut forests so that species were separated from one another, and populations declined. Humans reduced their populations to such low numbers they couldn't recover.

"And consider this: Homo sapiens went from maybe ten thousand to six billion in seventy-five thousand years. In the scheme of things, that is like the blink of an eye. Such a short time period might not even show up in the geological record. If the dinosaurs developed an intelligent species, maybe they all ended up in that black ash layer of the K-T boundary."

"That's interesting," Ramón toyed with the idea, "That a sign of intelligent life is a reduction in the numbers of species, but it doesn't feel quite right. That's it: humans only had an effect on other species when its own numbers increased dramatically, which only took seventy-five thousand years. All that data would be in the black ash layer. Which means it wouldn't show up. The lower numbers of species in the millions of years before the asteroid must have been caused by something else."

"Yes, let me think . . ."

"But your point may still be true enough. The ultimate species of intelligent life is just the ultimate predator. Which breeds its favorite food, is that it? And if they really like it, like something, like the passenger pigeon, well then, they kill them by the billions until they're gone. I like your theory," said Ramón.

"Well, it would seem that's the case."

"So, ultimately, intelligent life simply eats, gorges its way to extinction?"

"Not exactly, well, sort of. It increases the food supply, then it procreates to fill all the available space, *then* it eats its way to extinction. I suspect there are cycles within cycles for this sort of thing."

"Meanwhile poisoning the atmosphere."

"Sure, sending CO_2 and methane up into the atmosphere, filling up the land with their excretions, eating base species like coast-hugging fish. In general, screwing up the equilibrium. Creating all manner of ecological mess. Sure they learn to recycle, and do as much as possible, but maybe it's never enough."

"Because ..."

"Because, I don't know, it's never enough because they keep bringing more intelligent creatures into being, for example."

In a Few Thousand Years It's All Gone

"Dinosaurs in space. You idiot."

"Stop."

"You clown."

"Abner, it's just a speculation."

"Okay, I get your point. You want the reader to buy into your notion that 'intelligent life' is an oxymoron, like military intelligence and safe sex."

"I think you're on to something. Maybe 'intelligent predator' is an oxymoron."

"Because ultimately, the intelligent predator will over-reproduce?"

"High-level predators are usually only 2 percent of the population of animals in a given area. So, sure, a super high-level predator like man is likely to kill off his food supply, like the bacteria or mold that eats a slice of bread left out on a plate for a week. Once the bread's gone, no more mold."

"So, for bread read planet Earth."

"I'm just tossing it out there for thought. I mean, ultimately, do diets work?"

"Listen, if you're writing the *Decline and Fall of the Roman Empire*, it's been done before." Typical Abner.

"The Roman Empire? Small potatoes. I guess the question is: is human life different in any real sense from the bread mold? Are we compelled by our instincts, for example, to consume everything in sight and reproduce out of proportion to our food source? Usually reproduction is held in check by other predators. In our case, there don't appear to be any such checks. All top predators other than man are on the endangered species list."

"Back to the bread. Could bread mold, if it were intelligent, manage the bread any better?" Abner, considering the problem more seriously.

"Certainly, the bread would last longer if the bacteria were able to sustain a slower and even rate of growth."

"Dieting again."

"Smaller populations would last longer, but the example breaks down because the bread is not renewable, and the Earth is."

"Yes, the Earth is renewable. But there are still limits. Certainly, for the population that currently inhabits the Earth it may be continuable for a long time. But the prediction is that the Earth will double in human population in the next fifty years. And then how long will it take to double again?"

"So you're saying that, as the population increases, the size of the Earth becomes more and more finite."

"Absolutely, and less and less renewable. Of course, human inventiveness is astounding, and they'll be able to sweep refuse under the carpet . . ."

"And into the carpet."

"Exactly, with unbelievable creativity. This will appear to hide the basic fact that the Earth is a limited resource. Then they'll start putting people under the ocean, and there will be more and more levels, like a beehive. Honeycombs going further and further up and then further and further down. Kids, levels and levels underground, never get to see the sky, which is toxic anyway without the ozone to protect us."

"And the population will increase as resources appear to be great."

"Yes, that is my point. As the population expands to the very limits of all this renewability and creativity, does the planet's ability to sustain all this life come back, ultimately, to the bread mold?"

"So, some people see where this is leading. They smell something's rotten. Better get some off-planet backup."

"My point exactly. Dinosaurs evolved for almost every environmental niche. And if they produced the largest animals that ever walked on the planet, why isn't it possible that they produced animals with the largest brains, and then sent a sample off-planet?"

"And why did we never find any artifacts of this intelligent animal?"

"Artifacts? Who would ever find *our* artifacts? A hard disk is good for five or ten years, magnetic tape is good for twenty or thirty years, a CD-ROM they say will last fifty years, but we won't know if that's true for another twenty or thirty years. The best microfilm might be good for one or two hundred years, but again it will be years and years before we know that for sure."

"So, boom, after two hundred years all data disappears like Cinderella's dress at midnight."

"Magnetic tape from years ago is already deteriorating. Video tapes, tapes with scientific data from twenty years ago are already unreadable. The programs to read the data are gone with the tape. So even if you have a tape with good data, you still need tape with a good copy of the program, can't tell the players without a program. The issues multiply."

"So, in a thousand years?"

"Well, in a thousand years you might still find these shiny disks, with all the information on them gone, and without a device to play them, the disks would be useless anyway. They're just odd shiny disks. A clever species might speculate that they were information storage disks. But in a thousand years most of our culture will be gone. Most books will have deteriorated. Interestingly, I saw one company which intends to use acid-free paper to hold digital information for the ages because it's more reliable than the other media."

"So what happens in a million years?"

"A million years is a long time. I don't know about the deterioration characteristics of shiny disks. But I'll tell you this: I think oxygen will have oxidized the steel, and all our buildings will have crumbled. All culture has disappeared."

"And, say, in sixty-five million years."

"Well, that's a very long time. The Earth moves in that kind of time. San Francisco will have waved to Los Angeles on its way south. Things get buried, pressure makes everything unrecognizable."

"Maybe, but Leakey finds things on the surface near Lake Turkana."

"Five-million-year-old things."

"Yes, yes, yes. But they still find dinosaur remains on the surface. Aren't most such finds on the surface? And they're millions and millions of years old."

"Well, yes, but we're talking about fossilized remains. I doubt if CD-ROMs will fossilize. But the point is that they've never found any intelligent life on the surface from sixty-five million years ago, because usually, probably, intelligent life steers clear of the swamps."

"And no swamps, no riverbeds, no fossils, is that it?"

"You gotta have mineral transformation."

"Well."

"And let's not forget, if they had a huge population increase like humans did, all the remains are in the K-T boundary. But who knows what would remain from a highly civilized culture years and years hence?"

"I'm guessing a lot would be gone."

"A lot. After four or five thousand years the pyramids are still around, but you can see the signs of age setting in. They will be nothing but rubble in a million years. In sixty-five million years, everything but the odd bits and pieces is dust. But for that matter, who knows what dinosaur skeletons exist in the mantel, say a mile deep? Who can look for it?"

"It's just a matter of time. With ground radars and other imaging techniques, you wonder what will be able to hide from our scanners in the future? By the way, I liked the bit about how the predators keep the supply of their favorite food around. You should tip your hat to your father, he gives to Ducks Unlimited every year so that there will be plenty around to shoot. Your father, the happy hunter."

*   *   *

from the journal of Stephen Ambrose

Maybe the reason that the SETI people never acquired any nonnatural signal is because intelligence is such a short-lived phenomenon. Figure it out: Nonnatural signals, intelligent signals, are signals that are out of synch with nature. QED, intelligence is a short-lived thing, like the virus that kills its host.

Into Overtime

"Looks like the evidence is piling up for the dinosaur-bird connection." Amanda.

"Oh really." Stephen.

"Yeah, they found a bird in Madagascar that has a sickle-claw that resembles the one on Velociraptor and Deinonynchus."

"A bird? Flightless or not?"

"Looks like it could fly. Your dinosaur space creatures would have to come from prior common ancestors because in birds the front limbs become wings, your creatures have arms."

"Something like Velociraptor, huh? Though birds could have changed their wings back into arms and hands. Evolution is a remarkably random affair. Mammals develop on land and then go back in the water as dolphins and whales. What would a bird who had a more human body be like?" Stephen speculated.

"Might not sweat."

"Would it have our generalist tendencies? Bicuspids and molars? Would they eat meat *and* vegetation?"

Later, same conversation:

"Of course, at some point we cast out into space for more *Lebensraum*, as Hitler used to say." Stephen.

"Is it casting out into space, or is it escaping before we off the planet?" said Amanda.

"Off the planet. What would you call that? Lexical evolution, where prepositions become verbs."

"Isn't that what it is? Language evolution."

"Okay, I'll bite, how much land is necessary for life?"

"Depends on how you want to live. North Americans enjoy many times the land that each person gets in India," said Amanda.

"How will we know when we have reached the point where we have hit the limits?"

"We won't. That's the simple answer. We will linger on past the point of no return. It may be like many other problems, how will we know when we've killed the ozone layer? It varies from year to year."

"So, any idea when we'll reach the point of no return?"

"We may already have passed the point of no return." Stephen gave Amanda a funny look. "Okay. According to the study by Hubbert at Shell Oil, we've been into overtime on oil production in America since about 1972. We're taking more out than we are finding in replacement reserves." That was Amanda, up-to-date.

"So, we're already into extra innings. Great. So, you're saying that we won't notice a thing when we've reached the maximum population point. Only later. Great. Maybe I should make that the title of my story."

"What?"

"*Already into Extra Innings.* Well, if you're right, then the timing of my sci-fi story is right on. We'll need to get that sample of the species off the planet by end of the century."

"That may work for the American market, but you better find out what it is they go into if there's a tied score in what the rest of the world calls football, or what we call soccer."

"Sudden death?"

"A bit grim. Stay with baseball. What you want to express is that you're into overtime."

"Let me write that down. I'm sure to forget. What planets do you suppose we will be able to inhabit?"

"In our solar system? I suppose we might be able to make some use of the Moon and Mars and some of the other satellites in our solar system."

"Certainly some of them may have water on them, and they might be inhabitable to some degree. Europa has water, Triton has a nitrogen atmosphere," said Stephen.

"Even the Moon may have water. With the one-eighth gravity, it will make for a great retirement community. You can see the campaign. 'Arthritis got you down, move on up—to the moon where gravity is only one-sixth of Earth's.' And: 'Alice, to the moon.'"

"Very funny, Amanda. Well, there may be water on the moon, but I don't know if there is enough to support retirement communities. I think we're talking more in terms of base camps than new homes."

"What about Mars?" said Amanda.

"Well, they think there may be water under the surface, and they're talking about carbon dioxide machines to thicken the atmosphere, but I think we're still talking base camps for the foreseeable future," said Stephen.

"I see. So you see us as the enemy, like the aliens in *Independence Day*? Ignoring the existing population and taking over."

"Wait wait wait. You've gone from a hypothetical landing on what appear to be uninhabitable planets to an armed invasion."

"Yes, I guess I'm wondering if we really could observe a prime directive such as the one in Star Trek, not to assert ourselves over an existing population." Amanda.

"So that begs the questions, why a prime directive at all? If we are there, then perhaps we are there for a purpose, and that purpose may be to appropriate the resources of that planet for ourselves. The divine right of predators."

"Your father would probably say: the natural right of predators. Hell, why not use the population for sport like in the Arnold Schwarzenegger movie, *Predator*? As we have used the lesser-developed species on our planet for sport. That movie had its root in human behavior toward lesser species. Because, after all, a lesser-developed species is a lesser-developed species, whether it is a tiger or lemur or chimp on our planet or the lower orders of life on a planet in a star system light years away, right?"

"As a practical matter, it doesn't have much meaning at the moment."

"Au contraire," Amanda, the professional scientist was ready to weigh in: "We already have problems caused by alien species—Zebra mussels in the Great Lakes creating havoc in harbors and power plants. Argentine ants "erasing" insect populations in Hawaii, and if they kill off the pollinators, then poof: the spectacular and unique flower arrays disappear. The list goes on and on."

"Okay, okay. I'm getting it."

"No, you haven't. Of all the alien species, the one that has done the most damage to local environments is Homo sapiens leaving Africa. Homo gets to Australia, all the large marsupials disappear. They cross over to the New World—bam, 70 percent or more of all the large mammals gone. Meanwhile, in Europe and Asia, species were regularly disappearing. Nearly all the pachyderms—mastodon, mammoth, most elephants. And the damage keeps right on ticking—clear-cutting will destroy the rain forests pretty soon. And all this—without the benefit of extraterrestrial aliens. How could we ever be expected to honor a prime directive? Get serious. That's Hollywood stuff."

"I guess the rebuttal is that we're making progress. We're not hunting fowl or buffaloes to extinction, anyway."

"Nah, I don't buy it. The way they fish the oceans, dragging nets along the bottom. No way. Forget it," said Amanda.

Beauty and Symmetry

Tōparr found Eladia at one the of the ship's portals looking at the passing parade of white dots against the black backdrop.

"Looks like the black of a stage, before some drama unfolds," she said.

"It does."

"Have you ever wondered how the laws of nature can be reduced to neat mathematical formulas?" She looked at his forehead, which seemed a little different, the folds in the skin seemed a little less prominent. Must be related to coming out of stasis.

"Yes."

"Newton's law of universal gravitation. The Fibonacci numbers. It's almost too good to be true. Things like the simplicity and elegance of the DNA molecule? The whole idea of the cell."

"Sure, yes."

Surprised, she asked, "You recognize these names, Newton, Fibonacci?"

"Yes, I have been reading your literature."

"Well, as you know, no matter how small we go, we can parse particles but we cannot find God. We do not find the ultimate truth. Heisenberg gave us the tip-off. The smaller you get, the more you have trouble measuring your target."

"Indeed."

"And Einstein tried to put it altogether with a unified field theory."

"So have we."

"Any luck?"

"Some, but let me make a couple of observations. First, the mathematical formulations involved in physical laws suggests an intelligence on the other side."

"The other side of what?"

"The other side of the equation. I'm sorry. Allow me to be obscure because: I don't really know what I am talking about. I only suggest that if we can discover a law, the question arises: where did the law come from? And why can it be reduced to a mathematical formula? And the other observation is this: even if we can reduce the four forces (electromagnetic force, gravity, and the strong and weak nuclear forces) to a neat mathematical formula . . ." he said looking out the portal, "It will all still be here. After all, when your Einstein developed a formula for converting mass to energy, a bomb was developed for the uncontrolled explosive release of energy and so were nuclear reactors for a controlled release of energy. And it all is still there," he said, looking toward the absence of light.

"So is there any spiritual life among the Throdēop?"

"Not to devolve into a discussion of semantics, that depends on what you mean."

"Well, that is a good question. What do I mean? Good deeds, perhaps. Enlightenment, perhaps. Beauty."

"Well, science, as you call it, is all rapped up in the issue of enlightenment, isn't it?"

*   *   *

from the journal of Stephen Ambrose

Newton said, "Nature is pleased with simplicity." Einstein favored that quote, and the most famous equation of the twentieth century was his $E = mc^2$. Simplicity itself. It tells you a great deal in the shortest possible way. In the language of mathematics, it was sheer poetry.

Genetics is also simplicity. It's just four bases, that's all it is—adenine, guanine, cytosine, and thymine. Admittedly, the sequences are mindlessly long and exasperatingly complex in their interactions. But Alexander Pope could write heroic couplets until the cows came home, all you do is rhyme two lines at the end. And complexity, it seems, is just extended sequences of relatively simple components.

That's how you know they haven't figured things out yet—when the name they're using is The Standard Model. The name itself was a tip-off. You see: it's the best we can do. It's consensus thinking: The Standard Muddle, The Standard Standard. A theory only John D. Rockefeller could love. String theory had more beautiful mathematics, and extra dimensions, maybe eleven of them, but it couldn't predict anything.

No, the Rule Maker, the Game Maker, if such an intelligence among intelligences actually exists, favored simplicity. Otherwise, how could we reduce the seemingly haphazard events of the natural world to mathematical equations? But he has a tortured soul, he likes jigsaw puzzles of blue sky. Puzzles of points of light against a black night. He likes black better than yuppies and their black bimmers. Better than tango dancers like black garb.

But uncovering this simplicity is a daunting challenge. That is the genius of Newton. Feynman said, for example, the problem of superconductivity wasn't more experiments. He thought there were experiments enough; it was a new look at an old problem that was needed. The same goes for bringing together the four forces. Maybe extra dimensions are required, but only if beautiful, elegant mathematics led you there; that's what Dirac thought. Crick and Watson, looking at one of their early crude, ugly metal-shop models of DNA structure, knew they on the wrong track; it didn't look simple and elegant.

Though Stephen Wolfram might suggest maybe the Rule Maker liked both simplicity and complexity, because his simple program rules for cellular automata didn't always produce predictable results. Where Newton might be able to predict a planet's orbit a million years out, sometimes the only way to find out what Wolfram's a-million-step program would produce, is to do all million steps. The shortcuts don't work. What he called computational irreducibility.

And so where are we then?

Sex and Brains: A Mind-Expanding Combination

Ramón and Eladia were by equal turns intrigued and anxious: they could actually see the head of the Throdēop become slowly but noticeably larger.

Ramón asked, "Without meaning any offense, but Eladia and I have noticed that your head is becoming, well, slightly larger."

"Ah, is it?"

"We think so."

"Well, it is a phenomenon among our species that as a problem becomes more intriguing, our brains grow to solve them. Actually, our color changes a little, too. Have you noticed that?"

Ramón said, "Well, now that you mention it, you have become a little more reddish at the neck and more bluish above."

"There you are. Thinking is kind of a sexy thing for us."

Eladia said, "You mean this color thing developed as a sexual adaptation?"

"That and the larger head. Big heads are sexy. But when you say 'sexual adaptation,' you denude it of any innuendo. Innuendo being such a marvelous thing. The word 'head,' for example, has a very sexual meaning for us."

"No kidding."

"Why did you say that? Why are you laughing?"

"Oh, no reason. Please continue."

"In our distant distant past, the intricate singing of the songbirds was the thing which drew females to the males."

"Yes."

"And to do this singing, the brains of the males increased to do the songs."

"Really?"

"Well, it is what we have theorized."

"And this is still the case?" Ramón.

"Over time, the females also developed this brain-expanding capacity, too, presumably as a push-pull type of thing. Females needing more capacity to tease even greater displays from the males. But eventually, how can I say this in your language, to go back to our songbird ancestors, our songs came to be more duets than just serenades."

"So, how did this brain-expanding thing expand into things other than the mating?" Eladia.

"First, I am not sure it ever did. Let me explain, from our point of view, the solution of nearly all problems is a sexual display. Certainly, our desire to figure out the physical laws all comes from this. For us, almost everything is sexual. Though we, too, have had our share of Newton's. I mean—great naturalists who did not appear to engage in sex."

"So, this brain enlargement is still a sexual thing?" Ramón.

"Oh yes, females are attracted by the males with intriguing coloring and large brains who can present the most elegant solutions."

"And if there were no problems to solve?"

"Brains seem to contract to a more minimal state. Presumably because it is impossible to keep a brain at that high, excited level all the time. Witness your Sherlock Holmes, witness the deterioration of the successful of your species. Brains oftentimes take drugs when there's nothing for a brain to sink its teeth into."

"So to speak."

"So to speak. You humans have the same problem even though your brains do not expand as ours do."

"We developed this hard case to protect the brain from damage."

"Yes, it is true we have this soft shell. And we probably suffer brain injuries more frequently than you do, with more memory loss, but then . . ."

"You can grow new cells."

"That, plus there is no loss of cultural information because it is still there in our societies, our computers, and it can be reacquired much more quickly than you humans would be able to do. Our society is forgiving of such memory losses, but we often figure out what we lost."

"So, your brains had shrunk through inactivity, and this explains your rather unresponsive behavior at first."

"I'm afraid so. That and coming out of stasis."

"I suppose human brains also somehow rise to the occasion when confronted with a problem."

"In a less dramatic way."

"Right."

*   *   *

"Expanding brains? Get real." Nick.

"Everything I learn, I learn from canaries."

"How's that?"

"There was an article in *Discover* magazine about ten years ago about a zoologist named Nottebohm who came from Argentina."

"I suppose he dances the tango, too?"

"Bet he knows the music. Anyway, he was a naturalist who fell in love with Darwin, and went to Berkeley, where he studied with an expert in vocal communication."

"This is going to lead somewhere, I hope."

"That's it, even in conversation we want McDonald's. There's no leading up to the point. No, let's open the wine and let it breathe. No, let's smell the food as it's being prepared."

"Okay, I'm ready to appreciate the bouquet of your conversation."

"That's more like it. So, anyway, Nottebohm followed up on the work of a fellow named Thorpe, who showed that a young male songbird, some kind of a finch . . . didn't Darwin work with finches? Anyway, the male finch had to learn a song just before he reached sexual readiness. He learns his song from mature birds. If mature males were not around, his song was less appealing, less intricate. Would you call that culture?"

"Something learned from another, older member of a group. I don't know. In some sense I guess you would have to."

"Well, anyway, Nottebohm began to work with canaries. He correlated the song with the bird's brain. First thing he finds out is that these males are left-brained. If he cuts the right brain, the bird continues to sing quite normally. If, however, you cut the left brain, the bird no longer sings a normal song. From here, they looked closer. Everyone assumed male and female brains were the same, more or less. Not so. The male had a vocal center in the brain four times larger than the female."

"That makes sense. If the male songbird attracts the female with his song, it follows that he's going to need more brain matter to operate the vocal chords in the intricate way necessary for the songs, probably it will need more storage for the songs."

"Exactly. But here's the really neat thing. The researchers found that brains of male song-control areas changed dramatically seasonally. Brains grew quickly in the spring, and shrank at the end of summer."

"Sort of like a dick."

"Not sort of. They found that male brain size was affected by testosterone. And testosterone was affected by the amount of daylight. The proof that it was testosterone that made the difference was that when they injected females with testosterone, their voice-control areas doubled and they could suddenly make a more intricate, male type of song."

"I think it's pretty well-known that it is testosterone that controls sexual aggressiveness in both males and females."

"Well, from here Nottebohm found that brains of birds actually grow new cells, which humans don't seem to do as readily. They think this is something that comes from reptiles. Crocodiles produce new brain cells."

"So, you figure if reptiles grow new brain cells, and birds grow new brain cells, then the intermediate step, dinosaurs, could also grow brain cells."

"It's a logical conclusion."

"Yes, but how about brains increasing to solve problems?"

"Well, I figured that the same way that dolphins are sometimes willing to perform some tricks even without the food motivation, and as the brains of females increased, these dinosaurs with the enhanced brain matter would find other things to bear down on other mating rituals."

"I wonder about that."

"Well, muscles increase in size with exercise."

"And steroids."

"Which are hormones again."

"I suppose, in the case of humans, we would increase the braincase through genetics."

"Well, there are problems and problems to be solved with that. If the braincase is increased, then I don't know if even a C-section would get the baby out of the mother. But I presume that some kind of machine, some kind of birthing apparatus, will be set up so that women will not be required for natal development."

"Maybe something could be developed for humans along the lines of what you have worked out for these evolved dinosaurs. A somewhat soft braincase, which would allow for brain size to increase."

"And I guess researchers could find the on/off switch for neural development. So that brain size would not necessarily have to be fixed."

"Exactly."

"You know, I write this stuff, but you're making me kind of woozy."

"What's the matter? Don't you like skating out along the rim of the cerebral cortex?"

"Aren't there any limitations? Is gravity a limitation? Or are all these things just so many hurdles?"

"Annoying, isn't it?"

"We feel we are so clever as a species that we will figure out the key to the universe and be able to reset it at will."

"Sort of like an artist. This Big Bang didn't turn out so well. Let's do another, maybe it will be better. Stretch a new canvas. Start out again."

"Well, yes. And the more I feel that these things are possible, the more I think we are on our last legs. The same way whenever you reach the end of the stock market cycle, they say things like 'this time it's different.' And they come up with all kinds of reasons stocks will keep going up. Increased productivity will keep wages in line, and so on. There's always some reason. And then the whole house of cards collapses."

"Yes, I know. This time they've licked the business cycle. The Fed will micromanage the money supply, and lower interest rates just in the nick of time."

"But such management is sort of bound to fail. The cycle will come in like the tides and swamp the logicians. During the 1970s, Carter's administration, they couldn't manage it. Interest rates, wage rates went sky-high. It wasn't the money supply anymore, it was the velocity of money, or some damn thing. These formulas look good in retrospect, but are not necessarily great forward-looking vehicles. Times are good, and you think the Fed's doing the right thing. Times are bad and everyone's fucking up."

"Right. In the 1980s, during Reagan, the government cuts taxes and spends like no tomorrow, yet there's no inflation. During Carter there was nothing like that kind of deficit spending, yet inflation went through the roof. Of course, the oil price increase contributed greatly. And there are explanations for everything."

"But that's my point. It's only after the fact that we understand these things. It's just waves. In the thirties, margin was 90 percent, and they attribute the stock market crash to speculation, but now margin is 50 percent, so people borrow against their houses and get it right back up to 90 or 100 or 115 percent. You can't legislate against human stupidity. It's just waves. Eras of high speculation, eras of low speculation. Learn to be a surfer."

*   *   *

from the journal of Stephen Ambrose

Think it out, Stephen. Muscles increase with exercise, with steroids. Steroids are hormones. Bird brains increase with testosterone, i.e. hormones. Maybe human brains will also be found to increase with steroids, hormones. Maybe thought-lifting increases the hormones that trigger cell growth. Maybe that 15 percent larger inferior parietal lobe of Einstein's was the result of lifting heavy spatial/mathematical thoughts.

Getting Nervous

"I don't know about you, but I'm quite nervous," said Eladia.

"Absolutely, the more intelligent the Throdēop becomes, the more nervous I become."

"You're not alone. It's not clear at all what we are up against."

"Their computer was programmed to be quite shrewd. It learned our language without revealing their language. Same with the Throdēop himself."

"Insidious."

"Yes, I like your word choice."

"What will we do?"

"Try to find out what spices upset their digestion."

"You mean: you think we're a meal."

"At a minimum. Did you catch that perfect reference to Sherlock Holmes? Once they power up, they're terrific readers . . . information absorbers. I wonder if they can hear your thoughts."

"And the stuff about inhabiting planets without intelligent life?"

"Maybe that was their original intention. Maybe they're going through a midcourse correction, or maybe that is just their line for visitors. Deception being one of the signatures of intelligence."

"And they're from home, Earth."

"Dinosaurs of some description. Obviously quite evolved. No flesh-ripping big toe."

"And their teeth?"

"Well, I think they're generalists, too. You can see the front carnivorous teeth, I haven't seen them eat yet, so I cannot surmise about molars."

"How is it we have both molars and canines?"

"Interesting, isn't it? We have the long intestinal tract, indicating a preference for the vegetarian diet. The big cats, the predators, have a small intestinal tract."

"But the anthropologists say no meat, no big brains. They say it's the high calorie diet that supported the large brain development.

"Certainly, they must have reached a point where their diet evolved."

"Maybe. But maybe they're keeping us alive until we bore them."

"Maybe we should try to bore them, so they will relax and maybe their brains will shrink."

"Yes, it's taken days and weeks for them to get up to speed."

"How do you suppose you could get them to relax?"

"Ask them dull questions."

But the Tōparr was having none of it, "We know about your development. From the test samples we can see that 90 percent of our genes are in common. We think you developed from a small, furry creature that existed at the time of our emigration. A mammal, as you call it."

*   *   *

By now there were a number of Throdēop awake and going through this brain-expansion phenomenon. Very disconcerting for the fixed-brained humans.

What was it like to have a lot of brains and then lose them? Well, they just forgot a lot. In their reduced state they would say, "Oh, there's a word for that." And reliance on the computer also reduced the need for brain expansion. They would just ask the computer for the word, and the computer would come on like a Rothschild butler, who in nineteenth century England would say, "What kind of tea do you want? Indian, Ceylon, or Darjeeling." And then, "Milk, cream, or lemon, sir." And if milk, "Hereford, Jersey, or Shorthorn, sir?"

A talking computer was the perfect thesaurus.

*   *   *

Ramón asked the Throdēop what he knew of the era he had come from.

The Throdēop said, "We came out of an era of dramatic change. It was only a matter of a few hundred thousand years from the point our species had developed to the point where the growth of our culture had developed language, mathematics, and curiosity about our surroundings, which you humans variously call the natural world and science."

"And what transpired to bring you out into space?"

"Well, as I said, it was an era of dramatic change. The growth of our numbers was rather spectacular. We had hunted down many species. We tinkered more with the environment than probably we should have. But how do you know when you've gone too far? The Earth is a big place. I think our basic premise was that we were too small to have that large an effect on such a big thing as the Earth. And maybe we were wrong."

"Ah. And your mission?"

"Well, we were sent out as an exploration mission, but I think in the back of everyone's mind we were an off-planet reservoir of genetic material."

"Yes, I think we were, too."

Ramón wanted to know what the Throdēop knew of the asteroid impact. He had been dying to ask but he didn't rush it.

"I see. And have you kept in touch?"

"We did for a while. Then there was silence. Since your species has so greatly developed, we can only conclude ours has perished."

"Correct. But how long did you stay in contact with your home base?"

"Not that long really; less than a thousand years."

"What happened?"

"We don't know for sure, there simply were no more communications. Can you enlighten us?"

"I don't know if I can enlighten you altogether. Remember our species started to develop millions of years after you left. What I can tell you is what our theories are."

"Tell me."

"Well, the main theory is that an asteroid several kilometers in size struck the planet, and this triggered a massive conflagration and upset the Earth's crust, causing volcanoes, earthquakes, and contrecoup—devastation exactly on the other side of the planet. Although there is also evidence of huge eruptions prior to this event, the Deccan traps in India. There are other ideas as well. Disease—viruses, bacteria killed off large populations. But the long-erupting volcanoes followed by a huge asteroid impact is the main one. They sent up a cloud of dust which blocked out the sun for a couple of years, and this killed most plant and animal life forms that were left."

"Yes, there had been volcanos before we left. It was part of the reason for our departure. How do you know it was an asteroid?" said the Throdēop.

"Well they found large amounts of iridium, cobalt, and other minerals found on asteroids."

Tōparr said, "We know that Throdēop were developing very, very large nuclear devices as a protective measure after we left. It was large enough to break up even an asteroid of the size you are describing."

"In your terms, I believe it was a one-hundred-billion-megaton device."

"Really?"

"It's just a matter of scale." Realizing the glibness of his answer, he qualified it by saying, "If you have the technical expertise."

"Well, yes, but how did you get such a large device out into space?"

"Again, a matter of scale." He paused and said, "We have always wondered about the break in intelligence from our planet."

"Yes?"

"Well, some of our people were quite volatile, and we have wondered whether it was an asteroid, or whether the device itself got used on the planet, in violence."

"And you're saying that the site of such an explosion might also appear as an asteroid crater."

"You humans are so optimistic. That is the thing we have noticed about you. An asteroid. The beauty of the asteroid theory is that it proposes that the damage was done by an external force."

"And you don't believe that. What about the iridium?"

"Sure, external forces can be very great, we understand them very well. But we also understand *our* limitations. And my colleagues agree with you. The iridium does not suggest a nuclear explosive, but if you have a map of asteroids orbits, how hard would it be to change a trajectory a little? Anyway, why do you think we are in a state of sleep so much of the time?"

"Why?"

"Because we know about the problems of a confined craft like this. And we checked files on your computer. You yourselves have conducted many studies with rats. For example, if you put too many rats in a cage, they become irritable and aggressive. Even on Earth we had such population problems. Our population simply grew too fast."

"Indeed."

"If we are asleep, then we can do ourselves little harm. We have been in stasis for millions of years at a time."

"But you know what you are saying? You are saying that consciousness is a problem that you only seem to be able to solve through unconsciousness."

"Not exactly. I think we are saying that too much consciousness in too confined a space is a problem. And you humans haven't had such problems?"

"Well, yes, we have those problems, too. We have solved them in a variety of ways. Sometimes we allow one family to stay awake and have free run of the place for a week, or a month, or a year if they like. Other times, a few families are allowed to be awake.

"And you haven't had factions that were unruly and difficult to manage? There hasn't been any feuding? Like the Hatfields and McCoys, Montagues and Capulets of your literature."

"Yes, those are famous feuding families from literature. What is your point?"

"And this hasn't occurred on your ship? Feuding factions?" asked the Throdēop.

"Actually, yes. The two principal arguing groups are those who wish to have more children and those who would prefer to leave things as they are. Replacement births only."

"Ah, there, you see."

"And your people?"

"The same exact problem. Those who wish to have more offspring, and those who want replacement lives only."

"Rather surprising, don't you think?"

"Why do you think so? If the purpose of life, or the goal of life, is more life, then I think this would be the most natural thing in the universe."

"In that light . . ."

"And why should we be any different? The goal of life, the purpose of life, will always be extension of that life. By definition."

"Of course."

The Problem of Writing . . .

When he discussed science fiction with his brother, it was always the same.

"Science fiction? That's not the problem. The problem is writing anything at all."

"You're going to talk about the money thing again."

"Yes, of course, I am. Why knock yourself out for a year or two or three . . ."

"Or four or five . . ."

"Or six or seven years, over some novel that no one will want to read anyway."

"Upbeat as always."

"Hey, someone has to see things as they really are. And there's already a Stephen Ambrose in the stacks."

"Yeah, I know. I like his biography of Eisenhower. But he's not in the science fiction section. There won't be any confusion."

"You're a hopeless romantic."

"But it might be my retirement."

"You're not a hopeless romantic, you're delusional. Forget writing. Think IRA. Salt some of your computer programming earnings into a tax-free account. Think annuity. Think whole life—preferably with a mutual company. A stock company has to pay shareholders. Not that a mutual is perfect. Any organization where the managers ultimately become the owners without really having anyone look over their shoulders has got to be suspect."

"What about stocks?"

"Stocks, of course, better yields over time. Mutual funds, spread of risk. It's a simple thing. Just go to the library and see which ones have done the best. Check out *Morningstar* and *Value Line*."

"Anyway, I know that some science fiction interests you."

"It's the future imperfect that interests me."

"Sounds like a mythical tense, doesn't it? Past imperfect, future imperfect."

"Right. Who would have thought three or four hundred years ago that a radical concept like democracy would become such a popular phenomenon."

"And your favorite future imperfects?" asked Stephen.

"*Blade Runner*, of course. The dark rainy seedy texture was great. A man falls in love with an android full of self-doubt and strong feelings. That's my kind of android."

In an age when buying a book is as good as reading it, to be well-read in the year 1998 meant you knew your video. Books were relegated to door stops, window props, indeed, bookshelf props, and the one percent of the population with expanding circuitry, if not brains. His brother Abner was a well-viewed person. He knew his flicks.

"How about *2001*?"

"Great visuals."

"But what the hell was the story? I like *2010* more. Probably because it had a somewhat more understandable story line." Stephen.

"*Forbidden Planet* was quite advanced. Where did we see that first? Was it on *Saturday Night at the Movies*?"

"I remember. Black and white."

"Good story."

"Well, that's Shakespeare."

"And the Crell. Weren't they great? And the IQ machine. Very moody, and Walter Pidgeon almost does it all on his own. Of course today all the instrumentation looks tacky and oversized." Abner.

"Isn't that always the problem with science fiction?"

"What do you suppose instrumentation will look like in one hundred years, or two hundred years, or one thousand years?"

"Good question."

"Doesn't one hundred years seem like a long time from here? A hundred years ago, the automobile made its appearance. A hundred years later we still have the automobile. Still powered by burning gasoline."

"Television or video or whatever you end up calling it will all be flat screen by then."

"Unless we move into 3-D."

"And what about cyberspace? Here's the future: I lost my child to a video game. When he put on the headset he was a fine, cheerful kid. I came back a couple of hours later, he was a burned-out gamehead, no longer able to talk," said Stephen. "Maybe in a hundred years we'll all be wearing space suits, environmental suits. Ozone depletion will make us all vulnerable, or the South Atlantic magnetic anomaly or some other damn thing. Some chemical thing. Some of the satellites use nuclear power. On reentry they are subject to burning up in the atmosphere, spreading their bounty of radiation all over the planet. They say traces of the plutonium turn up everywhere. You may have an atom somewhere in your body. I can see the advertising line now: *Environmental suits, first developed for space, now can be used in your daily life . . .*"

"Always the dark side. Does intelligence always turn out badly?" Abner.

"Might not. Might be that we are just at the beginning. Somewhere I saw that it was thought that a really intelligent civilization could control the energy of a star. And a really, really advanced civilization could harness the energy of a galaxy. And if a galaxy is a collection of stars, and the universe is a collection of galaxies, then a really, really, really advanced civilization could direct the energy of a universe."

"A universe? Isn't that *the* universe?"

"Well, let's say out in deep, deep space beyond the end of our universe, there is another collection of galaxies, another universe, or universes so far away that the light hasn't gotten here yet. It's just a matter of adding zeros. Maybe it is so far away that before light gets here, we suffer the Big Rip. Dark energy tears our universe apart. Or maybe there are universes in other dimensions. That's what the physicists seem to want to tell us."

Abner: "What is it you always say: I think you've gone beyond the beyond."

"Hey, you brought it on. What I think is that we should stick to our own knitting. It's not clear that this planet has gotten safely past the dangers of its own industrial revolution."

A Treatise on Boobs

First off, no one writes treatises anymore. We can barely get out an essay. Sound bites are all anyone has attention for. One sentence, two sentences, maybe a paragraph. The whole planet suffers from attention deficit disorder. Did it follow from the advent of televison, and channel changing at commercial time? Well, this isn't a treatise anyway, it's a just a conversation:

Nick was lounging with Miranda after one of their sexsational fucks, and he was noticing the wonderful full and pendulous melons that draped off her chest.

"Really, you have wonderful bosoms."

"You like my boobs, do you?"

"Why would you use a word like that? Boobs. You're no boob-brained bimbo. Worse yet is when a girl talks about her boobies. Boobs is okay. But boobies, or titties. I hate that."

"I don't like titties, either. But boobs, you know, kind of describes them. They're kind of silly. The function they serve does not necessarily require a large shape to be effective. Even an A-cup will generate enough milk for a child."

"That's what they say."

"They kind of get in the way. Mine are so large that it makes running impossible. A bra that will hold them up is uncomfortable."

"Okay. But I think a word like boobies desexifies them."

"Probably intentional with a lot of women."

"What about breast?"

"No word for bosom should end in a 't,' I'm sorry. A bosom is not a bone, not a hard thing."

"So, that's the way you feel."

149

"Do you really think that a boob," and she cupped her hand underneath the right one, "should have a 't' in it?" Then she took the nipple, squeezing and extending it out.

"Now that. What you're doing now should have a 't' in it."

"'T' as in bite."

"Good, yes."

"Suck is better. The 'k' works."

"How about jugs? Do you like the sound of that?"

"'Jugs' is okay. If it works for you, it works for me."

"Melons?"

"I like melons. Full, luscious, delicious."

"You know what Desmond Morris says."

"Who's he?"

"Anthropologist, biologist, zoologist, whatever. He says that breasts were formed to appear as a front rear end. That when we started standing up, women needed a seductive front to attract the men."

"I wonder if it's true."

"You know that occasionally I like a tit-fuck."

"You like it all."

"Think about it, chimps don't have breasts of any size except when they're nursing. They do all their attraction stuff via their engorged and colorful pudenda."

"Uh huh."

"Let me ask, if you didn't use boob, what word would you use?"

"Bosom, probably."

Freedom is the Freedom to Run Amuck

from the journal of Stephen Ambrose

Eugene O'Neill kept a kind of work diary, which could be useful. You can imagine O'Neill's dilemma: Writers don't have to get up in the morning. They don't have to report to a boss. They have nearly complete freedom, and the consequent ruin which accompanies such freedom.[3] He needed to make a record of work accomplished. One has to establish a routine. Graham Greene counted out his five hundred words every day. Five hundred words and then he was free to go out and have his cocktail. He made no secret of either habit. It shows up in his novel, *The End of the Affair*. Same with Hemingway, write in the morning, drink in the afternoon and evening. He says it in one of his novels, *Islands in the Stream*. Joyce also observed the morning writing habit.

I love Joyce's biographer, Ellman, for the sequence he writes about Joyce and Hemingway. They are out on the boulevards at a cafe. Joyce picks a fight, but he's blinder than a one-eyed pirate, he's really pretty blind. And he picks this fight and then says, "Deal with him, Hemingway." A man who subcontracts out his fights. This is a man I can relate to.

It is little wonder why so many books come out of prison, they have structure. Hitler and Dostoyevsky, both wrote books in prison, but they are the tip of iceberg.

---

[3]   Editor's Note: The writer almost got it. In a democracy, freedom is the freedom to vote away your democracy. Hence the Germans in 1933. Hence oxymorons like The Patriot Act. And in the end, who cares what writers do with their time?

I must stick to some kind of schedule. A page a day, five hundred words, a block of time, an hour, something. Discipline turns out to be important, after all.

Money and Sex

"It seems to me you've always lusted after money."

"Nah, I don't have the energy. Gates has the energy for real money lust. Me, I'm a schlepper. I don't have that kind of greed down deep in my soul. I just fantasize about that kind of greed and lust. I don't have drop-out-of-Harvard greed like Gates." Abner.

"What good is money if you don't spend it? Gates is building his dream house. He's flying all over the planet. He's master of the best game on the planet—How Much Do You Have? He bought the da Vinci notebooks. It looks like he's having a great time. His buddy Buffett bought a corporate jet. That made it okay. I wonder if Gates finally broke down and bought one."

"And in the end, he plays a rubber or two or three with Buffett. Which anyone can do."

"Anyone can play bridge with Buffett?"

"Anyone can play bridge. And theoretically, I think Buffett plays bridge somewhere on the Internet. So maybe it's possible to play with him. Though I would be surprised if the Website didn't qualify the level of your skill."

"Years ago only the Rolls Royce had a telephone in a car, now everybody's got a portable phone. Everyone today travels faster than anyone two hundred years ago. Although two hundred years ago no one traveled any faster than anyone two hundred years previous to that. So, in a sense, technology has made us all wealthy. You read about Balzac in his diligence, a horse and carriage bus thing, going all over Europe. But to see his love Madame Hanska (married, of course) and to rub shoulders with Metternich he went to the expense of hiring a carriage to race to Vienna. It was an enormous expense, and the ride had to be a thousand times worse than even a bus trip today. And all this to have Metternich, the prick, not own up to having read Balzac when everyone was reading him."

"You kind of wonder if the carriage owner got paid."

"That far? Probably. Probably a cash up-front deal, I should think, though Balzac was a good talker."

Nick and Stephen were at Gibson's again, having come across the street from Jilley's. They saw a girl who certainly appeared to be a hooker. And Nick volunteered the following from his extensive reading on the subject:

"In Alex Adams's autobiography, *Madame 90210*, the biggest user of her services spilled a million point four a year. The next biggest spenders were a couple of Hollywood studio people, at 250 grand per year, or at $350 per hour or per fuck, that would work out to roughly . . . let's think, 700 fucks per year, or what's that, about 2 per day. By contrast, Money Bags, the biggest user, had 4,000 fucks per year to work with. Simple arithmetic puts that at more than 10 fucks per day. Very little jizz left at the end of the day."

"I would say so."

"But he usually spent more than $350, more like a $1000 per session. So, going back, recalculating, that would be 1,400 fucks per year, or 3 per day. More doable, but still not a lot of jizz left at the end of the day. So, to make things more reasonable, he would spend outrageous sums from time to time, ten thou for a hand job.

"He would audition hookers all day long. Madams brought over the best of their 'creatures' as Madame Alexi so aptly calls them. If the madams bragged that the tits were real, Money Bags would counter that he liked silicone, and often would treat a girl to surgery if he fancied her. He would make promises to put them in movies."

"Did he ever make any movies? Did you ever see those Andy Warhol things?"

"With Joe Dallesandro? Who could forget?"

"Queer bait for some flounder." A quote from Rocky and Bullwinkle, proving only that you cannot ever overcome your childhood.

"Whatever. Yeah, I think he produced a couple of movies. But here's my point. As much money as this big spender blew on hookers, it was still not his last dollar, or the end of an inheritance. His income was on the order of ten mil per annum. So, a mil-four works out to only 14 percent per of his annual income. Evidently, he was gifted in real estate."

"Right. Wasn't it Milton Friedman who said that people may be crazy, but money makes them sane?"

"Think about it. A divorce in California, with community property laws, we're talking millions and millions. He could actually be viewed as thrifty. His big mistake was falling for the worst possible chick, daughter of a mafia type from New Orleans. He paid her $2,000 per fuck, and bought off Alex to prevent her going elsewhere. No problem, she found other madams. They took Money Bags's cash and sent her out for the double-square payoff. So, keeping her in line was impossible. He got even by sending her a 1099 for half a mil, and the IRS descended on her. Unfortunately, he also spent enormous sums on coke. Enough that his father looked up Alex and offered her half a mil to get him off the stuff or into Betty Ford."

"Oh well. People get bored."

And Stephen was getting bored with Nick. Another trip to Buenos Aires to study tango would be the thing to clear his mind.

*   *   *

Nick had facial symmetry and great male hallmarks. And like those with facial symmetry, he had an early sexual initiation. So, it was clear from the beginning that he would be a busy bee, so he never saw the reason to marry. One girl, a certain Sylvia, had his attention for a year when he was twenty-three, but she was a sensitive Cancer and never pushed marriage. As luck would have it, he did not need to marry to get out of the parent's house or to keep a girl. Eventually, he got restless. He never got rid of Sylvia, he just moved on.

But the experience with Sylvia cured him of wanting to live with a girl. He felt bad about the parting with her, because she was so sweet. He wanted to free himself of the bad feeling, so he resolved to live alone and to have sex at the girl's apartment whenever possible. He could leave that night, or worst case, in the morning. No muss, no fuss. And, he felt the girls had had their fun. Girls have more intense orgasms with symmetrical men. He kept up on all the latest research. Symmetrical men were healthier; therefore, women wanted more to mate with them, because of a probably inborn notion, not in their conscious decision-making, that they will have healthy children. So it's a natural thing. The intense orgasm makes the cervix tent and dip into the sperm pool and improve the odds of conception.

*   *   *

"Well, I like your Throdēop." Nick. In the tennis lounge again, flat cushions. Balls being whacked every four beats.

"Why's that?"

"I've never liked close competitions. I liked Secretariat lengths and lengths ahead of everyone else. I liked Bart Starr taking the Green Bay Packers down the field, throwing deep. I liked the Chicago Bears beating the Patriots 46 to 10. I like Michael Jordan taking the Chicago Bulls to championship after championship. Winning games by 20 points. I like the Yankees in the 1950s winning pennant after pennant after pennant . . . Stengel, Mantle, Maris."

"And you don't think the humans have a chance?"

"Not against the Throdēop and their expanding brains. I mean: by rights. I don't know what you'll do with them."

"Maybe they wouldn't have such an advantage against chip-enhanced humans with their add-on computational abilities."

"Sounds like a cheat to me."

"I think it is a cheat, but . . ."

"But we'll all be using them, it's just a matter of time. That's what you think."

"It's not a matter of time. We already use enhancers. You wear glasses. That is a cheat, is it not? How many hours do you spend in front of your screen? It's just a matter of making it more convenient. First, there will be those tiny eyeglasses screens. They're already in commercials. The computer will speak to you through the earpiece. Eventually, they'll stick some kind of sensor right in your brain."

Whose Mission Are We On?

"That's an interesting thought about cross-pollination," said Nick after tennis, a week later, conversation being an ongoing process. The brain keeps tabs on conversations, time intervals are irrelevant.

"Why's that?"

"Oh, because I'm not religious, and I don't really think we're on God's mission. But you have to wonder, as smart as we think we are, if we're not doing someone else's business."

"You mean: individually, or you mean humanity as a whole?"

"Actually, I think I mean both."

"As an individual, you think you are doing someone else's bidding?"

"Well, most of the time we know we are doing someone else's bidding. Our employer's. Our wife's. Whatever. But I think there are times, perhaps even frequently, that we are doing someone else's bidding and don't know it."

"What do you mean?"

"Well, I don't know if I can describe it. It's sort of like the poor schlepper who introduces his girlfriend to some friend or acquaintance of his. The girlfriend and the friend become lovers . . ."

"And the schlepper's left out in the cold. At least until the next guy performs a similar favor," giving Stephen something he felt comfortable with.

"Exactly. There are two sides to the thing, are there not? And whose business is humanity doing?"

"Good question. Maybe it's just a few survivors of an alien crash, say a Roswell, who manipulate a few at a time, and they in turn persuade Congress to spend money on research . . ."

"What? To repair their spacecraft."

"Well, if it's only that, it's innocent enough."
"That's probably what it is, but I wonder."

*   *   *

from the journal of Stephen Ambrose

It would be disappointing to think Newton scored his colossal scientific achievement only so that he could become president of the Royal Society, and use that power to vanquish any claim of Leibniz to the discovery of calculus. A kind of pedestrian use of power. But apparently his achievements in the sciences were not used in any kind of mating ritual to attract a female. He never married. Although, it was never clearly established that he was a homosexual, either. Maybe he just never got around to making a decision. I wonder how this would square with Darwin, who claimed all decisions were made for evolutionary gain. God knows Newton took enough risks, losing his vision for three days after staring into the sun (via a glass) for three days.

Perhaps the thrill of finding out something others didn't know was thrill enough. Good enough to keep what he found out a secret. He kept calculus a secret for such a long time that we use Leibniz's notation. Fluxions never made it.

But maybe he serves to back up my notion that a Throdēop's brain might expand simply to solve a problem. Because Newton didn't seem to use his for anything else.

Miranda

"Miranda. You have the perfect name for this."

"Because my name is one of the moons of Uranus?"

"Listen, you can moon me anytime, sweetheart."

"I have a feeling you're going to give it some attention."

"Would you like that?"

"Sure, honey. You can mount me anytime."

"My, but you really have your lines down."

"Years of practice. Don't forget the lube."

Afterwards, she said, "Actually, you have your technique down pretty well, where'd you learn to be so . . . effective?"

"Videotapes. Isn't that how everyone learns?"

"No one could learn to do it that well from porno tapes."

"Honest, they help."

"Well, I suppose education is everywhere."

"That's what I think. Of course, practice helps."

"Practice makes perfect."

"I think it must be a German expression. It sounds like a German expression. Practica macht parfect."[4]

"The Germans."

"Miranda . . . I like saying your name. And not just because it's so appropriate. Your parents could never have known. No, I like the sound of it."

---

[4]   Praxis bildet vollkommen, that's the German.

159

"My parents named me Miranda because my father liked these camera magazine ads for Rollei cameras. There was a man in a black suit and bowler with a cane and this naked woman next to him named Miranda. I've seen the ads. Very sexy."

"Derivative. A takeoff from the famous painting by Manet."

"Probably, what isn't derivative?"

"So maybe your father had something like you in mind."

"At least they didn't name me April. I was born in April."

"So, you're an Aries."

"Head first. That's me."

"You have a great forehead." Nick often wondered what turned him on about foreheads. Was it the suggestion of great cerebral lobes behind the forehead? One of the ways paleontologists could tell a male from a female was the head. Females had higher foreheads.

"Yeah, I know what you mean a—great head."

*   *   *

"You seem to keep up on that vitamin stuff. Do you think they make any difference? I wonder what the research on twins would say about vitamins." Abner.

"I don't know that it says much yet. I think research on twins would tell you that twins would probably both end up taking vitamins. So where are you then? Tell you this much, stay out of the sun. I've seen pictures of twins. One who was in the sun a lot, one who was not. Just stay out. Environment can make a difference."

"Okay, okay. I get the message. So, which one ends up controlling, genes or environment?"

"It's a chicken-and-the-egg type of question. Stephen Pinker from MIT thinks that the genes rely on the brain cells to assist in the development of the mind."

"And the brain cells make a call on the environment?"

"Something along those lines."

"There you are. Barkeep, another beer here. What do you know about milk thistle?"

"Milk thistle? Sure, it's also called Sylmarin. How is it all you beer-a-holics know about milk thistle?"

"I'm alcoholic, not stupid."

"You're not an alcoholic."
"I said it for affect, weenie-brain."

*   *   *

from the journal of Stephen Ambrose

I saw the commercial with the monkey and cocaine again. I think the message is something like: given all the cocaine he could want, a monkey will give up food and sex. The monkey will consume cocaine until he's gone.

That's us, too. We'll consume until there's nothing left. Maybe it's not cocaine or heroin, maybe it's just consumption that does us in.

Tomorrow I'm off to BA.

PART II

Another World

On the plane to Buenos Aires about an hour from touchdown, the pilot came on and said, "Hope y'all are enjoying the trip. We're gonna go up to thirty-nine thousand feet shortly to dump some of this extra fuel, and then we'll begin our descent."

Going to Buenos Aires was like going to another world. And maybe it would be more of the same when we came to interplanetary travel. All the same rules of physics applied. Different expression, but the same laws. Sure, Mars was a red desert, but maybe you can find red deserts on Earth, too.

I felt like another person in Argentina. An observer. But observer suggests an out-of-body, astral-plane experience. And no one is just an observer; they are also an inhabitant, even if a temporary one, a consumer of food, a breather of air, a *milonguero*, a tango dancer. To think you are an observer is a kind of haughty fiction, no one gets off that easy. Neverthless I felt like I was an explorer, an adventurer, tango pioneer, terpsichorian astronaut. And at least I was away from my world. The one I shared with Nick was too corrosive. Thank God he had no interest in Buenos Aires.

*　*　*

It wasn't until my third trip to Buenos Aires that I got all my ducks in a row. The first trip I got a taste. But in two weeks, what can you accomplish? You go to the *milongas*, which is a confusing term because a milonga can be two things: a place where one goes to dance tango, but it is also the name of a particular up-tempo tango-related dance. At the milongas, we danced tango, *vals* (waltz), and the fast-tempo milonga, with the occasional swing or salsa number sprinkled in for spice.

I went to the dance halls, the milongas. Almagro was a famous desirable tango showcase locale with a great floor where you were seated by an older man with a distinguished mustache. El Desván was a loft hangout with the concrete floor. Regine, a dive. All of them now gone two years later. One learns the cycle of life. Birth, death, rebirth.

Regine. That was a case of foreseeable coincidence if ever there was one. On the opening night I was translating the Tanturi tango, "Mi Piba," with my tutor. She was curious about what was going to happen to the Regine location. We finished our translation and then we went over to El Beso, Regine's new moniker, where we "happened" to meet others from Monna's house, where I was staying. If I'd been back at Monna's, I would have been caught up in the chatter about the new milonga. So, I would have ended up at El Beso, no matter what.

Rebirth: the Regine location was reborn. The ugly duckling was reborn a swan. El Beso had a great floor. Lighting. Good music from Muscarello, who looked down sadly over his reading glasses from his disk-jockey perch, the man in the moon. But that was only after a great set from the orquesta Color Tango.

Some things happen as planned in your dreams. On that first trip, I did not plan to take any lessons, but I met the beautiful dancer from my videos, Mara Perelli, at a lesson before the milonga began at Almagro, and spent a bunch of moolah on *privados* with her. Picked up one good step. The step around after a backwards *ocho*. It is too much to expect more than one good step. She showed me the elements of milonga, the fast tango. All of this without her speaking a word of English, nor me a word of Spanish.

Well, this was not exactly out of my dreams. In my dreams I would never have her husky boyfriend, the *abogado* (lawyer) with the magnetic blue eyes, show up to translate. He only came once, thank God. She met him through his cousin, through whom she was taking English lessons. The friend I traveled with, Leo, kept remarking that she looked much older than her videos. I thought she was stunning nevertheless. It must be hell for actors to watch their old movies. *Yes, that was me back when I was young and stupid and beautiful. When every guy in town wanted me, and I only wanted the drunken alcoholic personal manager who stole all my money. Those were the days.*

That first trip I remember a dark-haired girl I danced with at El Desván. She had a very pretty face and very wide hips. If it weren't for the hips, she would probably be consigned to memory oblivion. I danced with her one tango, and thanked her. I was happy even to have one dance, but then I figured out that by thanking her we had ended our time together. And not to complete a *tanda*, a set of four tangos, was almost an insult, although I think she realized I was out of synch with the codes.

She looked at me when the next set of milongas started. The fast tangos. I looked away. I didn't dance milonga yet. Sure, Mara had shown me a couple of steps, but I was more out of synch with the music than I was with the dance codes. But she didn't know that. All she knew was that I looked away. Finally, and before she left, a nice set of tangos came on, and I went back and danced a whole tanda with her. In one of the breaks between tangos I explained my problem with the codes. She knew some English, and this was a happy conclusion to the evening.

The Second Trip

A year later, I made my second trip to Buenos Aires. This time I stayed for three weeks. I liked the hotel better. The Phoenix. It stood right next door to the fashionable Galería Pacifico, a very chic shopping mall in the downtown area called Microcentro. I arrived on a Tuesday, and slept most of the day. The next afternoon I was off to the Confitería Ideal, which was only blocks away.

Confitería Ideal was dilapidated splendor. Constructed around the turn of the century, it had grand marble staircases and columns from the era when it was the eighth richest country in the world, but Argentina did not have the money for this kind of opulence anymore.

The first floor was a restaurant for the old folks. It was never very busy. An old man on a platform played show tunes on an electric organ. Up the marble stairs and on the second floor, a woman sat at a fold-out card table with her metal box to collect the five peso entry fee. It was a large room with tall ceilings. It was broken-down glory. The ceilings were peeling, and it was hard to imagine there was enough money in that metal cash box to put anyone up on a scaffold to repaint it. On a good day maybe eleven out of fourteen ceiling fans were working.

The waiters were led by an old, dour-faced fellow named Jorge who never smiled. This is the face of Argentina. The face of Argentina is, when it is not in one of those Italian moments of joy and recognition, a poker face. Oddly, this is the face one would expect to find in Communist Russia. Joyless, hapless, beaten down—an exhausted face. I waited forever for this tall joyless character to see my hand raised for service. I gave him my instruction in tentative Spanish. "*Café con leche y agua sin gas.*" Coffee with crème, and bottled water without carbonation. Actually, it would be more correct to say "*agua mineral sin gas,*" but the less I said the better.

I have taken private Spanish lessons for two months prior to this visit, but it does not help much. My Spanish teacher in Chicago was a Gemini from Peru. A Peruvian who spent ten years in Ecuador when things were bad in Peru. She was in an American school there, so she spoke English from an early age. I slogged along on the three basic conjugations—present, past and future. It was very slow-going, but she is attractive with her big brown eyes. I'm trying to figure out her makeup. Indian for sure, probably Incan, but perhaps some part European, too. Great supple skin. She lets me know that she has a *novio* (boyfriend), so it's just lessons for me.

*   *   *

On my second trip to Buenos Aires, I had the best possible experience on my first night. It was a heroin type of experience. I am sitting alone at Salón Canning, but then Francisco Santapá, a tall handsome teacher, sends over a German guy who speaks English. We talked about the American economy before the Internet crash. He was an economist who thought Alan Greenspan, chairman of the Federal Reserve, was the most powerful man in the world. And I agreed, he was an influential man.

He thought they needed some northern European types to run the leading enterprises here. The politicians were corrupt, the managers were corrupt. No one was responsible here. You cannot depend on anyone. I told him that that was my take, also. He said that some day they will have to go off parity with the dollar, and devalue. All the jobs were going over the border to Brazil, which already had devalued.

We both spied a pair of young Argentines. I clapped eyes on one, and she nodded. She came to the edge of the floor and waited. That's the etiquette. My job was to walk over to her. I held up my left hand and she placed her hand in mine. My right hand came around and cradled her back. She was a *rubia* (a blond) who wore glasses which she left at the table. She was a decent dancer but a little stiff. When the tanda was over, I walked her back to her table, and then repaired back to mine. I told the German guy to give her a try. He danced with the other, the brunette.

Well, okay. I understood.

I watched him dance. Those Germans. They all seemed to be good dancers. I wondered how the hell this could be. But even though everything looked good from the table, I guessed it wasn't perfect because he didn't ask her again. I suggested he try the blond.

He tries the rubía. I dance with the *morocha*, the brunette. Now, this is dancing. I can't imagine what his complaint with her was. She was like an extension of my body somehow. She was with me. She mirrored when we were going in the same direction, and she was chest to chest (*pecho a pecho*) when we did the turns.

Chest to chest. This I learned in my private lesson with the famous Juan Carlos Copes in what must have been one of his last private lessons with his dance partner (and marriage partner early on), Maria Nieves. He says, "Lead from the chest." He showed me. If your chest moved to the right, the girl goes to the right. You don't have to drag her over there with your arms. She will follow you. It is an important lesson.

I am in love with Marisa. She is great. But my German companion leaves me. He is living in a house in San Telmo, way on the other side of town. It is two thirty. He's got a ride, and he's had enough. I alternate dancing with the rubía and the morocha. But at some point, it becomes obvious to the rubía that I prefer dancing with the morocha. I don't know quite how she figures this out. She is also quite lovely, and any other night if her friend the brunette were not around, I would be overjoyed to have such a partner. This is some special kind of hell. God gives me my perfect dance partner (or close enough), but then he gives me her friend as well. The rubía is in upset, so I am sunk. Well, they end up in the bathroom together, and I have no one to dance with.

I go there the following three weeks before I leave, but Marisa never comes back either by herself or with the rubía.

The Third Trip

On my third trip I have nailed down the basics. I am no longer in a hotel. Now I am staying at Monna's house in the Almagro barrio. I have my Spanish tutor, Aurora. I know all the main milongas. The ones I like—El Beso, Ideal, Niño Bien, Salón Canning. The ones I don't like, like Tasso. Tasso is always crowded and a bit of a dive. But it is always crowded, so it must be personal distaste on my part.

In some places they seat you, and this is something new for an American equal-opportunity seater like myself. Every table with a "Reserved" sign on it. Such signs are in evidence at many places. Ideal (EE-day-al) always seems to have them. Mostly I honor the signs, and sit in the back near the *baños*, which in the summer are very pungent, but it doesn't bother me greatly since I can't smell worth a damn. Three trips to BA, and I still don't know the system of reserved tables at Confitería Ideal.

At Almagro, a milonga named for the barrio Almagro in which it sits, all the tables were reserved, too. But now, Almagro, which I thought was a great place, is gone. And I was there for the *despidida*, the farewell night. All the luminaries were there. Robert Duvall, who had been coming down for years, and who had narrated a tango segment for National Geographic, occupied a table at one end of the floor. I saw my favorite couple, Javier and Geraldine.

There is all kinds of *chisme*, gossip, about what happened. Some of the gossip was that Fabbri allowed too many exhibitions, and the people who went there wanted to dance, not watch. Some said it was the chic clutter of La Catédral which was right around the corner, and which competed with them on Tuesday's nights. La Catédral was the creation of the Parakultural people, milonga operators who seemed to move from nightspot to nightspot with the adroitness of a black jaguar in the jungle.

La Catédral was another loft experiment. The floor was awful, nothing but warped boards, but it had the vaulted ceiling of a cathedral. Walk in, past the curtain, and to your left would be an old sofa, old chairs. There might be a mattress. Everyone sitting on the mattress next to the floor. Another sofa. Something that looked like a chair but wasn't. The music was very good, as it always seemed to be at these Parakultural locations. Most places organized the music around tandas. Three or four tangos usually performed by a single orchestra, with some kind of break music, a *cortina*, in between each tanda, which might be any kind of music—Elvis, Frank Sinatra, the Beatles, anything.[5] Oh Donna Oh at Lo de Celia. It would only be part of a song, one song at most. Parakultural played sets, but sometimes more than the prescribed four songs, and then the next set of valses or milongas followed without any cortina. That was very Parakultural.

---

[5]   In Chicago, Tom Barnard used the beginning of the Buena Vista Social Club as a cortina at Club 720.

The Invisibility

I went to El Beso on Sunday nights. A doorman was present to greet us, which was a feature that distinguished it from the other milongas. Up two flights of stairs, and you can feel the air-conditioning hit you. It cuts the humidity which the air is heavy with. I paid my five pesos, and walked to the end of the bar and surveyed the room. I saw my instructor's assistant, Annabella, across the room, so I ordered a J & B. I was still rattled that she had turned me down last week. I wondered what was the reason for such discordant behavior. When I first came into town, she dashed over to offer her cheek for a kiss. I thought we were on good terms.

Maybe being the teacher's assistant made her think she was something extra. That would be an Argentinian thing. They were desperate to be superior in some way. One of my favorite songs was "Gallo Ciego," the blind rooster. That was Argentina, in a nutshell. It had an exaggerated sense of itself which was only possible because it was blind, separated from the rest of the world by thousands of miles. As a teacher's assistant, by definition, she was better than a student. And I was the student, by definition. That is, I was paying. But she had only been dancing for a year, and I had been dancing for seven years and had taken lessons with the best dancers in the world. I only took the lessons with Marcelo because of her. She was adorable.

I figured it would be another night of nothingness. I ambled over to my friend, Gino, the Italian with the Swiss father, with a bald head that came out of one of da Vinci's notebooks.

"Are you invisible again tonight?"

"My invisibility is nearly perfect," which meant the women were not returning the invitations he was extending with his eyes.

I laughed.

"My invisibility is like a sheet of nonreflective glass. I am completely invisible. I am like the character in that movie with . . . Rens. What is his name?"

"Claude Rains."

"Yes, that's it."

"I heard someone say that was why tattoos are so popular now."

"Yes, why?"

"Because some people feel invisible, and think that people will see them with their tattoos."

"I think there is more going on there than that."

"The pain."

"Sure, the pain. And how does a tattoo on your thigh make you visible when no one can see it?"

"Yes, right, of course. Another theory for the junk pile."

He tuned me out. He was listening to the music and scanning the room. The dance floor was not particularly big, so shortly after the beginning of the first song of a tanda the floor was packed. So it was of necessity that they danced the *milonguero* style of dancing, sometimes called *apilado*, which Argentines translated into English as "close-embrace" for the norteamericanos. There was no room for fancy steps, no room for hooked kicks, *ganchos*. In fact, when it got terribly crowded, there was no room for anything other than the *cunita*, which was nothing more than rocking back and forth, the kind of close-dancing step that might not even be a tango step.

I tried to draw him back in. I said to him, "Listen, if you're so invisible, why come at all?"

"This is my cup of poison. This is the cup of poison I must drink."

I laughed.

With that his invisibility was interrupted. He had made eye contact with a tall rubía, and he put his glasses in his pocket and met her at the edge of the floor.

Then I spied a tall rubía. Late twenties was my guess. Her raised eyebrows met my raised eyebrows, and we had just cut a deal. She was sitting at the edge of the floor and stood up. I walked over to her.

I am tall and Argentinian women are short, so it was a pleasure to dance with someone so tall. The top she was wearing emphasized her ample bosom, which shoved into my chest. Poor me.

She was an excellent dancer, truly wonderful. She did not crowd me, but she was with me on every step. Whatever missteps occurred were seamlessly transformed into something else. She has the perfect follower's antennae. She has the cat whiskers that feel where I will move next. That's dancing. Only a really, really good dancer could see the difference.

We had a definite, unmistakable connection.

Every time a tanda came on with music I wanted to dance to like Pugliese or Calo (who was so romantico) or DiSarli, I found her eyes. This is kind of a high.

Her name was Mariela. Sometimes people take a full minute of a song before they begin to dance. I spoke in my elementary Spanish. She had been dancing for four years. A few lessons here and there, but mostly it was simply a matter of going to the milongas, night after night. Well, I had danced with some of those other night-after-night women, and somehow they never learned from the experience. They continued to be stiff, jagged, awkward dancers, night after night. She had learned from the experience. She felt right. It was a good feeling.

Where you might sit next to someone and engage them in conversation after a dance in any other country, in Argentina you walked them back to their seat and allowed them the opportunity to dance with others.

But I was on a roll. Before she left I resolved to get her phone number, and try to meet her for dinner.

* * *

E-mail from Amanda

Stephen Daedalus—

Looks like your puffed-up Argentines may have something to be puffed up about after all. The largest ever herbivore and carnivore were found there—Titantosaurus and Megaloraptor.

Love,
Amanda

* * *

Dinner. We met on a Tuesday, and I thought we could have dinner together on Friday. But when I got Mariela on the phone, she hemmed and hawed. She went to Estrella with her friend on Fridays, so it was *Lunes* (Monday). I tried

Saturday; she came back again to Lunes. I tried Sunday, and again it was Lunes. I said, sure, Lunes. *Claro*, Monday.

Then where to go was the next issue. I suggested either Puerto Madero or the outdoor restaurants in Recoleta. Puerto Madero was near the center, Microcentro, along the river, what must have been warehouses transformed into a chic and new dining area. Recoleta was a fashionable, wealthy, old part of town named for the famous cemetery. She thought both were good choices. She preferred Recoleta, which was fine with me. I liked the outdoor restaurants. *Restaurantes afueras.* It is well below freezing back home in Chicago. My breath would turn to frost on my mustache back home. Of course, I want to eat outside. Air-conditioning would be nonsense. I want to sweat. But at night it will be pleasant, it will be perfect.

Then we have to decide where to meet. I say, "Just a minute," and I grab my backpack and pull out the map of Buenos Aires. I'm scanning, scanning. Okay, I decide Junín and Vicente Lopez. She knows where it is, thank God.

An Impromptu Party

On Thursday night there is a party at Monna's house. It is one of these impromptu parties that never, ever seem to happen back in Chicago. Everyone contributes something, except me, which gets noticed, so I am sent on a mission to get paper plates and plastic glasses.

"You have to go to Disco."

"Why not Coto?"

"Coto doesn't carry them."

I am amazed. Coto is a huge grocery store. Marie and I agree that there are only three things that work in Argentina. The taxis, which are omnipresent on any sizeable street. The subway, called the *subte* (short for *subterraneo*), and Coto. Coto, we decide, must have studied American grocery stores. It is huge, and air-conditioned like a meatpacking plant. The employees are engaged in a way that most relaxed Argentinians are not.

It is kind of sad to see. I am a little sick of America. It was at the same time comfortingly familiar and disgusting when I saw a Blockbuster Video across the street from Almagro.

On my first trip, when I had no Spanish at all, I ate frequently at McDonald's and Burger King, barking out the number of the special I wanted, but hopeless when they would ask what I wanted to drink. Finally, getting the message, I would say, "agua mineral sin gas."

At the party, there was another rubía. Shorter than the ideal partner, Mariela, that I had met at El Beso. She could speak English, but she didn't think her English was very good. It was fine. She was an *abogada*, attorney. She was one of those brilliant people who claim they don't know anything unless they know more than everyone else, then and only then they say, "Well, I know something about it." This must be British understatement left over from the colony of English who built the train system.

This new girl's name is Sylvia. Sylvia is very attractive with lots of facial symmetry and a good butt, well-packaged. We danced a Pugliese number in the entry to the house, and several people clapped when we finished. She seemed embarrassed and turned a little red, and made off for the kitchen, but somehow, I am inclined to think she must have been pleased.

Gino follows her out to the kitchen, and soon they are in heavy conversation. She looks like she is greatly interested in him, and I feel all the points I may have gotten from dancing well with her have been lost. I was too tall. The points didn't matter, and that was that.

Before long they are in the stairwell kissing. I know that I am sunk. So I listen to old Carlos rasp his poem about tango back in the old days. Then someone whispers to me that Carlos, who does not dance that well in his 90s, never did dance very well; it's just that he is so old that he has become revered for being the oldest tango dancer around. Carlos, in turn, says that El Cachafaz, supposedly the best tango dancer ever, did not die in the arms of Carmencita Calderon after dancing to Don Juan. Carmencita also lives on into her 90s and still dances. Carmencita thrives from the love of tango dancers. I, too, gave her *un beso* at Sin Rumbo after she danced an intricate milonga and went around the room collecting kisses like a gardener snipping roses for her vase.

*   *   *

The thing is that I like Gino, and I did not want to compete with him over some girl. But I thought, he already has a girl. But men, being men, dream of harems and harems of women. And even if they cannot possibly satisfy them all, it's nice to have them around to bring you tea, massage your neck, to dance with, fetch your shoes, bring your reading material. Nevertheless, I am not happy with Gino. I avoid him for a while but finally he sits next to me at breakfast two days later.

"What's the matter? You have not spoken to me since the party."

"Nothing."

"It's not the girl, is it? Nothing happen. The girl, Sylvia, is an alcoholic."

"A little champagne."

"Not a little. Three bottles. I went around collecting the bottles. I pieced it together. One bottle here. One bottle there."

"I don't remember her polishing off a bottle."

"No, no. Not like that. She's more refined. She would take the bottle and pour for you and pour for Carlos, and check Marie's glass, and mine, and the others. But over the course of the night we went through ten bottles, and I think three of them were hers."

"You exaggerate."

"She ended up in the bathroom. Maybe one of them ended up in the toilet."

"Really?"

"Really. I gave her one of my T-shirts to get home."

"Are you going to Ideal?"

"No, I'm going to La Flaca's house." *La Flaca*, meaning skinny. That would be Carolina, his main squeeze.

"Ah."

"I behaved very poorly. I should not chase a woman right in front of her. She called me up, crying. She's very upset. It's normal."

I had seen her go upstairs, with that expressionless Argentine mask. I didn't quite know what to make of it. Evidently, not so expressionless after all. Carolina was a very smart woman, not to be underestimated. She was quiet. Whereas Ellen Fein, who wrote *The Rules*, thought that women should be quiet and demure, yet went on television and bragged about the happy state of her marriage. A sure sign that her marriage was in trouble. She hadn't watched her Ingmar Bergman, *Scenes from a Marriage*, and ended up filing for divorce before they issued the third book in *The Rules* series. Carolina would never brag about the state of her relationship with Gino. She was the model that Ellen Fein and Sherrie Schneider had in mind when they wrote their book.

"You left Catédral, but this Sylvia comes in. I have a nice dance with her, and so I asked Monna if I shouldn't invite her to our party."

"So, you invited her."

"You didn't know?"

"I wondered who she might have known. But all kinds of people come to these parties. I never know who invited whom. Nuts." Meaning Gino deserved first dibs, since he was the inviter. Now what?

"She is an attractive girl. Somehow she reminds me of someone."

"Me, too. I think it would be shame if nobody gets her. She has your T-shirt. It is a perfect reason to call her up."

"I will sometime," said Gino.

*   *   *

from the journal of Stephen Ambrose

I wonder how Sylvia reminds both us of someone. I'm wondering: does it have to do with the facial symmetry? That there is something basic about such symmetry, something archetypical, or is it as I saw in some Discovery Program, the common denominatorness of her face. Maybe it is no more than being reminded that we like symmetry.

The French

Staying at Monna's house were two French women, Madeleine and Georgette. Georgette was short with very thick glasses. She was of German-Jewish and French parents. But vivacious. In fact, too vivacious to be believed. No one has that kind of energy—it was shocking, it was repulsive to see such energy. Anyone with manners would know to hide it. For me it was like an extravagant show of wealth. Like a diamond ring that's so huge that the rock always turns and faces down. It's like she has so much gold jewelry her on wrist and fingers that you can barely see the flesh.

She gets up early, and she's fixing breakfast and laughing. Who can laugh that early in the day? Really, it's offensive. I like her, of course. Energy like that is contagious. There's nothing one can do but like her. It's just that I am sick with envy over her energy. I, who barely achieves consciousness each day, would trade all my treasure for such energy. I would do menial work for the rest of my life for such energy. Of course, that would be the deal, don't you know? The devil would say. Oh, sure, you can have all the energy in the world, but you will have to spend all that energy toting up sums on an old adding machine. I would never be lucky enough to get to use it to paint or act or direct or write.

Full of the devil, Georgette would say, "Ooo-la-la." Yes, I knew the French said that, but I thought it was passé, like "throw it around the horn" or "that's the bee's knees." She gave it new life.

Her friend Madeleine said nothing when I first met her. I didn't know if she spoke English or not. There was no special recognition in her eyes. Oh, she was in her mid-fifties, I imagine. When she was younger she must have been a knockout. A spectacular beauty. That French look. Catherine Deneuve. In 2000, both still beautiful.

We were talking about men and women. A common enough topic. One would think after a hundred thousand years, the juice would have run out on this subject but no.

Marie says, "I think male-female relations should be 50-50." Typical American.

Whatever 50-50 means. Then I get one of those shocks from Madeleine, who turns out to speak English after all:

"Relationships are never 50-50. This is what I expect from a man: I expect he will make the money. What do you call it in America?"

Marie offers, "Breadwinner."

"Yes, that will do. He is the breadwinner. And I expect him to dominate me. If the man does not dominate me, I don't want him. And I expect him to be hard for sex."

This I never heard in my life.

Marie protests, "No. I think women want a marriage of equals."

I say, "Marie. I think you need to do a little work on this. Here you are positively devoted to tango. Tango is a male-led dance. It is strictly lead and follow, and you are a follow. How many times have I heard you complain about the inadequacy of a male lead?"

"Well, that's for the dance."

"I think you need to do some homework. This guy you're so interested in, this former corporate exec, he is no pushover," which causes Marie to blush.

Madeleine smiles. I feel like I am basking in the sun. It is her first smile. And there is nothing like a smile from a beautiful woman.

The Setup

The set up was Gena. Gena was the friend of La Flaca, Carolina, who was the novia of Gino.

Gino says, confidentially to me, "I would do her if she wasn't the friend of Carolina."

This is by way of a recommendation. And it was true enough. He would do her. I was sure about that. It is becoming clearer and clearer to me that all's fair in love and war. No one seemed to observe any boundaries. This married person has an affair with that married person, and so on and so on and so on. I watched too much prime time and not enough soaps as a kid.

It was becoming clearer and clearer that we were just animals among other animals. And that "morals," a word which leaves such a foul, lingering taste in my mouth, were a convention that was mostly flouted. Yes, sometimes with consequences. But mostly we were just the agents of our basic modes of behavior. For men this means we pursue women, and we are possessive about our favorites. We try to keep our harem in the face of competition. And that's all it is.

The women want a protector, or multiple protectors, if at all possible. Backup. They want the best of all possible genes for their offspring. They're coded that way. Of course there is a trick to this, figuring out which of one's possible partners will generate the best offspring.

Anyway, Gena turned out to be another of these damned attractive dark-haired Italian-Spanish Argentines. She was divorced with a kid. As my cousin used to say, "They all got 'em," dropped a calf somewhere along the way. She was a relative beginner to tango but charming and easy enough to lead.

She had a little English, and I had a little Spanish. It wasn't quite enough. We went to La Calesita, an outdoor milonga. It was the first time I had gone to

La Calesita that it wasn't rained out. I enjoyed the night, but then I noticed it was getting later and later. I saw a girl frequently looking in my direction. I didn't give her the nod, though. Later, she sent some guy over to ask me to dance with her. I tried to understand this guy, but my basic Spanish was not up to the task.

Finally, Gino got tired of the exercise. "He wants you to go with him. Some girl wants you to dance with her. Just go."

I dutifully got up and followed the guy. He brought me to the girl, dressed in an attractive green dress. Not tremendously attractive but buxom and my best partner of the night.

Gino confided later that no one had ever sent an emissary to dance with him, but then, he added, "She wasn't *that* attractive." Naturally deflating the value of experience. Of course.

That night I wrote a sequence for my novel.

Gretchen, the German Girl

I was happy to be in Argentina. If I were in Chicago, I would undoubtedly spill the beans to my brother about my brainstorm of making my aliens good dancers. He would say I would say I was Looney Tunes, but I thought aliens had every right to be more interesting than they were portrayed by humans. Likely to be more interesting than humans.

But was there any reason not to believe that aliens could be dancers?

I took the long cab ride out to Sunderland, which was a basketball court in what appeared to be an Argentine Elks club. Even in such an inauspicious setting there were many good dancers. And I spied a tall morocha. Northern European of some sort, probably German. After the first song was over, we immediately started up in English.

"Where are you from?"

"Germany. And you?"

"Chicago. Have you ever noticed that some of these dancers are in a trance? The women close their eyes, and sometimes the men almost close their eyes. It's almost like a meditation. You cannot think of anything but the music and your partner, and where you are going."

"Yes, I think it is deeply spiritual. The problem with religion is that it confuses, or combines unhappily, a number of things: tribal ritual, the spiritual life, and the man's irritation that his knowledge of the universe is not complete."

"I can't disagree with that."

"As our knowledge increases, the less use we have for God. In a sense you could substitute the word 'God' for 'humanity's lack of knowledge,' if you see what I mean. The end point of his knowledge. God, or a god, which used to throw thunderbolts, now lies in the smallest things, particle physics, rolling quantum riddles our way.

"Indeed."

The music started again. *Cuidado con los 50.* And DiSarli was my favorite orchestra, the one which allowed me to dissolve into the music. One swayed with the rhythm, of course, but it also had very sophisticated contrapuntal melodies that allowed sophisticated steps with sophisticated ladies. When the tanda ended, she continued.

"And tribal ritual, well, that is always kind of with us, for after all, we are tango dancers. We become part of a very small tribe of dancers. Everyone thinks the spiritual life is dead, but it does not go away because of science. Although you see how enlightenment and science seem to come together."

Marvelling, he said, "I do."

"But what I am talking about in the spiritual life is a feeling, or a yearning for something higher. Higher knowledge, enlightenment. Art serves us in this. Music. Meditation, as you said. Speaking of which, what I find most annoying is to dance with a man who is somewhere else, not paying attention to the music or me."

All this in the second cortina, or break, between DiSarli's. Cortinas were less than a minute, and dancers often chatted another minute or two into the next song. An annoying thing for those who want to connect with the music and dance, but a very common thing in BA.

"You are a good dancer, so let's get on with it."

All this with Gretchen, the German girl who was an anthropologist. It seemed tango had more than its fair share of anthropologists. The Germans were great dancers, at least the ones I had danced with. Who would have thought the Nazis would be such great dancers? But then you have to then reconcile how the Germans who had developed some of the highest culture—Bach, Mozart, Beethoven, Goethe—could fall to the depraved depths of the Nazis. This train of thought called again to mind Walter Pidgeon as Morbius, waxing nostalgic about his poor Crell, who like the Germans rose to great knowledge and culture, only to fall prey to their own lust for war. The id.

The goose step was the tip-off. Germans would always be on the beat.

All of this triggered with my remark in the first cortina about tango and meditation. I had suggested that this tango meditation had supplanted religious ritual. Little did I know I had tapped into the main vein. We stayed on the floor through the cortina music of Louis Armstong's *What a Wonderful World.* It was unusual but not unheard of to continue into the next tanda. We exchanged basic information we had neglected in the first tanda. Why was her English so good? (Her parents had sent her to London for a year.) Where in Germany was she from? (Heidelberg.) Altogether maybe six breaks between songs. Perhaps we talked this out in between six minutes and twelve at the very outside. Before we were done, I had told her I liked Milstein's version of Prokofiev's violin concertos, and she was telling me I must listen to his version of Bach's Partitas.

She was brunette with glasses, which hid a rather pretty face. After the second tanda, I thought maybe I should try her for dinner. And I did look for her among the tables to dance again, but somehow she had disappeared. Didn't she realize I was her perfect foil? That I would have listen with rapt attention, that she was singing to the choir. I was in her camp a hundred percent.

And she was the right height.

Alien Tango

"We will perform a dance for you. Since such dances are always mating rituals, we think you will find them very enlightening as well as enjoyable," said Tōparr.

There were six individuals—three males and three females. Their music is hard to describe. Sometimes too fast for any of the humans to follow, sometimes deadly slow. The male Throdēop became a very, very royal blue in the face and purplish in the neck. This was probably what he thought the Primers would find so interesting. The heads of the females turned an intense chartreuse.

The dance seemed quite delicate and no one hesitated, everyone knew their role. But how would the people from Prime know if they made a mistake? They changed partners seamlessly, as in a reel.

Then Tōparr said, "We have studied your dance as well. We can do all of your dances, but we have decided to do one tango for you. We thought you might enjoy this."

Ramón said, "We didn't know you were studying our dance."

Tōparr dismissed this, saying, "Oh, we are naturally drawn to dance physiologically, as you know, and it is something we use to challenge our brains, of course. As you humans might say, something higher."

Then, the music of Argentine orchestra leader Carlos DiSarli began with Mi Refugio, and they swayed elegantly, simply walking, and then with feet occasionally darting effortlessly against legs, the one displacing the other. Then simply walking again, dancing head-to-head, in the style of the Argentines, but with their enlarged brains, it looked like they were passing thoughts directly from one skull to the other.

After the dance they left in pairs, disappearing into the nether parts of their ship, leaving the humans behind.

Only Eladia among the humans, the anthropologist, was familiar with the tango. Dance had gone in many directions during their long, long voyage, and no one else had taken the time to study this old form. She said, "Quite accomplished."

Ramón spoke for the lot, "Either they left Earth in an advanced state of evolution and culture, or they progressed greatly in the sixty-five million years since, even if they put themselves into suspended animation for five million years here and there."

Eladia added, "I have seen recordings of the tango, but I don't remember any as elegant, intricate, or as well-executed as these beings have done it."

A Woman After My Own Heart

The French woman Madeleine frowns a lot. It must be the hell of growing older against the backdrop of having been so beautiful. Imagine the lines that Marilyn Monroe would have had. Look at the pictures of Elizabeth Taylor. Then and later. A special hell for actresses when their old films turn up on Insomnia Theatre.

Still this woman was no fat slob of an Elizabeth Taylor when she went off on a binge. This woman was in perfect shape. I was kind of disappointed that she was so natural about her outward person, especially about the gray strands in her hair. Although usually I was Mr. Natural, I wanted her to color over the gray in her hair. After all, wasn't L'Oréal a French company?

But I decided it didn't matter, and I started to flirt with her anyway. I would tell her how beautiful she looked as she left with Georgette to go to some faraway milonga like that dive, Tasso. I took pictures of them both when they left, but then I would get her to let me take one especially of her.

It was easy for me to identify with her. Madeleine had all my neuroses. She couldn't sleep because of the telephone ringing in the morning. She couldn't sleep because of all the squeaky hinges. It especially won my heart when she was driven to the local hardware store to get oil for the doors, and offered it to me for my door. I accepted, of course. Anything could upset my sleep and did.

Finally, I said, "How come you never knock on my door?"

"Oh, Stephen." That was what she said all the time. "Oh, Stephen." I loved to hear it.

And when I asked her again why she never knocked on my door, she said, "Oh, Stephen, you are too late."

Too late, a dollar short, the train left the station. That was me all over. Perhaps I succeeded in doing a few things correctly, but mostly life was a boring routine enveloped in fear wrapped inside a cliché.

Merde

Buenos Aires was populated with dog walkers, and they walked a lot of dogs, sometimes I saw a brace of dogs ten-strong, walked by a professional dog walker. And there was the concommitent dog shit. A lot of it.

It made for a sometimes incongruous mix. You witness a beautiful-smelling woman pass you by, and then you immediately walk past the pungent odor of a freshly dropped bow-wow movement. It brought you back to Earth too quickly.

It suggested a moment in a film. Here's the setup: Argentina had produced a genius philosopher of aesthetics, a quite natural phenemonon arising out of its brilliant and well-educated populace coupled with an extraordinary attractive one at that.

The philosopher is crossing the street, waxing eruditely on the unusual juxtaposition of beauty and the jarring odious smells and unattractive people in Buenos Aires.

He says, "Even if the really beautiful people are only 2 percent of the population, that would be twice as many, on average, as anywhere else on the planet."

The philosopher avoids the noisome land mines with a casual nonchalance relying on his built-in radar. Meanwhile, the American who is interviewing him from one of the famous Ivy League schools has no such radar, and distracted by a passing beauty, dips his foot in a particularly smelly piece of shit.

The Argentine philosopher says, "Well, there are many beautiful people here, but of course, you do have to look out for the shit."

The Swiss

I met Karl at my Spanish tutor's office. He had finished up his lesson with her and was waiting for some study materials. I occupied the student's seat across from my tutor. He was sitting by the door. Earlier I had given him the bum's rush because he was so good-looking. I had told him I was a tango dancer, so I was in Buenos Aires to dance the tango and learn Spanish. Finally, two days ago I told him where he could learn the tango. This was big of me, I hated competition. Especially from such a good-looking man.

Anyway, he told me he was learning Spanish because he had just broken up with his girlfriend of eight years. I thought: What an honorable way of dealing with adversity! When faced with adversity what could one do? Blow out your brains. Blow out the brains of your adversary. No, learn a new language. I had to say I admired this. Before he left he told me the man who had stolen his girl was his best friend.

I left. I checked my email at one of the cybercafes. This place was just a beehive at the bottom of a grand old building, grand old staircase. After two hours, I decided to call Karl at my teacher's office just before the end of his lesson. I met him for coffee.

It turned out that he had learned English, which we were speaking, eight years ago when his wife left him. We were at the Galeria Pacifico in the elegant café at the bottom of the stairs on the right.

"I wanted to know where I stood in the marriage. Did the horse come first or did I?"

"The horse?"

"Yes, she had a horse."

"And . . ."

"She told me the horse."

"Brother."

"So, that's when I went to Miami for the first time. And signed up to learn English. But it wasn't so great. All these Swiss going out to the beach. We all ended up speaking German. It's a problem."

"I see. So, how old is your girlfriend?"

"Twenty-six. She was young."

"If you were with her for eight years, then she was eighteen when you met her."

"Yes, the same age as my daughter. It was a problem."

"Did you get along well with her?"

"Yes, very well."

"Then it wasn't a problem."

"I guess."

"So what happened?"

"Well, she went off with my best friend."

"Some best friend."

"Well, maybe he wasn't such a good friend. And it's odd because, really he's probably gay. He's kind of, you know, soft. His friends are kind of soft. They're gay. They say he's in denial."

"So, he won't own up to being gay. And he's your best friend. So, maybe he's in love with you." Karl nodded in assent. "Maybe he doesn't even necessarily admit to himself that he's in love with you. Yet he wants to be close to you. So, he gets close to you, close to your girl. And what does he do? He steals your girlfriend, which is to steal the person closest to you. And the girl, does she know about him?"

"Yes, she knows. But maybe it's a challenge."

"She knows, but she wants to give it a try."

"He's really something special. An artist."

"Well, you're very good-looking. You won't have any problem finding a girl."

"Oh, it's not a problem."

Such a line. Imagine being able to utter such a line.

"What do you do?"

"I'm a lifeguard. Like *Baywatch*."

"A lifeguard?"

Well, he was a good-looking man even at fifty. He was still very competitive. Young at heart, charming. Disarmingly charming. The karma of the disarmingly charming.

It turned out that he was a lifeguard for four months out of the year, but it was a grueling four months. From 6 a.m. until 10 p.m. every day for four months. No time to spend any money, so he was free for the eight months, and had a bankroll to spend. He sold Egyptian antiquities on the side. And he also owned a piece of a restaurant next to the swimming pool. A resourceful fellow, no doubt.

In Miami he would haunt the flea markets. It was a game to find the valuable stuff among the bric-a-brac. He wanted to know if I knew about any flea markets in Buenos Aires.

"There's the big one in San Telmo, Plaza Dorrego."

"Yes, I've been there." That felt like an understatement. One had the feeling he had set his eyes on every single item. "Do you know about any others?"

"Only the one on Rividavia, by the park. It's the last stop on the A line."

"I will give it a try."

"Mostly old books, magazines."

"I will give it a try."

"What did your former best friend do for a living?"

"He is an artist."

"He was able to make a living painting."

"No, he wasn't a painter, he was a sculptor. But he also had a bed and breakfast, a pension."

"Really, it's nice to know that artists can still generate interest among attractive young women. I do some writing."

"What kind of writing?"

"Science fiction."

"Science fiction is very popular now."

"Indeed. No one feels any limits these days."

"True enough."

"Einstein thought that the speed of light was a limit. That was as fast as one could go. But for at least fifty years, science fiction writers have been telling us that 186,000 miles per second was just a signpost on the side of the road. Pretty soon we'll be able to clone a human if we want to. We'll be mucking around with genes. From my point of view as a programmer, we will be rearranging, rewriting the code. Which is a possible thing, but I don't know if it is a desirable thing. The problem is: if you change the code, what else are you changing? It's very dynamic. I know that, in a program of thousands of lines of code, if I change one little thing somewhere in the code, it may affect other parts of the code."

He nodded. I could see English was an effort.

"There are examples. Let me think. Did you hear in Europe when AT&T's service went down a few years ago? Because one thing in the code tripped, it created a cascade effect. The entire network went down."

"Yes, interesting things are happening."

"Exactly."

"Think about it, even without the benefit of technological changes in genes, we are a species that has swamped the planet with our genetic setup."

"So what is your story about?"

"My story is about the nature of intelligence."

So, I told him about my accordion-brained dinosaurs. I told him how the Throdēop could outthink the poor humans. How the one Throdēop won a human female that the leader of humans, Ramón, could not make it with.

"Do you have a friend who is smarter than you, who won a woman that you desire to have sex with?"

Losers

My Spanish *profesoras*. Aurora, is another of my Gemini tutors. Dark-haired, short, and slim. She is the third of three Gemini Spanish tutors. Why they were all Geminis, I have no idea. Gemini, short trips, mental travel . . . It was just coincidence, this astrology stuff, something to correlate later, but in the meantime, things would come up to make me wonder—why was the Big Bang found to be in the constellation Leo, for example? Leo was associated with creativity. Perhaps all these facts will coalesce in a fully fleshed out theory later on.

Aurora is a whiz with languages. Spanish, Portuguese, French, Italian. English, the international language, of course. Plus Hebrew and a little Yiddish. She says Arabic was her waterloo. Four ways of saying "a" was too much.

One day I come for my lesson, and she says her laptop computer was stolen last night. She points to its proper place, my head rolls to the right, where I would expect to see it, and poof: it's gone. She starts lighting candles. I ask why.

"To drive off the bad karma."

There are other signs of strain in Argentina, besides theft. Counterfeit currency is a problem. Everyone is always holding paper currency up to the light to check the watermark, or putting it under a black light to check for streaks in the paper. I myself was stuck with a five peso note that didn't make it past the black light.

Remembering my invisible friend, Gino, I ask Aurora, "How do I say: 'a cup of poison'?" She laughs, *una taza de veneno*. Telling her the story behind the request, she says she's familiar with this sense of humor. I tell my friend Gino that we discussed his cup of poison at my Spanish lesson, and he says, "Yes, but did you tell her that you must drink every last drop?" This, she subsequently tells me, would be the *última gota*.

My Spanish tutor complains that the people who inhabit the milongas are *vampiros*. Indeed, it looks like some of the old tango dancers, the old milongueros, are feasting on the life force of the younger dancers. My tutor says they're losers. I ask, "How do you say 'losers' in Español?"

She laughs, "Losers. Same as English."

Indeed, there was a tall woman with black hair who was pale, and, with the makeup, she was positively eerie. And others seemed to have no job, which was maybe true, given the 25 percent unemployment rates. They came day after day after day. And the schedule was the vampire schedule. These people came out after dark, and disappeared just before dawn. Considering the black hair of these Italian and Spanish girls, the uniform de rigeur, tango black, and such a highly stylized dance, the only thing we are missing is a milonga with the right name. It won't be named Dracula or vampiros. It will probably be named for one of Anne Rice's characters—Armand, possibly.

*　*　*

I, too, like Gino, have had nights of invisibility. But I usually had decent luck dancing with other *extranjeros*, foreigners. And the Germans, Dutch, Swiss, Scandinavians are, generally speaking, very fine dancers. One Argentine instructor told me he thought the best average dancer was to be found in Amsterdam. One wonders if it isn't that damn, *maldita* Germanic mentality. The thoroughness of it all.

The Brazilians

I got up on Friday and new people had arrived. Two Brazilian girls were sitting at the table on the patio. One was young and bouncy. The other one was older and had the attraction of being rather knowing.

Young and Bouncy did not speak much English, but she could get by in Spanish. Forties and Knowing did speak English. Forties and Knowing was the tango student of Young and Bouncy. Such flip-flop things happened, didn't I know.

Young and Bouncy had a husband. Forties and Knowing had a boyfriend. Another flip-flop. At Salón Canning I took Young and Bouncy for a spin, and she seemed fine, but Gino said she was trying to lead. It is always confounding when a woman tries to lead. She can do it several ways. One way is resistance. She becomes sluggish and takes her own time to do an ocho or a *giro* (a turn all the way around, a kind of merry-go-round step). When she does this she is taking the lead away from the man. As my Swiss friend would say, resistance is a problem. The normal way of passing off control was when a man would stop at a lull in the music, giving the woman all kinds of time for embellishments.

The other way of taking control was to overanticipate, so that the follower moves into a step before it was led, in effect taking control because the man may not have had it in mind to lead the step that she moved into. Although he might have led the step, anticipation is a hit-or-miss game. The best follows always wait for some signal.

That was Young and Bouncy. It was a case of almost having too much energy. More than she could deal with. She just couldn't wait for the lead, so she would just make the step she thought was coming.

Gino said, "I don't know why you like dancing with her. She wants to lead."

"I didn't have any trouble with her."

Forties and Knowing couldn't dance for beans, but she spoke English. She told me about her Swiss boyfriend.

"How often do you see him?"

"Oh, I saw him five times in the past year."

"In Brazil or Switzerland?"

"Mostly in Brazil, but I went one time to Switzerland."

"How long were you there?"

"Two weeks."

"And you have children?"

"Yes, I have two children."

"How long were you married?"

"Seventeen years. Then he had a midlife thing."

"At least you didn't call it a midlife crisis."

"He found a younger woman. I waited for a year for him to come around. I was in love with him. Then, of course, I quit waiting, and his thing with the younger woman failed. And I think he wanted me back, but . . ."

"But you had moved on to this long distance fantasy thing of yours."

She laughed, "Do you really think it's so ridiculous?"

"How do I know? I don't know you. I don't know the guy."

"He says he wants to move to Brazil."

"Yes, well, does he have any business connections in Brazil? What would make it worth his while to move there? Are you going to support him?"

"He has business connections in Brazil."

"Well, then it's in the realm of possibility, isn't it?"

Forties and Knowing didn't seem particularly knowing after all. She was headlong into a long distance fantasy-evasion thing. But maybe that was all she was up for after devoting years to a marriage that her husband had trashed in a dash. Distance was her protection. Could it be, in the end, that all we really wanted was not actual bonding, but the hope of bonding?

*　　*　　*

Sylvia had given me her phone number, so what the hell, after a few days when it seemed like Gino was not going to pursue her, I called.

"Hola."

"Hola, es Stephen de la fiesta del viernes en la casa de Monna." (It's Stephen from the party on Friday at Monna's.)

"How are you?"

"Fine. I wanted to ask you to dinner."

"Tonight?"

"Tonight would be fine."

"I can't tonight. I'm going out to dinner just now. In fact I'm late, but he'll understand, he's Argentine, too."

"Of course. I'll call tomorrow."

"Call tomorrow."

I called the next day and the day after that and the day after that. But she was never home. I left my phone number, but women are not great about returning phone calls.

Mariela

Finally, Monday rolls around, and the date with Mariela, who danced divinely. I show up at the corner of Junín and Vicente Lopez a little early, the result of an upbringing with a Dutch mother. She is always prompt. She is always on time. She is always a little early. So am I.

The rubía is late. I stand on one side of the corner with the boulder, then on the side with the shopping center. Then back on the other side where I can lean on the boulder. And I wait. And I wait. But it is only a twenty-minute wait, which is the same as on time, Argentina-speak.

I kiss her cheek, more of the Argentina thing. But right away we run into my horrible Spanish, and she says in Spanish maybe this was not such a good idea. And I'm thinking the same thing, but only because that's what she's thinking. It is a long walk to cover all of the restaurants, and I want her to say she likes this one or that one especially, so that I can win the day, but she doesn't appear to have a favorite, putting the duty to find the right one back in my lap. Just like it is my duty to figure out what a woman likes when it comes to sex. It is nice when there is communication, and you are working together for a common goal, but it doesn't happen all that often.

Finally, I am tired of looking, and I choose a place which looks upscale. The hostess gives us a seat in the middle, which I hate, but already I'm running into the headwinds, and I've lost the willpower to oppose the forces which are conspiring against me.

She teaches history. One of my favorite subjects. Her specialty is American history, which I only have a high school knowledge of. She knows about how Americans stole this territory and bullied for that territory, all of which I never paid much attention to. My interest has always been in European history, although my father took us out to Little Big Horn where General Custer and his men were slaughtered. But that was the exception, wasn't it?

I ask her how she came to learn tango. She says that she took a few group lessons, but mostly she just goes to the milongas. And she dances and dances. She dances from midnight until 5 a.m. night after night. Then, she says, she collapses. A common Argentine phenomenon. My landlady does the same thing. She'll stay up all night, then stay up in the morning to meet the new boarders; go out again that night, and then, finally, crash. Sylvia tells me about her uncle, who brags that his one daughter comes home at 2 a.m. and the other leaves at 2 a.m. Buenos Aires is the ultimate for nightlife.

She changes the subject. She asks if I have traveled much. Some, I answer. Europe. We go through the names in Spanish. Gran Bretaña, Francia, Italia, Suiza, Holanda, España. I have been to Sud Africa del Sur. Capetown is one of the most beautiful cities in the world. She asks me how I like Argentina.

I like the climate, at least in February. It is hot and my bones seem to need it. This part is easy. Then I offer, "My spirits go up and down a lot in Argentina." I don't tell her that I have had some terrible nights. That I went to a Parakultural milonga, now gone, and never got a dance. Many looked away. One woman I asked to dance said she was smoking a cigarette. Another turned me down, pointing to her shoes, which were still on her feet, but the straps were unhooked. After a number of these rejections, I figured this was not my night and left.

She says, "I think Argentina is a roller coaster." In English she says this.

"Yes, I think so, too."

It seems she knows a little English but refuses to use it. Her mother forced her to learn English, so she hates it. And she hates norteamericanos. Somehow, I am not sure that I am excepted. I am a norteamericano who dances tango well, but does not speak Spanish. When I set out to learn tango, it was not clear that I would also need to speak Spanish; in fact, traveling to Buenos Aires was not even in my plans. But you keep dancing, the years roll by. Four years out, a friend decides to go, and I decide to go with him.

When I knew I was going to Argentina, I decided I should know Spanish. I bought books, the Barron's *Learn Spanish The Fast and Fun Way*. I bought. I bought. I bought dictionaries, verb books, idiom books, dual translation books, street Spanish books; I bought books as if buying the books alone would do the job. But I would look at the books, and in my mind I'm thinking, like I did on my very first trip to BA, "Oh, I have fourteen hours to kill with the connection in Miami, I'll study it on the way down." In a mere fourteen hours I will have the essentials down. The basic questions. Where is the bathroom? How much does this cost? And so on. The basic conjugation for regular verbs. I credit myself with knowing that the irregular verbs would be beyond the fourteen-hour time limit.

What happened? I watched the Tom Clancy movie set in Central America, which I can't follow. It is impossible to hear the dialogue over the jet engines. I watched the Discovery Channel. I drank vodka to knock myself out. They gave me two of the little airline bottles to start. I took one of Dr. Petrosian's tiny little Ativan tablets, which finally does knock me out for three hours, which was better than nothing. I had looked over this Spanish material for all of fifteen minutes at the best, and before I knew it they were serving breakfast and the captain was saying, "We're going to go up to thirty-nine thousand feet and dump some of this extra fuel before we begin our descent."

I knew absolutely nothing. *¿Donde esta el baño?* Yes, I had that one down. But nothing else, really. I couldn't tell the taxi drivers where to take me. I would hand them little cards with the address. Several times this was a disaster because old taxicab drivers don't always have their reading glasses with them, and I would have to read out the address. Number by number. Uno cuatro . . . Humberto Primo. That was another problem. I am saying "Humberto Preemo" when I should be saying "Oombeartoe Preemo." And the taxi driver would go, "Huh?" And I would say it again, and he would say "Huh?" again. Finally, I would spell out it out. "Ah-chay, ooo, m-ay . . ." Then recognition, "Humberto Primo."

"Si, Humberto Primo." Then the number again. Then we were off. Spanish language hell.

Well, the difficulty of learning a language is one more rude awakening in a lifetime of rude awakenings. Two months before my second trip I began the Spanish tutoring. This time I knew that fourteen hours would not be enough, but by the end of the two months I wondered if any amount of time would be enough to learn Spanish. I had learned my share of computer languages. First it had been Pascal, then Basic, and then C, C+, C++ (my grades in school). Every time I learned a new language, I would rewrite my astrology program to begin the process. Programming languages were different from spoken languages, but I felt there were more similarities than differences. Conditionals and tests and loops seem to dominate the computer. IF . . . THEN, DO WHILE.

In spoken languages we report the state of things. For example, last Thursday, the milonga Niño Bien was terrible. The heat and humidity were atrocious. There weren't enough fans. The people were packed in like sardines, but instead of being packed in olive oil, we were soaked in our own juices. A situation that was true enough. No conditionals, only a report of conditions. I am happy. I am sad. Still there were many similarities. I felt at home learning another language, but I was never that quick even with computer languages. There were always idiosyncratic commands, the management of dates, layout of the screen. Were the x,y coordinates for 0,0 at the top left or bottom left?

I didn't mind learning another language; I minded that my memory was so slow, that I would have to do that holographic thing. Come at something in as many ways as possible. I would have to be able to hear it, see it. Recognize from the sense of the sentence that blank blank wasn't blanque blanque. You get this from context.

It was all the repetition that I minded. I should think like a bodybuilder. You have to put in your reps. No reps, no muscle growth. That was the ticket. You had to put in the work. The trick was somehow to make the work interesting. Weight training isn't so bad if there are women around doing their various stomach crunches.

Anyway, at the end of the night I offered to take Mariela to Salón Canning. But she said she didn't go to Salón Canning, but she gave the driver the exact address, which I knew because I had looked at it before I left for dinner. If she didn't go there, how did she know the exact address? I made a mental note, and when I saw her at Salón Canning a week later, there was no surprise. It was a routine, run-of-the-mill humiliation. Nothing special. Just another little chink in the armor. But when she saw me, she came over and offered her cheek for a kiss, and asked, "Como estas?" It helped. At least she wasn't mean-spirited.

The Dutch Girl

On my last night, a Sunday, I figured I would go to El Beso and suffer the slings and arrows of anonymity when a French couple at the house, Daniel and Geneviève, persuaded me to accompany them to Gricel. I had not been to Gricel this trip. I have not had good luck there in previous visits. It seemed like a couples' place the Saturday I had been there before, but I thought, "Gricel starts two hours earlier than El Beso. I can go there with them, and I'll have some company, and if it does not work out, I'll go to El Beso."

We go. A group lesson had just finished as we came in, and no one was at the door to collect the cover charge. Someone stopped by our table later to collect. We sit at the far end by the restrooms at a table that does not have a "Reserved" sign on the table. This I continue to be mystified by. At the end of the night most of the tables with "Reserved" markers were still unoccupied. So why all the markers?

We are sitting next to a couple of attractive girls, but they have their backs to us, so I'm trying to figure out how to do the eye-contact thing when I'm looking at the back of the head of this girl. She has very, very blond hair. I have cousins with hair like this, platinum blond, I suppose. She has a perfect figure.

I watch a fellow come over to her table (unheard of), and ask her directly to dance.

Geneviève says to me, "See, I told you you should just go over to her table."

"He's probably a regular partner of hers. They probably know each other."

"I don't think she's from Buenos Aires."

"Why?"

"I don't know. Maybe it's her clothes, or the blond hair. She's a little tall. I just don't think she's from Buenos Aires."

I walk past her and then try to get her attention when I walk back, but she doesn't look up. Geneviève says, after another guy goes to her table to ask her, "You have to go over and ask."

So instead I dance with Geneviève. She is much shorter than I am. And it's difficult to do the plaster-your-body-against-mine thing that they do in Paris. Our first time out was a disaster, but this time we have a very good dance. Never quite finishing perfectly, but it didn't matter.

Finally, she nudges me to go over and ask the blond. And I do. The girl looks up and assesses me, and then nods a yes.

The first few steps are somehow critical. We are sizing each other up. She is tall. Her forehead nestles against my check. She's the perfect height. It's a tango vals, and I love the waltzes. I move to the rhythm and she is right there with me. She is an experienced dancer. I am greatly enjoying this. *Romance de barrio.* Neighborhood romance. My favorite vals. And then another and another. A good way to start. We come to the end of the tanda.

"Quantos años bailar tango?"

"Five years." In English.

"It's so obvious that I am English?"

"American. I think so."

"Your English is quite good."

"Yes, well, in Holland we study English from an early age."

"Holland. Yes, it seems like everyone there speaks English. It almost seems like an English-speaking country."

"In Amsterdam that would be true. But when you get a little further out, there is less English."

"I see."

"And you're from?"

"Chicago."

"Ah yes. Chicago. Al Capone."

"Right. Your hair is so blond."

"It's true of my family. It's pretty common."

"I have Dutch relatives with such light hair."

"You are Dutch?"

"My mother's parents came from Holland."

"So you have been to Holland?"

"Yes. Amsterdam. The Heineken factory. The Anne Frank house. The Rijksmuseum. The Municipal Museum. The Van Gogh museum. The Paradiso with all the drugs, the red-light district."

"You've seen it all, then."

"I wouldn't say that, but I've been there. What's your name?"

"Anna." At least her name wasn't Gertrude.

The music started and our dancing continued to be a well-connected thing. It is the synchronicity of the thing. The foot and shoe. Was this my Cinderella?

This was the high point of the trip, and I was hours from leaving. I had no time left to ask her out. Soon I would be back in Chicago, a continent away. I took her back to her table after the set. It felt like a heavy separation for me, but someone else asked her to dance the next set right away, seamless the way that happened, no interruption at all. Meanwhile, I'm starting to grieve already. She was back on the floor with her head passionately pressed against some other guy's head. Floor play with some other schmuck.

I, too, made the eye connection with someone. But the one thing that is hard to tell when someone is sitting down is how tall she is. She was short. No head-to-head here. But we nevertheless persevered through a tanda's worth of four songs.

I got one more set of dances with Anna before she left. I gave her my card and wrote down my e-mail address. And that was that. Brush your hands together, Stephen, it's done.

* * *

At Ezieza, the airport, on the trip home, I met a family who came from Montana to fish in Patagonia. They were stuck with several fake $100 Federal Reserve notes. To the untrained eye, there was no obvious tip-off that they were fake. More signs of a strained economy, I said to myself. These bumpkins were already over the shock and kind of bragged as they showed me the fake bills. The hicks were thrilled to be taken by these sharp, clever urban thieves. Their lives had not been lived in vain after all!

This was in the main area. Then I went to my gate at United, and met a technician who worked for a natural gas pipeline services company.

"What exactly does your company do?"

"We make the equipment to separate the carbon dioxide out of the natural gas."

"What do you do with it, the carbon dioxide?"

"Vent it."

"Couldn't you do something with it? Fill fire extinguishers with it?"

He put his finger at the hip of his glasses and pushed the thick frames back, "Actually, that's what I suggested. But they didn't want to spend the money on plant and equipment. Not a profitable enough business, I guess."

"Not profitable enough," I repeat.

"Ah, but that's nothing," he says, trying to cheer me up. "You should see the sludge they're pumping into the Amazon and some of these rivers."

I say, "I guess they must think no one will notice it out there."

On the plane the stewardesses were tired but cheerful. There are higher rates of cancer among stewardesses. The problem is the exposure to X-rays. The higher up you are the less atmosphere there is to deflect them.

This I kept to myself. I read too much. And I saw no need to bother everyone with my nightmares.

PART III

The Charmingly Cheap Girl

Shortly after Stephen left for Buenos Aires, Nick met a gorgeous girl one Sunday afternoon at a Civic Orchestra concert. The Civic Orchestra, which played at Orchestra Hall, now Symphony Hall, did not charge for its performances, which made it very attractive to penny-pinchers like Nick. And Nick *was* a penny-pincher. He rationalized that it made him more resourceful. Like a mathematician who is a little lazy and would like to find the easy way out of a problem, he would try to find someone else to foot the bill. Kind of a game. The idea was to pay for one beer, and get three from your drinking partner.

The girl was quite lovely—blond, long blond hair, a dancer's body with the exception of a handful for each hand.

Out of the blue she offered, "The great thing about these Civic Orchestra concerts is that they're free."

Naturally, this gained his interest. A girl who watched her dollars might watch your dollars as well. A girl like that in public office might do wonders for the national debt.

She continued, "That, and good music."

But not to miss a beat on the main theme, he said, "I wonder how many people would come if they charged."

"Depends, I suppose, on how much they charged."

"Let's say five bucks."

"Maybe half as many people."

"Why half?"

"Well, they're not the Chicago Symphony."

"But they are very good, or you wouldn't be here."

"How do you know that?"

"Well, you've come to a concert of Brahms Fourth. This is one of the great symphonies. In some way, it is powerful yet gives one some sense of serenity."

"I think you're overinterpreting. How do you know I don't come to every concert? Or maybe this is the first one in a year, just the luck of the draw. Or how do you know this isn't the first one I've ever come to?"

"From the way you said, 'These concerts are free.' Like you've been here before. My masculine intuition tells me you been here before."

"Your intuition is correct."

"How do you suppose they'd do if they charged ten bucks?"

"Not well, a portion of the main floor."

"Not a good value, or people are too cheap?"

"People are cheap."

Nick said, "Well, there are two ways to be rich. One is to have a lot of money, the other is make your money go a long way."

"I don't know too much about the former, but I've been known to put radioactive cobalt on a dollar to see where it went. It's value per dollar. That's what you have to look at. What I call the Squeeze Ratio."

"Very funny. I like that," he repeated her, "The Squeeze Ratio. Sounds about right."

"You have to squeeze the value out of every last dollar."

He laughed.

"Laugh if you like, but if we go out, you're paying."

Somehow, for a like-mind like this, he was willing to pay. But it would only be his favorite cheapie Mexican restaurant.

"And you can forget cheapie restaurants."

He laughed, "Okay, how about some reasonable Italian place?"

"What reasonable Italian place, exactly?"

And this was the small talk that led to their first date. And he needed someone to date. The thing with Ambrose would take a long time to work out. He was the mole. He was set in place and would have to wait for his opportunity. It could drag on for years.

Ecstasy

When I got back to Chicago from BA, I found we had lost the fourth floor of Tangier, the four stories of drinking and dancing where we had our tango in Chicago. Tangier used to be a candy factory years ago, and the smell of chocolate still scented the area some nights, coming from factories to the west which hadn't closed down yet.

We lost it because tango drinkers were not big drinkers, and drink paid for the place. But to be fair, it was difficult to drink heavily and do the intricate tango steps. First you become sloppy, and then next thing you're falling down. And human beings being human beings, many asked for tap water, for which there was no charge. Nothing was paid for the water, and no tip for the bartender. Yet many expressed surprise when we were shunted down to the second floor, so that owner could try a salsa band on the fourth floor. Salsa dancers were known to be big drinkers and big tippers.

On the second floor there were small windows overlooking the building across the alley. On the fourth floor there were tall windows looking out to the panorama facing east to the lake. For now, we were above the alley.

There was, in short, no comparison.

I accosted the bartender, Dave, "Hey, what happened while I was away?"

"When you figure the cost of lighting the place, the two security guys, you guys just do not buy enough to make it worthwhile. Hell, for the fifty bucks I make in tips, I'd rather come and drink with you."

"Yes, I knew it." I myself accounted for six of the fifty bucks. Two juices at three bucks (two for the bartender), and two drinks at six bucks each(four for the bartender). I didn't dance much at the end of the night, so it didn't matter if I drank or not.

"The cover charge for tango is only five bucks. On the weekends, it's twenty-five for guys, and twenty for ladies. And beer is six bucks, drinks are nine bucks."

"Wow, you guys make a fortune."

"My tips are four or five hundred bucks. It's not just the money, but some of the people here in tango are just plain rude."

"Oh, brother."

But I had heard the story before. No one in tango seemed to be bright enough to understand that a location like this was not a birthright, no matter how long we had been there. Egos needed to be massaged, and someone had to make a buck to make it work.

I said, "I noticed you were starting to sell bottled water before I left. In Buenos Aires, it's all bottled water. I would have thought you would have gone to that long ago."

"Actually, that's not it. We started selling the bottled water because of all the people taking Ecstasy."

"Ecstasy. Okay, I've heard of it. What's in it?"

"Crystal meth, heroin and LSD." Turns out that Dave had it wrong.

"My God."

"People on that stuff cannot drink anything else. Water is it. So I told Bob, 'Look, they're all going in the dark areas and taking Ecstasy. The only thing they can drink is water. So, let's get the bottled water.' Which he did."

"It seems like I am always off the money. I'm thinking, 'How can they make money on bottled water?' when really it's a matter of some drug making the rounds."

Dave laughs.

"So, tell me, Dave, have you tried this Ecstasy stuff?"

"What, do you think I'm nuts?"

This is Dave, the bragaholic who can drink me under the table easy. This is Dave, who is a thrill seeker on just about every level. Constantly telling me about women he's bent over by the windows after we've closed down. Dave, who is an air paramedic who swoops down out of thin air in a chopper to save people who've been sliced in half in a car accident. Dave, who married a woman connected to the mafia. Whose woman matches him infidelity for infidelity. We're talking about Dave who is the bartender in the hippest, most popular nightclub in Chicago. But he draws the line at Ecstasy?

"Dave, the thrill seeker, doesn't do Ecstasy?"

"Hey, the only ecstasy I want is the hormonal kind."

"So, Dave does draw lines?"

"You forget: I'm a paramedic. I've resuscitated some of these motherfuckers who take that stuff. I've seen heroin overdoses. Cocaine heart attacks. Come on, you think I was born yesterday?"

The Psychiatrist's Dream

"I had a dream last night."

Stephen, back in Chicago, back in his shink's office. This was her dream. Sophia's. It was this kind of thing that endeared her to him, even though it was probably just another ploy. Intimacy in exchange for customer loyalty.

"I dreamed that someone, maybe it vas you, brought a bag to me with a head in it. As I came closer, I saw that the head in the plastic bag vas my head. And it vas bleeding. And then I vas looking for a refrigerator, because I guess I hoped it could be put bagk on. So, I vas in this restaurant and I vent behind these panels and found a refrigerator, and I put the head inside."

"Your head."

"Right, my head. But somehow, in the dream, it doesn't seem like my head."

"I understand."

"Vhat do you tink it means?"

"I . . ."

"I know it reflects how busy I am that I'm always going this way and that way, like a chicken with its head cut off."

"You're picking up the idiom."

Her eyes flashed. Her head lifted. A compliment.

He continued, "You're dreaming in the idiom. Think how your English has improved."

"Is that idiom? Well, it just seems so appropriate that . . ."

"Well, at least it isn't a commercial for baggies."

"Maybe it was. I remember seeing the green that you get when both sides are locking."

Stephen laughed. "We can't help it. That's the society we're in. You see commercials, and then the next thing you know, you're humming their jingle, you're buying their product, and finally the product appears in your dreams. We're trapped."

"Yes, and I remember putting the head in the refrigerator, not the freezer. Because I knew if I put it in the freezer I would never be able to get it unfrozen without damage."

"You know there are snakes, I think they're red-lined garter snakes, something like that, which freeze in the artic regions, and unfreeze in the spring."

"That's interesting." But not to the point.

"I don't know if I have any particular insight which would be useful. I know that if I give it some thought I could probably come up with something interesting."

"Thanks."

He felt the sharing made him special among patients, but she tried the dream out on a few more people before the end of the day. And at the end of the day she tried it out on Nick, who said, "I was probably just picking up around your apartment, and found this head, and so I came to you and said, 'What do we do with this?'"

She laughed.

Nick continued, "I am no good at dream interpretation, that's your business."

Lunch at the Berghoff and a New Nomenclature

I met George for lunch at The Berghoff, a German restaurant on Adams which had been around for about a century. We were in the main room where sunny oak panels envelope you in their warmth. The ceiling was composed of undistinguished acoustic tiles which attempted, unsuccessfully, to damp down the chatter and clatter of humans and utensils.

The waiters wore the same black uniform and white smock that they always wore, though most of the waiters were Hispanic now. But this was a place where tradition outweighed all else; in short, they carried forward the gruff impatience of their German forbearers.

Blang! Bread and butter plopped in front of you.

"What do you want to drink?"

"Root beer."

And, "root beer." Poof, the waiter disappeared.

"It's too early for a stein of light. I'll never get any work done."

"Indeed."

"Well, George, the only solution as I see it . . ."

"Yes, yes. I'm waiting."

"The only solution to the population explosion is . . ."

"Yes, yes. Tell me."

"To eat humans."

He laughed.

"Look at the benefits. It reduces pollution, ozone depletion, and the decimation of the other species."

"I can see the ad campaign now: Save the Planet: Eat Humans."

"More to the point is: 'Stop Bad Thinking: Eat Humans.'"

"The New White Meat."

"Perfect."

"But I don't see it on the menu."

"Oh, that's because it's called Long Pig."

"Long Pig?"

"At least that's what the cannibals call it in Borneo."

"Ah."

I continued theoretically, "That's the thing about an idea. Intel gave the notion of cannibalism a boost when it brought on new semiconductors before the old ones had run their course. The bad thing about an idea is that it can spread, morph . . ."

"Witness another bad idea, fascism in the 1930s. It grew like wildfire in Europe and Asia. Almost got here, Republicans always felt FDR was a dictator."

"Another bad idea, the business franchise. I am sick of the spread of franchises: McDonald's, Wendy's, Burger King, Blockbuster Video, Citibank. Bringing ugly American banners to all parts of the globe. No wonder they all hate us."

"Cannibalism may yet become a Roman Coliseum-type event. We're not there yet, but the greater the population, the more dispensable humans become. I can see it now: Your son can be a gladiator, and win, not freedom this time, but financial freedom. A million bucks, two million bucks."

The waiter crisply placed the drinks in front of us. Pen to his pad, "What do you want?"

"Wiener schnitzel, creamed spinach."

"The same."

"Somebody jumped the gun on the nomenclature for Homo sapiens," I said.

"Homo sapiens sapiens. It was Carl Linnaeus, in the mid 1700s."

"I love it when people around me know stuff like that. So, that would be wise, wise man. But I still think they jumped the gun. That's the kind of name you might attach after the fact."

"So, don't keep me in suspense, what name would you assign?"

"Well, I think I might use a more descriptive name. Like man with a large head. That's descriptive."

"Homo capitus major. But what you really mean is large brain. Horses have bigger heads."

"I'm not sure that you could establish that modern day man, homo, has a bigger skull than Neanderthal, actually I think their's was larger, and they had more brain material."

"Well, it doesn't matter, I don't think the Romans had a word for brain, anyway. Head, yes. Brain, no."

"Right, and even brain may not be sufficiently descriptive. Whales and elephants have bigger brains. You would need to say the largest brain-to-body ratio."

"And the name is getting too long."

"Or how about: man who speaks."

"Homo loquor. But do we know for sure other species of homo didn't speak?"

"Well, they want us to believe the voice box was the problem, but have you heard the clicks the Bushmen make? I'm sure they made some kind of sounds, whether they got to language may fall on things we don't know about yet. Maybe the FOXP2 gene. I think we are best off with something even more neutral. Neanderthal was named for the river near where the first remains were found. I think they found really old remains of Homo sapiens at a river called Omo in Africa."

"Homo Omo."

"You took the words right out of my mouth. But something else I'm thinking. We don't want to go from the possibly inappropriate to the ridiculous."

"Well, they found 100,000 year old remains at a river in South Africa called Klasies."

"Homo Klasies. I think we've found our name."

*　　*　　*

from the journal of Stephen Ambrose

Martin Heidegger says the most thought-provoking thought in these thought-provoking times is that we are not yet thinking. If we are not yet thinking, what is it we are doing, and what is thinking? Herbert Simon of Carnegie-Mellon says that Deep Blue is thinking when it beats Kasparov. I'm not that clear. It is doing computing, that is for sure. And the current thinking of experts like Stephen Pinker is that this is what humans do. They compute. In the biz, they call it natural computing. But it is not doing what I would call awareness computing. It has no idea of its surroundings, where it is in the world. No idea if it is being threatened by the imminent removal of its electrical cord, and so on. But I suppose a subroutine could be set up to check the electrical cords, but could it develop analogies?

What does seem clear enough, is that specialized programs for various tasks, expert programs, like seeing and smelling, will be the key. My own experience with character recognition programs shows that this particular skill in computers has gotten better and better. It seems to me, as a program for vision develops, first a program may be run for faces, then one for things, then perhaps it converts everything to black and white, and does a quick character-recognition scan. All quite quickly. So, robots will improve step-by-step. Their programs will hear noises. Pick out words from voices. Pick out a language from the voices and so on. "You are speaking German, but I cannot make out that last word. Would you please say it again?" If that fails, then the computer will ask that it be spelled, what a human would do—because ultimately, computers, robots, androids are the sum of human ingenuity.

Programs will be developed to deal with speech, interpreting language, and on and on. It will necessarily be an ongoing progress. There will be Robot, beta version 1.0, and so on. Probably there will be common elements, cells, that can be used interchangeably. The human cortex seems to be pretty much the same throughout, allowing for the possibility of the blind to use more of it for hearing.

Will humans fall in love with robots? Some will, probably. Some have already fallen in love with their fuck dolls. The advantage of a fuck doll is that it doesn't present problems all over the place. *No static at all* . . . as rock group Steely Dan would put it. Unless of course that's your thing. Perri, the impossible fuck doll.

That's it: the sum of the sum of human ingenuity will be to perfect the android fuck doll.

The Follow-Up Date

The blond's name was Stephanie. And the Italian restaurant they ended up going to was a Lettuce Entertain You restaurant called Tucci Tuscana. Terrazzo floor, tall ceilings, simple furnishings.

"This is okay."

"Glad it meets with your approval." Nick.

"You will be."

Women could say such endearing things when they wanted to, and this was one of them. Foreplay already in the works.

"Why do you live so far out?"

"My job is out there."

There being Barrington, Illinois. Charming, monied suburb, far from the madding crowd.

"So exactly what is your job?"

"I'm an electronics engineer for Motorola."

"I see."

"What is that supposed to mean?"

"I guess I see electronics engineers as being nerdy guys with really thick glasses."

"I do wear thick glasses, when I wear glasses. Men seem to like the contacts better."

"Yes, you have lovely eyes."

"Well, behind fishbowl lenses you might not find them so lovely."

"Anyway, that explains why you live out there."

"So, what's on the menu?"

They spent a few minutes deciding what to have. She decided on a tomato-based pasta with seafood, and he had his usual, a carbonara. The house salad was a choice in common as was the wine, the house Chianti.

"Yes, I like the Chianti. It's not too dry."

"I agree. And the reds have iron, which I probably need."

"The red is the iron, you know."

"I'm in the sciences, remember, an engineer. But the value may be in the polyphenols. So what do you do?"

The problem with lies, or a second set of identities, is that you have to remember them all. Keep them straight. So, he told her part of the truth, which is easier, less problematical.

"I am an importer."

Also, an exporter.

"What do you import?"

"I import and distribute automobile parts for Korean automobiles."

"Are their cars any good?"

"Okay, I suppose. I don't drive one."

"That's a bad sign."

"Probably, but then they don't make a truly upscale car that I would want to buy, nor does America, for that matter. But there are all these global alliances now. Ford owns Volvo. GM owns Saab."

And this was how Nick saw the world. If there is only one world, what did it matter what secrets he sold to whom? The one hand of Vishnu passes a piece of paper to another hand of Vishnu. And he hardly felt like a thief. It was a matter of perspective.

Loyalty, in the old feudal sense, was under the gun. Women in Chicago who grew up with Marshall Field's, so intensely loyal many of them ended up working at the store somewhere along the line—out of school, in between marriages. After the turn of the century there would be no more Marshall Field's. Federated Department Stores decided to extend the Macy's brand. And with that, loyalties were up for grabs, many upscale shoppers switched to Costco.

Secrets were also in trouble. With the Internet, information was out there if you could figure out how to find it.

"I like it better when a man owns what he sells."

"It certainly makes selling easier."

"It makes it easier to sell because he believes in what he is selling, and that probably means it is a better product."

"I can agree with that."

He could hardly explain that the South Korean government, a friendly government, had set him up with one of its big carmakers to front for his activities and pay for his services.

Accidents

Accidents. It was an accident. No, it was a fortuity. Cross that. It was a fateful event that Nick met Stephen in the first place. They were sitting at an outdoor cafe on Rush Street at adjacent tables with chairs nearly next to each other when they both spied a stunning woman, all but whistling after her. They smiled at each other and Stephen said, "Do you suppose if all women were genetically engineered, let's say cloned to look like her, she would still have the same appeal?"

Nick, who had often tired of a particular beautiful woman, said, "Variety is critical. Wasn't it Kennedy who promoted 'diversity'? What did he say? 'If we cannot now end our differences, at least we can help make the world safe for diversity.' Of course, who knew then what he was talking about when he said 'diversity'?"

"Indeed."

"Beyond Fiddle and Faddle, and Gene Tierney, and Judith Exner, Jackie and Marilyn, there was a cast of hundreds."

"Joe was a great pursuer of women, so he passed the genes to his kid. So, was JFK great with the women because of the genes, or was it because of the model Joe established for him?"

"Isn't this always the question? You're leaning toward genetics, I take it."

"Have you seen the work with twins?"

"Only on television."

"It's really spooky. You see two women, separated at birth, they both ended up gigglers, both in the same career, maybe working for the same company. You start to think of the body as just an empty shell carrying out the instructions of a trillion-line program. There's your free will, it's just bumper cars. Your program, your bumper car, is fixed. In effect, your hands are off the wheel, the program makes it go this way and that. You run into other cars, and you think it's your decision."

"How many drinks have you had? I haven't heard this much bullshit since I was at college. Since whoever it was who wrote the *Consolation of Philosophy.*"

"Boethius."

"Maybe that's all it is, is consolation. You don't get the girl, you get consolation. Are you a teacher, professor? I want the girl and the consolation. I want it all."

"No, not a professor. Programmer. I couldn't get the girl myself, but I wrote the billion-line program that does get the girl."

"Is there some girl in particular you didn't get?"

"Not exactly."

"I don't know what that means, 'not exactly.'"

"To get her, or not get her, there has to be a point of attempt."

"I see. No attempt. So, what do you program?"

"Stuff for the government."

"What kind of stuff?"

"GAO. Government Accounting Office stuff. What do you do?"

"Wholesale parts for automobiles."

Silence as they watch the passing parade.

Nick inquired, "What does the no-point-of-attempt woman do?"

"Psychiatrist."

"Psychiatrist? How did you happen to come to know a psychiatrist?"

"I'm her patient."

"Oh, transference."

"Yes, well, there you are."

"The problem with going to a psychiatrist is that already you're in an inferior position. You're going to her. She's in the superior role. The control role. How is a man supposed to feel like he's in control when she's in the catbird seat? Bad for sex."

Why the Psychiatrist's Patients Never Get Well

Fast forward to: "You're an idiot if you think you'll ever connect with that shrink." Nick.

"Stop, now you sound like my brother," said Stephen. "Why?"

"You're her meal ticket. People like that know that if they convert the customer, the client, the patient, into a lover, they're going to be out a client, and that much less money for the coffers. And, you know, the patient they convert leaves them in the end anyway."

"That also sounds like my brother. Follow the money. But you forget, she wanted to throw me over because the PPO would not approve."

"That still sounds like another money decision, doesn't it? I know you're thinking: if you can just get her to break through that doctor-client barrier, you'll get an even greater ego boost." Also sounding like Abner.

"Probably. That must be it."

"Odds don't favor it. She's got her Mercedes to pay for."

"How did you know she had a Mercedes?"

"You told me. Don't you remember? You saw her come into the lot and park her 560SL, and your remark was that she probably loved the car more than her man."

"Oh, yes. I remember."

"So, she has car payments." More Abner.

"Maybe. But a lot of those immigrant women save their money. She might have paid cash."

"Well, then it's the next thing she wants to buy. Some expensive condo overlooking Lake Michigan."

"Yes, of course."

"Forget her. Focus on somebody else." Nick loved this. He knew the advice was spot-on, but he also knew that Stephen would do nothing about it, that he would go right on lusting after the girl who lusted after the Mercedes.

He wanted to tell him: forget it. The girl isn't that hot in bed. Being great in bed requires practice just like everything else, and she's always in the office. This girl spent her life in front of a mirror. So, the best part of her is looking at her, which anyone within eyeshot can do.

"You might get her, and find out she's not that hot. Happens to me a lot."

"Maybe I'm not that hot. Maybe we would be great not-hot partners together."

"Okay, I hadn't thought of that."

"So there."

"Nah. No. You almost got me. I think the hormones themselves crave something hot. I don't know if there is such a thing as lukewarm sex."

"Well, nearly got you."

Stephen and the Ladybug

In December, in January, maybe he day-dreamed about the Dutch girl, but the only company Stephen had was a ladybug. He would knock off a couple of keystrokes, and then suddenly the ladybug would come to life flying from the overhead fan to the bookshelf. He knew nothing about ladybugs. He couldn't imagine what it could possibly be living on. The beauty of ladybugs was that they didn't buzz around like mosquitoes, demanding your attention. A ladybug might sit in one place all evening. Perhaps crawl around. Every so often, and not really that often, the ladybug might fly to a new locale. Live and let live. I'll write my science fiction here, you investigate that part of the room over there.

The ladybug and his euphorbia were the perfect company for a writer. The euphorbia was an upright desert dweller that also required little attention. If Stephen had been a creature who needed to give something a lot of attention, the ladybug and the euphorbia would have been the wrong companions.

The ladybug seemed to be well-adapted. It walked along a surface, then it met a wall. No problem, it walks along the perpendicular, it meets another obstacle, the ceiling. No problem again, it walks along the ceiling. Perhaps next time around it will be an insect that develops the large brain. If it's the long back that's critical, then maybe it will be a descendant of the centipede.

*   *   *

from the journal of Stephen Ambrose

The brain is an adaptation to its environment. The senses develop to allow the brain to figure out its environment. First, touch develops as a tool for sensing the immediate environment next to your body. Taste and smell. Then vision and hearing develop to scout out the environment beyond what you can feel next to your body unit.

Perhaps the paranormals are on the right track. That the next way we will scout out the environment will be to read the thoughts of the person next to us. Maybe as an extension of hearing. It is an interesting thing how the two bones hinged together that are the arches or support for the gills in fish become the tiny, angelic bones of the inner ear. Primates in the jungle canopy feed at night, hence the need to distinguish among various smells. And this is how the smell brain became the cerebral cortex. That was one thought, consciousness came in through the nose, a heightened sense of smell, hence the expressions: Wake up and smell the coffee. Wake up and smell the Buddha.

Perhaps we will smell the thoughts of the person next to us.

After all, if dogs can be trained to smell cancer, then it seems possible that a person might be able to "smell" someone else's thoughts. Or "hear" them, or "sense" them.

Schipol

Looking for a place to sit at Schipol, Stephen spotted Sophia. There was at once apprehension and happiness in seeing a familiar face. Apprehension because psychiatrists were always at pains to maintain boundaries with patients. And nothing makes patients feel more like patients than boundaries.

Stephen had come to check out the best tango in Europe. He planned to start in Amsterdam, then go on to Berlin and Paris. That was the idea. He realized at once this was an opportunity to meet Sophia outside the limits of their circumscribed territory. He sat next to her.

"I knew you were going on holiday, but I didn't know you were going to Europe. I didn't see you on the plane."

"Yes, the best deal to Greece when I called my travel agent was through KLM, so it's a stopover for me. I used my flight miles to upgrade to business class. And you?"

"This is my final destination. But it always takes longer than you think for the luggage to come through. People rush like crazy to get to the baggage claim area, and all that happens is that they end up waiting and waiting. Then finally they turn on the ramp. They turn on the ramp and nothing comes through."

"What?"

"Well, eventually, you get your luggage."

Sophia was dressed to the nines. A deep red cashmere sweater, royal red, which nicely emphasized her bosom, and black velvet pants. A gold necklace with onyx and rubies, and a wide gold bracelet on her right arm. If she had just been traveling for hours in a plane, no one could tell. The hair was perfect. This was one girl who understood presentation.

"Very nice outfit."

"Tank you, Stephen. I'm jet lagging so baddly."

"Are you staying in Athens?"

"No, I have a friend in Voliagmeni, just outside of Athens, and vee vill stay dare for a few days. And den I vant to go to some of the islands."

"Vich vunns do you plan on seeingk?"

"Are you making fun of me? Mykonos and Santorini, maybe a few others. We'll see."

"Mykonos is very nice."

"You've been there?"

"Yes. It has everything. Beaches, restaurants, shopping."

"Shopping. Vhat shopping?"

"Practically everything. Clothes, Cartier."

"Cartier? Really."

"Well, they have to be ready for those impulse purchases."

"Impulse. I don't know about impulse. But tink about dis: I verk almost every day from sun up to sun down. I hardly have two minutes to put together to go shopping."

"And spend all your hard-earned money." The booty from psychiatry.

"Well, it's fun once a vhile."

"Once in a while."

"Tank you. And clothes. Dare are places to shop for clothes?"

"Many, many."

Life was a trick. Sophia was such a good-looking woman that she would never lack for male attention, but because of her eastern European, egocentric, overcoming-poverty background, she would always have a difficult time with the men. If she were one of those self-effacing, oozing-with-charm-and-compliments southern women, she would have a lot more fun. But she wasn't from the South, and her mother did not allow her to socialize as a kid. She never learned to pout.

"Don't you like to go to the beach?"

"Of course. I will need to buy a bathing suit."

The *leitmotif*, shopping.

"Well, I might as well check for my luggage. It is probably up by now. Yours is checked through to Athens, no doubt."

"Yes."

Where friends would kiss, they merely shook hands.

* * *

The chance meeting with Dr. Petrosian shook Stephen up. That was for sure. He didn't know why, but ten steps after leaving her his eyes watered-up and his nose started running. No full-blown crying jag hit him, but he was completely shaken.

Perhaps it was inevitable that Stephen, who paid for massages and psychiatrists and hairstylists, would end up paying for sex as well. And if that was the case, it would surely happen in Amsterdam.

In Amsterdam, where everything is bright and clean and clear as day. Where life is transparent, and everyone can see everything in everyone else's apartment, where men and women hose down the sidewalk in the morning. And where you can see the girls behind their storefront windows. Truth in advertising.

It was the meeting with Sophia that did it. He knew nothing would ever, ever, ever come of that. That, and the ease and proximity of sexual release in the red-light district.

But perhaps it was no surprise that he came to this realization in Amsterdam, the city where the mean IQ of 109 is the highest in the world. He read that somewhere. Then he thought, "Probably the hookers have an IQ higher than mine." Scratch that, he knew the hookers had higher IQs.

Lonesome, feeling like an idiot most of the time. Having to pay everyone for everything. No woman showing him any special interest, who might have said, "Really, you write the software for Patriot missiles?"

"And cruise missiles."

None of that ever, ever happened. For the obvious reason—no one knew what he was working on. If the Gulf War hadn't come along, even Stephen might have thought he'd been playing solitaire for ten years.

Lying in bed in his hotel, he was perked up by the idea of being with a beautiful woman, and he could do this with just the exchange of money. So he did.

He spied an attractive brunette in one of the storefronts. Attractive, but not threateningly so. If he gave it any thought, he would have said that she was ideal for the business. The girl knew French, English, German, but this was nothing special. Most of the hookers knew three or four languages including their native Dutch. This would be the argument that most of us aren't using our brains very much. That with our ten billion neurons and one hundred trillion connections/synapses, we could do a great deal more.

*   *   *

The second time Stephen headed out to the red-light district, he turned a corner and lo and behold—right there in the window was Anna! Anna from Buenos Aires, from Gricel. Wait wait wait. Anna was a hooker? Wait, wait. He ducked back behind the corner. He instantly turned cold and clammy. He needed time to assimilate this. Yes, it was all very well that tango originated in the brothels, but he didn't really expect that he would have to live up to that. That was the origin of the dance, but this was his life; what did he have to do with prostitutes? He went back to his room.

In his room he lay in his bed and rolled it around in his mind. He didn't want her to be a hooker. No, he didn't like that at all. This wasn't in his game plan. He was rather middle class about such things in the end.

He felt he was back in Buenos Aires, where his emotions seemed to rise and fall like a roller coaster.

But she was enormously attractive. He whittled down his own resistance. Meet her there, or meet her at the milongas. Try the milongas first, he thought. That would be best. But if it turned out there was no romantic possibility, he could at least treat himself to sex with her.

As it was, she didn't turn up that night or the next. It would have been so much better to meet her at the milongas where the fantasy of falling in love could play out (as opposed to the reality of paying for sex and company). But anxiety got the better of him. He would only be there a week, and three days were gone before he knew it.

The next afternoon he showed up in front of her window. She was stunning, even more beautiful than Sophia. She recognized him and she went to her door, and so did he.

"How nice to see you again!"

"I thought I might see you at the milongas, but . . ."

"Oh, sometimes I don't go for weeks."

"Ah. I should have known someone as beautiful as you would be in this business."

"You hoped for something else?"

"Well, yes."

"What is it they say? I think I saw it in movie . . . a plan is a list of things that never happen. Hope, I think, is a bunch of plans. Here we are. You are in my part of town not by accident I imagine."

"Yes, you are right."

"And you find me attractive?"

"Oh yes, very."

"Then I charge one hundred gilders for an hour. We will have a good time."

It was sweet that she would say "we." He sighed and pulled the money from his pockets, and gave her the bills. Not taking her eyes off his eyes, she put the bills in a drawer.

"Don't be sad. We will have a good time. You will see."

She came up to him, and gave him a very sensual kiss. First just on the lips, then plunging her tongue down his throat, which he sucked on. He was quickly transported. "It isn't fair that she can do this to me," he thought before he went under the anesthetic . . .

She took command and he was happy enough to let it happen. But when she slurped long enough on his lollypop, she fell back and said, "Get on top, please."

It wasn't that long before they were at it a second time and the time ran a little over an hour. He was happy to pay more but didn't want to sink back into money. Really, he liked her. Just as good in the sack as the dancing had prepared him for.

"You will come to the milonga?"

"Yes, sure."

"I wanted to ask you . . ."

"At the milonga, ask me there."

Time is money, and she needed to get back to work.

*   *   *

from the journal of Stephen Ambrose

Man develops a machine life form. It can reproduce itself through manufacturing, so it is not exactly like organic life, but has continuation. The machine-being, in its own pursuit of perfection, finds the adaptability of man interesting, and breeds humans for larger and larger brains to see what happens.

"You humans are silly. You have too many variables in your mate selection. Breast size, facial symmetry, ass shape, waist-to-hip ratios, penis size, pectorals, money, resources, resourcefulness, ability to dance and make conversation, and so on. We will breed you more appropriately for brains."

By this time, they don't need a female to carry the baby. They have machines for the whole thing. So, they can conduct their experiments unfettered by irrational human concerns.

The machines felt the organic, carbon model had not been exhausted.

*   *   *

Anna did come to the milonga, and Stephen monopolized her. He danced with her all night. She honored a few requests from other dancers, but mostly she kept him company. He didn't know why, maybe she liked the attention. He canceled the rest of the trip. He would have to check out Paris and Berlin some other time. It would give him two more weeks in Amsterdam.

He met her at her window every day to continue the great sex, and on the last day of the trip, she brought him back to her apartment after the milonga. This is the treatment you get for being a regular. A psychiatrist shares one of her dreams with you, and a hooker brings you back to the apartment where she really lives. Her place was, he thought, surprisingly homey. Sex was just a job? Her place was sparse and very Dutch, he thought, as though Vermeer had just left five minutes ago.

Science Fiction

―――――――――――

"David Cornwell, his circus mirror image George Smiley, whose stand-in Mr. Standfast, AKA Mr. Barraclough, that is, his literary doppelganger, John LeCarré, claimed in an interview on C-SPAN, that reading his Smiley novels now seemed like history more than anything else." Nick.

"You had fun with that, but I see your point. Everything becomes history ultimately. You must have worked on that for a week."

"Think of da Vinci. We still love to look at his ideas about future weapons. His notion of the machine gun, his notion of the tank and helicopter. Interesting history."

"Yeah, but nobody ever built them. Nobody ever used them. He was kind of a genius crackpot. It's a bad idea to be more than fifteen minutes ahead of your time. I'd like to see the figures on how well first editions of H.G. Wells's *War of the Worlds* are doing. Not well, I'll bet."

"Might be doing very well."

"You think? I don't think so. These books always fall on one or two notions. That book fell on the notion that Percival Lowell thought that lines he saw on Mars were canals. And if there are canals, then there must be intelligent life which made the canals. And if there is intelligent life, then that intelligent life might come to Earth," said Stephen.

"That's the proposition."

"Proposition, supposition, hypothesis, whatever. Crichton's book about the dinosaurs . . . Somerset Maugham once asked one of H.G. Wells's lovers why she was so attracted to a fat, undesirable little man."

"And?"

"She said he smelled like honey."

―――

"Uh-huh. What was it you were going to say about Crichton?"

"His book about dinosaurs falls on two notions. One, that you can get dinosaur DNA from a mosquito who sucked it off one of them, which then got stuck in tree sap, which crystallized into amber. Two, you can piece it together, splice it, maybe borrow some DNA from amphibians, and clone it. And three, make a fun park out of it. One two three. Bing bang bong."

"Yes, and Crichton pays attention to Aristotle. The unities. It doesn't happen in one day, but the drama usually happens in a short time, like a week."

"For a popular writer, I think he's very good. In fact, I think he could be a real writer if he set his mind to it. He does say important things about our society, which I feel writers should do. Lawyers, the problems with the Japanese, cover-ups, power and sexual abuse, and the scary stuff that science can come with when left to its own devices. But somehow, his plots require characters that end up being little more than chess pieces."

"Chess pieces? Don't you think you're being a little hard?"

"No. I like his chess pieces, but look at a novel by Saul Bellow, say *Humboldt's Gift*, and you'll see the difference. Or have you ever read Crichton's book *Travels*? That's the real thing."

"Yes, I have. Because I travel a lot I was intrigued by the title when I came across it. Loved the stuff at Harvard. The girl who came on to him."

"How is it that there is so little surprise, Nick, in learning that you know about the patient-slash-slut? Naturally, the girl who comes on to him is the girl who is out to lunch. I suppose that is one of those rules of life. Irony. If things are going your way, then you are just about to be knocked off in a traffic accident."

"I always liked his plots. Nearly always read them straight through."

"It's just the hand moving the pieces."

"Right. I envied his having two girls at once."

"Envied?" Stephen found that hard to believe.

"Enjoyed."

"Here's the thing. If plot is the main driver, then the characters are subordinate, stick figures. But if you base your characters on people you know, and Bellow has taken a lot of hits on that, doing portraits of friends of his, then your characters have endless depth, because the people you base them on have relatives and aspirations and girlfriends and houses out in the boondocks of New Jersey, and, well, you get the idea."

"So, that's why you like Crichton's book *Travels*. Because it's the real deal."

"Exactly. I'm not saying Crichton doesn't use snippets of people he knows, too, but Bellow is a full-fledged portrait artist. Plus you get interesting intellectual stuff, too. I love the Steiner stuff, the theosophy." He paused for a second, signaling a change of subject. "Would you ever marry a hooker?"

Practically choking, Nick said, "Would I ever marry anyone? First things first."

"Okay."

"It's hard to imagine I would marry anyone."

"Let's suppose you would. Now, what do you think?"

The question in Nick's mind was what to reveal. How distantly to answer the question. Should he reveal how he feels about Miranda? Compare Miranda and Stephanie? Or should he answer the question theoretically?

"Well, I have always liked hookers. There is a kind of honesty in charging as you go along. Like that program in Congress, PAYGO."

"Instead of, say, gambling on hooking the rich guy, and getting the big payday on the other end. You know, the divorce settlement."

"Well put, Stephen. And I like the pun on hooking. It's beyond you."

*　　*　　*

In a phone conversation, he quizzed Anna about her friends. "Any of your friends ever marry?"

"You mean: any of my hooker friends?"

"Yeah, that's what I meant."

"Of course, sometimes men can't help themselves."

"How do those marriages work out?"

"Not particularly well, but then, marriage isn't doing that well these days in any case, is it?"

"No."

"Your parents still married?"

"No. Are yours?"

"No."

Incalcs

I ask George, "Are accidents accidents? Here's why I ask: IF the orbits of all the planets and all the asteroids and all the comets are known, THEN we can calculate when all collisions will occur. It is simply a matter of computation."

"So accidents in space are just a matter of not doing your homework."

"Exactly. There are never any accidents."

"And so we should be able to figure out if some comet is going to hit the planet."

"Never mind that there are possibly millions of these objects in the solar system. Maybe billions if you count all the smaller objects. Maybe trillions, maybe zillions."

George said, "One at a time. One at a time. Find them and log them in."

There's a German for you.

"Yes, and getting the orbits right on objects the size of a quarter. And the effects of gravity on the orbits. So, my point is that there are never any accidents, just incalculables. Our vocabulary is short. We need a new word for accidents, something like incalcs, for an incalculable occurrence. Accident implies randomness. It's not randomness anymore, that's old-think, it's just that the complexities of computation make collisions appear random."

"Right. I should go to my insurance agency and tell them I had an incalc with my car."

"Okay, probably true random events occur. That's what quantum mechanics seems to tell us."

"Your point being that our lunch together is not an accident, or is it?"

"No accident. That would be a microcalc. A small event, which we both knew about. Anyway, I am off my intended subject." He paused and said, "Off my trajectory."

"Regroup, reconnoiter."

"Okay, I'm watching *Discovery* or some damn program last night, and I'm wondering, how does a Bonobo monkey know it needs the largest testicles in the primate family to assure the continuation of his genes? The evolutionists would have you believe it was a random process of mutation and natural selection. Mutations occur. I'm not saying mutations don't occur. They do. And the current theory, punctuated equilibrium, suggests that changes occur quickly in batches than in some slow, hit-or-miss way."

George says, "So, you don't think it's an accident."

"Are you making fun of me?" Stephen said with a facetious grin. "Yes, I wonder, and this is just out-and-out speculation, if there isn't some informing mechanism. I'm not an intelligent design guy, but perhaps there is some way our filled-out forms, our bodies, let the genes know that something needs to be altered. For example, there was a scientist who observed, in the Galapagos, I believe, that the beaks of finches changed size and form if the weather changed for a persistent length of time. I think that's going to turn out to be an epigenetic thing. Apparently, you can turn on and turn off genes by putting a methyl group or some such on top of a gene. Amazing really."

George said, "Wait. We have genes, gene mutation, and now on-and-off switches?"

"The on-and-off switches, the so-called epigenome, were there all along, we just didn't know about them."

"Adding a layer of complexity on top of the whole thing."

"Indeed. And apparently they can do stuff with them. Apparently, drugs, B-12, folic acid, and other stuff can affect these methyl groups. Which means that if some gene has gone bad and is causing cancer, maybe we'll be able to shut it off."

"Wow."

"But epigenes are only a good explanation as long as the gene is already there. And maybe it's all mutation and on-and-off switches, but I'm still wondering about this because the braincase of the advancing primates goes from 450 cc's to Homo sapiens 1,350 cc's in a mere three million years. The time it takes to get a good tan in the cosmic scheme. It begs the possibility of an informing mechanism."

"Maybe, but maybe it's just some eras have more solar flares, and more mutations."

"There's a thought. Yeah, I could swing that way, too. Maybe when the magnetosphere weakens, and solar flares spike, a lot more X-rays or whatever get through . . . then one would expect that besides humans there would be a lot of mutations in other species in that same three-million-year period. I wonder if that is true."

"Boy, are you wishy-washy today."

"Nah, I'm with Darwin, he still provides the best explanation, but you have to keep your mind open to all possibilities; otherwise, we're still using air, earth, fire, and water to explain everything. Whatever it is."

* * *

"Hey, you shouldn't worry about science fiction. I went to a used bookshop today and saw a Jules Verne on sale for $500." Nick.

"First edition?"

"First edition."

"How does that compare with a Mark Twain first?"

"Less, I suppose. But then, how does Jules Verne compare with Mark Twain?"

"Touché."

"The point is: science fiction holds up over time."

"Maybe. But collectors will collect anything."

"You're really negative."

"Well, you know, I don't want to get my hopes up."

"Ah. The problem of hope."

"Expectations really screw you up. I remember once I wanted a C so much in French that when I got my grades, I saw a C initially. Then, a second later, I saw the D."

"That really happened to you?"

"Really did. I looked and looked at that report card. I was sure that C had slipped away somehow."

"The Transformers do report cards. Here, Jimmy, turn that F into an A."

"What was it O'Neill said, 'hope . . .' I can't remember, but T.S. Eliot wrote, 'hope would be hope for the wrong thing.'"

"Well, those guys remind me of dried fruit. Shriveled up and miserable. You ever seen any pictures of O'Neill or Eliot? There's an argument to stay away from great literature. Although O'Neill is arguably a good-looking man. But I prefer the picture of Elmore Leonard. Now, he looks like he's having fun."

Family

"Really, our father is . . . kind of . . ." said sister Aimee. Youngest sister. The baby of the family, and bearing a smaller frame.

"Kind of what?"

"Well, not interested in us."

"I wouldn't say that."

"We're in the same town and he hardly ever visits."

"Times have changed. Koffeeklatsch is gone. There are no corner restaurants with wonderful bakery goods, and the smell of coffee drawing you in, and everyone living five minutes away. Did I ever tell you my Brookfield Zoo docent story? By the way, speaking of the smell of coffee, did I tell you I read it is the smell brain from which all our higher brain functions developed?"

"How do you ever come with stuff like that?"

"Actually, I think that book is old by now. Oh well, you know I read a lot. Television, wherever I can pick up something interesting. Also, I'm tall, maybe I have some neurons that are longer than normal neurons, and they make all kinds of unusual connections. It might be physiological."

"Stop."

"Okay."

"Back to your original point, brother dear."

"Did I already tell you my Brookfield Zoo story? Sometimes it seems like I only know about five things, and I tell everyone these same five things over and over again because I can never remember who I told what."

"You're funny."

"I was at the then-new primate house, and I'm thinking. 'Well, what do I have? Selfish parents, selfish siblings, selfish friends.'"

"That's for sure. All of 'em."

"And me, too. No sense leaving myself off the list."

"Fair enough."

"But maybe we're all like that, built into the genes. Dawkins wrote a book called *The Selfish Gene*."

She laughed, "Do you ever get to the point? No one makes more detours than you."

"Maybe we're meant to be that way. It's an evolved thing. We need to keep shifting our focus to keep an eye out for predators, some lion in the brush of the Serengeti. Attention deficit disorder is built-in, genetically. There is no cure for it. We're meant to be distracted."

"My God. Stop. I'm going to be your predator."

"Okay, okay. So, I'm in the primate house, and I'm watching these two monkeys with a baby monkey."

"Hmm-hmm."

"And so I remark to the docent. 'So, is that a family?' And she says, 'No, that's two females and a baby.'"

"Right."

"So I ask, because I'm thinking of Dad, 'Is the male ever interested in the babies?' And she says, 'Occasionally, they show an interest.'"

She laughed.

"Think about it. How far along are we as a species? The male tiger does a hit-and-run and he's never heard from again. The polar bear does a hit-and-run, and if he happens upon the kids later, they're lunch. You're crying for attention, just thank your lucky stars you're not a baby polar bear."

"I see. So, the male monkeys are kind of interested, and the females are very interested, but if they're human, they go wacko after fifty."

"Women really seem to have trouble with hormones after fifty. The hormones drop out of balance, and I guess the shots or patches or whatever they're using don't work. Is that it? Or were there too many hysterectomies, and that screwed up the hormone balance? An unforeseen consequence. Abner would love that, him and his unforeseen consequences."

"Who knows? I hope it's possible to go through menopause and still be sane; otherwise, I'm going to shoot myself."

"Don't commit so soon."

"Well, I still have a few years, maybe they'll come up with something."

"Let me ask you a question: I have a friend who's dating a hooker, and he's thinking of marrying her. What do you think of such a thing?"

"Have to know the girl."

"Not enough data."

"Why did she become a hooker? Where is she headed?"

"Right. What's her trajectory? I suppose that's the best approach, case by case."

"I think so." But it was not any help.

"Listen, I have to go. The plumber is here."

"What's the problem?"

"Sump pump failed during the last storm. Water backup."

"Oh?"

"Yeah, from what I hear it's all the dog owners. You know how they wrap up the dog poop with the plastic baggies?"

"Yes."

"Well, they flush them down the toilet and they become like a cement wall in the street sewers. Water can't flow, so . . ."

"It backs up into your house."

"You got it. Gotta go."

Attraction and the Loss of Control

The problem with Anna was simply that he was so attracted to her. She seemed so honest, but if they got closer, when would the honesty end? To be attracted strongly to someone is to lose control. There is a thrill in the loss of control. But ultimately we don't like to lose control, so we often sabotage relationships. Once the relationship is botched, control returns to the default setting, the factory setting. But then you're alone again.

So, in order for the thing to work, he would have to overcome the natural tendency to deep-six the relationship. This was a tall order. Even for the most attractive woman he had ever been with. Here was the problem:

He ran through the scenarios, and he couldn't come up with a single scenario where Anna did not resume being a hooker. It didn't matter that he felt all women were to some extent hookers (exchanging sexual favors for barter tokens). And when he thought it over, men were all a little like Jack Lemmon in *Irma La Douce*. They will do anything to herd their harems, even if it's only one female. As economist Stephen Frank would have it, if she's an attractive woman, what's to prevent her from moving on? Or Ambrose, if he found a woman just a little more attractive, knew just one more language.

As Frank would have it, marriage is like a lease. The owner makes a bargain with the tenant. The tenant may not be the best tenant in the world, but waiting for the best tenant may take forever. Same goes for the tenant. He might be able to find a better apartment. So, they strike a deal.

These days, the deals are more temporary. Everyone gets bored. Lack of necessity puts the apartment model of marriage in jeopardy. It's more like a hotel model. A man no longer needs sons to help him farm. And a wife's services can be bought piecemeal. Merry Maids can clean the apartment, Chinese food can be ordered in (or one can go to a restaurant), dirty shirts go to the cleaners in any case, sex can be got over the Internet, one can get a hug dancing the tango in the close embrace milonguero style, you can get a shrink for company and advice, and on and on. Same for the woman: she can get a man's services piece by piece if she looks.

So, marriages end when one partner decides to move on. Why bother to find a matching partner at all? What would be the future of marriage, when people live really long lives? Aliens are seldom presented by science fiction writers as having partners. There are single aliens, groups of aliens, but partnered, married aliens, almost never.

*   *   *

Nevertheless, he wanted desperately to talk to someone about Anna. The situation was so completely fraught with peril. How can one fall in love with someone who is all the time making love to others? No wonder Hollywood marriages never worked. *Honey, I know I was kissing the most handsome man in the world all day, but we were just trying to get the best take.*

Who would believe such a story? Both Mariette Hartley and Sally Fields admitted to being knocked over by smooches from Jim Garner.

On the other hand, fetishes are everywhere now; there are men who will only get involved with women who are married to other men. It's the only way he can get off. The Graham Greene syndrome.

He thought: She says she will leave the business, but she is eminently suited to it. She is an Aries with Venus in Aquarius, a free spirit. She will never want to be bound to a marriage, that's the worst bondage of all. She will tire of it. I will tire of it. We will both tire of it. Then we'll get divorced and she'll get all my loot, whatever I have. Eddie Murphy's best line, "Eddie, I want half." And she has a body that won't quit, that I cannot possibly satisfy enough. It's impossible.

Stephen was engaged in a civil war of the highest magnitude, an internal civil war. Was there such a thing as a brainstorm? Can one live with such extreme feelings? On the one hand, the girl of his dreams was, on the other hand, the girl of everyone else's dreams, too. Love seemed to be intimately connected with jealousy.

He felt he was burning out in this jealousy. A missile with explosive fuel burning, burning. Finally you reach outer space where there is no gravity. No feeling maybe. That's what happens.

* * *

This is hell. Even though I am attracted to this adorable sexy woman, I have to deal with this ancient brain. How will one feel about android fuck dolls? Will they only have cachet when they are new and rare and expensive and while possession is still important?

Of course I gave my view on androids to Anna. Long distance, into the mouthpiece. And she said, "We are all just fuck dolls to you men."

"Then all men are what to women?"

"Accessories."

I laughed. "Of course. Come on, really. What will women want out of an android?"

"Women will want something like what the man wants."

"A fuck doll."

"A dildo. When we're lucky . . ."

He cut her off, "Oh brother. Stop, I can't bear to hear. But wouldn't you want a man with drive and ambition, with charm and intelligence? Wouldn't you feel cheated with an android?"

"Wouldn't you feel cheated with a female android?"

"I'm not clear about that. There are stories and stories about men and their hormones. Like the two men who renounce women and move to the farthest regions of Alaska to mine gold. They go to the outpost and buy goods for a year. The owner of the general store stacks it all up, and on top of it he puts a board with a hole lined with fur. They say, 'What's that for?' The storeowner says, 'A year is a long time.' Next year, only one man shows up to buy provisions. The store owner asks, 'Weren't there two of you last year?' And the man says, 'Yes there were, but there was only one board.'"

She laughs, "I see your point, but women aren't exactly getting a man with drive and determination when they use a vibrator. Or are they?"

"You're wicked."

"Oh?"

"But it's like everything, you have put it into perspective. Evil is a spectrum disorder. I think that's what we get from Dante."

"And I'm not very evil, right?"

* * *

251

Nick hated driving out to Barrington to see Stephanie. It was a hell of a long way to go. And testimony to the youth of his hormones that an attractive female was still sufficient stimulus to make him endure traffic and an hour's wait.

He drove out in his old Jaguar XKE. Red. He only drove it on beautiful, perfect summer days. In the winter it sometimes failed to start.

She asked, "How much did you pay for that car?"

"Not that much. Didn't buy it new."

"Oh really."

"You don't approve. I should have bought it new, right?"

"Cars are all parts. New cars have new parts, and won't break down as quickly. On the other hand, a huge amount of the value of the car is gone in the first three years."

"True."

"And many cars come now with seven-year or ten-year warranties. I think a good three-year-old car with an extended warranty on it could be a very good deal. No fat on that."

"How is it women are grocery-store buyers no matter where they are? I don't like that steak, the butcher left on too much fat."

"It's just a matter of being efficient." With that, she put her hand on his crotch.

"Right."

"It's just a matter of getting to the root of things." Hand moving up and down a now-hardening cock. The girl was efficient. You had to admire her economy of movement.

"It's just a matter of getting things in hand." Zipper, swoosh. Unhook the pants. Over the top of the drawers. "Don't you agree?"

"Hard to disagree."

She laughed. "Hard, anyway."

He had his hands on her ass, kissing her ear. "You're good."

"I think this thing needs mouth-to-cock resuscitation."

"Actually, it doesn't exactly need resuscitation."

"Okay, then we'll forget it."

"Okay okay okay. You're right. It needs . . . whatever it was you were talking about."

"Mouth-to-cock resuscitation." There was something very efficient and direct and sexy about her. She was modest most of the time, but then she could be disarmingly direct. Sexual chiaroscuro. Light and dark. Modest, modest, and then whorish.

Meanwhile she had moved down to her knees. Pulled it down with her hand, and let it spring back up. She licked on it like an ice cream cone. She looked up for approval.

"Do you think I'm doing this thing right?"

"Oh my God."

Then she put it in her mouth, careful to cover the teeth. She was perfect.

He thought, cock on a bed of tongue. This girl is just too good, I'll have to keep making these trips out here.

"I'm not sure I'm doing this right. I think I need some instruction."

"I'll give you some instruction." At this point he just holds the back of her head and fucks her mouth until he comes.

The come dribbles all around her mouth, certainly some of it on purpose. She smiles and gives him that look of recognition that lets him know that she knows she's great. And somehow that is part of the high, the experience. She swallows and wipes the rest off with a Kleenex, rather ladylike by now.

Nick thinks, "Damn, she's rather too good at this." He never thought he could find a woman this good in the civilian population.

"Just let me fix my makeup and then we can go. You will return the favor later."

"Absolutely."

*　*　*

Even if Stephen had decided that nothing would ever, ever happen with Sophia, seeing her was a hard, hard habit to break. Habits were comfortable. Too much change wore you down, aged you. So, he continued seeing her.

"What do you suppose the odds would be for a man if he married a hooker?"

Sophia made no immediate response. "Is this hypothetical, or is this a real possibility?"

"Hypothetical."

"But this is something you might contemplate?"

"Well, I'll tell you why I'm thinking about it."

"Why is that?"

He had thought long about how to propose this: "I saw a program on Howard Stern. This guy was saying that he had had much better experiences with hookers than those outside the trade. They were more interested in sex."

"And sex is that important?"

"If you were a man, you would not even ask such a question."

"I see. And other things are not important?"

"Of course other things are important."

Sophia was a little crestfallen by this discussion, though she gave no indication. What hurt was that she knew that her power over him was great. He came even though there was no insurance coverage. He came even though they discussed very little sometimes. For him to overcome his reserve and bring up such a subject, even hypothetically, was a disappointment because even though he was not her type exactly, she liked the attention. He was always there in reserve, in the lineup. After the vice president, and the Speaker of the House, and the Senate pro tem, and the secretary of state, there was Stephen Ambrose, programmer.

"I have never treated a hooker, that I know of, and I don't know any, so naturally, any observations I made would lack direct experience."

"I know. I know."

"Well, it seems to me it's a lifestyle that works against relationships. Against male territoriality. Not that women are not territorial."

"Yeah, right."

"That means you have to live with her going off with other men. And if that's the way you met her, you know that she might fall for one of them. Correct?"

"Correct."

"Then if you decide to take her private . . ." She must have picked that up from some stockbroker. The business lingo was popping up everywhere. But maybe it was appropriate. A hooker's in business, after all. "Then you run up against other problems. What will she do with her time?"

"No skills other than hooking."

"No skills other than hooking, but also, there's an ego thing there, I can imagine. She's getting all this attention. Men are telling her how gorgeous she looks. Men are putting in her hands a lot of money for her services. Then all of sudden, nothing . . . I can imagine what would happen to me if I had a stroke. If I couldn't be a psychiatrist anymore . . . You can tell that my insurance agent has been by recently."

"For the annual scare."

"Exactly, but say it happens. I'm getting my disability check. But I'm not really a doctor anymore. And doctor status does count for something. I no longer have my own parkingk space at the hospital; people no longer look to me as an autority. No nurses coming up to me and asking, 'Vhat shall we do with the man in 501?' I'm no longer prescribing. I tink I might go into a deep depression because I've come to expect those things now."

"That reminds me of an interview I saw with Paul McCartney. He talked about the breakup of the Beatles. He said he'd felt he'd given up the best job in the world, being a Beatle. He said it made him sympathetic to others who had lost their job. He said he went into a depression."

She nodded, raised her eyebrows in agreement.

"Right," she said, "Of course, if a woman were occupied. Perhaps if she had a child . . ."

"A new occupation." It always came down to gainful work. That was her main theme.

The Visit

Finally, Stephen succumbed and asked Anna to visit him. He charged an airline ticket for her on his VISA. Some combination of the sexual impulse and curiosity drove him to ask her to visit.

He couldn't expect her to pick up the ticket since she was giving up a week or more of filthy lucre. Filthy something anyway.

He collected her at O'Hare, and he took her on the Kennedy leading into the city and then out to Oak Park.

"You don't think I could do anything else? Listen, I was an excellent student."

"I'm sure you were."

"Don't worry, I can find a job. I could easily become a manager at a hotel, for example. There's lots of things I can do."

"Well, you're English is good enough, so that won't be a problem."

"So is my French, my German, my Dutch, and my Italian."

"Italian?"

"Yes, I like Italy and I spent some time there."

This was a problem he was going to have to conquer somehow, if he was going to hook up Anna: Stephen would like to know what she did in Italy, but how could it not involve her occupation? And this was not necessarily something he wanted to know about.

"I had a boyfriend there for a while."

That was some kind of answer. Anna seemed to like Chicago immediately, and was very cheery. It was really difficult for Stephen. He wanted also to be cheery, but he couldn't figure out how this could ever work.

She was constantly cutting him off at the pass. "Don't worry. I have no problems with a fair prenup. I'm beautiful and interesting, and if things go sour, I'll land on my feet."

She was beautiful and interesting, no doubt about it. But such optimism seemed to him against nature. Nobody he knew was that optimistic. And that was another problem: How could he believe her, if no one in his experience was that optimistic?

They went to the milonga at Tangier. He took her to look out the tall windows, and they looked out at the Chicago skyline. He danced a great set of DiSarli with her. DiSarli's melodies provided the beat necessary to dance, but also variations so natural it felt they sprung out of nature. Men in Chicago had no sense of decorum, so a woman like Anna caused something not unlike a feeding frenzy. She danced continuously for the rest of the night.

*   *   *

Finally, after two weeks, she had to go back. "I've got rent to pay." But before she left, she knocked him off his feet. She could do those tricks you see on Howard Stern. Girls swallowing bananas and whatnot. It's all technique, but she learned it somehow.

She was completely at ease with sex. A little like the French woman, Madelaine. Stephen was not particularly so at ease. A lifetime of women's lib had addled his sexual equilibrium. He'd once had a conversation with a pre-transexual named Brenda (Ricky) who seemed a lot more at ease with her/his orientation than Stephen was.

Tango had helped to reorient him, though it was still a work in progress. But he hadn't planned to take it back to its roots, its roots being in the brothels. That was all an accident, at least he thought it was an accident. But maybe some powerful alien was looking over his shoulder having an alien's idea of fun twisting around the events of this poor human's life.

Make Your Best Deal

"I watched Court TV again last night."

"The trial of Jeffrey Dahmer. When was that on—two, three?"

"Two."

We were, both of us, horrible sleepers.

"It's our family. Angry mother, passive father."

"You've watched that trial before. Stop."

"No. Really."

I had to distract him or I was looking at an hour's tirade: "I was reading last night this book about Marion Davies."

"And who is she?"

"She was the longtime paramour of Hearst. I don't think they were ever married. I think he left her all his money even though they weren't married. But she turned it over to his kids."

"The problem of marriage is the problem of money."

"Always. Get a load of this: I know a woman from tango. She had an illegitimate kid by one fellow, married another, dropped a kid; divorced, married yet again, and had another kid. Now, of course, she's divorcing this guy, too."

"First question. These guys have money?"

"Yes. All of them."

"So, she's getting, what, child support on the one out of wedlock, and two alimonies plus two child support payments. Hell, she's in business. She's a going concern."

"It's what you always say."

"Make your best deal." He repeated it, "That's it. Make your best deal."

The unsaid thing was that it was impossible to know exactly what your best deal was.

"Anyway, I guess when George Hearst, who made the family fortune in mining, went home to marry his childhood sweetheart, he made her sign a prenup."

"Maybe that was her best deal. What happened?"

"They had the one kid, William Randolph Hearst. I think George, the father, bought a Senate seat, and when he died he left his widow a pile of money."

"Nothing wrong with it. That shows that a prenup does not necessarily mean that a marriage will fail. Absolutely. I think they should invoke some kind of vesting law in marriages."

He didn't have any such agreement, of course.

"Ten percent a year for ten years?"

"IF she's with me when I die, THEN she's 100 percent vested, and I leave her everything."

"Let me ask: do you think it would be possible to marry a hooker?"

"Only you would ask a stupid question like that." And then: "What brings on that question? I wondered why you didn't go to Berlin and Paris."

"What do you think?" It was a mistake to bring this up with Abner; he would want to know what hooker exactly. But maybe he could do a quick hit-and-run.

"My first thought is it would work if you have enough money."

"Right. They got in the biz because it was easy money. So, she might take on a permanent one-client-only relationship if there was enough money."

"Follow the money. Wasn't that what the advice was in the Watergate thing. Follow the money. Who stands to benefit?

"Sounds like Balzac."

"Balzac?"

"French writer. Master of self-interest. In one of his stories, a collector of junk, bric-a-brac, was ignored by his landlady until she found that the stuff was worth money, and then she became interested, if you get my meaning. He got sick, and she looted his apartment."

"In the best deals, everybody makes out." And that was the closest Abner got to explaining what your best deal was.

*   *   *

Anna hadn't given up her profession, so Stephen visited hookers himself.

"So, this hooker is, you know, licking and whatnot, and she's telling me about her boyfriend."

Stephen is speaking with Sammy.

"Her boyfriend? Why would she tell you about her boyfriend?"

"She started in. My curiosity. I probably encouraged her."

"Well, that's your first mistake."

"Anyway, she's working on me, and she's very good. Very enthusiastic."

"How old?"

"Thirties. Probably late thirties."

"Good age."

"So, anyway, I'm curious and I'm asking her about her boyfriend. And then she tells me about how she got home early last week from one of these out-of-town engagements."

"Where's she from?"

"Pittsburgh, or somewhere nearby."

"And?"

"And she goes on and on about how she followed him to some other girl's apartment, and then went home and waited for him. But. But he doesn't come home that night."

"So meanwhile she's going on and on about this guy while she's licking on your nuts."

"Well, right. She is. And I'm trying to figure this out. Let's see, it's okay for her to suck off anyone who drops by in the city of Chicago because it's for money, I guess, but her man is supposed to stay idly by."

"Yeah, but he always comes back. I'll tell you why. When they first met, she gave him the blow job of a lifetime. This was such a good blow job that every blow job after that was just trying to reclaim that first blow job."

"That reminds me of interviews with junkies, heroin addicts. It's always that first high gets them hooked. Every time after that, they're just trying to get back to that first high. More and more stuff, and still can't quite get there."

"Yes, but what do you think of my theory?"

"The knocks-him-off-his-feet blow job?"

"Yeah."

"What can I say, I go and see her every time she's in town."

"That proves my case. You're a regular. You didn't even get the full treatment, and she still knocked you over. So, I think that's what he is. He's a regular but he got the special treatment."

"I'm just trying to figure out what that special treatment might be. She's pretty damn good as it is."

"Anyway, he's getting good sex when she's in town, but then she leaves for a week or two at a time, right?"

"Right."

"And so, out of sight, out of mind, he doesn't think about it too much. But he still does sometimes, and that drives him nuts. So, his only protection is to seek out another girl, a fallback, a shield, revenge. Call it whatever you want. The evener."

"But meanwhile, she feels that he should be loyal since he's getting special treatment, is that how it works? She must somehow block out the fact that she's blowing and fucking men like crazy when she does these out-of-town gigs. I imagine she must work it around in her mind that she is just going out of town on a job. And a job is a job. 'You can come in my mouth if you want.' It's just a job. Like that Elton John song, 'Rocket Man,' he's an astronaut, but *It's just my job five days a week.*"

"It's got to be something like that."

"And she gets very jealous and possessive. Meanwhile, she's telling me that she's got him by the balls. If he breaks up with her, she'll claim her rights as a common-law wife. I guess they've been living together for four or five years."

"There you are. By the way, what became of the hooker from Holland?"

"The happy hooker from Holland."

"Yeah. What? What? What?"

"She's still there."

"You went back to Holland twice to see her. That counts for something."

"Yeah, and I'm going back again."

"Wow!" Sammy, who resembled a Jewish Buddha, but who always sounded like a kid with a new toy.

"But you know how long distance relationships go."

"No, how?"

"They don't work out."

"So, make it a short distance relationship. Bring her here."

"You're always in such a rush."

"We're not here forever."

"You keep reminding me of that."

"It's important to remember."

"I don't know if she wants to come here. You're the one who said the only reason she would come is to get a green card."

"Probably. But you're way out on a limb. Find out. Ask her."

"Stop. You're way too direct."

"Okay, go your own way, but at some point I think you have to ask. Or, you can stay single and keep eating at McDonald's and going to the movies alone."

"I never eat at McDonald's."

"You get my point."

"Yeah, I'll bring her back so I can recite this whole story again from the point of view of the boyfriend of this hooker I was telling you about, only this time in the first person."

"Maybe, but you're a writer, you can get something out of the experience."

"Do you think that someone could marry a hooker successfully?" Sammy was the guy to ask. Sammy saw hookers all the time. His wife was only bothered from time to time. Why? Because Sammy knew about making your best deal. He put the company in her name and made her president, and taught her how to run the business. He knew women craved security, and he knew how to provide this.

"Well, I think it is possible." But Sammy was a gambler, so it was hard to take him seriously because he probably lost a lot of the time, though the losses, like income from cash businesses, went unreported.[6]

---

[6] Sammy's favorite movie was *Ben-Hur*, which led Stephen to have this dream sequence: Sammy is chained to a stool at a Blackjack table in one of the gambling boats. The pit boss says to him: "We keep you alive to serve this ship. So bet well and live."

Property

Abner said, "You're in the right place with software. Intellectual property will be the thing. Warren Buffett will chase after those old fashioned values; meanwhile, right before his eyes, everything changes. His insurance companies use software code, his newspapers and insurance companies can't get on anymore without technology. They use it to run the printing presses, to input and edit copy, and yet he says technology lies outside his circle of competence."

"You suppose, with a friend like Bill Gates, it's an ego thing. He can't possibly admit his pal is in the right place at the right time."

"Well, it is hard to know which technology will rule the day."

"One could check with Buffett's companies to see what they're using and place a few bets."

"I'm confident that's the way to go." His brother would latch on to an expression for a while, and "I'm confident" was the current one. He did not use it without a touch of irony.

"We are in a bubble, but nevertheless, things are continuing to change quite rapidly. Before long we'll all be able to hit a satellite to make a phone call. Nowhere will be too remote."

"Yes, well, the Japanese thought like that in the 1980s and their PEs went through the roof, the Nikkei hit 39,000 in 1989 and now ten years later it's 14,000, and maybe it's not finished going down."

"Certainly the Japanese had it all for a while. Cheap money, low interest rates. Technology that wouldn't quit. Remember when the U.S. set up that semiconductor alliance because they thought the Japanese would eat our lunch and dinner and midnight snack and breakfast the next day?"

"Sematech. Wasn't that what it was called?"

"I don't remember the name. Then Intel came roaring back, and then the biotechs came on and the telecommunications thing grew. And then the United States came back like it did after Pearl Harbor. Evidently, still a nation to be reckoned with, and for the same reasons it has always been a nation to be reckoned with."

"And what's that?"

"The immigrants. There is something about the immigrants. They have more drive. More chutzpah. Lower MAO levels. Possibly more brains. Look at the CEO of Intel, Andy Grove. That can't possibly be the name he was born with. He's a Hungarian immigrant."

"Let's get back to property." His thing. He owned a large house. He owned a piece of Loop real estate.

"Okay."

"The problem with property in America is that even when you own it, you're still only renting it."

"Property taxes."

"Absolutely. Let's say you're Rip Van Winkle and you fall asleep for one hundred years. Not even that. Let's say five years. When you wake up, all your property has been confiscated by the government for property taxes and sold off."

"So, owning real estate is really just a matter of having a long-term lease from the government."

"Right, exactly. It is a lease without an end, theoretically, as long as you pay for the perpetual care. The rent, the taxes."

"So, other kinds of property are really better bargains. If you buy stock, in a hundred years you still have the stock, no property taxes."

"And a copyright is another pretty good deal. If you do a Rip Van Winkle and fall into a coma for twenty years, when you come out of it you still own the property. Copyright is good for the writer's lifetime plus fifty years. You should write a program that would be a big seller."

"Or a sci-fi novel."

"Don't make me laugh. They say the intellectual property laws will change again when Disney's rights on Mickey Mouse are about to run out again."

Stephen said, "Don't you think, in a sense, all property is intellectual property? The idea of property is an intellectual notion. Tigers don't have a notion of property as we do, but they do have a notion of territory, which they mark out with scent. Is the tiger's idea of territory an indication of higher thought? The etymology of property should somehow include territoriality. That's the root."

"This is my hunting ground, you stay out. Could be."

"Look at the apartment building. First it was a building owned by one person and rented to others. Then the notion of the co-op developed. Then the condominium developed. You own one apartment in an apartment building. Then time-sharing develops. You own the right to stay in an apartment for a certain week or group of weeks in an apartment building. You have to wonder: how will ownership be further subdivided as time goes along? Or will it finally dissolve?"

"Who knows? Listen, you're a consultant, just be sure to put some of your programming loot into a Keogh."

"Right."

*   *   *

"About the hooker thing again."

"Yes, what?" Sam, on the phone.

"Here's my problem: I once saw a porno actress on a talk show, and she claimed she fell in love, however briefly, with every man she had sex with."

"And you think, if your girl . . ."

"My girl?"

"Okay, have it your way. If this hooker-friend-whatever of yours ever has sex with another man . . . I don't have time for this nonsense. I have work to do."

"It's not nonsense . . ."

Click, line dead.

*   *   *

from the journal of Stephen Ambrose

I cannot tell Sophia, but Darwin would probably claim she was dead right about the therapeutic value of work.

Darwin suffered various symptoms from about the age of thirty to the age of sixty. "For twenty-five years extreme spasmodic daily and nightly flatulence: occasional vomiting, on two occasions prolonged during months. Vomiting preceded by shivering (hysterical crying), dying sensations (or half-faint) . . . ringing in ears, treading on air and vision (focus and black dots) . . . (nervousness when E. [Emma, his wife] leaves me)—What I vomit intensely acid, slimy (sometimes bitter) consider teeth. Doctors (puzzled) say suppressed gout—No organic mischief, Jenner & Brinton . . ."

Symptoms flared up just before the birth of his first child, also when his father was dying and after he died.

It was thought that the symptoms suggested a psychosomatic disease. But an organic cause has also been suggested, Chagas's disease. One of the problems with this is that he had palpitations and pain around the heart even before he left on the *Beagle*.

Anyway, the point was that it was work which distracted him from his ailments: "I was speculating yesterday how fortunate it was I had plenty of employment . . . for being employed alone makes me forget myself."

And again he writes, "My chief enjoyment and sole employment throughout life has been scientific work; and the excitement from such work makes me forget, or drives away, my daily discomfort."

And again, "I have hopes of again someday resuming scientific work, which is my sole enjoyment in life."

To his friend and competitor in the race to advance the notion of evolution, Alfred Russel Wallace, he wrote the following when Wallace suffered a broken engagement: "Do try what hard work will do to banish painful thoughts." It was what he did himself.

Only Travelers

The Throdēop and the humans speculated about the intelligent life. Eladia began the conversation:

"You are the only other intelligent species we have ever run into, and you come from the same planet."

Tōparr agreed, "Yes, that is true, but I don't think that intelligent life is limited to the planet Earth. We only traveled to a few other star systems."

"Yes, but have you not noticed something common to us both, which is that your species developed only shortly before the end of the age of dinosaurs, and ours came at the end of the age of mammals."

"So, you are suggesting that intelligent life is only a short-lived thing?"

"Except for travelers, maybe. What do you think?"

"Yes, well, to state the obvious, we lack the data to make broad statements."

"That's the easy way out. You know what I know. Which is that the number of species on Earth suffered as our brain capacity grew."

"Yes, that appears to be true for us as well."

"We consigned all other top predators to zoos."

"So did we. And many disappeared through sport."

"The same thing happened with us."

"What are you getting at?"

"Only this: that ships such as those that we are both using required the manufacturing plant of a planet. A capability we both lack at present. We can make repairs, but we no longer have the capability of making everything that runs our ships."

"We, too, can make many parts for our ship, but your point is well-taken."

"And that we ruined the planet which supported the life required for the fabrication of our respective ships."

"Yes . . ."

"So that we are in essence on our own."

"I am still wondering what your point is."

"Simply this: that perhaps intelligence, whenever it occurs, is only capable of lofting a few travelers into outer space before the self-destruct sequence they triggered, perhaps unwittingly, when they reached the point of industrial revolution."

"So, this is your point?" Tōparr reflected for a while, and said, "Well, it is an interesting broad speculation on intelligence, and it deserves some thought . . ."

"But your first thought is . . ."

"Only that there is a precociousness about intelligence, a child thing, a sandbox thing. It cannot help but play with things, and they always get out of hand before the consequences can be figured out. And it could turn out that way every time intelligence pops up. That's possible."

"Yes, that's it. I think that's my point." Eladia.

"So, all there ever is is a remnant of civilization that scoots around the various heavenly bodies. A remnant of a planet with billions of beings."

"Travelers. That's all that ever survives. We have some capability for making replacement parts, but this craft is the product, more than that, the culmination of a manufacturing capability, plants and fabricator facilities of an intelligent population in the billions, which we cannot possibly duplicate on this small craft."

Tōparr agreed, "Nor can we, but we could plant a seed on a planet."

"Ah."

Art, the Quest for Knowledge, and Games

George said, "Let's see. The last time I saw you, you were touting the next thing in white meat."

Stephen, "Indeed, I was. My point was, I guess, that the only thing I get out of human beings' huge gift of intelligence is that they can reproduce without limits."

"Who can argue with that?"

They were again at the Berghoff, in the back room, which was a little quieter than the rest of the restaurant, but the golden oak was still there eavesdropping on them. The waiter banged down a plate with bread and butter, and they gave him their drink order.

"What is there to do with one's brains, if not to seduce the female and make more humans?" George.

"Well, there's always art."

"I agree, there's art, and there's the quest for knowledge."

"Art and the quest for knowledge, I think that's it, isn't it?" Stephen ventured, "Playing games."

"Ah. I guess so."

"More and more. Games. The sanitary time fill. But it is one of those things which make you feel that everyone not pursuing art and knowledge is a patient."

"Ugh."

"In the future, it will be: play this game or we give you Thorazine! Or Prozac. One of those drugs."

"Surely, you jest."

"I don't know, am I kidding? Well, maybe it won't come to that. It's probably in our genes that we love games. Think of cats and their prey. I saw a cat once get a lot of fun out of playing with a mouse before he swallowed it."

"Maybe it's just a matter of finding the right game."

"That's it. It will be the quest for knowledge, art, playing games, and spectatoring."

"Spectatoring. Is that a word?"

"If it isn't, should be. Sure, there will always be slugs who do nothing but watch. They will watch sports, games, movies."

"You are not a hopeful guy."

"Well, the universe is a big place. There has to be room for everything, hope has to be in there somewhere, but today it's raining out."

Safety on the Outside

That's where Nick wanted to be. He wanted to be on the outside of the relationship. To be on the inside meant that you were exposed. That the woman, the partner, might be disloyal. Cheat was the word women used. Men were cheaters. Men didn't think in terms of cheaters. You were loyal, or you weren't. You could be counted on, or you couldn't.

Women thought of men as womanizers. Nick thought of himself as charming, irresistible, a ladies' man. A womanizer sounded like a meat grinder.

It was always best to be on the outside of a relationship, especially if the female is attractive. If you're on the inside, you're protecting, you're building defenses along the English Channel. You're building the Atlantic Wall, you're planting mines, and putting up barbed wire. You're building pillboxes and positioning your panzers.

It's a bad place to be. You want to be on the attack. Maybe your partner is loyal. Maybe she says, "I was always a loyal partner." Loyal but bored. She counted ceiling tiles, and speculated on how she might redecorate the bedroom. She was never there with you.

To have a partner is to slow you down, to distract you, to weaken you. She might leave you, and then where is your morale? Down in the dumps. So, you must always be on the attack. On the hunt. Alexander the Great. "Advance. Always advance."

It was Stephen who provided all the backup support, the intellectual framework for staying on the outside. He would report things from the science magazines that female birds might connect with a resourceful, scrawny male who found a great nesting location, but if a big bruiser was nearby, she might end up with eggs from both.

This would be further supported by television programs such as *What Do Women Really Want?* which would say that women liked men who could dance. And the work with birds. A female would opt for the best of both worlds if she could get it, and the blue bird female in the program did. She went for the smaller guy who had the best pad, the best nesting place, and then she had a little on the side with a big, robust suitor. So she had babies by both. Smaller, resourceful ones by the home provider and big healthy ones by the big guy on the side. A shorter distance between nests resulted in more extra-pair copulations.

Nick always preferred to be the guy on the side. Why get stuck with some female who might not be loyal anyway? Not loyal and probably a shrew. Although one could get a loyal partner and still end up with a shrew. There were a million ways things could fail to work out. But it never felt like there were also a million ways things could work. That was the problem.

Nick was just playing the odds. He saw himself as a keen observer of nature, and borderline amoral. The code of conduct among humans was a fabricated thing, like clothing, which draped over humans in all manner of ways. It was not a thing he felt he could count on. He did not flagrantly violate those codes, but neither did he really view them as law. Law was more like his favorite African savannah programs. The lioness hunts for the smaller, weaker animal. The lame animal. Or a larger animal if isolated and she has help. It was an issue of the stronger and the weaker. Or the smarter, or more agile, and the dumber. Occasionally, a lion might make a meal out of a monkey. But mostly the monkeys kept out of range. And they were not without humor. On one program, the baboon ran up a tree and peed on the lion below.

Monkeys seemed to have laws that more approximated human laws. If a monkey found food and did not share it, then he was punished by the other monkeys. The rule of social law.

When Nick approached a woman, he used all of the weapons at his disposal. Conversation, good looks, compliments, and he practiced constantly. A man married to a woman for years was no match. When was the last time the husband told his wife how good-looking she was? And, even if he did, compliments coming from the same source lose their power, their effectiveness. They become bland, oatmeal, vanilla compliments. She doesn't even hear them.

She'll say, "Nick thought my hair was like a willow."

"A willow?"

"Well, I don't have any curls in my hair. You know, it hangs down—like a willow tree."

"Interesting that Nick should take such a keen interest in how your hair hangs."

"Why shouldn't he? I'm attractive."

"Don't I know."

And so on. This was the effect that Nick could have.

* * *

Nick perspired constantly. It seemed to be the only weakness in the otherwise perfect man. But just when you thought that would be a negative, some woman would come up and say, "I like a man who perspires. It shows that he's really working out."

Stephen was chagrined, but then he thought about it, and wondered why women seemed to crave that male demonstration. He once spoke to a Latina who told him, "I like a man who is jealous. No, I insist that a man who wants me be jealous."

When they spoke further she clarified it. "I don't think if you really care about someone you can hide those feelings."

As they were walking off the court after a long set, Nick said, "I really sweat a lot."

"It cools you off."

"Yes, but it's kind of unsightly."

"Did you know that birds don't sweat? They actually have a salt gland. Perspiration might have a bad effect on flight."

"No kidding."

"Figure it out. Early hominids developed the bipedal walk for a couple of reasons. He could see above the grass, and follow an animal in the savannah. He could walk faster and farther than the monkey, which are not great distance walkers."

"So you think early man just outran his prey."

"Perhaps to begin with. And walking upright accounted for part of the cooling system for the brain. If you are bipedal there is less exposure to the sun than if you are a four-legged animal like a cow. An enlarged brain needed more cooling. Otherwise, the heat would constantly destroy brain cells."

"Well, with this Scotch, I reckon I'll destroy a few."

"And that is why the first massively parallel computer is the human mind. If cells are destroyed it is not of great moment because there will be other cells making the same connection through some other route."

"Don't you ever stop?"

"And it's adaptable. The proof is that they can see in the blind man's MRI, or whatever, that he is using not only the usual area for hearing but also part of the vision area of the brain. So, probably his hearing is more acute. Better interpretation of data. Not that the basic equipment is any different, the ear's the same. A reasonable analogy would be to say that the software is better, like when we sent Patriot missiles from Germany to Israel. Hardware was the same, it was the software that was much improved."

"Is that so? I don't remember seeing that."

"It was in the news."

"Something you know about?"

"A little. Interesting, isn't it, that they can see from an MRI that a blind man uses some of the visual area of the brain for hearing? Also, when they use certain dyes they can see that the image a man is looking at is reflected in his brain. I think the test case was a bull's-eye."

"You're not getting enough sex."

"Why's that?"

"Because you must spend all of your time soaking up these useless facts."

*　*　*

Nick turned in reports to Seoul, but he wondered if anyone ever read them. He grew fond of the movie *Pascali's Island*. The man who was everywhere but powerless, impotent. He lusted after a beautiful woman, but he didn't have the nerve. Later he ended up in bed with a young man. Pascali sent endless reports from the island to Istanbul, but no one ever acknowledged his work.

He wondered, "Does anyone look at my reports?"

*　*　*

from the journal of Stephen Ambrose

Reading up again on Malthus. Both Darwin and Alfred Russel Wallace—coincident discoverer of evolution—were influenced by Malthus.

Malthus's father had been a friend and admirer of David Hume and Jean-Jacques Rousseau. His father was a critic of the educational system, so for a time Malthus was home-taught. At eighteen he was sent off to Cambridge, graduating with distinction in mathematics, and became an ordained Anglican clergyman. At age thirty-two he published his famous work, *An Essay on the Principle of Population as It Affects the Future Improvement of Society, with Remarks on the Speculations of Mr. Godwin, M. Condorcet, and other Writers.* This came twenty-two years after the Declaration of Independence of the North Americans, and nine years after the start of the French Revolution.

The first edition of the book was published anonymously. And well it might have been. An essay that runs flat in the face of life. The purpose of life being its continuation and propagation at every opportunity. But an essay that recommends that there be fewer poor people, meaning fewer poor people to put on the dole, would easily attract the attention of the elect, the aristocracy, who were handily more brilliant and valuable to mankind. And besides, the poor couldn't read, so they wouldn't know he was their enemy. And if they cannot read, they cannot write. So, no hate mail. Those were the days.

So, naturally, when the essay became a success, and he acquired a certain fame, he attached name to the work. His contention: populations increased geometrically, food arithmetically. His idea was that population would outstrip food supplies. There were no worthy scientific statistics to base this on, but never mind.

He did some work on gluts, which presaged later work by Keynes and others on inventory accumulation and consequent imbalances in production and consumption, which caused recessions and depressions. A decent intuitive thinker. No Newton, who would want to see the data, the astronomical observations for himself.

Man turned out to be cleverer than Malthus could ever have imagined. Problems in food supply were solved in various ways. Better grains were developed (i.e. tinkering with DNA), better techniques of farming, the use of fertilizer, and so on.

*   *   *

Nick argued, "I think you should have one of your evolved dinosaurs want to mate with a human female. After all, I'm sure you have somewhere in your library of pornography, photos of women having sex with dogs or horses."

"That's an interesting thought."

"What's that?"

"Do you suppose a human has all the genes of a dog, so that a subset of human genes could be used to create a dog?"

"I don't know, but I like it."

"No, probably it wouldn't work. Dogs evolved other genes along the way, which is where you'd run afoul. You could only create the species that modern man and dogs had in common, whatever that was. Some rodent thing. A chimpanzee would be closer, which is supposed to have 98 percent or 99 percent of our genes. That would be a better subset, but they also branched off and have their own genes."

"Good, I never got off on the human-monkey thing. I'm sorry, it doesn't work for me aesthetically. Woman-dog thing works. Woman-horse thing works. But chimps? Chimps are not inherently sexy like horses. Zebras are sexy. Even giraffes are sexy. Or a big cat."

"I see your point. I could never see the Leda and the swan thing either."

"Why is it never the male with one of these other animals?"

"Shepherds and their sheep."

"I see that as kind of an emergency-safety-valve type of thing."

"Don't you suppose that is the male fantasy thing? To debase the female makes you a little more powerful. It's the humiliation thing."

"Anyway, the point is: the cross-sex thing is okay, might outrage some, but draw in others. But make it a Throdēop male and a human female."

"Has to be."

"Why's that?"

"Because, remember, brain enlargement is a sexual thing with Throdēop, and the male brain will increase to entice, to mate with the human female."

"Right, your canary thing, or was it finches?"

In Which We Continue the Science Fiction Plot, However Thin

The Throdēop asked the ship's counselor Ada: "What do you think of our shape? How do we look to you?"

"Well, unusual-looking but not without features of interest."

"Not without features of interest. That is, how would you say, academic? Not very revealing."

"Maybe I didn't mean to be revealing."

On the screen he put pictures of a tiger. "Do you think that is a good-looking animal?"

"Tigers? Oh yes."

"They are kind of lean, are they not? Lean and powerful. I like all your big cats, tigers, jaguars, panthers. Like a dancer."

"Yes, that's very perceptive."

"Well, that is my gift. I should say that is our gift."

"They move gracefully. Their bodies seemed designed, streamlined for speed and agility."

"Like a dancer's."

"Yes, like a dancer."

"Did you ever want to be a dancer?"

"I am a dancer."

"Ah. Throdēop are drawn to the dance, as you know. Well, you have seen us . . . How can we tell the dancer from the dance?"

"You're a poet, are you?"

"Not really. No. I just did a search of your computer on dance with reference to poetry. It is a line from a poet of the twentieth century, William Butler Yeats."

"It's a famous line, famous poem, famous poet. It is an interesting line of thought, moving from tigers to dance to poetry."

"Thank you."

"But this is your gift. We have a pair of tigers on our ship. Would you like to see them?"

"Indeed."

*   *   *

The Throdēop attempted to find out about the human female sexual characteristics from the males.

"Do your females ever do exotic things when they're in heat? I mean estrus. When they ovulate."

"Like what?"

"Well, I have read about the Greek women being orgiastic. Like the mother of Alexander the Great. Rituals with snakes."

The curious Throdēop really wanted to meet with a human in a back alley and get the lowdown, but he had instead to deal with this scientist.

"Yes, there have been such things written about our early culture."

This was not working the way Throdēop had in mind. He wanted to ask if there were any sexual maniacs on board the ship.

"Which of your shipmates are the most sexually aggressive?"

"Why would you want to know that?"

"As you know, our brains resulted from a natural selection process which favored brains which grew large in order to attract our mates, and I was simply wondering if the same process developed in your species. I thought I would conduct an informal survey."

"I see. Probably it does play a part in the mating process, along with subliminal thoughts about the health of the possible mate, for which symmetry seems an indicator."

"I agree."

"Well, you might speak to Carlos or Javier."

"They are sexually aggressive?"

"Aggressiveness is not exactly the right term on the ship, since we've become so bored that nearly everyone has had sex with nearly everyone else. But Carlos and Javier have higher testosterone levels than others, so they have sex more often. We do not look on it as necessarily an indicator of sexual preference anymore; we just see it as part of the biochemical profile. So and so has a mole on their cheek. Javier has higher hormone levels than most people."

"That seems a very sensible way to view it."

Of course, the Throdēop knew that sensible explanations often masked the unruly, uncontrollable underneath.

*   *   *

Tōparr with his sandy tones and freckles had been given free access to Prime. And he wandered around and spoke with Carlos.

"What is sex like on Prime?"

"Well, we've all been here so long that we have had sex with everybody on the ship."

"No holdouts. No forever loves?"

"Are there forever loves among the Throdēop?"

"There were before the age barrier was broken. When we started living 200 years, 300 years, things changed. Originally, our life spans were not unlike yours, 30 years or 40 years. Then 70, 80 years. But the really active sex period was only 30 to 40 years."

"And then?"

"And then. Well, you start living 300 years with an active sex life of 250 years, everyone gets bored. Even the true loves."

"So, then everyone had sex with everyone."

"More or less. And on your ship?"

Carlos provided him with the *chisme*, the gossip, "We have the same situation. But there are a few holdouts. Ramón, our leader, is very attracted to Ada, who does not find him appealing, but who is, nevertheless, his good friend and his confidant. How come you have not woken up more of your compatriots?"

"I will, sooner or later."

"You want to scope out the scene before your favorite females wake up. You don't want to deal with the jealousy and envy."

"Territoriality, you mean. That may very well be true."

"What kind of abnormal sex practices are there among you? I am imagining after all the boredom, odd things may have cropped up."

"I don't know what to say."

The Throdēop knew to keep his silence.

"Well, here all manner of things have popped up. Our knowledge of hormones maybe juiced the whole thing. There are all kinds of bondage and discipline things. The adage around here is: the only unnatural sex is the sex that you cannot, you know, physically accomplish. That's the rule. If women had nostrils big enough, men would stick a cock up there. The women are pretty randy, and so are the boys. Which reminds me, there are toys, of course. Then there is too much with the toys, and all toys get abandoned. People seem to go through certain cycles. Some women, although quite beautiful, are not creative lovers, like Ada. I have had sex with Ada many times. She talks a good game, and it's always nice to have one's orgasm. I can't understand why she doesn't want to have sex with Ramón. One girl, Nanci, is altogether too close to her dog. That's kind of exotic."

Bingo.

* * *

"I'm not that foreign. We have many genes in common; in fact, most of our genes are the same. Ninety percent. I don't have three sex organs, only the Earth-standard one. And like the human animal, our male organ developed to be rather out-sized."

"Stop. I don't want to hear," said Nanci.

"I don't know. I thought all females like to hear about outsized sex organs."

"Stop."

"We are rather creative lovers. Sex is all in the brain, and we have exceptional talents that way. You think you understand humiliation. You think you understand your need for humiliation and the male's need to humiliate, but you do not begin to understand. You will be dripping. You will be so open that only our very thick male organs will create the necessary tight friction of a piston."

"Oh my God."

"Why resist?" Understanding perfectly that resistance was all part of the game.

"You don't understand. You're not just a different race, you're a different species."

"Well, that may very well be, but another of your shipmates told me that some female crew members have experimented with their dogs, and they are, after all, a different species."

"Stop."

"What kind of chemical enhancers have you tried?"

"Stop."

"Well, we have some things that are held in high regard by the females of our species. Maybe you would like to try them."

"An aphrodisiac?"

"Well. That is a bit of a romantic term, but I guess it will suffice." And then, "You are a little bit different from your comrades. Smarter, and as you know, smarter is sexier in our species. I think it always is."

By this time he had put his hand around her breasts. It looked like something out of H.R. Giger.

*   *   *

from the journal of Stephen Ambrose

Male and female.

In *Australopithecus*, males were nearly twice as big as females. In early hominids, males were only 20 percent bigger.

Even now the braincase of men is still 8 percent larger than females.

The IQ Boost

Abner, over the phone: "You idiot. What are you drinking now to jack up your IQ?"

"Green tea with ginkgo biloba."

"Not exactly the IQ boost machine of *Forbidden Planet*, is it? And you're the one who thought the Discovery Channel would bring us enlightenment. Instead, we got Monster Garage and American Chopper. You're ridiculously optimistic."

"That's because optimism is our only choice. Pessimists are people who don't understand that their only choice is optimism."

"Yeah, right."

"Well, get sick one time, and you'll see what I mean."

"So what's ginkgo biloba supposed to do?"

"The theory is that it increases the oxygen to the brain."

"It better had, brainwad, your brains are for shit."

"Well, for now there is not much you can do about the genetic, unless it turns out that you can tweak the epigenes. So, you have to play with whatever is left."

"Yeah, I remember when you found that thing with Linus Pauling and vitamin C. It was supposed to raise your IQ five points. Did it ever do you any good?"

"Did I feel five IQ points smarter? Not really."

"See, there's my point. It's just money down a rat hole."

"If you're going to tell me to put my money in an IRA account, save your breath."

"That's a good idea. Forget the novel. Focus."

"There's a buzzword if ever I heard one. Focus on what?"

"Your programming. Go private. Consult."

"Yes, I remember. The Keogh plan."

"Okay, okay. So, what else are you taking to increase your IQ?"

"Phosphatidylserine, glutamine."

"And what's that supposed to do?"

"Phosphatidylserine has a role in neurotransmitter function and synaptic communication."

"What a sucker you are. It goes down into the stomach, gets taken apart, and never makes it to the brain. I've always sworn by the traditional drugs."

"And those are?"

"Coffee and alcohol."

"Yeah. There is something about coffee. Who'd a thought that kids who grew up on Frosted Flakes would ever become addicted to something with the bitter taste of coffee?"

"Anyway, forget the supplements. You spend thousands. You at your computer?"

"Yes."

"Check your Quicken. How much you spend on vitamins last year?"

"Wait a second . . . Reports . . . $1,896."

"That's almost an IRA contribution. You could buy a great stereo system for that. Or a digital video camera."

"Yeah, well, vitamins. You don't feel their effects necessarily, but if I fall off the wagon, I notice that I get colds and stuff."

"And dumber, I suppose."

No answer.

"You don't have to answer. Everyone knows it's the truth, dick brain."

*   *   *

from the journal of Stephen Ambrose

Brazilian street children are capable of doing advanced math for their street businesses, but nevertheless, flunk math in school. Researchers found that these astute handicappers implicitly used a complex model with up to seven variables, and that their ability to do this did not match up with their IQ scores.

Love is Grief

_____

From the Journal of Stephen Ambrose

One sex researcher working with finches easily fooled the males with a finch sex doll. It was a taxidermist's delight with special plastic cloaca. The males didn't seem to mind. They didn't have to chase; in fact, no static at all.

It's so disheartening. Males are not all that discriminating. It's always the fuck dolls. So, girls, when you see a man and wonder just what he sees in that ugly, overweight creature, or that pretty brainless airhead, think of the taxidermist's delight that the zebra finch males go for, and relax, it may be nothing at all. Just a place to put it. Not love.

Proving, of course, that men will fuck a knot in a tree, something we all knew.

Love was another matter. Scientists pretty much tried to stay away from love. They like to talk about mating. Sex responses, for example, can be measured. Love, well, there's a trick. Grief when a partner is gone. That, the scientists think, is as close as we come to love. They think it is love because they do not see what purpose it serves. Grief does not bring a human female into estrus as it will in tiger females. Grief does not drive a man to fuck. In a video about macaque monkeys in Japan, the baby dies. The mother macaque is in grief and will not leave the dead baby. She carries it with her. The zoo caretakers steal and hide the dead baby macaque, hoping she'll forget, but it only serves to send her into further paroxysms of despair.

*   *   *

"Anna, you know, I find it very agreeable that I can chat with you about monkeys and grief." And easier still to talk about love theoretically, and easier still over the telephone.

"Thank you for saying so."

"Did you go to college?"

"What, you think because I am a hooker that I have no education?"

"Well, I shouldn't. It seems these days that one out of three hookers got started paying for an education."

"And you thought it was just a cover story."

"You're altogether too smart. So, what did you study in college?"

"Psychology."

"Why is it so many women study psychology?"

"Oh, I suppose they want to make human behavior seem more understandable, predictable. More manageable."

The Big Extinctions

We met roughly every three or four months, me and Amanda. Amanda and I. I was going down to Powell's used-book store on Fifty-seventh Street to hunt for books on evolution, so it was a natural to suggest lunch. So, I quizzed her on the big extinctions.

Amanda said, "There are various camps. Peter Ward claims there have been two big extinctions, Leaky says five. Ward does not really deny the others, it's a matter of magnitude. Both think we're in the middle of another big one.

"Both would say the current big extinction event has come on with homo. Both cite the appearance of the Clovis people in the Americas at the end of the Ice Age, about twelve to fifteen thousand years ago, with the disappearance of 70 percent or more of the large mammals there.

"Some would like to claim it was the Ice Age. So you have this back-and-forth thing. Was it an external agency, say, the thawing of the ice pack because of a change in the shape of Earth's orbit, the bursting of an ice lake, or another asteroid or comet, or was it some other agency—say, an intelligent species, like man?

"Here's my cheat sheet," and she proceeded to write down on a napkin:

End of the Ordovician	440 million years ago	65% species gone
Late Devonian	365 million years ago	65% species gone
End of Permian	225 million years ago	95% species gone
End of Triassic	210 million years ago	65% species gone
End of Cretaceous	65 million years ago	75% species gone

She continued, "And for the big extinctions, what has been cited as the causative agents? Global climate change, mostly global cooling. Marine regression is a big one. And everyone knows about extraterrestrial bodies like an asteroid or comet. Then there are volcanic events going on for a thousand years that would also darken the atmosphere, the Siberian traps, the Decan traps. I saw on the tube there is a caldera at Yellowstone the size of the park or something. Huge. If it goes off, big global effect. Of course, one could cause the other. An asteroid might jostle the Earth's crust enough to cause earthquakes and volcanoes in response, multiplying the effect of the asteroid, right? And there's the contracoup, the effect on the opposite side of the planet."

"Isn't there a theory about a dark star?"

"There are theories for everything. That theory supposes that we live in a two-star system, and the other star orbits Sol about every twenty-six million years. When it does, then it creates all this havoc among comets out in the Orc cloud, out beyond Pluto, and meteors, and comets are jostled out of their orbits and more likely to hit Earth, especially when this dark star comes close to the Sun."

"Dark star—sounds like a television series."

"What, another franchise?"

We thought alike.

"Here is an interesting theory: At the end of the Permian Age, which was the worst, the continents came together to form Pangaea. The idea is that separate continents have more shoreline. And more shoreline will support more shallow water marine life. One continent and you have less shoreline, and shallow water marine life is one of those critical links which supports the larger forms. Cut that off, and apparently you cut terrestrial animal life off at the knees.

"Further, it is suggested that if continental shelves lay exposed during an ice age, organic matter would oxidize, that is, as the organic matter rusted, it would take oxygen out of the atmosphere, and oxygen would be converted from O^2 to carbon dioxide, dropping atmospheric oxygen to half today's levels. The shift created by this mechanism alone would knock out many species. Then there's the idea that if you warm up the oceans by five degrees, then frozen methane starts to bubble up, and it's an even more potent greenhouse gas than carbon dioxide. Then things really get warm."

Stephen sat back and said, "All I can say is that the asteroid thing is very attractive for its simplicity. Less shoreline seems arcane. There wasn't any asteroid in the Permian?"

"Maybe there was an asteroid. They're investigating near the Falkland Islands and Antartica where they think there may have been an asteroid event. But I'm thinking it was multi-causal. The Earth opened up in Siberia. There was what they call a flood basalt eruption, on top of which a huge coal deposit burned raising methane levels. Lots of particles and gases released into the atmosphere. Global warming. If the oceans were warmed up by five or ten degrees, then all the methane frozen on the bottom might enter the atmosphere, and methane is much worse than carbon dioxide as a green house gas. So, then you've warmed up the planet ten or twenty degrees, and everyone thinks that would just about do us in. Bad things happened to the ozone layer. Lots of deserts. 95 percent of species gone. That's like saying life on Earth was near extinguished. But an asteroid is a lot easier to explain than to argue we are in the midst, right now, of an important extinction event. Sure a few obvious species are in trouble. The tiger, and so on. But it appears life is still abundant. Dogs and cats are everywhere. The counter argument to the alarmist talk is that there is more diversity of life at this moment than at any time on the planet."

"Well, I am sure there are those who would argue that there is no need for diversity, no problem in sameness. Warren Buffett would love the dog and cat franchise. The massive distribution of sameness."

"Well, you could argue a similar case for human beings. There have been multiple species of homo at the same time. I think Homo erectus, Neanderthal, and Homo sapiens all existed at the same time. Now, it's all Homo sapiens. They got the franchise."

"Did you see that program where this group of people retraced David Livingston's path in Africa? David Livingstone hardly ever ran into people. The retracers could hardly avoid them. Massive poverty."

"Personally, I'm not overwhelmed by human intelligence. And why should I take the big view, when everyone is out making out like rabbits? If we keep conceiving like laboratory animals, then pretty soon we'll be treated like laboratory animals. Think about that."

"By whom? Other humans?"

"Sure, but who knows. The universe is a big place."

"Whenever I say 'but who knows,' why is it that I usually expect the worst case to happen?"

Amanda: "No one cares, we're all morons. It doesn't matter that we're killing the habitat we need to live on. Intelligence is just too weak a force. It's like what I read about consciousness. It's just a slight thing on top of all the other duties the brain manages: walking, balance, sight, smell, the internal works—pumping the heart, peristalsis, reproduction. Reproduction, now there's a force to be reckoned with." And then she said, "Watch, one of the these days I'm going to ambush some poor slob of a man."

"Ambush?"

"Yeah. Men are such idiots."

"Who could argue against that, but what do you mean? Exactly."

"I mean, I'll do a little research on some poor unsuspecting sperm donor, and make sure he has good genes, and then I'm going to tease the guy to death. And he's going to let loose some of that genetic treasure of his, and I'm going to grow one of those cute little human monsters. But I'll only have one."

"Nah, you're just talking. And by the way, tone it down a little. You're not going to have any friends soon. I can't imagine what your friends think when you say things like 'Six billion and one' when they have a baby."

"Too late. I got into trouble yesterday. Julie said to me that she was going to have a second baby. I told her: not necessary. But she defended it . . . tried to convince me that replacement is okay. I said, 'Yeah, like we need to maintain six billion people to keep the species alive.'"

"I'm sure she loved you for that."

"Then I got into a rap about this TLC program I saw about anacondas. Some village found a big one, and one of the villagers went to the scientists and told them they should move it before it got killed. There's no habitat. What's more important? Anacondas or humans? Well, it's going to be humans every time. It's going to be humans until there's no rain forest. But I think that did it. She rang off when I told her ecology was a complex thing, we might need anacondas."

"Almost every species feels that way about their own. What would you call it? Professional courtesy? Well, I'm sure even a million humans, spread out, would provide adequate reserves to guarantee the survival of the species against most kinds of adversity."

"Given that there are only ten thousand tigers around I would hope so."

"That's it. That reminds me: I saw on NOVA or some History Channel or Discovery program that there was a bottleneck about seventy-five thousand years ago. Humans were nearly wiped out, down to ten thousand people. Imagine: from ten thousand to six billion in a mere seventy-five thousand years."

"So, what you're saying is that the surplus human population is like six billion, give or take a million. Well, I can see a lot of women thinking, wouldn't be nice if a disease came along and wiped out almost all of the population except for pockets here and there. She'd get to keep her husband and child. And a mission to have ten more babies. It would be like heaven."

"Either some disaster happens, or we'll be stacking humans in the ocean. We'll be building enormous honeycombs underground."

*   *   *

from the journal of Stephen Ambrose

Leakey and the elephants.

The human devastation of elephants is an indicator of human predatory tendencies. From 1979 to 1989, the number of elephants in Africa dropped from 1.3 million to 625,000. But that doesn't tell the whole story. In Kenya, only 22 percent of the elephants were male bulls (should be 50 percent or thereabouts). In Tanzania, only 1 percent of the elephants were male bulls. Male bulls have the tusks which are in great demand.

Evolution: male bulls without tusks are becoming more prevalent.

Monkey See

Nick tried his hand at programming. It was not that it was beyond his ability. He could do things step-by-step. After all, as he said to Stephen, "What I'm doing now is monkey see, monkey do."

"That's what I did at the start."

"You didn't study programming in school?"

"No. I hadn't found programming yet when I was still in school, but I had a few majors. English, Physics, Economics."

"That's unusual."

Stephen responded, "It didn't feel like it at the time, it felt like another course of this or that. It did tack on an extra year."

"What did you think you would do with all that stuff?"

"Go to engineering school, rise in management, develop five-year plans, and finally end up making speeches to cheer the troops."

"And use all your majors."

"Sure, why not?"

"So, what happened?"

"I went to engineering school, did some work in plate tectonics, and worked for an oil company for a while. I got laid off in the mid-eighties when oil collapsed. The IBM PC had just come out. I learned BASIC and played around with PASCAL. Then C came around."

"How did you learn these languages?"

"Oh, I would rewrite my astrology program every time a new language came along that I wanted to learn. It was, like you say, monkey see monkey do. I'd stay up all night doing compiles, seeing if it worked, debug it, compile it again (that is, converting my higher level language stuff down into machine code), run it again, look at the error messages, make corrections, maybe look for a more elegant way of doing things, and then do just one last compile. And by this time the sun would come up."

"I didn't realize you were so obsessed."

"It doesn't feel like obsession. It just feels like one more time."

"Sounds like obsession to me."

"Maybe it was just that the computers were so slow back then. Compiles took forever. My shrink says that there is a thing called clinical obsession, which is a serious condition. But then she'll flip-flop and say all the most successful people are compulsive and obsessed. That's how they get to be good at what they do. Perhaps there's a fine line between clinical obsession, and the obsessive-compulsive who are so successful, like Jerry Seinfeld."

"Well, I do a little with this programming thing, and then I get bored."

"That's it," Stephen said glumly. "Success with computers is a low-intelligence thing. I don't get bored doing simple things requiring many steps. That's the key to my success. I'm a little dull. It's like seeing the Sears Tower from Oak Park. You know where it is, and you set off in that direction. Walking. Walk and walk and walk. You can see the damn thing from time to time as the landscape of the buildings gives in to an empty lot, a burned-out building. That's programming."

"So, A may be smarter than the B, but because A gets bored writing up these small steps to get to a finished product, A will never be a great programmer."

"Probably not."

"Somehow seems odd to me."

"That bright people can't do everything?"

"Yes, I guess I wanted a high IQ to mean something more. Like having a superpower."

"Like you had the powers of a Marvel comic book character? Super IQ, he outwits his opponents with a single thought."

"Something like that."

"Meanwhile, the ants build their anthill."

"I guess that's it."

"It seems like that to me. I'm just one of many worker ants, or worker bees. A sexless worker bee, working for the good of the colony. Not that I really realize I'm working for the good of the colony. I'm just doing my thing. You know, just one more compile."

"Won't there be computers doing your programs?"

"I think so, yes."

"How soon?"

"Kurzweil thinks it'll be in the next ten years."

"Kurzweil?"

"A gifted programmer, developed early optical character-recognition programs, speech recognition."

"But not yet?"

"Well, the tools keep getting better and better. The languages keep improving. And the development of reusable code, modular code, called objects, has speeded up things a lot. If you don't have to write out routines every time, like—look to see if anyone else on the network is using this file, or check to see what time it is, say, for automatic backup programs, then the whole thing gets done faster.

"I don't know when computers will knock out code on their own. But I see the tools getting better and better. Perhaps things like Java will help. A language for every platform. A sort of universal language. Microsoft wants to gum up the works by making its own dialect. This will slow things down. But eventually, there will be some kind of universal computer language tool, which will write things in any language, or the best that can be done in a particular language."

*   *   *

from the journal of Stephen Ambrose

When we exit our baryonic flesh containers and become dark matter spirits, we will enter another dimension and actually occupy the same space as another body. We will be like neutrinos scooting through floors and walls, gliding into someone else's body, seeing everyone as they see them. So, we can follow along a brother or grandchild and see things through their eyes. Why not? Any scientist will tell you we're mostly space to begin with. Matter is a kind of fiction or convention.

What is a Genius?

from the journal of Stephen Ambrose

Charles Darwin was predestined to write *The Origin of Species*. His grandfather, Eramus Darwin, a famous physician and versifier, wrote about evolution years before his grandson's birth. So, it was already in the air. His cousin, also a grandson of Eramus, was Francis Galton, famous for his writings in the field of eugenics. It's a sure thing that Galton thought that he himself had a high IQ. Writing about eugenics has to amount to a self-justification of some kind or other.

But all of this thought in the same direction by three family members suggests a genetic map. The point is that they were in related fields. Darwin took the only adventure of his life at age twenty-two on board the *Beagle*. He was on that ship for four years and nine months. He looked at nature constantly; in short, he was obsessed. And he was looking at what animals had in common. For example, he never came across a large animal with three eyes. They all had two eyes. Two fore limbs, two rear limbs. When he got home he noticed something interesting in the breeding of dogs and horses and dairy cows . . .

Along comes Lyell, who writes of geology and eons. Long periods of time where things can change. Somehow, seabeds can end up at the tops of mountains.

Along comes Malthus, who writes of population explosion. Malthus suggested that populations increased geometrically, and are kept in check only by adverse factors, such as famine, wars, disease, and so on. This gave Darwin his major insight. And it's economics. Where resources are scarce, the struggle for existence will be fierce. The question becomes who survives and why.

Darwin writes in his *Autobiography*, "In October 1838, that is, fifteen months after I had begun my systematic enquiry, I happened to read for amusement Malthus on *Population*, and being well-prepared to appreciate the struggle for existence which everywhere goes on from long-continuing observation of the habits of animals and plants, it at once struck me that under these circumstances favorable variations would tend to be preserved and unfavorable ones destroyed. Here, at last, I had got a theory by which to work."

Born in 1809, he was twenty-nine years old. A power thinker. But he was not alone. Alfred Russel Wallace came up with much the same theory at around the same time. What is the IQ of such a person? Terman assigned him an IQ of 135. On Stanford-Binet, that's 1 in 70 people. Speculators in intelligence in the year 2000 give him a higher IQ of 165, which is 1 person in 41,174. But it's ridiculous. He and Wallace answered this question for all mankind.

Even if we view this on some numerical scale, which I am not particularly comfortable with, Darwin and Wallace would be 2 in a world population at 1.2 billion (or 1 in 600 million) for the year 1850. Or a Stanford-Binet IQ of 195.

Psychometrics might give you a high score on a test, but I object to the term "genius" for a person with a high IQ. You can only apply the term "genius" to someone who's done the deed. For his achievement. Only Darwin and Wallace came up with a viable theory of evolution. Only Leibnitz and Newton came up with calculus. Only Shakespeare wrote *King Lear*. The psychometrics people should alter their vocabulary to high IQ, or very high IQ, or very, very high IQ. But they must let go of the term "genius." It is an after-the-fact term, not a before-the-fact term, not a term of potential. Moreover, even if they are correct about what Darwin would score on an IQ test, and 1 in 70 would test as high as he would have, he had the unrelenting curiosity plus experience, which at that point in time was an immeasurable advantage.

It's a nice thing that a young kid like a John Stuart Mill knows some Greek at the age of three, but it just doesn't matter.

Footnote on the Last Chapter

Charles Darwin's cousin, Francis Galton, may have only been a very smart guy, but he was *very* smart. If intelligence can be reduce to a single number, his IQ has been estimated at between 170 and 200. He was reading at two, knew some Latin and Greek by age five, and by age six he had moved on to adult books, and soon after he could quote long passages of Shakespeare. There were a couple of years devoted to the study of medicine. But then he went traveling and wrote a book called *The Art of Travel*, a best seller, still in print today.

Then he went on to make the first popular weather maps, did work in regression mathematics, fingerprinting in criminology, but he was gripped by a cousin's work (whose IQ is never estimated as high Galton's), especially the early chapter describing breeding among animals. He naturally wondered what implications this would have for humans, and ended up writing a book *Hereditary Genius*, but had no children himself.

He was one of the first to suggest the study of twins, to see if those who had grown up in different environments had the same abilities. And he was one of the first to suggest the use of metrics to test those abilities.

Another of similar abilities would have to be Thomas Young. By age fourteen, he knew Latin and Greek, and had some acquaintance with French, Italian, Hebrew, Chaldean, Syriac, Samaritan, Arabic, Persian, Turkish, and Amharic. He is famous for making the first progress on understanding Egyptian hieroglyphics from deciphering some of the Rosetta Stone. He felt his most important contribution was to the wave theory of light, which Einstein praised when he wrote an introduction to Newton's *Opticks*. Like Galton, he seemed to shine a bright light on whatever he seemed to be interested in at the time, be it actuary science, or tuning instruments, or medicine. A linguist, he brought the term "Indo-European" into general use. Andrew Robinson thought he was *The Last Man Who Knew Everything*. Neither of these brilliant, brilliant people came up with Darwin's penetrating theory of evolution. A theory, by the way, he developed without benefit of Mendel, or Watson and Crick. But nevertheless, these two clever men make the rest of us feel like we've been twiddling our thumbs, playing solitaire.

So What Did Happen to the Dinosaurs?

"Okay, fancy pants, if you think you know everything, why did reptiles and birds survive and dinosaurs did not?" Stephen to Amanda, continuing their luncheon conversation at Aimee's birthday party. "There were all kinds of dinosaurs. Large ones, small ones. Why did small ones not survive? Velociraptors were no larger than crocodiles, yet crocodiles survived. Was it the water that protected, insulated the crocs?"

Amanda replied, "They did a study at Hell Creek, Montana. Scientists looked below and above the K-T boundary (the Cretaceous-Tertiary boundary), the layer of rock that lies at the moment of the dinosaur extinction.

"One thing the facts tell us is that anything large, over forty-four pounds, suffered much worse extinction rates."

"Okay, I guess it makes sense that the smaller life forms would have better chances."

"Let's see if I can remember this. Of sharks and rays, five species were found below the K-T boundary in the Cretaceous era, none were found above. This would appear to be 100 percent extinction. But sharks and rays both survived, so what does that mean? It means that the sample above is not all inclusive.

"Of seven species of frogs and salamanders found below the K-T boundary, all were found above. Meaning 100 percent survival.

"Out of seventeen species of turtle, fifteen survived. Only three out of ten species of snakes and lizards survived, although four out of five crocodilians made it through.

"Of mammals, in the late Cretaceous period there were found ten species of rodentlike creatures; five had descendants above the K-T boundary. Fifty percent extinction.

"All in all, as I recollect, 52 out of 107 species survived. Why did crocodiles make it and dinosaurs did not? There certainly were dinosaurs that were smaller than the forty-four-pound break-off point. Crocs are cold-blooded, dinosaurs were probably warm-blooded. Perhaps cold-blooded animals had an advantage. They could survive for long periods without food in cold weather. There's a snake that freezes during the winter and is able to thaw out in the spring."

"Yes, I know about that snake."

"Perhaps there are multiple reasons for survival. Birds survived because they could fly out of harm's way. They had the best mobility for finding areas which allowed survival. There is a theory about being at the right place at the right time. And not necessarily the best and smartest survive in those cases. It might be a turtle that found a protected shelter. Turtles are cold-blooded."

"Yes, but five out of ten mammals survive, and they're warm-blooded. So, why didn't warm-blooded dinosaurs survive?"

"Right. Those mammals were all small. When the hot particles that were thrown up into the atmosphere rained down, the lucky ones burrowed, or found a cave. Smallness was an advantage (even if a large animal holed up in a cave, what would it eat when it came out?), cold-bloodedness looks like an advantage, the mobility of birds was an advantage. Perhaps some were at the right place where there was some sunlight, water. Perhaps there is no universal explanation. The disappearance of the dinosaurs is a sticky problem. There's a theory out there about a dinosaur disease, virus, or bacteria that knocked them all out. Maybe some had a better immune system. Probably it was still a combination."

"Birds are going to turn out to be dinosaurs, so they did survive. That's the short answer. But not bad, Sis. Keep at it."

*   *   *

from the journal of Stephen Ambrose

Dogs used to find bodies at the Oklahoma Federal Building bombing would get so depressed from finding dead bodies that the human managers would put live bodies (other investigators) among the wreckage for the dogs to find. It helped to cheer them up. Interestingly, dogs respond well to the same antidepressants used by humans. A similar chemistry would explain their success. What happens when we decide we are not the only sentient beings on the planet?

The Best Line in a Porn Film

"You know the best line I came across in a porn flick?" Nick.

"No, what?"

"Stretch my throat," he said. "Who would ever say that in real life? It's the kind of line you dream about, but you would never ever hear. What's the best come-on line you've ever heard?"

"This is why we can't be friends."

"Why's that?"

"You ask impossible questions. 'What's the best come-on line I've ever heard?' Hell, I don't know if I have ever heard any come-on line from a woman."

"You have, but you've blocked it out because you didn't respond, and you're kicking yourself. So, you forget: it's a defense mechanism."

"Okay, what's the best come-on line you're ever heard?"

"'I have a high pain threshold.'"

"Oh wow. Someone actually said that to you?"

"What a girl! Disturbed, of course. But a good disturbed, if you know what I mean."

"Well, that will be the future. There will be 900 numbers manned by computers. And we won't know if it was a computer or a woman who said 'I have a high pain threshold.'"

"The new Turing test."

"Where you have to figure out if you're speaking to a woman, or transsexual, or transvestite, or some expert program called SexTalk?"

"Brother . . ."

* * *

301

"What can you say to a woman in that situation? You are just too excited, my dear. You are so open and so juicy, I can't feel anything. I need the friction, baby. It's not you. It's just an engineering thing," said Nick.

He continued, "I have a real problem with condoms. In a way, the girls like them. I just go on forever. They say, 'What? Are you going to fuck me to death?' But after a while, they get tired of the whole thing. It's not sexy anymore, it's just a chore. And I'll have them jack me off."

"Now you're talking about something I know about. It's an engineering thing. You have to have a certain amount of friction to keep your erection up. There's probably an equation. So many strokes per minute for a given tightness and slipperiness of the hole equals erection, and then eventually ejaculation." Stephen, the software engineer.

"Sometimes fast, though, does not equal orgasm."

"Yes, well, fast, slow, there's a trick. But I'm sure some damn scientist will figure it out, and his work will turn up in the world's best fuck doll."

"In a way, I feel it's kind of a shame that that fuck doll is so far off. I don't know if they will create one while I'm still alive."

"I hear you. Probably beautiful, but perhaps in some offbeat way if you want. Like the slight asymmetry of Mimi Rogers."

"But you know, if they build these things based on human circuitry, they'll probably develop their own minds."

"Damn."

"But you would get bored if the creature had no spunk."

"Well, maybe, but I'm pretty simple sometimes. I can get off on the same scenario again and again."

"You're speaking of porno videos."

"Of course."

"Me, too. But after a while . . ."

"Maybe a week. Maybe a month."

"Sometimes longer. But eventually I want to move on to some other video."

"Yeah, right."

*   *   *

They were nearly the same height. The Throdēop, Tōparr, was slightly taller than Nanci. She was intrigued. She asked, "You have not been very forthcoming. Dinosaurs became extinct except for birds about sixty-five million years ago. What happened?"

"I don't know."

"What do you mean you don't know?"

"Well, I wasn't there, was I? If I had been, we probably would not be having this conversation. I would just tell you."

"True enough."

"What was the status of things when you left?"

"I don't know that either, really. It was many generations ago that my relatives left the planet. I was born on the ship, millions of years later."

"Your computers must tell some kind of story."

"They do up until the time when we no longer had communication."

"What do they tell you?"

"They say that our forbearers, what you call velociraptor and deinonychus, made kills with their claws. We came along a few million years later. We were organized. We would build fences around our favorite meal and care for them and make sure they had plenty of plants to eat, and then we had machines carve them up, and grind them up, and they would be frozen and distributed all over the planet. And we hunted down the velociraptors, like you hunted down tigers. Very similar."

"Rather like what happened during the human tour of duty."

"And what did you do?"

"Beef. Cows were grown and fed and given antibiotics to fight disease and fatten them up, they were given plenty of grass which they converted into flesh that we liked to eat. And then we sent them through meatpacking plants where they were killed, grabbed, and cut open while they were still nearly alive, because, you know, it kept the meat fresh. But some were still frozen and ground up and sent all over the planet."

"See, you are no better than we are."

"Yes, we're dirty filthy flesh-eating animals, too."

"And you're a little pig."

*   *   *

from the journal of Stephen Ambrose

Jane Goodall at the end of her 1999 program for American Public Television makes her way to the edge of Gombe Park. "Thirty years ago I could look out over this valley and there were forests stretching into the distance. Chimpanzees living there. But today all the trees are gone, the chimpanzees have gone. And it's the same all the way around the park."

Jane then takes comfort in the fact that the park is a safe haven for the chimpanzees. The park is twenty square miles. Figure it out, that is an area of four miles by five miles.

Private jet owners will need more and more need more and more exotic destinations. And what could pay better for wilderness than a tourist destination?

Jane, who went to Gombe as an anthropologist, might end her career as a park docent, telling, first the filthy rich, and then the wave of upper middles, about Fifi and Freud. The park will be known as Disney's Gombe Park after they give $100,000,000 to increase its size by a factor of 3. Then they will spend multiples of the gift to increase the park size to build a fabulous resort around the park, with more forest that some of the chimps will migrate to, which will be just adorable.

As humans crowd the planet, it will seem more and more that we are keeping the chimps alive, saving them from extinction. Heroic work. Which only means, of course, the chimps no longer hold a vital place in the ecology. Where formerly they could make their own way in the world, now they are the walking dead. Relying on humans, all living at the pleasure of his Royal Highness, Homo necare.

Duck Decoys, Fuck Decoys

"You know when they first spoke about ATM machines, cash machines, I thought, 'No, I'll always stick with a human teller.'"

"But you didn't, did you?" Abner.

"No, it's the damn shame. I only use a human teller a few times a year. Hardly ever."

"Well, the cash machine is so much faster. It's the ease of the thing."

"We're suckers for that, aren't we? That will be the epitaph of Homo sapiens, 'He took the easy way out.'"

"Point taken."

"The thing I should be working on are the computer fuck dolls. That's the thing."

"Fuck dolls?"

"Well, they say we'll have androids by the end of the twenty-first century, and there is really only one good reason to develop them. And it's not to send them to Mars or the Moon, or do the paintwork at a Ford plant, or to do dangerous work down in the heat of the Earth's mantle, or at volcano sites, or at the bottom of the ocean. Well, maybe that stuff, too, of course. But the real problem of man is overproduction. Too many humans."

"And your idea is to fool men."

"And women."

"And give them decoys."

"I think decoys are going to turn out to be great collector items. Duck decoys, probably, in particular."

"And you think men will be fooled?"

"Are not male turkeys attracted to female turkey heads?"

"You're telling me that male turkeys get turned on by a head only?"

"That's the deal. They start doing their male display stuff before they even see if there is a place to put it. So, I think the silicon fuck dolls will be like cash machines used to be, and it will happen again: 'No, I'll never use a cash machine.'"

"But you do."

"Of course."

"You think men will go for these fuck dolls of yours."

"Think about it. It might look like Marilyn Monroe, and gush like Marilyn, and fawn over you. And ask you if you have any diamonds for her. And once they get her voice patterns down, they can mimic her voice for any kind of situation."

"Oh great."

"Might be. She'll be charming and alluring. And say things like, 'Oh, I would never do that.'"

"But she would."

"Maybe. Maybe not. Depends on how she's programmed. Maybe she'll hold you off for a month before she gives it up."

"Oh my God. A bitch android. Sounds like heaven."

"Let's not get into the mechanics, but you get the idea. Men get unprotected sex with their dream dates, no fear of disease, no fear of any babies. Populations decline to reasonable amounts."

"It wouldn't be a pendulum thing where men no longer want real human women anymore, and the population sinks to nothing? Where men come to prefer the decoys."

"Men. Get real. Men. They already prefer videos to the real thing. Where have you been? Looked in your closet recently? They already prefer the decoys."

"You exaggerate."

"Okay, maybe a little. I suppose the men making the videos have a good time. They get to act out their fantasies."

"I think the camera takes some of the fun out of it."

"I don't know about that. I know men who video their sex performances. For them, it's a boost. The guy from *Hogan's Heroes* was into that. Crane."

"For now, anyway, maybe the best way to solve the population problem is to make everyone rich, because sociologists have been saying for years that, generally speaking, the richer the family, the less children they have."

"So, if everyone is rich, the population will decrease."

"That's the idea."

"It's a theory, who knows if it's true? But if it is, then with less people there is a corollary benefit."

"What's that?"

"More freedom. More space. More space, more freedom. If there are less people, then I don't have to pay for parking anymore. I hate to pay for parking. I think it's a male thing, men feel that free parking is a right protected by the Constitution."

"Out in the hinterlands there is hardly anyone around to call shit on you, because there *isn't* anyone around—for miles. Even kids in Alaska learn how to fly, just to visit their pals."

"Freedom is a spatial thing, to some extent anyway."

* * *

The lounge area, after tennis: "They are predicting computer intelligence will be indistinguishable from human intelligence by the end of the twenty-first century."

"Because the cost of chips is heading to zero and they're making progress in programming, I suppose that's the deal." Nick.

"That and we'll map with extrasensitive MRIs the circuitry of the brain, so maybe we'll be able to duplicate exactly a human's thought processes."

"They also say we'll find something faster than the speed of light. Like the speed of gravity. I don't know from shoeshine about this stuff, but I'd say there will be a few stumbling blocks along the way. At the end of a stock market top they're always saying things like it's different this time. Romans had a relatively high state of technology, but it was nearly lost during the Middle Ages or the Dark Ages."

"Okay."

"In 1929, the Dow hit 328. I'm fond of asking how long it took to get back there. Want to take a guess?"

"If you insist, probably during WWII when the economy ramped up the war machine. I'll say 1942."

"Completely wrong, the market tanked when the war began. But I like the thinking behind it, the logic. Just shows how wrong our thinking can take us. Very instructive. No, 1952 was the year. It took the war economy plus the postwar boom to get back there, plus the prospect of a great general as president."

"Wow, twenty-three years. I didn't think it took that long."

"They don't call it the Great Depression for nothing."

"Yeah, but it did get back to the old high, and then higher highs."

"Right. But the pattern repeats. Look at the Japanese. Low interest rates, high technology. They thought the stock market would never stop going up. Nikkei hit 39,000 in 1989, it's never looked up since. It's less than half that now. We're ten or eleven years out. Maybe it will be twenty-three years before it gets back there."

"Well, okay, maybe machine intelligence doesn't get there by the year 2100 because there's a long period of economic depression, but it does get there by 2150."

"Your point is that it does get there."

"That's my point. But I don't think androids will create much interest until the military understands their potential. Then the money will kick in," said Nick.

"Right, of course. Has to be. No need to send soldiers. Just send in the 'droids."

"Get in there, boys!"

"But androids will be too expensive."

"To begin with."

"Then the price will come down."

"Everyone will have his own android. His butler."

"His companion. His agent."

"In my case, a female companion."

"And when a human female gets to sixty or seventy years old, she'll buy a male android that will look like twenty-five."

"What's wrong with twenty-three, or twenty-one for that matter."

"Could be any age you want, fourteen, if you fancy that."

"Nah, I like them fully developed. Eighteen is good."

"Buy an android." He repeated it to get a sense of it, "Buy an android. I have a feeling that is going to sound bad in the future."

"Racist?"

"I don't know for sure. Something like racist. If they turn out to be sentient beings, as they're so wont to call androids on *Star Trek*, then how can you buy them without invoking the old notions of slavery?"

"Slavery. I have the feeling this is an idea that hasn't lost all its juice yet. Look at the sex ads."

"I have a sense about where you're taking this and . . ."

"Give me license to complete the thought. Maybe it's just one of those permutations which never transpires . . . Anyway, you can see the S-M thing develop over time. First, it's in the basements and back alleys."

"Then it moves to the front room."

"Sure, everyone will wear their earring that signifies dominance or submission. Women, who formerly were women's libbers when men were pigs, will now start adoring those pigs. You can see it. 'He's my pig, and I'm standin' by him.'"

"And wear her black eye as a badge of honor."

"Black eye, shmlack eye. You're moving too fast for me. Probably some of course will want their black eye. Those will be the ones in the forefront."

"It won't be the slavery of the past. It will be a voluntary slavery. It will be a sex thing. People who realize their preference will pursue it more actively. There will still be boundaries. And people will assault those boundaries. Some will end up in prison, and others on the cover of *Time*."

"After all, if Monica can get on the cover for a blow job, everything's up for grabs."

"Things swing back and forth. The pendulum is always in motion. There might be an age of repression somewhere in there."

"Repressions can be interesting."

"You're thinking of the Victorian Age."

"Repressives are always around. Remember, the Puritans only allowed Shakespeare, that great voice of the human soul, to put up his dramas on the other side of the Thames. And remember also, boys had to play the female parts."

"And today we have the Fundamentalists."

"Fundamentalists, Puritans. It's all the same. Perhaps they have a role to play."

"That role is to prevent *Huckleberry Finn* from being taught. And removing Darwin from the curricula. The world, the universe was formed in 4004 B.C."

"Oh well."

The Six Pack Girl Revisited

"So the alien seeks out the Six Pack Girl," said Nick.

"That's it."

"I don't think the Six Pack Girl makes it with dogs."

"You see. You present an idea, and right away everyone has their own idea behind the idea. And you resent my appropriating your notion."

"Well, think about it. The Six Pack Girl is the girl you take to the motel. She's not necessarily the girl you take to a sex party. That's a different animal all together. That's the Circus Girl. She's a performer. Three guys working on her, or five, or seven."

"Where are you getting these numbers? The first three I've got but the others?"

"One for each hand makes five. And one guy at each breast makes seven."

"I got you. Just so we're on the same page. Is she lactating?"

"Is she lactating?"

"I'm just trying to create a little interest."

"So, you've got her going with all these people, and then you've got the onlookers. You know, I think I prefer the Six Pack Girl. I've never been into team sports. I always preferred chess or tennis."

"What if it were the other way around? How about you with, let's see, one two three four five girls? What if the Six Pack Girl brings a friend?"

"Well, for the experience, yes, but once again, I think ultimately, that we're talking too many. It's distracting. Orgasm is one of those things that requires concentration."

"Concentration and Orgasm. Sturm and Drang. Crime and Punishment. Let me work on that."

"Haven't you ever had to hold some image in your brain even as you are fucking some unbelievably sexy girl?"

"Only when she's a dud. When she doesn't keep me involved with some verbal cues. But yes, I've had the experience."

"Okay, and even when she's communicating this stream of verbal cues, isn't that really an aid to your concentration?"

"Yes. I suppose."

"So, my point is that too many distractions get in the way. Perhaps you may be conditioned through boredom into too many situations so that you may have overexposed yourself to sex, and run out of interesting scenes. In which case I suppose Circus Girl will save the day."

Stephen: "So, are you that far gone?"

"Well, we're all trying to get back to that first time."

"That first time?"

"That first sex experience. That first drug experience. That first time you heard Bach's Concerto for Two Violins. That first time in the back seat."

*   *   *

from the journal of Stephen Ambrose

I dreamt a missile was coming after me. All sorts of thoughts are coming at me as I get the video feed from a missile, maybe from some astral plane location. Even though I have designed the software for this missile, I am wondering how it is homing in on me. Can it detect my bad breath or defecation trail? I know that if I were lower down in the Earth I would be safe, because I can visualize the stairways going further and further down. I am closing the fire doors behind me as I go down the stairwell shaft. Yes, at some point I would be safe.

But I am not down there. Safe? I am up on land in the desert with no means to protect myself. This missile, which I designed, is homing in on the silver amalgam fillings in my mouth. Damn, I should have had those replaced with porcelain. The silver amalgam wasn't good for me anyway. What the dentists didn't tell you was that your silver fillings were over half mercury, and of course, that's poison.

Then I realize that it isn't the silver amalgam that the missile is homing in on. It's homing in on the electrical signature of my thoughts. That's it. It's brain patterns. The grey matter etchings that develop the code for the missile are the tip-off, that's how the missile detects me. Because, now I realize, the missile is sent out to destroy the makers of missiles. The missile was not aimed at me but aimed freely at whoever makes such missiles, and homing in on the signature of their thoughts.

It's a flaw in the programming, I realize. Damn thing has buggy code. No beta versions released. There should have been some way to make sure it knew how to recognize me and not attack.

*   *   *

from the journal of Stephen Ambrose

> An idea is like the wind.
> You can see a tree swaying
> to the music of an acoustic rustle;
> or tulips deflect an airy punch;
> You cannot see an atom,
> but you can see its angry path in a gas chamber.
> Genes dictate behavior,
> but you cannot speak to one.
> You can only speak to its filled-out form,
> the Punch & Judy into which it stuck its hand.
> Let me put it another way:
> You can speak to me,
> but you cannot speak
> to that which made me.
> Me: I'm just a puppet.

Idea for a Story

from the journal of Stephen Ambrose

Idea for story.

"Of course I remember meeting you. You had on a blue shirt and a very colorful paisley tie, and you were with a stunning android babe. Her name was Samantha. Whatever became of her?"

"Well, dating a human was just a passing fancy for her. I couldn't hear music like she could, you know, in the higher registers. And I didn't like fast music."

"Funny how important music is for those in the higher intel groups."

"And you know how acute their sense of smell is. She could smell my defecations long after I passed one. She was very sensitive about that."

"Yes, I know how hard it is to please an android. You feel like you're a relic, like you're all reptile brain, and she's somewhere out there."

"We played chess once. That was enough."

"Didn't you click on your enhancer?"

"I did. I would look at the screen in my glasses, and make my move. We played to a draw. But it's all phoney-fakey. She calls out the names of the openings. I mean, who's ever heard of the Winawer variation of the French Defense? And she kibitzes about strategies, and I don't know what she's talking about. I just get the next move from the enhancer. I'm just kind of a robot moving pieces."

"It's a drag."

"Yes, and you know how androids are about pattern recognition. They really almost get inside your brain. And they're not using probes or anything. It's not telepathy exactly, but they hear you talk for a while and they know what's coming next."

"Yeah, I've had that. Where they finish your sentences."

"I hate that. Some are more polite than others. Some will keep their mouths shut."

"Yeah, but then you can read their facial expressions. The new ones really have a hard time keeping a poker face."

"Ultimately, maybe it's impossible to be polite."

"How was the sex?"

"The sex was great, of course, in a technical sense. I don't know what she's getting out of the deal. She does this great sex act thing, and they have their orgasm thing, whatever that is."

"Right. I know what you're talking about. So, you just end up doing it for money."

"Yeah, androids pay well for a short period with humans."

"Don't I know."

"And I need the money. That's how they've got us. Who would have thunk a hundred years ago that androids, who didn't even exist then, would turn humans into wage slaves. It's not force exactly. It's not eighteenth century America slavery. We need the dough, and they've got us."

Not Ready to Face the Traffic

Abner, the 5pm-and-I'm-not-quite-ready-to-face-the-traffic call: "Hell, we're all wage slaves."

"I don't know for sure, but I think my psychiatrist would say that work is good. She would probably say she's a slave to her job. In fact, I think she has said it."

"You and your psychiatrist. You need a psychiatrist like I need a psychiatrist."

"Maybe you do need one. You never sleep well. You're always irritable. Angry most of the time."

"Get real. Nobody sleeps well. Do you sleep well?"

"No, but then I'm seeing a psychiatrist about it."

"Hasn't helped, has it? I can remember one night about a year ago. I happened to speak to everyone in the family. Dad was up at two. You were up at two. Mom was up at two. Amanda was up at two. Aimee was up at two. Everyone in the family was up at two."

"What's your point?"

"The family that is up at two together is dysfunctional together," he laughed.

"Couldn't quite get that to work, could you?"

"You would have the whole family doing psychotherapy. Besides, I read that talk therapy isn't that effective anyway. Drugs are the thing."

"That's what my therapist would say."

"See what I mean? Does she prescribe anything for you?"

"Yes."

"Does it work?"

"Yes."

"Then what are you seeing her for?"

Relatives can get to the point sometimes faster than nonfamily. They care less about subtlety. There was no way Stephen was going to let his brother razz him about the fact that he was attracted to his shrink. He would never hear the end about how silly that was.

He would say that she would never go for a weakling on therapy. That's for starters. She would never go for someone making less money than her. Thirdly, she would never give up a paying customer.

"Let's talk about this some other time. You're just needling me."

"No. Let's keep going."

"Stop."

"No, no, no. I think this is a breakthrough session. There must be something else. Oh, that's it. You're in love with your shrink."

"Everyone falls in love with their shrink. It's called transference. You're bored. That's the problem here. You don't want to work. You're the one who said they're going to write on your gravestone, 'He wrote change orders.'"

"You're just trying to distract me. We have to keep working on this."

"Stop."

"Is she attractive?"

"Just a second. Do you want to hang on? I've got another call coming in."

"No, I'll go, penis brain."

There was no one on the other line. Discomfort sometimes requires a subterfuge.

Hookers, Yet Again

It was a big deal to go back to Amsterdam again—time and money, so meanwhile Stephen responded to the occasional ad in the adult pages of the *The Reader*, or increasingly, some Internet ad.

But print ads don't tell you anything. Sometimes a word like *zäftig* appeared, which was interesting. And the Internet ads can be just as bad. Maybe you see just a giant pair of boobs. You meet the girl and everything is big. Huge. Especially, her middle. Or you get the face, which is pretty, even gorgeous, but again she weighs a lot more than you do. Sometimes, you can see the whole body and face, and everything checks out, but she has a terrible personality. She's got an appointment with her hairstylist, and she just wants to get the party over with.

So it was that Stephen responded to an ad for Marilyn. She was blond, buxom. She had a studio, obviously a place of business, on Oak just off Rush Street. $400. Plus parking, so add another $15.

Stephen comes into the room, and it's nice. Very bordellowy. Four-poster bed, thick melon-colored plush carpet. A fainting sofa. Obviously an apartment designed to have sex anywhere. There were two mirrors, strategically placed.

She opens the door and let's him in. Then she gives Stephen a big kiss. This is unusual. Girls in the business don't like to kiss. She smells great. Already Stephen's sold.

"Take off your jacket."

"Thanks."

Stephen sees on the entrance table a VISA bill for Miranda English. Boy, he thought, that's careless.

"I've been drinking a lot of coffee."

"The bathroom is right there." She points.

When Stephen came out, the VISA bill was gone.

"So you're Stephen Ambrose. Are you Stephen Ambrose of the Richmond Ambroses?" This in a thick fake southern accent. He loved it. This girl was great.

"So do you say the same thing if the guy's name is Polinski? Are you Paul Polinski of the Richmond Polinskis?"

"No, silly." Then she says, "I would say, 'I Are you Count Polinski?'"

I laughed. This girl was a diamond.

The girls don't usually like to kiss, there is something a little too intimate about it. He put his hands on her ass, and pulled her to him.

*　*　*

Stephen was paying this Marilyn or Miranda or whoever she was, but he had had his chances to do her thing himself. The sex-for-money thing. He had been hired to set up a Web site for an older woman, Summer. She needed a Web site for her hospital league. They worked together closely for a while.

Summer was an attractive full-breasted woman. In her early fifties was his best guess. Stephen was forty-five. A few years behind. She was divorced. He assumed from her Lake Shore Drive condo and Mercedes Benz, that the settlement had left her a woman of substance.

"My husband was busy all the time. Traveled a lot. He's a good-looking man."

"And the women are drawn to him, are they?"

"I should say so. But divorced twice before I met him. Three kids. The man had a lot of baggage. This guy was on safari with six porters carrying suitcases."

He laughed. This is what one would have to do to earn your money. Listen to her rattle on about her ex-husband. He didn't follow it up because he figured it would mean that he was interested in being . . . what? She was already picking up the tab on expensive meals at the Four Seasons. What else would she end up paying for?

"Do you travel much?"

"I like to travel, but I can't get away that often."

"I love to travel. I'd like to do the Greek islands. I understand they're delightful."

Travel. Would she pay for me to accompany her?

"Never been there."

"You're not attracted to Greek culture?"

Greek culture meant only one thing in the sex magazines. Could this elstwise high class society woman really be suggesting such a thing? Backdoor adventure in an exotic locale?

"As an amateur etymologist, of course, I run into Greek roots all the time."

"Greek roots. Yes, I guess a lot of words have Greek roots."

Oh brother. This sure had all the appearance of opportunity. He didn't pursue it, but he heard she later bought a place in the Greek islands. She had the money, so maybe he had missed his big chance to try sex for money (more or less). So, she would end up paying for everything, and Stephen would be in Norma Desmond's thrall. That is how it would work out. Maybe he was jumping to conclusions.

Stephen believed in tradition. Men should pay for sex. It just works better. They pay for sex. They appear to have control. Maybe. Generally speaking, the appearance of male control is good for good sex. Although the sex literature is full of men with foot fetishes. Mistress, may I suck your toes?

How were men in control if women paid? Stephen kept his distance, and things went on amiably enough. He felt kind of sorry for her. She had all this money, but it was wrong ways up for him.

* * *

"Ideally, you would get two women with alternating periods. Problem is: if they become friends they'll synchronize their periods, and then where are you? True harems must have been a disaster."

"You're thinking negatively. Periods. You should be thinking ovulation dates. Ideally, you should have twenty-eight different women with twenty-eight sequential ovulation dates. They go off like firecrackers, one per day." Nick.

"Probably they shouldn't know each other."

"Exactly, you don't want them to synchronize, which they absolutely will do if they know each other."

"I have to admit I think you're on the right track about the ovulation dates. One of my friends. His wife wanted to have a baby. She gave him the thrill of a lifetime. Best sex he ever had."

"And?"

"She got pregnant, of course. He had to quit law school and get a job to support the baby."

"That's it. Right. You should have known with that tip-off, 'the best sex he ever had.' In this life you don't get that without some consequence."

*　　*　　*

"Snakes, Stephen. Snakes." Nick.

It was a very warm night in the 80s Fahrenheit, upper 20s Celsius. The girls were in full bloom. Halter tops, long naked backs. It was the beginning of June and we were at an outdoor cafe on Rush Street watching the passing parade.

"Nick. The trouble with you is that you don't get enough sex."

"If I don't, then who does?" he laughed. "But you're right, of course, it's like Jell-O, there's always room for more. Although, I must confess, sometimes just looking, like we are doing tonight, is enough."

"Then you could get into the Japanese thing, voyeurism?"

"Kinky watching. Of course. But only as a passing thing, just to check it out. I like to watch. Who said that?"

"Peter Sellers in *Being There*."

"Occasionally, you can find that particularly sexy girl. That's what I live for. That is the algorithm I'm working on."

"Well, there's an algorithm worth working on. What are your parameters?"

"There are certain things I need to have in the way of a body, but I am surprisingly broad in my outlook. A good dirty mouth can make up for a lot."

"You're not speaking of oral sex per se, I take it," said Stephen.

"We live for great oral sex, but you're right, I'm talking about someone who's worked a 900 number. And I've tried that, too. A girl named Gia was great."

"Gia, huh? What do you suppose it is? We get older and need to hit more sensory centers to get to orgasm? Touching is not enough. We need to hear something. Smell something. See something. Engage the brain in some fantasy scenario."

"Possibly, but denial can also work. If I let it go for a few days, then I'm really ready."

"So what are your other parameters?"

"Well there is something to the research that women show more skin when they're near ovulation. It gives you a little bit of an advantage when their chemistry is working with you. Hell, women are constantly taking advantage of men's chemistry. Look at how many men still marry in California in spite of the community property laws."

"Yeah, I saw Al Goldstein on some goofy program or other. He claimed that one of his wives screwed him so few times that he figured each session was in the thousands. Maybe ten thousand. That's a lot for sex. I have a friend who thinks a hundred bucks is all it's worth."

"What can he find for a hundred?"

"Your're right, it's not great stuff he's finding. Hookers in their forties, fifties. Second—or third-tier hookers. A lot of the time, he tells me, they have some defect or other."

"There's a hunter for you. He picks off the young, the weak, the lame. Sounds like a speech or a credo, doesn't it? We all do that from time to time. But I'm looking for something other than just young or weak."

"You're hunting for the elusive nymphomaniac."

"Something like that. Nymphos are usually a little nuts."

"That's a deterrent?"

"Well, it can be a problem."

"Right, you want a nympho when she's in her good element, before she makes a grab for the knife."

Sam

Sam was born in Germany in the 1930s. His father just barely escaped from the Nazi death camps, cutting fences to get out. They migrated to forbearing Holland. Sam spoke Dutch as a kid, but lost it as he grew older. Then they caught the last boat for America. As a teenager Sam had a bout with cancer. He was the guy who thought it was only worth a hundred bucks.

"Why are you always moaning? Life is good. Let me set you up with Masha. You can have her for a hundred."

"Thanks, Sam. I'll think about it."

"She has small titties. I know you don't like that but she'll lick your ass. She'll drive you nuts."

"Where did you meet this one?"

"On the boat."

"Which boat?"

"The Empress in Joliet."

"And how did you meet her?"

"She's a concierge. She gets me free passes, free meals. Stuff like that."

"And how did you . . ."

"Oh, the usual stuff. I paid her a lot of compliments. I told her I would love to lick her pussy."

"Ah."

"You're ridiculous. You don't do anything to get a woman. You don't do anything, and nothing happens. Big surprise. If you want something to happen, then you have to do something. Join something. You need exposure."

"You're right, of course."

"You're the worst. You concede everything, and don't do a thing. Listen, life is going to be over soon."

"You remind me of my brother who is always saying they'll put on his tombstone, 'He did change orders.'"

"That's it."

"The other thing he says is that at the end of your life, no one wishes he'd logged more time at the office."

"That's it. He's on the right track."

"Mostly lip service, I'm afraid. Must be a family trait. He spends most of his life in the office writing change orders. You're the one out doing something."

Sam was like a breath of fresh air. He had the unbounded optimism of a happy sociopath. The laws of man he held at arm's length. He honored them most of the time, but wasn't above flouting them when he felt like it. It offended his sense of freedom not to do as he wished when he wished.

"My father died at fifty-two."

"Yeah, but you said your father was a smoker."

"True. But you could hardly blame the man. Just to get through Germany in the thirties . . ."

"What happened to your relatives?"

"Auschwitz, most of them. Terrible things. Throwing babies out of windows and ending up on bayonets."

"I think that's why you're so lucky."

"Why's that?"

"The spirits of all your relatives are looking over you. Providing you with protective cover. And I think they're using you as a vessel to work through all the lost opportunities."

He laughed, "Hold on. My other phone's ringing."

Click. He came back on the line. "Where were we?"

"I was explaining to you how you were able to win fifteen consecutive times at the boat, and get the girl."

"Girls."

"Have it your way. Who else?"

"Luwanda."

"Luwanda?"

"I love that black stuff. You know what they say, 'Once you go black, you don't go back.'"

"What is it you like?"

"They're uninhibited. I had this one in the shower, and she grabbed the bar and put her legs around my shoulders and shoved her pussy in my face."

"It's nice when they show a little interest."

"You have to eat their pussies. That's it. You have to do it."

"I'll bear that in mind."

"'I'll bear that in mind.' You idiot. Just do it. The meter's ticking."

"Doesn't work for me. Scare me to death, and what you get is Stephen scared to death. I end up in bed wrapped in covers. Not necessarily Action Steve."

"Well, listen, I have to go. I've got a chess club meeting to go to. There's a bunch of young kids that are going to show up."

That was Sam. Sex and chess. He was a good player, but it was emotional for Sam. His fondest memories were of playing chess with his dad. His dad was gone, so now he sponsored chess clubs, chess matches. He sponsored chess scholarships. A lot of his closest friends came out of chess.

With Mars and Jupiter conjuncted in Scorpio, he was a sex maniac.

Waiting for Amanda

I had been waiting a long time, and now I was really pissed off. My first story had been accepted for publication, which had also taken a long time, and I wanted to celebrate. But as it was, Amanda was late. Amanda was the one to celebrate with, but if this had been a first date, then there would never be a second. I was waiting a long time, and this wasn't Argentina, where no one was on time; this was sensible, grid-city Chicago. Beyond that, I didn't anticipate her being late, and I didn't have any reading material with me.

"Where have you been?"

"Sorry, car trouble." Amanda.

"And no cell phone still?"

"Hey, I'm a student. How can I afford a cell phone?"

"Well, car trouble on the south side. I should think a cell phone would be mandatory as a safety precaution. I thought you had one of those European cars that never break down."

"Yes, it's a Volvo, but it died like a Fiat."

I laughed, "You're distracting me," and laughed some more.

"Of course I'm distracting you. So, I'm a little late. This isn't worth bothering about. Have you heard from Abner recently?"

"Sure I've heard from Abner. He thinks we'll still have the same government and currency twenty years from now."

"What?"

"So, I should saving for retirement."

"Yes, he told me I'd better write a book," said Amanda.

"Oh really, why? Wait. Let me figure it out. The university thing—publish or perish. Publish and you can get a better job. And secondly, for the income. Which he wanted you to salt away for retirement."

"Right."

"Well, he's always telling me to forget my book."

"Oh really, why's that?"

"Because I should become a consultant. Consultants make bigger money, and, get this, I could put more money away in a Keogh plan than a regular IRA."

"That's Abner, all right. Abner the squirrel."

"Well, there's something to be said for providing for the future. That's my point. That we're all consuming like mad. Is man really that destructive?"

"Are you asking me in my professional capacity?" said Amanda.

"Why not?"

"Man is pretty destructive. They think modern man developed, let's say a hundred, two hundred thousand years ago. They've found remains in South Africa on the coast by Klasies River mouth that are about ninety thousand years old. And it seems they traveled hugging the coastline where they knew how to fish, and made it to Australia about sixty thousand years ago."

"Presumably over the water."

"Well, if a lizard, a Komodo dragon, can travel great distances over water, certainly a man could find a way. Anyway, we know they were there because we found remains. But get this, by thirty-five thousand years ago, while Cro-Magnon was painting in caves in the South of France, most of the large marsupials disappeared in Australia."

"And you don't think it was an accident?"

"No."

"And the marsupials that survived?"

"They were fast and agile, or they were night animals."

"I see."

"Most elephant species—mammoth, mastodon, were gone from Asia about twenty thousand years ago. And twelve thousand years ago, all elephants were gone in Europe."

"I get the idea. Anyway, we can celebrate the ephemeral event of my getting a story published."

We clinked water glasses.

"Here's looking up your old address."

"Chin-chin. Science fiction I expect."

"Yes."

"I knew you'd publish. And you'll also publish your novel. I like what I've read of that. I've always wanted you to abandon the work on the missiles."

"I think I'll lose half my audience over the male songbirds."

"Why?"

"The males are the ones with the brain expansion."

"Have more confidence in females, we're more resilient than you think. You keep up on the literature, but something may come up and turn the whole thing upside down. And think about this: someone has to make a judgement about male singing performance, and that will require brainpower. There's your push-pull."

"I guess that makes females the ultimate critics," he said. "I'm reminded of the blue bower bird doing its dance for the female. He's raising his wings and doing all manner of stuff, and she's turning her head so one eye then the other eye can judge the spectacle, and then she flies off." Amanda raised her eyebrows.

He continued, "This male-female stuff doesn't bother you because you have established your claim to brilliance. You have your Ph.D. in paleoanthropology from the University of Chicago."

"It helps."

"Well, it's just one story. And even if I publish a novel, that does not make for a career."

"Oh, you'll do it. You and your compiles. It's always just one more compile and just one more and just one more. You never give up. Now it will be just one more rewrite. And when you run up against a brick wall, you have a good way of figuring a way around. You think you're a plodder, but you have you have your moments. And I like your balloon-brained Throdēop."

"Technically, they're bandoneon-brained," Stephen kidded.

"You're such a nut. I suppose that's from tango."

"The bandoneon is the accordion-like instrument that is the heart of tango music."

"Of course. Ever notice how the humans in your novel have these Latin names?"

"Actually, it never crossed my mind. It's an accident."

"You call it an accident. I call it too many trips to Buenos Aires."

"I suppose that would support the hypothesis that consciousness is a slight thing. I use the Latin names and am not even realizing what I'm doing."

"And you see yourself as a Ramón? Interesting."

"Wow," I thought. Regaining my equilibrium, I said, "Well, of course that would be the natural conclusion. You really want to do this analysis thing?"

"Not necessarily."

"What do you know about ice ages?"

"What do you want to know? Most of the time the planet has been quite warm, sometimes even at the poles. Most of the time there is no ice. Evidently there have been three big ice ages, and we're in one that's been going on for two and a half million years, since volcanos closed the passage in Central America and cut off the currents."

"And so we're in a temporary warming between cold periods."

"Right. There have been seventeen warm periods during that two and a half million years. I'm not going into the causes of ice ages, that's not my interest. There's the Serbian guy with the wobble in the axis and temporary change in the orbit. You'll have to look that up on your own. I think when the Earth's orbit is nearly a circle, it's warm and when it becomes more elliptical it gets cold. Anyway, here's my point. Seventeen warm periods, and the megafauna, the large animals . . ."

"Yes, I know what megafauna are."

"Okay, you know what megafauna are. But think about this. Somehow they survived one ice age after another. These are animals that have been around in one version or another for millions of years. But suddenly, seventy to eighty percent of the megafauna are gone in a matter of a few hundred years, maybe a thousand years. How come? What made this thawing different from every other thawing? There's a theory that a comet or asteroid hit the glaciers in Canada and a flood ensued."

"I feel like a defense attorney. That's your case, huh? Circumstantial evidence. As Adam would say on *Law and Order*, where's the smoking gun?"

"The smoking gun? What are you looking for? Where the bullet entered the body? Some kind of Chicxulub-type collision site? It doesn't always work that way. How about a hut made from mammoth bones, would that work?" Amanda.

"Really, they've uncovered such a site?"

"Two hundred eight bones at one site. But there is even more condemning stuff."

"What stuff?"

"Work on mammoth tusks. It seems the tusks have rings like tree rings, and from this they can tell two important things.

"One is that in times of starvation, the rings are small."

"Okay, that's logical."

"And the other thing that they can tell is, in females, how many births they've had because the calcium in the diet goes to the fetus. Evidently, they can tell that they were having births every four years."

"So?"

"It seems that African elephants, when they are under distress from overhunting, increase their birthrate to make up for the lost animals. Guess how often they breed in that case."

"Every four years."

"Exactly. Usually, they have births about every six years."

"And what about the rings? Get back to the rings and starvation."

"Yes, you might expect that starvation at the end of an ice age. Dislocation, floods. Travel into unfamiliar territory, but that wasn't the case. The animals do not appear to have suffered starvation, and were well-fed."

"So, they died suddenly."

"And how are sudden deaths caused?"

"Humans with spears."

"Like humans with flint spears. There could be some other cause, but what would cause mammoths to fire up the birthrate?"

"Humans killing baby mammoths."

"Hey, what is veal, after all?"

"The meat of calves, baby cows."

Therapy, Sessions, Classes, and Dinner

Sophia was beautiful today as always. That was the great thing about women, and especially beautiful women. They always kept up appearances.

"I think there are only four things in life," said Stephen.

"Let me guess—air, earth, fire, and water?"

"Very funny. Therapy, sessions, classes, and dinner."

She laughed.

"For me, this is therapy; for you, this is a session."

"Well . . ."

"I write programs for a while, that's a session, or therapy, depending on how interested I am. Then I go for a massage, that's therapy. I come here, that's therapy. I take a Spanish lesson, that's a class. I go for yoga instruction, that's a class. And what's left? Dinner."

"Yes, well, for some of my clients anyway, dinner is therapy."

"And if they eat too much, then they come to you . . ."

"For more therapy. And maybe from a different perspective doing these sessions with you is therapy for me."

"Well, it may be therapy sometimes. That's possible. But I imagine that it is sessions most of the time."

"Well, I can imagine these meetings are sometimes sessions for you."

"Rarely, they're mostly therapeutic."

"I'm glad to hear that."

"I suppose dinner is mostly a therapy."

"So, then we're down to therapy, sessions, and . . ."

"Classes."

"And classes?"

"Yes, they're probably either therapy or sessions. So, that means everything is either therapy or sessions."

"Or both."

"I liked my original statement. I don't like it being reduced to a dichotomy, a binary statement. We're either 0 or 1."

"I agree with you."

He said he had a dental appointment next week, and that he would call to reschedule, but he never did.

*   *   *

Stephen waxed on about machine intelligence, "In the future you can see some android saying about the machine that beat Garry Kasparov. 'Oh, that thing was just a machine. Deep Blue. Get real. It's just a program with a brute of a computer behind it. Humans thought it could think. Get real.' Of course, the human brain is also a computer, a calculating machine. An organic thinking machine, you can see the android saying, 'Quite remarkable really, that an organic machine can do such higher level computing.' That'll cheer you up."

"Yeah, Deep Blue was just a specialized machine, like an anteater," said Abner.

"The Turing test is okay. Can someone at the end of a telephone line tell which of two parties at the other end is machine or human? That's a test. But a machine capable of reproducing itself. Now, you're talking. There's a test. Now you're talking about continuation."

"Is it reproduction, or is it continuation that is the issue? Because maybe a machine can be made that will continue ad infinitum. This part fails, that part fails. Everything is modular. You just plug it in. Plug in a new arm or leg."

*   *   *

"Well . . . I'm trying anyway to give her a feeling for the environment. I go to parks a lot, and the zoo." That's what Amanda said. She was pregnant. No father anywhere in sight. She followed her program just as she had laid it out.

"Parks. You mean those areas where commercial developers have not been allowed to develop . . . yet. And zoos. The pens we build for the living extinct." Stephen.

"They're not extinct if they're still living and in zoos."

"Okay, have it your way. Get me on a technicality. But if the zookeepers are prevented from feeding these animals for a few days, then poof: they're all gone. They cannot fend for themselves in a cage. So, I'm calling them extinct. Or call them pre-extinct if that makes you any happier," Stephen said. "In fact, in fact, I've got a good story for you. There was a species called the heath hen, lived in the northeast. A favorite meal of the settlers, some people think the heath hen was the first Thanksgiving dinner, not the turkey. Well, as humans occupied more and more of their territory, there was less and less room for the heath hen. And on top of this, humans hunted them to near extinction. By 1908, there were only something like fifty of them left off the mainland, in Martha's Vineyard. That's what happens if you become a favorite meal of humans."

"I hear you. So, what happened?"

"Oh well, humans tried to save them, created a reserve for them. By 1915, the population had increased to two thousand. But then they suffered a bunch of disasters. Gene rot, you know, inbreeding; there was a poultry disease, and then a fire reduced them to thirteen birds in 1927. By 1932, all gone."

"It's a good story. Your point is even when we try to save a species, we muck it up."

"Maybe it shouldn't be up to us. A top predator, a lion, a pride, will eat a Cape Buffalo, which is a big animal, but that's all until it's hungry again. But man, he sends Bill Cody to shoot buffalo, and he shoots so many, he has such a massive population to feed, that he comes back 'Buffalo' Bill. That was another animal almost hunted to extinction. Game reserves, parks, and so on help, but really the only thing that will make a difference is to reduce the number of humans. Habitat then increases for these endangered species."

"But as it is, we're headed for twelve billion."

"Right. When we're all underground because we've fucked the ozone layer, and your daughter takes your grandchildild to the playground, which is just a very big room a mile underground with a very bright light, she'll be able to say to her kids. 'Back in the old days we used to actually see the sun. And the clouds would sometimes block the sun. No, don't look at that bright light, child. It's not the sun but it's still very bright.'"

"And the kid will say, 'Mom, can we go to the top sometime and look at the sun?'"

"'It's too dangerous, child. But they're trying to fix the ozone layer. Maybe someday.'"

Wrapping up the Loose Ends:
The Demands of the Throdēop

The Throdēop demand was completely unforeseen. They appeared to be cooperating, but there was always the little thing about their heads continuing to expand and turning deep purple.

They felt the humans were little more than pets. Clever pets, but pets. They would send them out to do little tasks, and then the humans would come back with the bone or frisbie they sent them out to fetch. The humans never seemed to tire of the game. How well the Throdēop understood the human and his love of games.

The Throdēop started to think about how they might use the human spacecraft. It would give them resources that would otherwise might be difficult to come by. They could reproduce further. Perhaps send the craft off in another direction to try and find a new planet to occupy.

*   *   *

The confrontation was a brief one. The Throdēop simply said, "We have decided that we need your ship to increase our chances of finding a satisfactory planet. And it will temporarily solve the demand of some of us to have children."

Ramón said, "I see."

The Throdēop said, "We feel you should not alarm your people because there is, after all, nothing they can do about it. We have by far superior resources. You have not experienced our power of suggestion. Think back to the 1990s. We are playing chess. You are Kasparov. Brilliant, driven. We are Deep Blue. We are Germany 1939, and you are France. You are the Starship Enterprise, we are the Borg."

"I see." It was annoying how much of human culture they could pick up with their expanded brains.

The Throdēop said, "Since your chances to overcome us are so remote, I hope you will see the sense of the plan I am about to propose."

"What plan is that?"

"Well, we don't want to cause all kind of alarm and unhappiness among your crew, so we felt the best thing to do would be for you to go back and say that we've had a nice visit and now we are going to go back on our respective paths."

"Yes, and?"

"And put your people back into deep sleep."

"From which they will never recover . . ."

"Probably not. We think it would be the Throdēop thing to do. What you would call humane."

"Well, I suppose from some point of view it is a thoughtful thing to do."

"I don't suppose you would want to keep some of us alive as specimens?"

"It's a thought."

"For the genetic material if nothing else."

"Oops. Not for that. We'll keep cell samples for that."

"Of course. Right," remembering that that was the same argument that those who wanted children had used for extinguishing the animals in the zoo. With cell samples they could grow them back at any time.

"I don't suppose there would be any point in saving a culture, would there?"

"We have plenty of data samples in your computer. Video, three-dimensional, and so on. So, I'm afraid not. But good try."

"No. I won't do it. You'll have to find someone else to impose your plan."

But it was only a courtesy that the Throdēop requested their help. They didn't need to because the Throdēop were the next step in evolution. They did not require all the paraphernalia of speech, the mouth, the larynx, vocal chords, and the rest. All these were vestigial remnants of their DNA which had not yet disappeared. They could communicate through telepathy.

The Throdēop had never demonstrated this capacity because it was a weapon in their arsenal. To reveal it would not do.

So, in a combination of sending voices that people recognized to their victims combined with an hypnotic suggestion the humans had no means of defeating, they all went to their sleep shells.

*   *   *

Nick kept turning in reports to Seoul, but he wondered if anyone ever read them. He used to watch *Pascali's Island* once a month. Now he was watching it every week. The man who was everywhere but powerless, impotent. He lusted after a beautiful woman but ended up in bed with a young man. Pascali sent endless reports from the island to Istanbul, but no one ever acknowledged his work.

Meanwhile, Stephen sold another story, the one he made out of his notes on a new ice age. He celebrated by seeing a hooker, since Anna was in Holland.

*   *   *

Stephen offered to bring Anna to the States for another extended visit. He was surprised somehow that she agreed to come. He mulled it over, and there was only one conclusion—the green card. Although Holland was no third world country. And Chicago was not necessarily an improvement over Amsterdam. He concluded it must be advertising. All the movies take place in America. Sean Connery got his Oscar for a movie about Chicago. *ER* took place in Chicago. It must be something like that.

Once she was back in Chicago, he was reluctant to let her go, so he had to find a way to get her to stay. So, after the three months of visitor's visa wore off, they went to Canada to get another three months. Then the pressure began. She had the rent on her window to pay, the rent on her apartment. Meanwhile, he investigated. Marriage, work permits, education permits. These seemed to be the only options. He went for the work permit.

Stephen was surprised at how much he was willing to go through to keep her in Chicago. This bonding thing was much more powerful than he could have imagined. He thought, what if one bonded with some kind of shrew, monster bitch? What then?

He worried. She was beautiful. He might only be one rung on the stairway. First the green card, then a suitable partner.

So, should he, as economist Stephen Frank would have it, look for another apartment? Was the rent too high? Maybe the rent is okay now, but will rent increases make it, the relationship, impossible to maintain?

He was swamped by the calculations. Too many variables, too little information. You could spend years running background searches and conducting psychological tests, and after all that you still might not know enough to plug in numbers for all the variables. So in the end, one spent the rest of one's marriage figuring out if the shortcut calculations you made at the time were right.

Meanwhile, she was quite nonchalant as his brain went in overtime, calculating, computing. She would tell him about her experiences.

"You know," she would say, "for many of the men . . . my regulars . . . I am some kind of surrogate love figure. They are so sweet. They tell me all about their lives like I'm they're shrink. I think they think they are in love with me. In psychology they call it trans . . ."

"—ference."

*   *   *

Amanda, "Yeah, that's the theory. They think modern man killed the young of the mastodon and mammoth. The skin of the young animal is thinner."

Stephen, "Easier for their flints to pierce."

"That's the theory. If you relentlessly kill the young, the old die, and as populations get smaller, they become dislocated and have a problem finding suitable mates."

"Wow."

"Although I think there is evidence that they scared a herd off a cliff, young and adults."

"Really?"

"So maybe it wasn't just the young. But killing the young was probably a big part of it. Sure, there may have been other agencies. An asteroid. Massive ice age floods have been proposed. And you have to ask, okay, floods might explain North America, but South America also lost 70-80 percent of their large mammals. What floods were down there? And even if the floods killed many, the humans were there to mop up."

"To finish the job."

"Just so."

Anticlimax

As Tōparr walked Ramón to his sleeping berth, he started to turn a sickening yellow.

"I am becoming quite faint," and then he lapsed into Bop, which none of the humans could make out.

The euthanization of the humans was postponed. And the best physicians among the humans were awakened, and the Throdēop began to give their leader medical attention. The yellow was a sign of liver damage. His blood was analyzed and a bacterium was found, common enough to humans, but deadly for the Throdēop. In the end, only six Throdēop had been restored to consciousness, and all of them took sick. Throdēop brains were expanding to solve the problem, but the bacterium was growing faster than the brains.

The leader, Tōparr, dying, dryly observed in English, "It's all macrocosm/microcosm, isn't it? My body is the host for this disease. Life, bacterial life, is growing at a phenomenal rate in my body. A few bacteria—now billions, probably soon to be trillions—will overpopulate my body and cut off important pathways in the body, and I will cease to function."

It was an effort to speak, and he was urged by the humans to relax, "When it runs through and conquers my entire body, and the others, it will have nowhere else to go. Incinerate us. It will destroy the bacteria. You understand we did not mean you any particular harm, but we have been looking for years for a place to allow our females to raise additional children. In lieu of finding a suitable planet, your craft was determined acceptable. The fate of those in stasis will be in your hands."

* * *

Abner: "A virus? A bacteria? It's been done a million times. Didn't you see *War of the Worlds* with Gene Barry? And that was way back in the fifties. What a numbskull you are. It'll never sell. Get back to your code."

"We think we're done with bacteria and viruses, but then we find that viruses are causing cancer after all. Remember, for every cell authored by your DNA, you have maybe ten bacterial cells."

"I'm not convinced. This is old stuff."

"Of course Ray Kurzweil would send in the nanobots to knock out the bacteria."

"See."

"What do you know about it? I just told you about the nanobots."

"Then put it in the book."

"That's a Crichton novel. I'm about inevitability and endless cycling and recycling, hence I circle back to bacteria. And I wonder if nanobots will work as smoothly as Kurzweil suggests. And soon as they invent nanobots, someone will invent evil nanobots. I mean: who would have thought of computer viruses fifty years ago?"

"Who is Kurzweil?"

"An inventor. He invented the first optical character recognition program."

Of course the ending would never work for Abner. Always you have to overcome your relatives. Maybe he can't do the eaglet thing and push me out of the nest. But he can still try to trip me up along the way.

*　*　*

An interesting thing happened after the Throdēop leader died. Ada suddenly became available to Ramón. It was like a switch was turned. She was suddenly around him all the time. Stroking his back. Telling him how happy she was that he had said he would not be the instrument of the Throdēop.

He liked the attention even if he felt it was unwarranted.

Eventually, they made love.

*　*　*

Nick didn't want to go all the way out to Barrington to see Stephanie anymore. But he also was not drawn to go and see Miranda. He was not making any progress in getting the code from Stephen, and he started drinking Pepsi nonstop. But he did his best to spoil Stephen's fun.

"The humans survive in your story because of a virus or bacteria?"

"Yes."

"Cop-out. What a romantic. What a softie. That's like saying the buffalo survived because Buffalo Bill caught a cold."

"Buffalo Bill?" Stephen.

"Yes, yes, I know, the buffalo survived, but in your case, in your book? They're toast," concluded Nick.

"I have a bias against unhappy endings."

"That's because it's November—dark most of the time, and cold. It's what I call that trash compactor time of year when everything is caving in. Finish it in May. Then you can be more objective."

Certainly things were caving in for Nick. He drank Pepsi and listened to Barry Manilow records. His apartment, which had always been neat, became cluttered, then dirty. He superficially maintained his routine, and if asked he would never say he was depressed. He would say he was a little tired, or bored. He still made his reports back to Korea, and aside from the occasional money drop, it didn't seem they needed him much. The drops didn't require them to have read his reports, he could have been hired out of the secret temp pool. He was just told where to get the money and where to drop it.

The reports he sent back were in English. If he had just used his brains, he told himself, he would have learned Korean, and then they would have looked at them. He was too proud to ask if anyone ever read his reports, it would have been devastating to hear that no one ever did. Or worse, they might say:

"Where did you send them?"

Or: "We have them all. They're in our files." No one reads them, of course, but they're neatly filed away.

It had been some years that he had been sending in his reports, and no one had ever asked for a follow-up, or an update, or a close-up, or any damn thing. And he had known by now that his reports counted for nothing, and it ate him up. He had been duped. They had wined and dined him, and told him he would have to do a little chore for them once in a while. And they asked him to send an intelligence report. A digest. They knew he was an English major and would be a sucker for this kind of thing. And he dutifully sent his reports, thinking himself a Graham Greene. But all he had ever been for the Koreans was an errand boy. They had distracted him with what could have been a computer game called Intelligence Reports.

The girl. Well, really he was crazy for the girl, but his morale was sinking like a ship off in the Atlantic. He could not respond to the girl, Stephanie.

So, after drinking a Pepsi, he and Stephen went out to play a set of singles. In the midst of the match, he suddenly said to Stephen,

"Listen, I can't continue."

"Why's that?"

"I'm seeing things."

"Seeing things?"

"Yes, I'm seeing things . . ."

"What would you like me to do?"

"Drive me over to my mother's house."

"What will happen to your car?"

"Forget it. Let's go."

Stephen drove Nick to his mother's house, where he waited until she opened the door and took him in.

Nick was hospitalized for a while. He was quiet for a week. A liver imbalance caused by chain-drinking Pepsi's had caused the hallucinations. After he got comfortable in the hospital, he seduced another of the patients. An attractive blond in on a drug overdose. Then, he seduced a nurse, a brunette, who could not resist his charm and facial symmetry. The doctor on his rounds was a redhead. And soon after meeting her, dreams of a democratic foursome—himself, patient, nurse, and doctor—danced in his head.

Meanwhile, there was a break in the intelligence reports.

Oak Park, Buenos Aires, Villefranche-Sur-Mer

Acknowledgements

All roads seemed to lead ineluctably to and from Saul Bellow. My adviser at university, Keith Opdahl, wrote a book on his novels. My friend, Tim Redman, loaned me his best novel when it came out, *Humboldt's Gift*. My uncle, Burt Barnard, had an insurance agency of which he was a customer, and where I met him. Another writer friend and life-guide, Stephen Vizinczey, was enticed to meet with me after reading praise from Bellow. Indeed, such contacts, when they become mentors, and eventually friends, are critical in life. Bellow read hundreds of pages, and each time he would write or call and give me his take. Beyond that, he published my first story in *The Republic of Letters*. His company and conversation were a high water mark in my experience, and helped to fortify me considering most of my friends and family, and beyond them, editors, publishers and agents have been "an admiring bog." Writers: you know what I mean.

I am grateful to Keith Opdahl for seeing something in me beyond my desultory performance in university.

I am happy to have friends like Tim Redman, who are able to make up their own minds, and let you know when you're on the right track, and put you on to great books like *Humboldt* even when its writer is right under your nose.

I rely on the judgment and stalwart friendship of Stephen Vizinczey, who also wrote one of the novels I most admire (*An Innocent Millionaire*), and who put me on to Balzac, who is incomparable, by giving me his copy of *Lost Illusions*.

My uncle, Burton Barnard, inspired me. I went to work for his insurance agency not because I had any interest in insurance, but because he was an extremely well-read man with unerring judgment, who admired great writing, and I wanted to be around someone like that. His encouragement has been like sunlight piercing through the clouds of an overcast Chicago winter.

I would also like thank my readers not mentioned above: Dennis Huey, Robert Kinsell, Mike New, Gloria Vizinczey, and Tom Frank.

Lastly, it is perhaps not possible to approach the subject of intelligence straight on, we don't even know exactly how the brain works, though we're getting there. It is possible, for example, to read Jeff Hawkins book, *On Intelligence*, sans all the underlying science. However, we can see the effects of intelligence even without popping the hood. Scientists often report on the effects of chemicals, drugs, without understanding the underlying mechanisms. And that is the viewpoint from which I operated. The books of Richard Leakey (in particular, *The Sixth Extinction*), Peter Ward (*The End of Evolution*), and Edward O. Wilson were instrumental as I developed my thinking about the larger theme of this book. I commend them to anyone interested in the issues of this book.